# NAUGHTY BOOK THREE:

## IT'S JUICY NO MATTER HOW YOU SLICE IT

# NAUGHTY BOOK THREE:

## IT'S JUICY NO MATTER HOW YOU SLICE IT

### BRENDA HAMPTON

URBAN Renaissance

www.urbanbooks.net

Urban Books, LLC
78 East Industry Court
Deer Park, NY 11729

Naughty Book Three: It's Juicy No Matter How You Slice
It copyright © 2009 Brenda Hampton

ISBN 13: 978-1-60162-241-9
ISBN 10: 1-60162-241-4

First Mass Market Printing January 2011
First Trade Paperback Printing October 2009
Printed in the United States of America

10  9  8  7  6  5  4  3  2

Distributed by Kensington Publishing Corp.
Submit Wholesale Orders to:
Kensington Publishing Corp.
C/O Penguin Group (USA) Inc.
Attention: Order Processing
405 Murray Hill Parkway
East Rutherford, NJ  07073-2316
Phone: 1-800-526-0275
Fax: 1-800-227-9604

# 1

## *JAYLIN*

*B*USTED was written all over my face. I stood between Scorpio, the woman I loved, and Daisha, the woman I desired for the moment. When Scorpio reached up and tried to punch me again, I quickly grabbed her wrist to stop her. I wanted to mess her up, but since I knew I was wrong, I pulled her inside of Daisha's house and comforted her in my arms. Daisha walked by us, excusing herself. Scorpio didn't say a word; she was numb. When I opened my mouth to apologize, she shoved me backward and abruptly walked off.

I had some explaining to do to Daisha, so I stood in the doorway and watched Scorpio leave. Her eyes met with mine, and even though she hadn't said much, I could tell exactly what her thoughts were. Obviously, she was tired of my bullshit.

What in the fuck was I thinking, though? I tried to be the man Scorpio wanted me to be, but the news about Daisha being pregnant kind of messed up everything. I didn't want to leave Daisha hanging, and as for my child, the thought of not having him or her in my life was bugging me.

Fucking her last night was wrong and I knew it, but I couldn't help myself. I ain't never been the type of brotha to turn down no good pussy. Thing is, I didn't know what Daisha wanted from me. By the looks of things, she must have thought I was ending it with Scorpio to be with her. Scorpio, though, had something that no other woman had, other than Nokea once upon a time, and that was my heart.

Scorpio drove off in my Porsche and I closed the door, taking a deep breath. Daisha was sitting on the couch with her head on the armrest. I put on my clothes then sat next to her, holding her hand. Her eyes were watery, so I held her close to me for comfort. She laid her head on my shoulder and closed her eyes.

"You still love her, don't you?" she whispered.

"I never stopped, but that doesn't mean I don't want to be a part of my child's life."

"But what about what you said last night? You told me you loved me and said—"

"Daisha, honestly, I can't remember what I said. I was full of alcohol, stressed the hell out, and had no business coming here. Seeing you naked last night made me—"

"Freaky as hell." She laughed.

"Okay, if you say I was, then I guess I was. I didn't mean to mislead you in any way. I'm trying to deal with Scorpio and you being pregnant, and it ain't easy."

Daisha sat up and her eyebrows rose. "You're kidding me, right? Is she really pregnant too?"

"Yep. I thought you knew, especially since y'all tried to set a brotha up this morning."

She shook her head from side to side. "No, sorry, but, uh, that's not how it happened. When I pulled up, she was already outside."

"Really?"

"Yes. After I got out of my car, she came up and asked if you were here. Seeing how angry she was, I wasn't about to lie to her."

Thinking about Scorpio, I stood up and felt my pocket for my keys.

"I . . . I really need to go home and—"

"Go handle your business, Jaylin. Whenever you have time, you and I need to talk. Soon. I told you once before I didn't want to interfere, but I'm not going to allow you to run to me when things aren't going smoothly at home. It's not fair to me, nor will it be fair to your son."

I smiled at Daisha's news. "So, it's a boy, huh?"

"Yes. A wiggly one at that." Daisha took my hand and placed it on her stomach. It excited me to feel him move, so I sat back down and pressed my ear against her stomach.

Daisha laughed. "What are you listening for?"

I rose up. "I was listening to my son telling me what a wonderful mother he's got; how much I should appreciate her for understanding me, and for not being mad at me for saying and doing what I did last night."

"Like I said before, we'll talk later, okay? Besides, I kind of took advantage of the situation anyway."

"You did, didn't you? If I don't remember much about last night, I do remember you unzipping my pants and riding my thang like you did."

Daisha chuckled and held my hand as we walked to the door. Before I stepped outside, she rubbed her fingers in my curly hair and stared into my eyes. "I can't wait to have our baby, Jaylin. I hope our son has your hair and beautiful gray eyes."

"If he belongs to me he will. In the meantime, take care of yourself. I'll be back to see you soon."

I leaned forward to embrace Daisha, but she didn't want to let go. She sniffled, and when I pulled away from her, I saw that her almond-shaped eyes were filled with tears.

"Damn, Daisha, you're making me feel like shit. I said I was sorry, and—"

She touched my chest and motioned for me to leave. "Trust me, it's okay. I'm just emotional right now, but I understand that you have a critical situation to work through."

"Are you sure you understand? I mean, you have to know I never wanted to hurt—"

She nodded. "I know. Just call me later, all right?"

I gave her another hug and left.

On the drive home, I thought about LJ, the son I already had, and how delighted I was to be having another one. He and LJ would be good for each other, and I would give them every opportunity to grow up together.

I knew the whole situation wouldn't sit right with Scorpio, and I pondered what I would say to her. I was sure she'd seen Daisha's stomach, and my lie about Daisha being one of Stephon's ladies wasn't going to work. I figured she was probably already packed and on her way out with Mackenzie.

Thinking about Scorpio taking off with Mackenzie, even though she wasn't my biological child, I hurried, not wanting her to leave. When I pulled up, I was surprised to see my Porsche in the driveway. I was even more surprised when I walked into the kitchen and saw Scorpio at the kitchen table reading the *St. Louis Post Dispatch* with Mackenzie's dog, Barbie, in her arms. She ignored me, so I sat at the table to get her attention.

"Do you see the mark you put next to my eye?" I asked.

She continued to focus on the paper. "Good. I wish I would've done more than that."

"Where's Mackenzie and Nanny B?"

"Gone."

"Do you know where?"

She looked up and snapped. "To the grocery store."

"Cool, then we got time to talk, right?"

She huffed and slammed the paper on the table. "About what, Jaylin? How sorry you are? How this shit is never going to happen again? Or maybe about how much you love me?"

"Yeah, well, a li'l of that, but more so, you need to understand why I went to Daisha's house last night."

"Oh, I see," she said, raising her voice. "I need to understand why you're out there fucking other women when I have sex with you almost every single day? Whenever! However! And wherever you want it! You have got some nerve coming in here telling me what I need to understand!" She pointed her finger at me, continuing to yell. "You're the one who needs to understand that the bullshit stops here and now. There was no reason for you to do what you did to me last night, and I will never ever forgive your ass." Scorpio tossed the newspaper on the floor and scooted her chair back. I grabbed her hand so she wouldn't walk away.

"Are you finished?" I asked casually.

She snatched away. "Hell no! As a matter of fact, I'm just getting started."

"Well, let me know when you get finished so I can tell you what really happened. And if you leave before I can at least explain myself, then your loss, not mine."

"Leave? Uh-uh. I ain't going nowhere. You dragged my butt out of Denver, gave me this . . . this bullshit-ass ring!" She pulled the ring off her finger and threw it at me. "So now you're stuck with me, bastard! Remember, for better or worse, for richer or poorer, in sickness and in health . . . and nothing, Jaylin Jerome Rogers, will keep us apart. So use me whenever you want—that's all I'm good for. Your doormat I will continue to be, so feel free to step all over the woman you claim to love."

"Come on now, baby. I know you're upset, but it ain't even like that. If you would just listen, I'm sure you'd understand." Scorpio folded her arms and tapped her foot on the floor. "Would you at least sit down?" I asked politely.

She rolled her eyes and plopped down in the

chair. I shamefully lowered my head and then looked over at her pretty self sitting close to me. Her long hair was resting on her left shoulder, her light skin had a silky glow to it, but her seductive eyes were red and swollen from all the tears that had fallen. Never seeing her react so coldly toward me, I rubbed up and down her shapely legs and then placed my hand on the side of her face. She sat motionless, and when I leaned in to kiss her, she turned her head.

"Don't try to manipulate me, nigga. Just get to the point," she yelled.

I quickly backed up. "Nigga? You have got to be out of your motherfucking mind disrespecting me like that. Now, I've sat here and listened to you go on and on, but I will fuck you up, Scorpio, pregnant or not. I understand your pain, but I will not be called a nigga by my own woman, especially if she ain't one hundred percent black her damn self. Either you're gonna sit here like you got some sense and listen to what I have to say, or we can have this discussion some other time. The choice is always yours."

She scooted the chair back and got up. Before she pushed the kitchen door open, she turned to me. "I'm in no mood for one of your pep talks. And how dare you talk about respect? What a joke." She walked out.

"You're damn right I want respect," I yelled out. "As long as you're in this—*my* damn house, you'd better remember what the definition is!"

I was pissed off, but at the same time, I tried to understand how hurt Scorpio was. Thing is, though, I wasn't going to walk around my own house being miserable. As far as I was concerned, if she was that unhappy, then she could leave until things cooled off. I had much love for her, but if she didn't want to listen to what I had to say, what else could I do?

I sat in the kitchen for a while and came to the conclusion that maybe I was wrong. Scorpio was dealing with a lot too, and it was time for me to put the shoe on the other foot. I went upstairs to my room and saw Scorpio lying across the bed, looking at the plasma TV on the wall. Barbie was in bed with her.

I stood in the doorway and cleared my throat. "Now, you know I don't play that. Please get the dog off my bed."

"You don't say nothing to Mackenzie when she puts—"

"Scorpio! Put the damn dog on the floor before I—"

Scorpio put Barbie on the floor and she ran up to me. I picked her up and took her into Mackenzie's room. I placed her on her doggy bed beside Mackenzie's bed and rubbed her. I told her to stay, and then hurried back to my room. The shower was on, so I went into the bathroom and sat on top of the Jack and Jill sinks to watch Scorpio wash herself.

Moments later, she turned around and noticed how mesmerized I was by looking at her body and her barely poked-out belly that had my baby inside. It was evident that she tried to cover up her tears by allowing the water to fall on her face. I felt terrible. There was no justification for what I had done. I wanted—no, I needed her to understand how sorry I really was. I stared back at her, closing my eyes to fight back my own hurt. When she pushed the glass doors open, I hopped down from the counter. She didn't come out, so I stepped inside of the shower with her, fully clothed.

"Why do you keep doing this to me?" she said while pounding her fist against my chest.

I held her in my arms and kissed her forehead. "I didn't intentionally try to hurt you. I love you, baby, and you have got to believe me when I say that."

As her body trembled, I squeezed tighter. I lifted her chin and placed my lips on hers. She accepted my kiss. Wanting to make love to her, I hurried out of my wet clothes. I backed her against the wall and she held on tightly around my neck. I lifted her, and when she straddled my hips, we stood full of emotions while looking into each other's eyes.

"Baby, I don't know what is wrong with me," I admitted. "I . . . I need you. Please don't think about leaving me. I promise you we'll get through this, okay?"

"Whatever you say, Jaylin. It's whatever you say."

I slid myself inside of Scorpio and felt relieved. She closed her eyes, leaned her head to the side, and sucked in her lips. As I worked her insides so well, she lowered her legs and turned around so I could work her from behind. Trying to show her how much I wanted her, I massaged her butt cheeks apart, got on my knees, and licked her from front to back. She shook all over, and as I was all into it, it seemed as if she still couldn't stop crying. I was hurt too, but damn. Her being so emotional kind of messed up my mood.

The sex was over before it got started. I turned off the water and sat on the seat inside of the shower. I held Scorpio's hands as she stood in front of me.

"Are you going to forgive me?" I asked. "If not, let me know now. I still have something I need to tell you, and once I do, I hope like hell that we can move on."

She loosened her hands from mine and left the shower. As she reached for a towel in the closet, I took it from her and wrapped both of us in it. Scorpio stood motionless with her head against my chest, not saying a word. Maybe reconciling with her was going to be more difficult than I thought, but there was no way in hell I would accept losing her.

# 2

## *SCORPIO*

Words couldn't express how hurt I was. I'll be the first to admit that Jaylin's good loving, along with his smooth talking, had me all messed up. He had no idea how much he had broken me down, and I was doing everything in my power to stay strong.

After we had sex in the shower—and that's all I seemed to be good for—I stayed the night in one of the guestrooms. The nanny who took care of all of us, Nanny B, came in to check on me, but I told her I needed some time alone. She told me that when I was ready to talk, she'd lend me an ear. Thing is, I was devasted about Jaylin going back to the playboy he was, and I didn't quite know where to turn or what to do.

For months, I had a private detective keeping an eye on Jaylin. Before I decided to go through with our marriage, I wanted to be sure he was a changed man. So much for that. I was so glad that

I hadn't become his wife just yet. He was almost perfect—up until last night.

When I called the detective, he had given me Daisha's address, told me where I could find Jaylin. I couldn't resist going.

My heart ached when I saw his car parked outside of her house, but more so when I saw her get out of a car and noticed her swollen stomach. I knew he wanted to tell me the baby was his, but would he also be honest about what happened between them that night? Realistically, Jaylin spending the night with a woman and not having sex with her was impossible. I knew something had gone down, and frankly, I was too damn hurt to face the truth.

I lay in bed gazing out at the blue sky, thinking about the control Jaylin had over me. Lying around and feeling sorry for myself had to stop. I'd never let any man upset me like this, and I couldn't believe I allowed him to keep on doing it.

By 9:30 A.M., I got out of bed and went into our bedroom to put on some clothes. Jaylin was still asleep, but when I opened the closet, he rolled over and looked at the alarm clock.

"Where are you getting ready to go?" he mumbled.

"Out."

"Out where?"

"Somewhere. I don't know."

He pulled the covers over his head. "If you're not back by midnight, just make sure you call."

I ignored his comment, changed clothes, and

headed downstairs to the kitchen, where Nanny B, Mackenzie, and Barbie were. Nanny B had breakfast on the table, while Mackenzie sat next to Barbie, rubbing her.

"Good morning," I said to Nanny B, then bent down to give Mackenzie a kiss on the cheek.

Nanny B said good morning back, and so did Mackenzie. "Mommy, why did you sleep all day yesterday? Daddy said the baby needed some rest. Is that true?"

"Yes, that's right honey; it did." I picked up a piece of toast. "I'm on my way to the doctor for a check up. Would you like to come with me?"

"No, that's okay. Nanna's taking me to the toy store today. I'll go next time."

"You promise?"

"Yes, I promise."

"Scorpio, you need to eat a little bit more than toast, don't you think?" Nanny B said.

"I'm not hungry. Besides, I'm trying to watch my weight as much as possible."

"If you insist. Just make sure you eat something later. I know you're trying to avoid looking like me with all this meat on my bones, but you have to eat for the baby."

"I'll eat something later, especially if you make a pot roast. I'll be the first to dive into it."

We laughed as Jaylin came into the kitchen. Nanny B handed him some orange juice and he took a seat at the table next to Mackenzie. He played with her and Barbie. After I excused myself from the table, he finally said something to me.

"Say, uh, I forgot where you said you were going," he said.

"I didn't say."

Nanny B shifted her eyes from me to him. Obviously, she could cut the tension with a knife. "She's going to the doctor, and she shouldn't be going alone. I'm taking Mackenzie to get some toys, and before I come back, I'm stopping at Nokea's house to get LJ. Jaylin, since that leaves you with nothing to do, why don't you go to the doctor with Scorpio?"

"Uh-uh, Nanny B," I declined. "That won't be necessary. Besides, I'm going shopping after I leave the doctor's office."

Jaylin scooted the chair back. "Then that's my cue. I don't need you spending any more of my money, so let me go put on some clothes right now."

I rolled my eyes as Jaylin hurried out of the kitchen to change clothes.

Nanny B glared at me. "What's going on with the two of you now?"

"Trust me, you don't even want to know. Besides, I'm sure Jaylin will tell you all about it. I really don't have the energy to discuss it right now."

"Well, whenever you feel like talking, just know I'm here."

I kissed her and Mackenzie on their cheeks and told them I'd be home by the time they made it back.

As I was about to back out of the driveway, Jaylin ran outside, shirtless.

"Damn, can't you wait? I said I was going," he griped while pulling the shirt over his head.

"Well, hurry up."

I unlocked the door so he could get in. "I'm a little nervous about you driving my car. Do you mind pulling over so I can drive?" he asked.

"I've driven your car before, so what's the problem all of a sudden?"

He shrugged. "I don't know. You tell me. You've been on this . . . this emotional roller coaster, and I don't want you messing up my Porsche 'cause you're upset with me."

I pulled over to the side of the road. "You don't have any sympathy for me, do you? Not only that, but you haven't a clue what I'm going through."

"Yes, I really do. But how can I fix things if you won't even listen or talk to me?"

I folded my arms. "So, okay, I guess you want to tell me Daisha is pregnant by you, right?"

"Yes, she is. If you hadn't stayed in Denver fucking around for as long as you did, then maybe—"

"Maybe, my ass. If I were here in St. Louis at the time, she'd still be pregnant. Besides, I wasn't in Denver last night when you took it upon yourself to go fuck her."

"Why are you assuming that I slept with her last night?"

"Because you did! Don't sit there and try to lie about it, Jaylin."

"I should plead the fifth, but I was under the influence of alcohol. I had just found out yesterday that she was pregnant too, and I didn't want anybody's feelings to get hurt."

"So screwing her was your way of making sure she didn't get hurt?"

"No, I didn't go there to fuck her. I went there to find out about my child. I passed out on the floor, and, uh, things kind of . . . you know."

"No, I don't know. Things kind of what?"

"I can't remember. I told you I passed out."

"So, she initiated sex, not you?"

"Yes, she did."

I tooted my lips. "Are you trying to tell me this woman raped you?"

"No, but she was very persistent."

"In other words, you knew that you were about to get some."

"Sort of."

"Don't bullshit around with me, Jaylin. Did you want to have sex with her or not? Yes or no, and I'll leave it at that."

He smiled and winked at me. "You promise?"

"Yes, I promise."

"Then yes, Scorpio, I wanted to have sex with her."

"Why?" I screamed and slammed my hand against the steering wheel. "Why, when I give you everything that you need?"

"I can't answer that because you just made me a promise. You said that after I told you, you would leave the situation alone."

"I know what I said, but I will never understand you. For the past few months, we've been so happy, and now you've messed up our relationship for one night in the sack with another woman. Accepting the baby is one thing, but allowing this relationship between you and her to continue is—"

He reached over and put his fingers on my lips. "Listen. All I can say is it won't happen again. I tripped and I'm sorry." He reached in his pocket and pulled out my engagement ring. "Now, would you please put this back on?" I snatched the ring from his hand and looked at it. "I'm entitled to a few mistakes, aren't I?" he asked.

"Zero," I said, giving it back to him. "That ring means nothing to me if you're not going to be right."

Jaylin put the ring back in his pocket and I got out of the car to let him drive.

When we got to the doctor's office, he stayed in the waiting area to finish his phone conversation with Stephon. I was called to one of the examination rooms. When Doctor Birch came in, he patted my leg.

"How have you been feeling, Scorpio?"

"I've been okay. I haven't been as hungry as I thought I would be. Sometimes I feel as if I have to force myself to eat."

He gazed over my chart. "You haven't picked up much weight, and for you to be . . . nearly five months."

My heart dropped to my stomach. *It couldn't be*, I thought. "Four. I thought it was four."

"No, five. The ultrasound showed your conception date to be roughly in November."

"No, I thought you said December."

"I don't think so, because according to this chart,"—he showed me the chart—"I wrote down November. I could be wrong, so we'll set up another ultrasound today and go from there."

"Thank you."

When Dr. Birch walked out, I couldn't help but think about my time in Denver.

Jaylin came in and interrupted my thoughts. Seeing that I was naked underneath the white gown, he got on the examination table and playfully kissed me.

"Come on," he said, unzipping his pants. "I don't think I've ever gotten down on an examination table."

"And you never will, so get up."

"Damn, you ain't no fun. All I need is five minutes."

I thought he was playing, until I looked down and saw how hard he was. "You can get that thing up anywhere, can't you? I can't believe you're serious about this."

"Don't I—I mean my dick look serious? Shit, I ain't playing."

I couldn't help but laugh, and when Jaylin walked over to the door and locked it, I knew just how serious he was. He aimed Monster Dick in my direction and stood at the end of the table. He noticed the stirrups and pulled them out.

"Damn," he said, laughing. "I have always wanted to do this shit."

I was kind of curious myself, but I was still upset with Jaylin for what he'd done. Deep down, I knew he loved me, but he sometimes had a funny way of showing it. Today, I wasn't giving in to him. There was no way I could see myself opening my legs to him after what had happened between him and Daisha.

When Doctor Birch and his nurse came back

in, Jaylin was on his phone and I was reading a magazine. Doctor Birch said he was ready to do my ultrasound, so I asked Jaylin if he wouldn't mind leaving the room.

"Why? I wanna see the baby too."

"I'll show you the picture later. I don't want you to know what sex it is. Please . . . let it be a surprise, okay?"

He pecked my lips. "You're lucky I love you like that. I'll be in the waiting area, and if not, look for me in the car."

"Will do."

Jaylin left, and Dr. Birch and his nurse continued with my ultrasound. After all was said and done, he confirmed the baby I carried was conceived nearly twenty weeks ago, which put me in Denver, Colorado at the time. In shock, I dropped my head and let the tears fall because I knew there was no way in hell this baby was Jaylin's. It had to be Rick's baby, the exterminator that I slept with twice because of the loneliness I felt from losing Jaylin.

I had gone to Denver just so I could get away from my Jaylin drama, but I wound up bringing more drama to myself. When the condom tore, I was deeply concerned. I hadn't even enjoyed my time with Rick, and my feelings were not there. It was simply something to do to pass my time away, to minimize my hurt.

I couldn't believe this saga for nothing in the world. Somebody or something didn't want us happy together. The thought of being pregnant by Rick did cross my mind, but as much as Jaylin and I had sex, I was almost positive the baby was his.

Unable to come out of my trance, I sat in the room alone and tried to figure out my next move. Jaylin had come clean about his situation with Daisha, and as angry as I still was about what had happened, I now had an even bigger fish to fry. There was no way in hell he would understand my situation. I couldn't let him go on thinking this child was his, but I didn't know where to begin with telling him the truth.

After I put on my clothes, I went into the waiting area to find Jaylin. He wasn't there, so I went outside. He was in his car, talking on his cell phone. He smiled as I walked toward him, and I knew he couldn't wait to hear about the baby. When I entered the car, he ended his call and pecked my lips again.

"So, do we have ourselves a girl or a boy?" he asked.

I put on the fakest grin ever. "We have a healthy baby, and for now, that's all I'm going to tell you."

"I'm sure I'll get it out of you. Did everything else check out okay?"

"Yeah, it's fine. Dr. Birch wants me to eat a little bit more, that's all."

"Well, I'm taking you to dinner tonight. Stop worrying so much about your weight, baby. You look spectacular."

"Thanks." I leaned over and kissed him again. "I needed to hear that."

"Why? I always tell you how beautiful you are, don't I?"

"Yeah, you do. I just don't know if my being beautiful is going to . . . never mind."

"Hey, what's in the past, let it stay in the past.

After today, I don't want to talk about anything that's happened before. You understand?"

I nodded.

The ride back to the house was quiet. I told Jaylin I wasn't feeling up to dinner that night, and Nanny B, LJ, Mackenzie, Jaylin and I watched *Madea's Class Reunion* in the theater room downstairs. I could barely concentrate on the movie because I knew time wasn't on my side. Jaylin had to be told the truth, and delaying the news wasn't going to help either of us one bit.

# 3

## *NOKEA*

Things between my new man, Collins, and I were off the hook. I felt as if I were over Jaylin, after years and years of loving him more than life itself. Because of our son, LJ, our relationship had become one of the friendliest, respectful, and most considerate relationships. Had I known we could get along this well, I would've suggested us breaking up a long time ago.

Jaylin confided in me a lot, and I did the same with him. I'd finally met Collins' ex-wife a few weeks ago, and nervous about meeting her, I called Jaylin to address my concerns. He told me I didn't have anything to worry about, and gave me the confidence I sometimes didn't have when it came to other women. Jaylin stressed how beautiful I was and talked about my inner beauty as well. We both laughed when he made me a bet that Collins' ex was ugly, and when I saw her, I laughed because he was right. She wasn't anywhere near as attractive as I was, but I knew Collins was attracted to her because of her intelligence and her body—for those were the only things she seemed to have going on.

As for Jaylin and Scorpio, I knew sooner or later something was bound to happen. He called the other day and told me things weren't working out too well for them. When I asked what had happened, he insisted we'd discuss it when I picked up LJ from his house on Friday.

When Friday rolled around, I hurried to Jaylin's house from work so I could make it to Collins' place by seven. He promised LJ and me a home-cooked meal, so I didn't want to miss out.

I was quite surprised to see Scorpio open the door, when Jaylin clearly said things weren't working out between them. However, I knew she always had a way of smoothing him over, and he the same.

"Hi, Nokea."

I stepped inside. "Hello, Scorpio. Is Jaylin here?"

"No. Him and Stephon went somewhere. He said they'd be back soon, though."

"Oh, okay. If you don't mind, I'll wait for him in his office."

"That's fine with me. LJ's upstairs taking a nap. If I would've known you were coming this soon, I would've had him ready to go."

I looked at Scorpio's finger and immediately noticed the blinging ring wasn't there. "I'll go upstairs to get LJ," I said. "But can I talk to you for a few minutes?"

Scorpio turned on the lights in Jaylin's office and we went inside. We sat face to face on the circular leather sofa.

"I don't mean to pry, but when I talked to Jaylin he said you guys were having some problems. I know it's not my business, but I couldn't help but notice your ring is gone."

Scorpio sat back, folded her arms, and crossed her legs. "Nokea, I really don't feel comfortable talking to you about my relationship with Jaylin. And our problems ain't nothing we can't work out. For Jaylin to tell you anything other than that, he was out of line."

Her attitude was funky, but I didn't take it personally. "Maybe so, but you do understand how close we've always been. Again, I'm not trying to interfere, I'm just a bit concerned about him, that's all."

"Don't be. He's a grown man, and I'm sure you know he doesn't have a problem taking care of himself."

"No, he doesn't. He's still the father of my child, and I care deeply for him."

"Oh, I understand. And if your question is did our one-day breakup have anything to do with him cheating on me, yes, it did. I'm sure you know better than anybody that Jaylin has a serious problem keeping Monster Dick in his pants."

"That was definitely too much information, but I know better than anybody how that is. I really thought he would settle down, but I . . . I'm sorry to hear he hasn't. Was it with that, uh, Daisha chick?"

"So you knew about Daisha?"

I shrugged it off, not knowing much. "He briefly mentioned her before. I also heard him talking to her one day in his office."

"Then you know she's pregnant?"

I uncrossed my legs. My mouth hung wide open. "By who? Him?"

Scorpio nodded. "Yes. And just in case he didn't tell you, so am I."

My mouth got wider. "You have got to be kidding me. Scorpio, I can't believe what you're telling me."

"It's called the truth. So you can pretty much understand what I'm dealing with. I love Jaylin, but this is so much more than I can swallow."

"I'm sure it is. I'm stunned by this. He hasn't said one word to me about this."

Scorpio and I continued our conversation. I couldn't believe how disturbed I was by Scorpio's breaking news. LJ wasn't even two years old yet, and Jaylin was already running around St. Louis making more babies.

When Scorpio and I heard him and Stephon coming through the front door, I called his name and they walked into his office. He was looking fine, as fine could get. Body was tanned, gray eyes were glowing, curly hair was freshly cut, and goatee was fitting his chin well. As for Stephon, who followed closely behind, he looked just as spectacular. Head was cleanly shaven with a shine, his body was looking downright workable, and his goatee was doing him justice as well. Just for a moment, I reminisced about being with both of them in the past, and as hard as it was, I quickly got my mind out of the gutter.

"Shortay!" Stephon yelled, then walked over to give me a hug.

"Hey, Stephon," I said, hugging him back. "What's up, honey?"

"Honey?" Jaylin said.

"Yeah, nigga, honey. You got a problem with that?" Stephon joked.

"Naw, I'm a li'l upset 'cause I ain't been nobody's honey in quite some time. Ain't that right, baby?" he said, looking in Scorpio's direction.

"You're always my honey. You just need to learn how to be sweeter to me, that's all."

"If I get any sweeter, everybody gonna be thinking I'm gay or something. And we for damn sure know how much I love me some pussy."

Stephon and Jaylin laughed and gave each other five. Scorpio and I found no humor in his comment.

"So, honeydew," I said, looking at Jaylin, "where have you two players been?"

"Players?" Jaylin said, pointing to himself. "Now, that's kind of cold, Nokea. Do I look like a man who likes to play?"

Scorpio cleared her throat. "Don't put yourself out there like that, baby. I'm gonna leave now before I start running off at the mouth like you've apparently been doing lately."

As she walked out, Jaylin smacked Scorpio's ass, lifting her long shirt up in the back so Stephon could see her butt. She quickly pulled her shirt down and punched Jaylin in his chest.

"That's a bad booty right there, man," he said, laughing.

"Don't ever do that again!" she yelled. "Don't you have any fucking respect for me?"

"Damn, why you tripping? I was just playing."

"I don't like to be played with like that!"

"Okay, I'm sorry. I'll never do it again." He picked up her hand and kissed the back of it. She snatched it away and walked out.

"Women. Damn," he griped as he sat down. "It ain't like Stephon ain't never seen her naked ass before. She wasn't too worried about brothas seeing it when she was stripping."

"Whoo-wee. You are something else, aren't you?" I said. "For her being a woman you claim to love, that was very disrespectful."

He waved off my comment. "Whatever, Nokea. Why are you over here anyway?"

"I'm here to get my son, remember? Or have you forgotten, since you can't keep up with all these crumb snatchers I hear you're expecting."

Jaylin and Stephon looked at each other. Stephon grinned, shrugged his shoulders, and handed Jaylin a piece of paper.

"I'm outtie, my brotha. Don't forget to take care of that tomorrow."

"I'm taking care of this tonight." Jaylin winked. "If I have time."

Stephon said good-bye and gave me another hug before he left. I stayed in Jaylin's office so we could talk.

"So, what's on that piece of paper? And why didn't you tell me about the babies?"

He looked at the paper, folded it, and put it in his pocket. "If you must know, Miss Nosey, the paper is the phone number of a nice young lady I met today. As for the babies, I can't wait to be a father again."

"Are you serious?"

"About the phone number, or the babies?"

"Both."

"Yes, I'm very serious."

I shook my head, disgusted by his actions. He wasn't my man anymore, so I tried not to be so discouraged. "Jaylin, when are you going to stop hurting people? I was just talking to Scorpio and she seemed so upset about your encounters with other women. Can't you even imagine what she's going through, especially being pregnant with your child?"

"Look, don't worry about Scorpio. I got her all taken care of. Besides, she wasn't worried about you when I was sticking it to her, was she?"

"That's not the point. As your friend, I'm encouraging you to stop bringing about so much drama. One of these days, your mess is going to backfire on you and you're going to find yourself in a heap of trouble."

"As my friend, you need only to offer your opinion or advice when I ask for it. I offer mine only when you ask."

"But—" My phone rang and I reached into my purse to answer. It was Collins. "Hello," I said.

"Hey, baby, it's me."

"I know who you are, and I'm sorry I'm running a little late. LJ and I will be there shortly."

"Okay. Just checking."

"What did you cook for us?"

"You'll have to see when you get here. Trust me, it's going to be good."

A huge smile came across my face and my voice softened. "It always is good, isn't it?"

Referring to sex, we laughed, gave our good-byes and hung up. I put my phone back in my purse. Jaylin was glaring at me.

"Why are you looking at me like that?" I asked.

"It always is good, isn't it?" he said, mocking me. "I hope you were talking about the food."

I grinned. "Don't tell me you're still jealous of my relationship with Collins."

"I have never been jealous of anybody in my entire life. I told you before I'm happy for you. You're the one who's jealous. That's why you can't stay out of my business."

"Please. If anything, I'm just concerned about you." As I walked toward the office door, Jaylin smacked my butt hard. "Hold up! This is not your booty anymore, so stop playing like that."

"Who says I'm playing? Besides, I couldn't help myself. Your petite body always turns me on, and I am digging the hell out of your short spiked haircut. You're looking more and more like Nia Long, and you know how I feel about her."

"Well, thank God she doesn't have to put up with you. And in the meantime, keep your hands to yourself, please."

"Whatever. My hands will go wherever they choose to, and there ain't nothing you can do about it. Besides, you know you miss me. I'll put some money on it that you still love—"

"You're so right, Jaylin," I said sarcastically. "I dream about you every night. I wake up in a sweat thinking about how good you used to be to me."

"Okay, you're laughing now, but I bet you that

shit is true. Not only that, but I'll put some money on it that says I can have my booty back any time I want it."

"Don't flatter yourself. Collins is handling his business extremely well."

I couldn't believe Jaylin's arrogance. On our way out of his office, he pressed his thang against my butt.

I turned to face him. "Stop, Jaylin."

He innocently held out his hands. "I couldn't help it. You shouldn't have come over here looking as good as you do."

"And you should have just a tiny bit more respect for your woman, especially if she's in the house."

Jaylin shrugged off my comment. Once I gathered LJ's things, Jaylin walked us to my car.

As I drove to Collins' house, Jaylin was on my mind. Indeed, I had dreamt about us being together, but I knew a future relationship with him would never be. No doubt, it was hard moving on without him, but my relationship with Collins had turned into something I never thought was possible. I wasn't about to give that up for no one.

# 4

# JAYLIN

After Nokea left with LJ, I didn't have much to do. Scorpio and Mackenzie went to visit her sister, Leslie, and when she asked if I wanted to go, I looked at her like she was crazy. Leslie had too many out of control kids, her house was nasty, and her smart-ass mouth was liable to get her hurt. I passed on the invitation and decided to stay home.

Earlier, I'd hung out with Stephon and a few fellas at the shop. I was trying to clear my head from all the bullshit that had been going on. And yes, I did meet myself a new lady friend, but I had no intentions of calling her any time soon. As for flirting with Nokea, I liked joking around with her because I loved to see her smile. We had an undeniable connection, and I couldn't even imagine her not being a part of my life.

I was still deeply in love with Scorpio, but something didn't seem right with her. She was too forgiving about Daisha being pregnant, and whenever she'd have sex with me on demand, I knew she was trying to whip that thang on me to fuck up my mind. Pussy was spectacular, though, and with her being pregnant, it felt even better. Whatever her motive was, I was definitely buying into it.

I lay across the bed, thinking about Daisha for a while. She was so forgiving, and I couldn't get the vision of her beautiful, teary eyes out of my mind either. I dozed off thinking about how she'd thickened up a bit and her hips seemed to have more curve to them. Her breasts, damn; being pregnant had them swollen. I remembered holding them in my hands and sucking them deeply into my mouth. Her lovely, one in a million face that my baby would have made me smile. Since we could easily pass for brother and sister, I knew my son would be off the chain.

I realized I hadn't called Daisha since I left her place, so I reached for the phone to call her. Daisha picked up the phone sounding somewhat disappointed when she heard my voice.

"If you want me to call you back, I will," I suggested.

"That won't be neccessary. I was taking a nap and need to get up anyway."

"Are you working today?"

"Jaylin, I work every day. Everybody don't have the benefits of staying at home like you do." Her tone was dry, and I could tell she was still mad.

"But what about the baby? Standing on your feet all day can't be good for you."

"I do okay. Trust me, I take plenty of breaks."

"Make sure you do. I know you said we needed

to talk, but I've been busy trying to work out things with Scorpio."

"That doesn't sound too hard to do. I'm sure she's already forgiven you."

"It wasn't as easy as you think, but, uh, do you need anything? I told you I want to be there for you, and I intend to."

"No, I'm fine. I would, however, like to discuss a few things with you. Can you come by?"

"How about tomorrow? I'll pick you up around lunch and we can talk then."

"That's cool, Jaylin. I'll see you tomorrow."

We hung up, and shortly after, Mackenzie and Scorpio came home. I wasn't sure where Nanny B was, and as it got later, I asked Scorpio if she knew. Scorpio said Nanny B told her she had a date.

"A date? And you believed her?" I asked.

"Why wouldn't I? She probably needed a break from all the chaos that's been stirring around here."

"There's no doubt about that." I looked over at Mackenzie, lying in my bed asleep, cuddled up with Barbie. She looked too adorable, a spitting image of Scorpio: butter-soft light skin, you'll-give-me-anything-I-want light brown eyes, coal black wavy long hair, rosy cheeks, and high cheek-bones.

I smiled. "I guess those rug rats at your sister's house wore her out, huh?"

Scorpio pushed my shoulder, defending her family. "Don't be calling my nieces and nephews rug rats. I just happen to love them a lot."

"Love them or not, they still some rug rats." I

picked up Barbie and put her on the floor. "Why do y'all keep putting this dog in my bed? All these other beds around here, and she's got her own bed, but y'all insist on having her in mine."

Barbie looked at me, wagging her tail. She had pink bows on her ears and had worked her charm on me as well. Feeling bad, I picked her up and carried her to her doggy bed. When Scorpio came in carrying Mackenzie, I put Barbie in bed with her so they could sleep together.

Scorpio insisted that she was tired, so she headed for the bedroom, and I went downstairs to watch a movie. Al Pacino was my man, so I stayed up for several hours watching *Scarface*. As the movie neared the end, I realized I'd dozed off a few times. I turned down the lights and headed back upstairs to go to bed.

When I entered the bedroom, I saw Scorpio lying sideways on the California king bed. She was wearing a white fishnet shirt and she was bare underneath. Thinking that she was asleep, I laid my body on top of hers and pulled the white satin sheets over both of us.

When she turned her head to the side, I noticed dried tears on her face. I eased over next to her.

"Are you still upset with me?" I asked with a puzzled expression.

"No."

"Then why do you keep crying?"

"Because something is telling me this isn't going to work out. As much as I want it to, and as much as I do believe you want it to as well, I don't think this relationship—"

"You're saying that because you're giving up on us. I know I fucked up, baby, but there is no such thing as a perfect relationship. I enjoy being with you, and I still would love for you to be my wife, so stop stressing yourself. You're not going anywhere, and neither am I."

Scorpio leaned forward and gave me a kiss. When I rubbed her pussy, she grabbed my hand. "Baby, please, not tonight. I'm tired, okay? Don't you ever get tired of having sex?"

"With you, no, I don't. I thought you felt the same way."

"I do, but just not tonight."

I pecked Scorpio on the forehead and fell asleep while holding her in my arms.


By morning, I rolled over and Scorpio was gone. I was still tired from staying up late, so I went back to sleep.

Mackenzie and Barbie jumped in my bed and woke me. When I looked at my alarm clock, it was already 11:00. I told Daisha I would meet her for lunch, so I rushed out of bed to shower and change clothes.

"Mackenzie," I yelled from the bathroom, "get Barbie off my bed and ask Nanna to fix you some lunch."

"She's already fixing it!" she yelled.

"Where's your mother at?"

"I don't know. She was gone when I woke up."

I finished shaving my goatee, and after I put on my clothes, I went downstairs to the kitchen.

"So, where were you at last night, Miss Lady?" I asked Nanny B.

"Now, you know better than to try to keep tabs on me. If you must know, I was on a date."

My eyes widened. "A date? And I haven't had a chance to meet him yet?"

"You will. Sooner than you think. Now, where are you going?"

"I have a lunch engagement. After I leave there, I'm gonna stop by the shop and holla at Stephon for a minute. Did you see Scorpio before she left this morning?"

"Yes, I did. I'm a little worried about her, Jaylin. She hasn't been looking too good lately. She—" Nanny B paused when Scorpio and Mackenzie came into the kitchen. I could see the stress on Scorpio's face.

"Baby, are you feeling okay?" I asked.

"Yeah, I'm fine. I forgot to tell you I had a short computer class this morning." She looked me up and down. "Where are you going? I'd like to go with you, if you don't mind."

"I'm, uh . . ." I looked at Mackenzie and Nanny B staring down my throat. Then I took Scorpio's hand and walked her into the living room. "Baby, I told Daisha I'd meet her for lunch so we could talk about the baby. I hope you don't mind." Scorpio stood stonefaced and I felt defeated. "Come on now, baby. I hope being pregnant don't have anything to do with how evil you are. You're making me feel guilty, and this is getting ridiculous, don't you think?"

She threw up her hands. "Look, just go. At this point, there's not much I can say or do."

"Listen, if you don't want me to go, then I won't. All you have to say is no, and just to show you how important your happiness is to me, I'll stay right here."

Scorpio paused before saying a word. "I . . . I don't want you to go. I am so uncomfortable with you being around her, and I'm so afraid of losing you."

"Enough said. I told you I wouldn't go if you didn't want me to, so forget it." I removed my jogging suit jacket and tossed it in the chair.

A huge part of me felt frustrated. Her insecurities were really starting to bother me. Scorpio had always been a confident woman, but this thing with Daisha really seemed to throw her off her game. I walked into my office and closed the door.

It was already way after one o'clock, so I called Daisha and cancelled. "Something came up. I'll call you next week, okay?"

"Don't bother, Jaylin. I knew you would make up an excuse so you wouldn't have to see me."

"Trust me, I do want to see you, but I promised Stephon I would take care of something for him today."

"Well, what's more important: our child, or what you promised Stephon?"

"Please don't go there. You know damn well how important this baby is to me."

"So important that you haven't asked to go to one darn doctor's appointment with me. You haven't talked to me about what to name him, or about his expenses. I refuse to deal with a man who's a pretender. Either you're going to be there, or you're not. You make the call."

Daisha hung up.

I was getting sick and tired of these grumpy-ass women in my life. I knew Daisha was right, but I was in a no-win situation: damned if I do, damned if I don't. Feeling horrible about reneging on my promise to her that I'd be there if she needed me, I put my jacket back on so I could go to Stephon's shop. I went upstairs to tell Scorpio I was leaving.

"What time are you coming back?" she questioned.

"Shit, I don't know. It won't be late, though."

"What I consider late is totally different from what you consider late."

"Damn, baby, I'm just going to his shop. Do you think that's going to take all night? If so, come on, you can go with me. Since you don't trust me, get your purse and go with me."

Not thinking that she would take me up on my offer, I was surprised when Scorpio grabbed her purse and said she was ready to go. When she saw how frustrated I looked, she laid her purse on the nightstand and sat on the bed.

"Go ahead. Have fun. And call if you're going to be late," she said.

"Are you sure you don't want to go?"

"I'm positive. And I'm sorry for sweating you like that."

"No problem. I'm just not used to all of this."

I gave Scorpio a kiss and jetted. I wanted to stop by Daisha's place to talk, but I didn't want to complicate shit between Scorpio and me even more. She was becoming a pain in the ass, and I didn't like this side of her one bit. If her intentions were to keep me away from my child, that wasn't going to happen. We'd have to come to an agreement soon, because I knew Daisha was in need of some serious support from me.

# 5

## *SCORPIO*

I felt like I was losing my mind. Jaylin didn't get home from Stephon's shop until almost two o'clock in the morning. He called a few times, but with all the noise that was going on in the background, it wasn't no telling what they were into.

There was no doubt that the minimal trust I had for him was gone. Every time he left the house, I was in a frenzy. He'd get mad at me for feeling the way I did, but I was reacting this way because of his cheating. When I reminded him of that, he apologized and hit me with his famous questions: Do you want to go with me, or do you prefer that I not go at all? Nine out of ten times I would say don't go, and he'd either go into his office and slam the door, or go downstairs to watch a movie.

As for sex, well, the other day when I told him I had a computer class to attend, I actually did what I thought was best for me and terminated my pregnancy. I had no other choice, because I didn't want Jaylin to be responsible for raising another man's child. Hell, he was already doing everything for Mackenzie, and if I had to throw another baby on him, I knew it would be over. I was so mad at myself for having sex with Rick. Doing so had cost me more hurt than I could handle.

All week long Jaylin wanted to have sex, but I couldn't. I bled like crazy, and I wasn't prepared to tell him about the baby yet. I knew I couldn't keep it a secret for long, because he was always doing investigative shit behind my back to find out things. More so, he knew my doctor's appointment was tomorrow, and he talked about going with me.

Trying to avoid him for the rest of the evening, I helped Nanny B clean the kitchen after we ate dinner. I then chilled in the living room for a while and paged through an *Ebony* magazine. I continued to keep my eyes on the bedroom, and when the lights went out, I gave him a few minutes to fall asleep before heading upstairs.

When I entered the bedroom, I almost lost it. To my surprise, he sat on the white leather chaise, with his birthday suit on. Several lit candles surrounded him, and he was leaned back with one leg on the floor and the other one on the chaise. His smooth dick lay long on his stomach, and he stroked it up and down. He took a sip from the glass of wine in his hand, and then placed it on the table next to him. While focusing on me, he licked his lips from one side to the other.

"It's been kind of cold in this room lately. I was hoping you'd have the pleasure of warming me up tonight."

I stood mesmerized by his fineness. I couldn't get any words to come out of my mouth. Instead of saying anything, I walked over and kneeled down in front of him. Wanting to give him some type of satisfaction, I reached for the hot cinnamon gel he had next to him. I squeezed it onto my tongue and licked around his head until I heard him moan my name. I used my hands to help with my stroking, taking all of him deeply into my mouth. It was rare that he'd come like this, so I had my work cut out for me. I sucked in my jaws and made sure that every entrance made it to the back of my throat. By how tense he was, I could tell he was pleased. I worked his jewels and tightly squeezed my lips over his thick head to make him come. When he tightened his fingers in my hair, I closed my eyes and swallowed.

"Take off your clothes," he whispered.

I ignored him and continued to clean him up with my tongue.

"That was good . . . very good, but I want my pussy."

I stopped and looked up at him. "Not right now. Just let me finish, okay?"

He was too excited to respond, and he lay back so I could finish the job. Moments later, he pleaded to go inside of me, but this time I refused.

"What's the big deal?" he yelled. I watched his dick deflate in my hand. "Are you fucking around with somebody else?"

"No, Jaylin. I just don't feel like it tonight. Maybe tomorrow."

He gave me a hard stare, and without saying one word to me, he got in bed. His eyes followed me as I went to the bathroom to get a towel. When I wiped him with it, he grabbed my hand.

"If you're fucking around on me, I'm gonna hurt you, Scorpio. I will not tolerate a cheating woman."

How dare he not tolerate a cheating woman when I'd tolerated a cheating man? Jaylin's controlling ways were making me crazy, but now wasn't the time to deal with them. I definitely had a bigger fish to fry. "I'm not messing around on you. Being pregnant just makes me this way, so be patient. It's not that often that this happens."

He let go of my hand and mumbled something underneath his breath. After that, he turned his back, and thirty minutes later, he was sound asleep.

I felt horrible. I was in no position to argue with him about his actions. This was my fault, and continuously lying to him wasn't making things better. I wanted him inside of me so badly, but I had to wait until I somehow worked out this mess.

By early morning, I crept into the bathroom to check my blood flow. It wasn't too heavy. I got in the shower before going to my fake doctor's appointment. As I was in the shower, Jaylin knocked on the bathroom door. Normally I'd leave it unlocked, but I knew after I turned him down last night, he'd want to join me.

"Baby," I yelled, "I'll be out in a minute, okay?"

"Unlock the door," he said, turning the knob.

"Can I have some privacy, please?"

"You can have all the privacy you want after I piss. Now open the door."

"Can't you go to another bathroom?"

"Scorpio, open the damn door!"

I turned off the shower, grabbed a towel, and unlocked the door. When Jaylin came in, I quickly covered myself with the towel. He cut me like a knife with his eyes, and then sat his jaw-dropping naked body down on the edge of the Jacuzzi tub.

"What is up with you?" he said, rubbing his eyes.

"Nothing. I just needed some privacy, that's all."

"For as long as you've been in this house, you've never locked the bathroom door or demanded your privacy. If you're not going to forgive me for what I did, then maybe it's time for us to call it quits. I'm not going to live my life like this; I'm not going to be in the same house with my woman and can't even touch her, and I'm not going to stay stuck up in here because of your insecurities."

"I understand," I said softly. "And I'm not asking you to. All I wanted was some privacy this morning. Nothing more, nothing less."

He grabbed my waist and sat me down on his lap. I held the towel tightly above my breasts so it wouldn't slide down.

"Tell me honestly," he said. "Do you still love me?"

I placed my hand on his face and looked into

his to-die-for eyes. "Yes, I love you, but being in love with you is a scary thing. Just give me a little more time to get over this and I promise you, I will."

I rose up, and Jaylin stood tall in front of me. He wrapped his arms around me and squeezed tightly.

"Don't be afraid to love me, because I'm not going to hurt you again. We've come too far, Scorpio, and I hope you're willing to work this out with me. So, let the towel go, and let me make love to you this morning."

"We're going to be late for my doctor's appointment. Can we do it later?"

Jaylin didn't buy my excuse. "It's six-thirty in the morning. Your appointment isn't until ten o'clock. How in the hell are we going to be late?"

"You ain't no five-minute brotha, Jaylin. And once we get started, you're not going to stop."

"We'll have to see about that."

Jaylin pulled the towel from the back, and not being able to hold on, I let it go. He moved my wet hair away from my face and leaned down to kiss me. I held my hands tightly together in front of me, feeling myself about to lose it. As soon as he gripped my butt cheeks and swayed his hand across my coochie, I backed up. At that moment, I wanted to lie and tell him that I'd had a miscarriage, but we had already lied to each other enough, and I just couldn't go there. If he found out I lied, he would never forgive me. I had to be honest and come clean, but I also had to do so when it felt convenient for me. Now wasn't the time or the place.

"I'm sorry, I can't," I said, backing away from him. "Not right now."

"And why not right now?" he yelled. "I'm about to explode." He held his hard dick in his hand. "What in the fuck do you expect me to do about this? I thought you were my woman. I guess not."

He opened the bathroom door and slammed it as hard as he could. One of the potpourri crystal vases fell from the counter and broke.

I hurried to clean myself up. Not saying a word to Jaylin, I went into the closet, changed clothes, and hurried to go. Having no cash on me, I stopped at the doorway and turned to face him.

"So, I guess you don't want to go with me, huh?" I asked.

He wouldn't even look up at me. "Nope."

"Then can I have some money?"

"You already got some money."

"Trust me, I don't. The last time I checked my account, I only had twenty dollars in there."

"Then check again." He picked up the phone and held it in his hand.

I dialed my bank's 800 number then entered my code. The recorder said I had ten thousand twenty dollars and some-odd cents in my account. I hung up and looked at him. "Thanks for thinking about me."

He didn't say a word. I headed toward the door and turned to him again. "Are you sure you don't want to go with me?"

"Positive."

\* \* \*

Having no doctor's appointment at all, I drove around for a while to keep myself busy. I had breakfast at Denny's on Manchester, and then stopped at Frontenac Plaza to shop. Thinking about how good Jaylin had been to me, I shopped for him at Saks Fifth Avenue, and then bought a dress for Mackenzie as well. I didn't want to leave out LJ, so I bought him a blue jean Polo outfit and a pair of shoes to match.

By the time I finished, it was almost one o'clock. I called Leslie's house to see if she wanted some company. From the sound of my depressing, low voice, she sensed something was wrong and told me to come over.

When I got to her place, she was arguing with her boyfriend, James. The kids were crying, and she had a bat in her hand, about to crack his head wide open.

"Come on, you black-ass fool," she yelled with tears streaming down her face. "If you call your bitch on my phone one more time, I'm gonna fuck your ass up!"

"Girl, you better put that damn bat down before you get beat up in here," he ordered.

Leslie swung the bat hard and hit James in his arm. After that, they were throwing down. The kids were crying even harder. Unable to separate Leslie and James, I called the police.

Several minutes later, the police came, and James flew out the back door. One of the officers saw him and chased after him. They took a statement from Leslie, and she lied about who hit who first. Since James had a warrant out for his arrest, they hauled him off to jail.

I calmed the kids and went into the bathroom, where Leslie stood looking in the mirror at the bruises on her face. Having different fathers, she was much darker than I was, so the bruises were easier to hide. She pressed a towel against her lip, wiping blood from it.

"I'm so sick of this mess," she said, throwing the towel in the sink.

"Well, why don't you just leave him alone?"

She tooted her lips and cut her eyes at me. "I know you ain't talking. If anybody needs to leave anybody alone, you need to leave that no-good-ass Jaylin alone."

"Leslie, there's no way you can stand there and compare an animal like James to Jaylin. For your information, Jaylin loves me, he takes care of me, and he would never put his hands on me the way James just did you."

"Whatever," she said, walking out of the bathroom. "Abuse is abuse. It comes in all different shapes, forms, and fashions. If you want me to be honest about it, your situation ain't no damn different from mine."

I put my hand on my hip and defended my situation. Again, there was no comparison, and Leslie knew there wasn't. This was her way of taking the heat off her situation and putting it on mine. "Now, I don't want to argue with you about this, but think about the children, please. You're destroying them, girl. One thing I can say is Mackenzie has never been subjected to Jaylin and me beating the hell out of each other. If anything, you should know how it feels to watch your mother get beat all the time. We watched it for many years, and you know it's not a good feeling."

Leslie lit a cigarette and sat on the edge of her bed. The whole damn house was a mess, and I was so disappointed to see her living like she did.

"Look, I know you're right, and that nigga ain't coming back here ever again. He's smoking that crack, and if one more bitch call this house looking for his ass, I'm gonna kill him."

"Girl, please. He ain't even worth it. Then your kids would really be messed up without no mother."

"You got that right." She took a few more puffs from her cigarette then put it out. "Anyway, why you been coming over here lately? The only time I see you is when shit ain't going right with you and Jaylin."

I sat on the bed next to Leslie. "That's not true, but we are going through something."

"Who he done fucked this time? Don't tell me he's on his way back to Nokea."

"No, it's nothing like that. But, uh, he has another baby on the way."

Leslie's eyes widened. She looked like she'd seen a ghost. "Other than your baby? He got another baby?"

"Well, something like that."

"See, that's what I'm talking about. And you just a fool for sitting back letting him."

I had to get my secret off my chest. Maybe it would make me feel better to tell someone, and who better to tell than my own sister. "Leslie, the baby I had wasn't Jaylin's."

Her eyes got even wider. "Well, who in the hell's baby is it?"

"It was Rick's baby. You remember the fine-ass exterminator I told you I met in Denver?"

"Yeah, I remember. But you never said anything about having sex with him. And why in the hell would you not use a condom?"

"We did, but it tore. Twice. I didn't tell you because I didn't want anybody to know. I found out that it was his baby, and I had an abortion the other day."

"Does Jaylin know all of this?"

"No, he doesn't."

"Well, I'll get you and Mackenzie's bed ready in the basement. I'm sure after you tell him, you'll be right here with me."

I couldn't agree with Leslie more. Jaylin acted as if I had no feelings and no right to be with anyone other than him. There was no way he'd understand my need to have sex with Rick, even though he'd been doing his thing with Daisha. He was so one-sided. It was always up to me to put a stop to the mess he continuously dished out. I knew it wasn't fair, and it would be just a matter of time before he'd have to deal with the reason I turned to another man.

I laid my head on Leslie's shoulder. "Our relationships are such a mess, aren't they?"

"*Was* a mess, baby girl. I'm getting out of this shit and soon."

"Me too."

I stayed at Leslie's house and helped her clean up until almost six o'clock. When I called home, Nanny B said Jaylin wasn't there and told me

Mackenzie was in the backyard playing with her best friend, Megan, and Barbie. I told her I'd be home soon.

"Big sis," I said, "I'm getting ready to take off. Do you need anything?"

"About fifty dollars, if you got it. I got a disconnection on my gas and electric bill and—"

I reached in my purse and gave Leslie three hundred dollars. She looked at it. "Thanks. I guess that damn fool you got is good for something, ain't he?"

"More than you will ever know."


By the time I got home, I was hoping Jaylin would be there, but he wasn't. I called his cell phone and he didn't answer. During a late dinner, Nanny B could tell how moody I was, and she encouraged me to stay strong. I tried to, but it worried me so much when I didn't know where he was.

I went downstairs and watched television with Mackenzie and Megan. Seemed like every five minutes I gazed at my watch. By midnight, I was fuming. I zipped Megan and Mackenzie's sleeping bags so they could stay warm and headed upstairs for bed.

Jaylin didn't come home until almost 3:45 in the morning, and when he did, he was drunk as hell. He crawled in bed and kissed all over me.

"Would you move, please?" I said, shoving him off me.

"Come on, baby. Open them legs up and let me in."

"Hell, no! Get off of me, Jaylin."

He continued touching me, and when he tried to force down my panties, I smacked his face hard and got out of bed. He jumped in front of me as I headed to the bathroom.

"Don't ever put your hands on me again," he said calmly. His breath reeked of alcohol, so I did my best to ignore him. "If I can't make love to my woman, then . . ."

I ignored his threats by going into the bathroom and closing the door. When I came out, he was gone. I looked outside and saw him speed off down the street in his Mercedes. I was so sure he was headed Daisha's way.

# 6

## *NOKEA*

At almost five o'clock in the morning, the door-bell was ringing like crazy. Panicking, I rushed to the door only to see Jaylin standing outside. When I opened the door, he stumbled in. He removed his shades and his faded black jean jacket. His matching wide-legged jeans were cuffed, and his red stretch shirt hugged his muscles. When his phone rang, he slightly lifted his shirt, looked at the number, then turned it off. I got a glimpse of his six-pack, and instantly noticed the normal hump in his pants. I turned away and yawned, attempting to ignore my attraction to him.

"What are you dong coming over here this time of the morning?" I asked.

"Where my son at?"

"He's outside playing golf. Where do you think he is?"

Jaylin walked down the hallway to LJ's room, and his shoes made a loud noise on my hardwood floors. I ran down the hall to stop him from waking LJ.

"Please don't. He's been crabby all night and I need some rest. You can spend all the time you want with him later today, okay?"

Jaylin looked at me but didn't say a word. He walked into my bedroom and looked around. "Where your man at?"

"At home. Hopefully getting some rest."

"Why ain't he over here with you?"

"Because he was just over here the night before."

"Did you fuck him?"

I smiled at his question, as it had caught me off guard. "Are you crazy? That isn't any of your business."

"You're right," he said, sitting down on my bed. He lay back, placed his hands behind his head, and looked up at the ceiling fan. "You know I've been thinking a lot about you, don't you?"

"No, I didn't know." I walked over to the bed and sat next to him. "But did you have to come over here this early in the morning to tell me?"

He turned his head and looked away. "I was out. Besides, I've wanted to tell you how much I've missed you for a long time. I just didn't have the courage."

I was bothered that he was coming at me like this; after all, we'd both decided to move on. Still, there was a part of me that would always have some feelings for Jaylin. "Look, Jaylin, don't do this. I know you're going through something right now, but telling me something you really don't mean isn't going to solve your problems. The alcohol doesn't help either."

"I do mean it. Hell, I miss you like crazy. Been missing what we shared for a very long time." He looked at me for confirmation. "But you're in love with Collins, right?"

"Yes, and you're in love with Scorpio. The two of you have a baby on the way, and—"

"And it's still not going to stop me from missing you."

"So what do you want me to do? Hey, I'm happy with who I'm with. You are so wrong coming to me like this, and you know it."

"Why? Because you're feeling the same way about me? I know you are, Nokea. I can tell."

"Just like you can tell I've been dreaming about you too, right?"

"That's why I'm here this morning. I sensed your dream and came here to make it a reality."

In an effort to cut the tension, I laughed. I stood up to turn on the TV. He grabbed my hands on my way back over to the bed. I stood in front of him, and he rubbed his hands together with mine.

"Jaylin, go home. Work things out with Scorpio."

He closed his eyes and placed his head against my stomach. When he sat up straight, he reached for the belt on my robe to untie it. I held my belt. Seeing that I wasn't going to let him undo it, his hands swayed to my legs. Searching even further, his hands went up my robe, and he reached for my panties to pull them down.

I was foolishly caught up in the moment, and

while stepping out of my panties, I pulled his shirt over his head. He scooted back on the bed and removed his pants. Lying naked in bed, he had me hooked. We stared at each other and waited for the next move.

I looked at his goods that had already expanded past his navel, and willing to take the next move, I dropped my robe to the floor. I eased my way up to him on my knees and came face to face with him. He cradled my face in his hands. The moment our lips touched, there was no turning back for me. Past feelings resurfaced.

I laid my body on top of his and felt his long, hard muscle pressing against my stomach. Taking control, he rolled on top and kneeled down in front of me. He held my legs together and pushed my knees close to my chest. Having a clear vision of my insides, he rubbed himself against me and forced his way into my wetness.

I took deep breaths and backed away from the man I still had a difficult time handling. He could feel how tense I was, and inched his way slightly out. I guess trying to make it easier for me, he took his time and refused to give me all of him. His eyes were focused in on his insertions below, and I could tell he was concentrating hard on making me come.

Moments later, the heat was coming down, and Jaylin was teasing my clit in a way only he knew how to do. He widened my legs, and feeling every bit of him now, I covered my face. I couldn't believe this was happening. The lovemaking was perfect and almost brought me to tears.

He saw how into him I was, and leaned in to

whisper in my ear. "Collins ain't working my pussy right, is he?"

I had the nerve to agree, and responded with the truth. "No, never. Never like you."

He smiled and continued to stroke. "Well, if your pussy ever needs me again, remember, I'm just a phone call away."

"We need you now, so hush."

Jaylin rubbed my hair back and looked deeply into my eyes without moving. He pecked my lips with his. As he put me into another position, a noise came from LJ's room. My bedroom was so quiet that you could hear a pin drop. Neither one of us wanted this to end, so we listened for LJ to make another noise. He didn't, so we continued. Jaylin smiled and so did I. He drenched my insides again.

After we were getting deeply into it once again, LJ cried out loud. Jaylin lowered my leg and dropped his head on my chest.

"Damn," he said. "You have got to let me finish."

"I . . . I wish I could, but I can't," I said as LJ's cries got louder.

Jaylin let out a deep sigh and eased himself out of me.

"I'm sorry," I said, getting out of bed.

"Don't be. Just promise to make it up to me some other time."

I made no comment, put on my robe, and hurried to see about LJ.

Jaylin slid into his jeans, and when I put LJ down by the doorway, he walked over and tried to climb in bed with Jaylin. With my bed being up so high, Jaylin reached down and picked him up.

"We make a cute little family, don't we?" he said.

"Please don't go getting any ideas. You know more than I do that sex between us should have never happened."

"Well, it did. You can't change it, and you for damn sure can't say you didn't want it to happen."

"So you made my dream a reality. Now, would you get out of here before my man finds out you're over here?"

"Damn, just throw me out. Use me for my shit and then tell me to get to stepping."

"It's not like that. I want you to go home because I'm sure your woman is looking for you. Remember, I've been in her shoes before, and I can only imagine how she would feel if—"

"Okay, I'm leaving. Right after you cook breakfast for me and my son."

"Breakfast? I'm not cooking you any breakfast."

"Then I'm staying right here. You already got me leaving empty handed." He looked down at his goods. "And then you don't want to feed me?"

"You need to talk to your son about why you're leaving empty handed. It wasn't my fault."

Jaylin looked at his watch. "I got all day, baby. As soon as you get breakfast over with, I'm outtie."

Seeing that he wasn't going anywhere, I whipped up a quick breakfast. Collins was expected to stop by this morning, so I rushed Jaylin to leave.

No sooner than we finished eating, Collins rang the doorbell. I rolled my eyes at Jaylin and made my way to the door.

Collins could barely get inside. "Is Jaylin over here?" He looked at Jaylin's Mercedes in the driveway.

I leaned in for a kiss. "Uh-huh. He's in the kitchen with LJ. He just stopped by for breakfast with his son."

Collins headed for the kitchen, and I followed behind him, fidgeting. Jaylin was finishing up his orange juice, with LJ sitting on his lap. Jaylin had a wide, smirky grin as he reached out to shake Collins' hand.

"Hey, man. What's been up?" Jaylin asked.

"Too much," Collins said. "All this hard work has been killing me."

"I wouldn't know nothing about that, but don't stress yourself too much."

"I try not to," Collins said, sitting down. "I'm on my way to Detroit tonight. A couple fellas down there been embezzling money from the business and selling our products at a discount. I gotta go find out what's going on before it's too late."

Jaylin leaned back in his chair and looked at me. "Are you going too?"

"No. I have plans to do something else."

He rubbed his goatee and gave off a soft snicker. "Well, I'm getting ready to take off. Can I take LJ with me, or do y'all have plans?"

"I'll bring him by later. Maybe after I drop off Collins at the airport."

"Cool," he said, standing up. "Collins, good seeing you, man. Take care of my babies for me."

"Always."

I walked Jaylin outside, and when he talked about finishing up what we started tonight, I shook my head.

"No, Jaylin, and I mean it. I'm calling Nanny B to come get LJ later, because you and I will never be alone again."

"Why? 'Cause you can't handle it?"

"Maybe I can't. But I don't get a kick out of hurting the people I love. I'm not going to allow you to interfere with my relationship."

"You've already allowed me to do that. But if you didn't learn anything from our encounter today, I hope you see now how easy it is for you to cheat on somebody you say you love. Happens to me all the time."

"Good-bye, Jaylin."

"Adios, Nokea."

He got in his car and left.

I thought about what Jaylin had said. Never in my wildest dream did I think I would be so willing to go there with him again. Especially since I was so happy and in love with Collins. I waited an entire lifetime to find someone like him, and there was no way I was going to let Jaylin have the upper hand. I promised myself to never let something like that happen again, but I also knew that promises could be broken.

# 7

## *JAYLIN*

On the drive home, I couldn't stop thinking about what had happened between Nokea and me. She was tighter than a motherfucker, but as usual, her pussy was just how I liked it. And the truth of the matter was, I had been missing her tremendously. For many years, we had each other for support, and if a brotha like Collins ever thought he could permanently take her away from me, he was sadly mistaken. I knew Nokea would always be there for me, no ifs, ands, or buts about it. I just never thought that getting her back in bed with me would come so easily. I seriously thought, out of all people, she would be faithful to her man. But again, that's just what I thought.

As for Scorpio, I wasn't trying to play her like I did, but I'd had enough of her rejection. I didn't know what the fuck was wrong with her. She acted like she didn't even want me to touch her. If I even looked like I wanted to make love, she'd clam up and act like she wasn't feeling me. Now, what woman in her right mind would turn down what I presented to her the other night? I'd be damned if I put myself out there again, and if I found out she was giving my shit up to somebody else, only the Lord knew what was going to happen to her. As for her seeing another man, the signs were definitely there. I wasn't going to be a fool for anyone, and I hoped she wasn't going to try to play me for one.

I had some regrets about having sex with Nokea today, but I always had to somehow, or some way, protect myself from being hurt. I'd had enough hurt from past women in my life, and it didn't make sense for me to ever let my guard down. Until I found out what was up with Scorpio, if some pussy that I wanted was within my reach, I was taking it.

I got home at almost ten o'clock in the morning. Nanny B was in her room catching up on some rest, since Mackenzie and Scorpio were gone. When I asked where they had gone, she told me she didn't know, and asked me to close the door on my way out.

Since Scorpio wasn't around, I used the phone in my room to call Daisha. I'd left several messages for her, but she hadn't called me back. When she didn't answer this time, I left a message saying I was thinking about her and my baby, and told her I'd call back later.

Afterward, I called the barbershop to holla at Stephon. He asked me to hold on and gave the phone to Mona.

"What's up, Mona?" I asked.

"Daisha's going to kill me for telling you this, but she was admitted to the hospital yesterday."

"For what?"

"I don't know. Something with the baby."

"What hospital is she at?"

"Where does she work?"

"St. Lukes?"

"Yes, Jaylin. And please don't tell her I told you, okay?"

"I won't, and thanks for telling me. Let me talk to Stephon."

"Yo," he said.

"Have you seen Daisha lately?"

"Naw, man. Mona just told me what happened today. I know they've met up a few times; other than that, everything's been kind of hush-hush."

"Well, I'm on my way to the hospital. I'll catch up with you, Shane, and Ray-Ray later."

"If we ain't at the shop, come by my place."

"Will do."

I hung up and hurried off to the hospital to see Daisha. When I got there, I had a hard time finding her. Finally, when I saw Carolyn, a chick I used to hang out with in college, working there, she told me she knew who Daisha was and walked me to her room.

Daisha was sleeping. Trying not to wake her, I took a seat in one of the chairs. I was thirty minutes into watching *Judge Mathis* when one of the nurses came in. She asked if I was Daisha's brother because we resembled each other. I informed her that I was the father of Daisha's baby and asked her Daisha's condition. As she was about to tell me, Daisha's eyes slowly opened and connected with mine. She had a disturbing look on her face. The nurse asked if she needed anything, but Daisha told her all she needed was privacy.

"Do you want me to leave?" I asked.

"I wasn't talking to you. I was talking to Judy."

Judy smiled at Daisha and closed the door on her way out.

She sadly looked at me. "So, you finally found some time for us, huh?"

"Woman, please. I've been calling you like crazy. I told you if you needed anything to call me."

"That's what your mouth said," she snapped. "All I wanted to do was talk. You never made any time for us to do that."

"I tried . . . really, I did. Besides, I'm here now. So how are you feeling?"

Daisha took a hard swallow and her eyes watered. "I'm feeling as good as I'm going to get."

"How's the baby?"

With attitude, she gave me an angry stare and spoke sharply. "Why don't you go see for yourself?"

"You had him already? You still had at least three to four months to go, didn't you?"

"He's premature, Jaylin. He only weighs a pound and a half, and the doctors—" She covered her face with her hands.

"The doctors said what?"

Daisha started crying and refused to say anything else to me. Dying to know what was up, I left the room and looked around for Judy. When I found her, I asked her to take me to where my baby was. She did, and when she pointed to my son, I damn near wanted to cry myself. He was so tiny that he could have fit in the palm of my hand. He was in an incubator with all kinds of tubes attached to him. The sight of him fighting for his life sent chills through my body.

Knowing that I was his father, Judy told me to wash my hands and made me put on gloves and a gown to cover up. Once my mouth was covered, so I wouldn't spread any germs, she held my baby in her hands without removing him from the incubator.

"If you'd like to hold him, you'll have to hold him like this," she said.

I reached for my son, and not able to hold him for one damn minute, I put him back down and lost it. I was full of emotions as I snatched the gown away from my chest. I tossed the gloves in the trash and stormed out, removing the mask from my mouth.

I fought back my tears all the way to Daisha's room. When I opened the door, I fell beside her bed, touching her hands. "I'm so damn sorry," I yelled and pounded my fist on her bed. "Why didn't you tell me?"

At first, she didn't say anything, but when I dropped my head on the bed, she reached over and rubbed it. "It's not your fault, okay? A few weeks ago, my doctor told me that I'd have a difficult pregnancy, but I didn't listen. My blood pressure was way up, and I have diabetes. He advised me to cut back on my hours, but I thought working would keep my mind off the stress I'd been under."

I gathered myself and sat on the bed next to Daisha. No matter what she said, I still felt at fault.

"What are his chances of surviving like that? And don't go making up shit so you don't hurt my feelings."

She took another hard swallow, and a few tears rolled from the corner of her eyes. "His chances are slim. My doctor said there's pretty much no way he's going to survive. I'm trying to remain hopeful, but this isn't the first time I've lost a child."

I figured that was what Daisha wanted to speak to me about, and I felt like a fool for not going to see her when I had a chance. I got in bed with her, allowing her to rest her head on my shoulder. "Don't give up yet, okay? You don't seem like a person who gives up so easily, so don't go doing it now."

I stayed all night at the hospital with Daisha, and neither one of us could get any sleep. Deep down, we both knew the baby wouldn't make it. When Judy came in early in the morning and broke the news to us, we held each other and released our emotions. My pain was because, just maybe, had I been there for her, things would have turned out differently. And no matter how much Daisha played it down like she wasn't tripping off me not being there, I knew she somewhat held me responsible.

I didn't want to make the same mistake with Scorpio, so I called home to tell her where I was. Nanny B answered, and after I mentioned to her what had happened, she told me she was sorry to hear that and then gave the phone to Scorpio.

"Listen, I apologize for not calling you sooner, but I've been at the hospital with Daisha all night."

"All night, Jaylin? For what? I don't care what was going on; you should have called me. I've been worried. We really need to talk, because I can't go on living like this."

I knew she was upset with me about my bullshit, but I just couldn't leave Daisha's side. "I understand your concerns. We'll talk as soon as I get home."

"Fine. Now, is everything okay?"

"Not really. Daisha lost the baby, and I'm just trying to offer her my support."

"I'm sorry to hear that, but how are you doing? Are you okay?"

My throat ached. "Uh-uh. But I'm happy that I got another baby to look forward to. Take care of my baby, all right? And I'll see you soon."

"I'll do my best. See you when you get home."

"I love you."

"I love you more."

I stayed with Daisha almost the entire day. We talked about the baby and agreed to take our friendship one day at a time. She was glad to have me with her, and I couldn't think of any other place I'd rather be.

Later that day, I think Daisha kind of got tired of me being around.

"It's time for you to go home. Besides, I'm getting sleepy," she said.

I kissed her forehead and eased out of bed. "Since they're releasing you from the hospital tomorrow, if you call me, I'll pick you up and take you home."

"You don't have to. Mona's taking me home to-morrow. I don't think I'm ready for us to be see-ing each other like that yet."

"Can I at least call you? And you know we have to make some arrangements for our son."

"Let's just keep it simple. I've suffered enough."

I nodded, kissed Daisha on her cheek, and then jetted. Before I left the hospital, I looked in the empty incubator where my baby had been. I held back my tears until I got in my car because I didn't want anyone to see how much I was really hurting inside. I knew everything happened for a reason, but why did bad things have to keep on happening to me? Especially when it came to my children.

The house was cozy and quiet. Everyone was asleep. Having a banging-ass headache, I took two Tylenol and went downstairs to be alone. I sat in one of the soft leather chairs and turned on the theater-size TV. It blasted loudly, and I quickly lowered the volume.

I was almost an hour into checking out *Bad Boys II* when I felt a wet tongue licking my ear.

I closed my eyes. "Umm, Barbie, get down girl," I joked.

"No, my dear, I am not Barbie," Scorpio said in a seductive voice. "I am the woman who loves you." She kissed me on the cheek and laid a red rose in my lap. "Who will do anything for you." She kissed my other cheek. "And I am here for you whenever you need me." She moved face to face with me, looking into my eyes. "However, we still need to have our talk about why you felt the need to walk out on me and not call. I don't want for us to disrespect each other like that, and the next time you get that angry, just go to one of the guest rooms, okay?"

I nodded, but she pushed. "You look tired, so this conversation is over for the night. Let me know when you're ready to have a real discussion about what's been going on between us."

I nodded again.

Scorpio got some blankets from the closet and spread them out on the floor. We rolled ourselves in them together and crashed out on the floor. My mind was a little more at ease, as I thought about Scorpio's and my baby. I was going to be there for her every step of the way to make sure nothing happened to her or to the baby. I thought deeply about my son, and the memory of seeing his handsome little self would stay with me forever.

# 8

## *SCORPIO*

This lie I lived was killing me! I planned on telling Jaylin everything the other night, but he never came home. And when he called to tell me about Daisha's baby, how could I tell him about my baby? No doubt about it, I was losing my mind. Since Daisha had lost their baby, he'd been waiting on me hand and foot. He constantly asked if I needed anything, and if he left the house, he'd come right back. There were no more late nights, and he took me almost every place he went.

Feeling so badly about the situation, I'd been losing sleep. My eyes looked tired, and when Nanny B questioned me about not gaining any weight, I didn't know what to say. She had a look as if she knew something wasn't right, and I knew if there was anybody I could talk to about my situation, it was her.

Jaylin asked if I wanted to celebrate Stephons's birthday with him, Shane, and Ray-Ray. I wanted him to have a good time without me, and I definitely did not want to see Shane because of my previous bedroom encounter with him, so I declined. I figured it would give Nanny B and me a chance to talk.

I lay across the chaise in the bedroom with Mackenzie and Barbie, as Jaylin got dressed to leave.

"How do I look?" he asked. I laid my book on my lap, searching him over from head to toe. Mackenzie looked him over too, and tilted her head from side to side.

I wet my lips. "Turn around so I can check you out from the back."

He turned around and stood with a confident smile on his face. I picked the book back up and covered my face with it. "You look a'ight."

He walked over and took the book from my hand. "A'ight? That's all the credit you can give me, and you're the one who picked out this suit?"

"You look sharp, Daddy," Mackenzie said, holding her hand up to give Jaylin a high five.

"Thanks, baby. I knew I could always depend on you for the truth." He puckered up and Mackenzie gave him a kiss.

There wasn't any doubt in my mind that my man looked spectacular. He had on a single-breasted pin-striped dark brown suit, and a silk cream-colored shirt with an oversized collar. Having no buttons on it, it showed the thickness and smoothness of his chest. As for his hat, it really set him off. It was a silky brown with stripes on the band that matched his suit. He wore it slightly to the side to show his neatly trimmed curly hair and thinly shaven beard. As for the goatee, well, that always spoke for itself. I'll be the first to admit, Jaylin was banging. *GQ* magazine didn't know what they were missing. After he sprayed on his cologne and covered his gray eyes with his tinted brown shades, I knew I'd better set a curfew for him tonight.

When the doorbell rang, Jaylin ran downstairs to get it.

I heard the fellas loudly coming up the steps and quickly lowered my head to pretend I was all into my book. When they all stepped into the bedroom, I looked up and smiled.

"Hello, everybody," I said. They all spoke back, and Stephon made it his business to walk over and personally say hello. He lifted my hand, kissing the back of it.

"Hey, lovely lady. How have you been doing?" he asked.

"Watch it, nigga," Jaylin said, walking into the bathroom. "Don't be getting too damn friendly with my woman."

They all laughed.

"I'm fine, Stephon. How about you?"

"I'm fine too, but never as fine as you."

Jaylin pushed him in the back and tried to nudge him away from me. "Back off, bro. You getting too damn frisky for me."

Stephon straightened his jacket and smiled at me. "Woman, you are lucky—"

"Chill out, Stephon," Shane said. "Why you all up on Jay woman like that?"

"Shane, don't say nothing to him," Jaylin said, putting on his shoes. "When his ass laid out on the floor from this blow I'm about to give him, don't y'all be mad at me."

They all laughed again, and when Ray-Ray mentioned the last time Jaylin and Stephon had a fight, the room got pretty noisy. I wasn't paying attention to what Ray-Ray said at all. My attention was focused on St. Louis' finest men that I had standing in my presence. These brothas looked flawless and would definitely be considered what I called metrosexual men. If Stephon's to-die-for smile, his hazelnut eyes, or his ocean blue casual linen pant suit didn't catch my attention, Shane's thick and cut muscular body dressed in a black fitted V-neck ribbed shirt and black wide-legged slacks damn sure did. His twisties were freshly done, and bedroom eyes were bound to get him laid tonight. I'd been there before, of course, and could only think about the licks he gave me between my legs.

As for Ray-Ray, well, he needed some more work to keep up with the fellas. His outfit didn't even come close to theirs. My baby, though, looked the best. I couldn't stop staring at how fine he was. I dared any woman to put her hands on him tonight.

Either way, they were all groomed to perfection: fresh haircuts, beards neatly trimmed, and cologne lighting up the whole room. *Jesus!* was all I could scream silently to myself.

When they bragged about whose outfit cost the most, I had to tune them out. Nobody could even afford to look like Jaylin and he knew it.

"Baby, would you tell these fools how much this suit cost?" he yelled.

I rolled my eyes. "Totally irrelevant, but if they must know, it cost almost two grand."

"See, I told ya. And that don't even include the shirt, the shoes, the hat, the jewelry, or my underwear."

"Man, quit trying to perpetrate," Ray-Ray said. "I saw that motherfucking suit at Tesse's Thrift Store in Pawn Lawn last week for seventy-five cents."

"When you was there picking up your suit, right? Nigga, please. If you saw this suit there you should have bought it your damn self instead of coming out in that tight-ass motherfucker you busting out in."

They all fell out on the floor and on the bed, cracking up. Not being able to keep quiet, I chuckled as well. Quiet as it's kept, though, Ray-Ray's suit was a little snug.

Shane sat on the bed and wiped his tears from laughing so hard. When he caught my eye, he blinked and looked away. I was a little uncomfortable with seeing him, but I'm sure he knew Jaylin and I were happy together and the past was the past.

Before they left, Jaylin came over and gave me a nice, long, wet and juicy kiss. Knowing they were about to get their clown on, since Stephon was turning thirty-five, I reminded him of all the strippers I knew and suggested they not take a ride to East St. Louis. When Ray-Ray yelled, "Strip clubs, here we come!" I gave Jaylin a stern look, as if he'd better not go there.

"Baby, you know I ain't going to no strip club tonight."

"No, I don't know. But be careful and call if you're going to be late. You know I worry about you."

"Aw, ain't that so sweet," Stephon said sarcastically.

Jaylin turned around and gave Stephon a devious look. He pecked my lips again and they all left.

Once I tucked Mackenzie in for the night, I headed straight for Nanny B's room. She was in bed reading.

"That is really an excellent book," I said, taking a seat.

"I know. So come back in an hour or two after I'm finished." She smiled, closed the book, and looked at me with many questions on her mind. "Out with it, Scorpio."

I sighed, unable to give her eye contact. "Well, first of all, you do know how much I love Jaylin, don't you?"

"Uh-huh."

"Well, with that being said, I . . . I've been keeping something from him and I don't know how much damage it's going to cause if I tell him the truth."

"The truth about what? You losing the baby?" I immediately looked up at Nanny B. "It doesn't take a rocket scientist to figure out you're not pregnant, Scorpio. And it's going to be just a matter of time until Jaylin notices you're not gaining any weight. You look as if you're losing it. Since I do the laundry and take out the trash around here, it's hard to keep something like that from me."

"But I didn't lose the baby, Nanny B. I had an abortion."

She frowned and shook her head with major disappointment in her eyes. "Oh, chile. Now, why'd you go do that?"

My eyes watered. Nanny B told me to come sit by her. She wrapped her arms around me and squeezed me tightly. I wiped my face. "The baby wasn't Jaylin's baby. It was a man named Rick, who I met in Denver."

I shamefully dropped my head again, but Nanny B lifted my chin and pointed her finger at me. "Listen, people make mistakes all the time. But continuing to lie and hurt the ones you love is unacceptable—on your behalf and Jaylin's. If you love him as much as you say you do, then don't keep anything like that from him. He's running around here excited about a baby that doesn't even exist. Deception can hurt a person more than anything. And if you lose him for telling him the truth, then deal with it. Maybe it just wasn't meant to be."

"But I don't want to lose him. He means everything to me, and I could never see myself being without him again."

"Chile, you remind me so much of myself. But when God brought you in this world, you were without Jaylin. And trust me, when He takes you away, you'll still be without him. You have only known him for less than two years, and if you made it before, you can damn sure make it after he's gone."

"I know you're right, but you know more than I do that Jaylin is going to act a fool. He was so hurt about losing his son, and I don't want to hurt him again."

"He'll get over it. He always does, doesn't he? And so will you."

I thanked Nanny B for listening to me, and before I left the room, I told her I needed more time before telling Jaylin the truth. She promised me she wouldn't interfere, but warned me the longer I waited, the more damage it would cause. I felt the same way, but as smooth as things were going between us now, I didn't want no fuck-ups.

# 9

## *JAYLIN*

I wanted to make sure that I came in at a decent hour, so Shane and I rode in my car and Ray-Ray and Stephon rode in his BMW. If I let Stephon drive, I knew Scorpio wouldn't see my ass until early morning.

We were on our way to the Eagle Crest Mansion, a place where the most extravagant and rich folks partied. A friend of mine owned the place and let me rent it out for $15,000 a night. Normally he'd charge $30,000, but since we were cool like that, he cut the cost in half.

It was Stephon's thirty-fifth birthday, so I couldn't help but go all out. He had no idea where we were going, until we drove up a long, curvy road near Eureka and parked our cars. The place was already packed, and having been here on another occasion with me, Stephon already knew what was about to go down.

"Man, no you didn't!" he yelled after we got out of our cars.

"Only the best for you, cousin." Stephon gave me a hug and we all stood for a moment, looking at the bad-ass mansion in front of us. From the outside, it looked like a castle. There was a swimming pool at the side of the house that stretched around to the back. On the inside, the room where the party was going down had craps, blackjack, and poker tables. A buffet with food for days was in another room, and it had a get-down-and-boogie dance floor with a DJ that kicked it down so loudly that you could hear music nearly a mile away.

Inside, I was surprised to see so many ladies, because at midnight, they all had to go. That's why I didn't mind asking Scorpio if she wanted to come along, because the *real* party wasn't going to start until after the women were gone.

When I tilted my hat to the DJ, that was his cue to change the music. He blasted "Happy Birthday" and everybody came out of the woodwork to sing to Stephon. Needless to say, he was touched, and when the singing was over, I saw his sensitive come down. I punched his arm.

"Don't be acting like no bitch, man." I laughed.

"Thanks, y'all," he said, nodding to everybody, and then looking at me. "Suck my dick, man. You ain't even have to do this shit."

"Aw, you gon' get your dick sucked tonight," Ray-Ray said. "And then some."

We laughed and gave each other five.

The dancing room was overcrowded. I didn't even know about fifty percent of the people there. I wasn't trying to, either, because it seemed as if some of the brothas were checking me out harder than the ladies were. Jealousy was a motherfucker, I thought, but tonight belonged to Stephon and me.

I was kicking up a sweat on the dance floor. When I looked around for Stephon, I couldn't find him. I saw Shane at one of the blackjack tables, with this light-bright chick sitting on his lap.

"Are you winning any money, man, or what?" I asked.

"A li'l bit." He looked at the chick sitting on his lap. "Jay, this Stacy. And Stacy, this Jay."

She spoke and I spoke back.

"Have you seen Stephon?" I asked.

"The last time I saw him, he was on the dance floor. Things looked as if they were getting pretty heated, so ain't no telling where the brotha at."

I patted Shane on his back. "All right, I'll be back." I looked at Stacy. "Nice meeting you, and enjoy yourself."

I walked off and continued to look for Stephon. I could barely make it from one room to the next without all the females throwing themselves at me. Pussy was everywhere and nearly every woman that I came in contact with had made herself available. I tried to stay focused, and after a while, I had to sit down and have myself a drink. I couldn't even do that in peace, because ladies surrounded me.

Just as one chick slid her number into my pocket, I caught a quick glimpse of Stephon on the dance floor and excused myself to go talk to him.

"Where in the hell have you been, fool? We 'bout to do this shit in ten minutes, my brotha."

"Man, I've been everywhere." He leaned over

and whispered in my ear while still dancing. "Did you see that cold-ass gal out there by the swimming pool?"

I shrugged. "Shit, which one?"

"Uh-uh. This one is in a category all by herself, trust me. When I say *cold*, I mean put on all three of your fur coats cold. When you get a minute, go check her out. She got on a white sheer two-piece bikini with tiny strings on the side. Body just . . . damn! And them titties," he said, shaking his head.

"Please don't have a heart attack on your birthday."

"Just go look, would you?"

I left the dance floor and walked over to the tall glass doors that led to the pool area. I looked around, and not seeing anyone like Stephon had described, I put my hands in my pockets and stepped outside. I scoped the set for a while, and just as I was about to go back inside, I saw her get out of the swimming pool. Instantly, my dick shot up. I was so stunned by her beauty I had to take a triple look. I rubbed my goatee, licked my lips, and watched her dry off with a towel.

When she caught my eyes, she smoothed her long wet hair back and placed the towel on a lawn chair. Things seemed to be moving in slow motion as she showed her pearly whites and headed my way. Her skin was a silky caramel brown, thighs were thick. Her hips had a hell of a curve, waistline was tiny, and titties were poked out right at me. I'd already peeped her plump and smooth heart-shaped ass when she got out of the pool. There was no doubt this sista was a vixen, straight from a rap video.

It was obvious that the look on my face said what I was thinking, but I couldn't help myself. When she walked past and ignored me, I grabbed her hand.

"So, you gon' ignore me like that, huh?" I said, displaying my charm.

She laughed and squinted her slanted eyes. "See, you thought I was coming to say hello, didn't you?"

"I was hoping that you were coming to do more than that."

"I was—until I realized who you were."

I pointed to myself. "Aw, so you know me?"

"Very well. Besides, who doesn't? Jaylin, right?"

"In the flesh."

She held out her hand for me to shake it. "I'm Mercedes."

"Mercedes? I like to ride my Mercedes every chance I get—or I just might like the way it rides me."

"We do ride so well, don't we?"

"I'm sure you do."

Mercedes snickered and twisted her long hair to squeeze the water from it. I glanced over at her nipples that were visible through her bikini top and looked down at her hairless pussy that showed through the sheer white bikini.

"You don't have no shame in your game, do you?" I asked.

"No, I don't. I love my body and take good care of it. By the looks of things, seems like you do as well."

A loud roaring noise sounded off. I looked at my watch; it was five minutes to twelve. That meant the ladies had to leave. Not wanting Mercedes to go anywhere just yet, I asked her to stay.

"Are you sure? These other females might get a little upset if I stay here with you."

"Correction. I didn't say stay with me. I said hang out for a while, okay?"

Mercedes nodded and strutted away. I took a few sips from my glass of Remy and watched her tie a wrap around her waist. From a distance, she saw me checking her out, and she couldn't do nothing but smile. I gave her a wink before returning inside.

There was no doubt about it that my ass was in trouble tonight. There wasn't no way possible for me to leave without fucking Mercedes and I knew it. The only thing that could save me was Scorpio being here in the flesh, and with her not knowing where I was, that was impossible.

All of the ladies quickly left the premises to make room for the new ladies. Months ago, a few fellas and me gathered up thirty-five of the coldest female dancers there were and invited them to provide the entertainment. Each one of them cost me one thousand dollars a pop, and promised the fellas and me the best time ever.

When they arrived, they came in five black Lincoln limousines, courtesy of Jaylin Rogers, of course. The loud sirens continued to go off, and brothas were going crazy. Stephon, being the man of the night, took a seat in the king's chair in the middle of the floor. The sirens stopped, and when ten fellas pushed in the largest fake birthday cake I'd ever seen, the new ladies stepped out one by one.

The fellas and me circled the room and watched.

Stephon had a welcoming smile on his face, and as each one of the ladies had their way with him, he leaned his head back, screamed out loudly, and closed his eyes. Occasionally, he looked over at Shane, Ray-Ray, and me. We were all dying to be in his seat.

The ladies tied up Stephon, lightly spanking his ass thirty-five times, with one to grow on. When the last chick rose out of the cake in mid-air, butt naked, I had seen it all. She stepped out and strutted toward Stephon as if she were the winner of *America's Next Top Model*. She was a deep dark Hershey's chocolate, wore a big Afro, and had a bone necklace tied around her neck. Her body looked as if it had been soaked in baby oil, and her backside had many spectators' mouths wide open.

When she reached Stephon, he slid down as if he'd melted in his chair. She winked at him, and after straddling his lap, she placed her tall, slim legs on his shoulders. She leaned backward, and not being able to resist, Stephon dropped his face right in.

Everybody started going wild. The DJ kicked up "Salt Shaker" and the dance floor quickly filled. Women circled Shane, Stephon, Ray-Ray, and me. I danced next to Stephon, and as we made our way down to the floor, nothing but booties shaking stared us right in our faces. All I could do was shrug my shoulders.

"Hey, what's a man suppose to do?" I asked Stephon.

He licked the chick's ass who danced in front of him, then licked his lips. "That's what a man's supposed to do," he said. "You only live once, my brotha."

When Stephon noticed Shane leaned against the bar, talking to Mercedes, he tapped me.

"That's who I was talking about, bro. Look at her! She bad, ain't she?"

"Trust me, I know. Is this your move, though, or can I take it?"

"I got the African princess tonight. You g'on ahead and knock yourself out."

"Will do."

I quickly wrapped up my dancing and made my way over by Shane and Mercedes.

My forehead was sweating, so I took off my hat and laid it on top of the bar. I asked the bartender for another shot of Remy and looked over at Shane and Mercedes, who stood close by.

"This shit is wild, ain't it?" I said, talking to Shane.

"Hell, yeah. Y'all brothas messed me all up." He walked closer to me and left Mercedes standing alone. "And just when I thought I was on the right track."

"Shit, how do you think I feel? Scorpio gon' kill my ass tonight."

"Man, don't throw away your relationship for one night up in here. You got yourself a decent woman at home."

"Trust me, I know what I got. I got a fucking hard-on right here and right now. That's what I got."

"I suggest you go home and work that off. But if you can't make it," he yelled, "I truly understand."

Shane held his hand out and I slammed my fist against it. He told Mercedes it was nice meeting her, and went back on the dance floor with Ray-Ray and Stephon.

Mercedes eased over next to me. "You are having yourself a good time tonight, aren't you?" she asked.

"I'm hoping the night will only get better."

"It might. But I'll let you be the judge."

I rubbed my goatee and observed her. "Well, the judge has ordered you into his courtroom. Are you with it or not?"

She smiled. "If I say no, then I'll be arrested. I think it's best that I follow the judge's orders; that can only be beneficial to me."

I put my drink down and escorted Mercedes to the elevator. My partner who owned the place had given me a key to the lower level, just in case I needed some privacy. When we got inside the elevator, I hit the button for the ground level, and the elevator took us to an area that had an oval-shaped marble Jacuzzi with four black columns around it. Plasma TVs were on nearly every wall, and a fireplace burned in the far corner. For our drinking pleasure, a bar made out of nothing but glass was nearby, and black leather swivel chairs sat directly in front of it.

Wasting no time, I turned on the power jets so the water could warm up and bubble. Mercedes didn't waste any time either, and once she got in the Jacuzzi, she motioned her finger for me to come to her. The reflections from the dimmed lighting bouncing off the water made her look even sexier. The mood was set by the lit fragrance candles and soft jazz that echoed in the background.

I took off my clothes and rested my head on a contoured headrest once I got inside of the Jacuzzi. Mercedes made her way over to me, and when she straddle my lap, my hands couldn't wait to grip her ass cheeks. I massaged her hairless soft pussy and removed her string bikini so I could rotate my fingers inside of her. Getting much pleasure from my touch, she took off her top and exposed her suck-me-right-now hard nipples. I covered her breast with my mouth and she was on fire.

"Put it in me, Jaylin," she ordered. "Show me what all the fuss is about."

I intended to do just that, but for some reason, my dick wasn't cooperating. It was somewhat limp. Mercedes worked it in her hands to help it grow. I didn't know what was up. This was the first time some shit like this had happened to me, maybe because I was feeling guilty about playing the shit out of Scorpio. She had been on my mind all night, and to my surprise, so had Nokea.

I tried to wash the thoughts of them from my mind, and turned Mercedes so that her back faced me. I just knew that hitting it from her firm backside would arouse me, but I still couldn't get with it. She seemed frustrated with me and suggested giving me some head. No woman could bring me to an eruption like Scorpio could, so I decided to wrap it up.

"We gon' have to try this another time, all right?" I said.

Her face showed frustration. "Why? Just sit back and let me do what I do best."

"Not tonight," I said, already getting out of the water. I dried myself and slid back into my pants. Mercedes had a blank and almost embarrassed look on her face as she got out and leaned against the bar next to me.

I grabbed a napkin and a pen from behind the bar. "Write down your number for me," I said.

"Why? So I can get dissed again?" she said, rubbing my bare chest. She tried to excite me by kissing my lips and wetting my nipple with her tongue. Still, I wasn't feeling her. I took a few steps back and looked into her beautiful, seductive eyes.

"This ain't happening tonight. Again, would you write down your number so I can call you some other time?"

She snatched up the pen and scribbled her number on the napkin. I apologized for not being able to perform, but was given no response. We left and went back upstairs.

I looked around, unable to find anyone. Stephon, Shane, and Ray-Ray were missing in action. When I asked around, nobody seemed to know anything. I glanced at my watch and saw it was already three-thirty in the morning, so I decided to call it a night. Mercedes asked if I would take her home, and feeling as if it was the least I could do, I agreed.

As we walked to my car, I saw Shane and some chick leaned up against it. I was worried about dents being put in my car, so I yelled his name.

"What's up?" he said.

"Back off the ride, man. There are plenty of bedrooms inside."

He laughed and held the chick around her waist. I tossed him the keys to the elevator inside. "Take the elevator to the lower level and have yourself a wonderful time."

"Thanks," he said, catching the keys, making his way back toward the house.

Mercedes lived close by, so dropping her off was no problem at all. She invited me in, but I declined and promised her that I would call her soon.

I pulled in the driveway at five past four in the morning. I found myself keeping up with the time more than ever, trying to make it home early so Scorpio wouldn't trip. I hurried to my bedroom.

I was horny as hell after seeing her naked in bed. I took off my clothes and slid in close behind her. She slightly turned her head, and when I saw the puffiness in her eyes, I wondered if she'd been crying or had been sleeping.

"Do you know how much I love you?" I whispered in her ear.

"Yes."

"Then why are you upset with me?"

"I'm not. I just don't want to lose you."

"Baby, you aren't going to lose me, so stop saying that." I eased on top of her and kissed her entire face to make her smile. She reached up and massaged her fingers through the curls in my hair.

"I love you, Mrs. Rogers. When are you going to proudly wear your ring and represent your name?"

"Hopefully soon."

We kissed and did what we do best—made love.

If anything, tonight proved to me that Scorpio would be hard to replace. Many would disagree, but in a situation like I was in tonight, Mercedes' sexiness was not enough to keep me from coming home to my woman. The only other woman who could loosen Scorpio's grip on me was Nokea. I still had much love for her, but my feelings had to be put on the back burner. I wanted, needed for things to work out between me and Scorpio, for the sake of our child. Yes, it was four o'clock in the morning, but I was here. And for me, that was a miracle!

# 10

## *NOKEA*

I was quite surprised I hadn't heard from Jaylin, especially after what happened between us the other morning. Normally, he'd call just to say hello, but I guess he was trying to keep his distance, as was I.

After Jaylin left that morning, I couldn't even look at Collins. I was so ashamed of myself for cheating on him, and more than anything, how wrong of me to do so. Just when I thought all of this was behind me, there I was thinking about Jaylin again. When I took Collins to the airport, I almost had an accident because my mind couldn't stay focused. If it weren't for Collins reaching over and grabbing the steering wheel so I could avoid this truck clear as day in front of me, we'd all be messed up.

He could tell something was on my mind, and when he got to Detroit, he called and tried to get it out of me. I would have been a fool to tell him how I really felt, especially after how far we'd come in our relationship. Truth was, Jaylin still had a huge part of my heart; that I was so unwilling to admit.

And then, for me to sleep with a man who was engaged to someone else, I really knew better. Jaylin or not, I was wrong. Scorpio had been going through some things, and being in her shoes before, I couldn't understand how easy it was for me to let sex between us happen. As usual, he played with my emotions. He knew exactly what to say and what to do to get me where he wanted me. I was sure he left here on cloud nine that day, feeling good about sleeping with a man like Collins' woman.

I was nowhere near oblivious to the situation and knew I had a soft spot for him. Stupid, I guess, but we shared so darn much in the past that it was hard to let go. So, did I believe him when he said he missed me? Yes. Did I believe he still loved me? Yes. And those were just a few reasons why I had a difficult time letting him go.

Pat was on her way over for dinner, since LJ was with Mama and Daddy for the weekend. He spent so much time at Jaylin's house, my parents had barely gotten a chance to see their own grandson. Daddy was hurt, too, and had threatened on occasion to go by Jaylin's house to take LJ. When I told Jaylin that Daddy was on his way to get LJ, he angrily told me that no man would take his son away without a fight. In so many words, he said if Daddy even tried, he would have to disrespect him. I called Daddy that day and begged him not to go over there. Then, in an effort to keep the peace, I promised my parents that LJ would spend every first weekend of the month with them. Jaylin wasn't too thrilled about it, but he had to learn how to share.

I waited for Pat to show, and since dinner was already finished, I called Jaylin's house to see what he was up to. Collins wasn't coming back until tomorrow morning, so I wanted to talk to Jaylin before then.

When he answered the phone, I thought he was screwing, but he told me he was just waking up.

"It's almost four o'clock in the afternoon and you're just now getting up?"

"Shit, I'm tired. And I got a slight hangover."

"You've been drinking a lot lately. Did you go out last night?"

"You know Stephon's birthday was yesterday. You didn't get a chance to call and wish him a happy birthday?"

"I forgot. Kind of had a lot of other things on my mind."

"I guess I don't have to ask what, do I?"

"I haven't been thinking about you, so don't flatter yourself."

"Then I guess that's why you called, huh?"

"I called to tell you that your son is with his grandparents today. He won't be back until Monday, so don't be whining 'cause you haven't seen him."

"I should go over there and take him from your punk-ass daddy. Your moms is cool, Nokea, but I don't like his ass."

"Hey, watch it. If you don't have anything nice to say, then don't say it at all."

"Okay, then I won't. But, uh, is your man back yet?"

I hesitated before anwering, knowing what was coming next. "He . . . he'll be back tomorrow. Why?"

"Because I thought you might want some company later on."

"No, thank you. I'm spending the evening with Pat."

"How boring. I thought you might want a little excitement in your life tonight."

"I already got plenty. Besides, haven't you and Scorpio made up yet?"

"Don't we always? And if you must know, my shit with Scorpio is tight. Ain't nobody slipping through the cracks of our relationship but you."

It was good to know that, but . . .

"You're starting to talk a bunch of crap now, so let me get off this phone. You know darn well there are a whole lot of women slipping through the cracks, so don't make me feel privileged."

"Seriously, no it ain't. Y'all women need to stop thinking like that. I am faithful to my woman, and have been for a very long time. I would have remained faithful if you hadn't slipped through the crack and put something on my mind that I'm having a hard time forgetting."

"Okay, now, blame it on me, right? You couldn't be too faithful if you have a baby on the way with Daisha. You're talking like you're in denial."

"Well, that thing with me and Daisha didn't work out," he said, lowering his voice. He paused for a moment, as if he really didn't want to talk about it. "The . . . the, uh, baby was born prematurely and didn't make it."

I knew how much love Jaylin had for all of his children, and just from listening to his voice I could tell that losing a child had taken a toll on him. "Oh, I didn't know Daisha was having difficulties with her pregnancy. I'm sorry to hear that. Why didn't you call to tell me?"

"You know me better than anybody, Nokea. I was hurt and really didn't want to talk about it."

"But you know you can always talk to me, don't you?"

"I know, and I appreciate more than anything what we have. It hurts me, though, that I have never seen any of my children come into this world. I feel as if I've missed out on something. But, of course, you wouldn't understand."

"I do understand, more than you know; and I regret not telling you LJ was your child from the beginning. It was the biggest mistake of my life, so please don't make me feel guilty all over again. Hopefully you'll have your moment with Scorpio, and whatever you seem to be missing out on, maybe you'll find it."

"I hope so."

My voice softend, but I wasn't about to go there with Jaylin again. "I gotta go. Pat's here, so I'll call you later."

"Tell her I said hello."

"I sure will."

Jaylin and I hung up, and just that fast, our conversation changed my whole mood. He still seemed bitter about LJ, but there wasn't anything

I could do to change what happened in the past. More than anything, I hoped he wasn't still holding a grudge about my mistakes and past plans to marry Stephon. I was sure that he had forgiven me, and it was good to know that he'd been thinking about our encounter the other morning as much as I was.

Pat came in with the usual: a bottle of wine and two movies for us to watch. Neither one starred Denzel Washington, so I tossed them on the couch.

"Now, you know I can't make it through the weekend without seeing him in action."

"Girl, forget you. The rental store was out of every movie he's in. It's evident that you ain't the only one who got the hots for him."

"So, you're telling me they didn't have no *John Q, Training Day, Antwone Fisher, Out of Time, Hurricane, Malcolm X, Pelican Brief, Devil in a Blue Dress, Mississippi Masala, Remember the Titans, Courage Under Fire, Crimson Tide, Philadelphia, The Debaters, Mo' Better Blues, Inside Man,* or *American Gangster* on the shelves? I would go on, but . . ."

Pat looked at me like I was crazy. "But you need some help. That man is married, Nokea. He ain't thinking about your butt."

"That's okay; however, I do enjoy watching him in action. That's enough for me."

"And so do I," Pat said, shaking her body as if the thought of him gave her chills.

After we fixed our plates, we stretched out on the living room floor, eating and watching a movie. Our conversations turned to the men in our lives, so we didn't even pay attention to the movie. When I told her what Collins had done to me the other night, she was tuned in.

"Now, that's nasty," she said. "He do look like a freak, though."

"He doesn't look any freakier than Chad. And from what you told me he be doing, it doesn't get any nastier than that."

"I guess you're right." She laughed. "But, girl, Collins looks like he can tear a sista up! You know them quiet kind always come out in the bedroom. Besides, who needs Denzel when you got him?"

"I do!"

We both laughed.

"If anything, it's the ones like Jaylin I be worried about. I don't believe for one minute he be setting it out there like you say he do."

I pointed to my chest. "Would I lie to you? Just the other day—I mean, the other . . . a while back . . ."

Pat's mouth hung wide open as she looked at me with a stone face. She moved her plate aside and stared into my eyes. "You hoochie-ass skeeza." She laughed. "You are still fucking him, aren't you?"

"No, I'm not. You know better than to assume something like that. Besides, who needs Jaylin when I got Collins?"

She tooted her lips. "Uh-huh. Go ahead and lie to your best friend, but I know better. I knew you and him would get back together! I knew it!"

I felt defeated; my best friend knew me all too well. "Pat, please don't go rushing to judgment just yet. It was one time and that's it."

"One time, huh? Well, get ready to break Collins' heart because that one time is going to turn into two, three, four plus five more times real soon. I can't believe you are hooked again."

I stood up and held my plate in my hands. "See, that's why I didn't want to tell you."

Pat picked up her plate and followed me into the kitchen. "Tell me what? That you still love him?"

"No. That him and I got caught up in the moment, we screwed, LJ woke up, and that was it."

"And let me guess; you were so glad that LJ stopped you?"

"Actually, no, I wasn't. I know you don't want to hear this, but girl!" I yelled and dropped my plate in the sink. "His penis inside of me damn near made me want to cry."

"Dick, Nokea. It's okay to say dick."

"Okay, then not just dick, but Monster Dick. That's what Scorpio calls it anyway."

"Y'all a mess, but Monster Dick got you doomed again. His dick is just a *powerful* thing and has you and these other women out here doing whatever it wants you to do. You got yourself a good, fine-ass man that treats you like a queen and you cheating on him?"

"Since I've been with Collins, sex between Jaylin and me has only happened one time, Pat. It's never going to happen again, and I can promise you that."

She shrugged, reaching forward to give me a hug. "If you say so. Just remember I love you, and I support your decisions, but I don't want you to allow him to hurt you again, okay?"

"Never again," I said, returning to our movie in the living room.

\* \* \*

The movies were over and Pat headed for home around twelve o'clock that night. Unable to sleep, I lay in bed looking around my room, thinking. When the phone rang, my heart raced because I thought it was Jaylin calling. Instead, it was Collins. He never called in the middle of the night, so I was shocked to hear his voice.

"Are you asleep?" he asked.

"I was on my way. Pat left not too long ago and I just got in bed."

"Well, I won't be leaving out until Friday morning. It's a mess down here and I need to stay and straighten out some things."

"I'm sorry to hear that, but I understand. In the meantime, I miss you."

"Same here. I can't wait to get home and hold you in my arms again."

"Don't even make me think about it."

Collins laughed. "Why should you not think about it? I can't seem to get you off my mind. Are you naked?"

"Partially. Are you?"

"Yes."

"Then hold on." I pulled my navy blue silk nightgown over my head and lay back on my bed. When I picked up the phone, I laughed. "Okay, now I'm feeling you."

"Um, um, um . . . all I can do is let my imagination run wild. Why'd you do that to me?"

"Because I want you to hurry home so you can make love to me. I'm so lonely without you."

"I'll be home soon. Until I get there, take my

picture off your nightstand and put it in bed with you. Then hang on tight, and sweet dreams."

"I will."

"I love you."

"I love you too."

I reached for Collins' picture and held it close to my chest. I truly wished he were here with me, and maybe, just maybe, my thoughts of Jaylin would go away.

# 11

## *SCORPIO*

Jaylin picked me up from school and we took a long, romantic walk in Forest Park. He was extremely playful with me, but still feeling very uneasy about the baby, I was a little moody. He suggested we stop at Talayna's to get something to eat, and after we ate, we headed for home.

Nanny B had been giving me funny looks all week long, and I honestly feared she would tell Jaylin the truth before I did. She was so overprotective of him that it sometimes drove me crazy.

I was kind of glad she had this new man in her life. Hopefully he'd keep her occupied and out of my business. She told Jaylin and me that we'd meet him soon, and when we got home, his car was in the driveway. I'd seen it at the house before, but I never got a chance to meet him. When I told Jaylin he was there before, he laughed and said Nanny B was trying to keep him a secret because he was probably very old and unattractive.

We walked into the house and could hear a conversation going on in the kitchen. Jaylin stood in the foyer, flipping through the mail. Feeling a little tired, I headed upstairs. Before I reached the middle stair, Nanny B came out of the kitchen and called my name. She asked Jaylin and me to take a seat in the living room. I felt as if she was getting ready to bust me out, so I walked nervously to the couch and sat down. Jaylin sat next to me and asked Nanny B where Mackenzie was.

"She's still at school. I'm going to pick her up after I talk to the two of you."

I touched my chest. "You're scaring me. Is everything okay?" I asked.

Jaylin looked flushed. "Please don't give me any bad news. I—"

"No," she interrupted, "it's nothing like that."

We were relieved, and when Jaylin sat back on the couch, so did I.

"Jaylin," she said, "there's someone here I want you to talk to. I was skeptical about you seeing him, but it's not my place to interfere anymore. Please listen to what he has to say, okay?"

Jaylin's eyebrows raised and he leaned forward, gripping his hands together. When this light-skinned, slim but well-built man came from the kitchen, the curious look on Jaylin's face had vanished and turned to anger. Obviously, he knew who the man was.

Jaylin jumped up and yelled loudly, "Get him the fuck out of my house, NOW!" Nanny B grabbed him by the hand and he snatched away from her. For the first time, he gave her a look that could kill. "How you gon' let him come in my home after what he did to me?"

"Jaylin," the man said in a deep, strong voice, "just calm down. I know you're not happy to see me, but—"

"Man, get the fuck out of my house! I don't want to hear shit you got to say." Jaylin rushed over to the front door and opened it.

The man looked over at Nanny B. "Hey, I tried." He headed for the door.

"Stanley, don't leave this house until you make some kind of peace with your son," she said. "You haven't seen him in years, and Jaylin needs to understand why you walked away after his mother's funeral and he had to live in an orphanage. You need to explain that to him, not me." She pointed her finger at Jaylin. "Your father is sick, and you—"

"I don't give a rat's ass about him being sick. Sick or not, he needs to get out of my mother-fucking house. And if you don't like it, then I suggest you get the fuck out too."

Nanny B took a few steps back, stunned by his reaction. So was I. Never in a million years would I expect him to disrespect her.

His father walked toward the door, and after he walked out, Jaylin slammed the door so hard that it shook the whole house. He rolled his eyes at Nanny B and hurried upstairs. I heard his bedroom door slam, and we both jumped in our shoes. Nanny B pulled her apron over her head and reached for her car keys on the table.

"I'm going to get Mackenzie. I'll be back." She looked hurt.

"I'll go get her. Please, go sit down and just talk to him after he calms down."

"No, that's all right. You go upstairs and talk some sense into him. If I have to go, I'm afraid I'll say something that I might regret later."

I nodded and gave her a hug. After she left, I went upstairs to talk to Jaylin. He was already on the telephone, and as he cursed out loudly, I heard what he was talking about. I couldn't believe he'd gone upstairs to call Nokea. What in the hell was that all about? How dare he call her before even speaking to me? I figured she must have known more about the situation between him and his father, since I'd only known Jaylin for a couple of years and she's known him since they were children. I tried not to trip.

"I swear, if he ever come up in here again, Nokea, I'm gonna kill his ass." He paused. "Yeah. . . that's what I'm saying. Nanny B knew better, didn't she?" He looked up at me. "Let me hit you back in a li'l bit."

Jaylin slammed down the phone and picked up the remote to turn on the TV. Before I could say anything, he tore into me like I had something to do with it.

"I don't want to hear it, Scorpio. I can already tell you got something to say."

"Pertaining to how you disrespected Nanny B, yes I do. As for your father, I'm staying out of it."

Jaylin looked at me as if I'd told him to go eat dirt. "Father? Please. That cocksucker ain't been no father to me not one day in my life. I don't give a shit if he lie down and die tomorrow. He knew better than to show his face around here."

"I haven't a clue why you hate him so much, but those words are really cold. Again, I'm staying out of it, but please talk to Nanny B when she comes back. I'm sure her intentions were not to hurt you, and you know they weren't."

"She needs to stay the hell out of my business. If it wasn't for him, my mother would probably still be alive. Fuck that! I have no love for his ass."

Jaylin wasn't trying to hear me, and I didn't want him to. It was evident he was standing his ground, and when he acted this way, I got as far away from him as possible.

By the time Nanny B got back with Mackenzie, Jaylin had already left. He didn't tell me where he was going, just simply said he would be back. I was slightly bothered by his reaction. What little information I knew about his father, Jaylin felt that if his father had been around, then his mother wouldn't have had to work as hard as she did. He insisted that if she didn't have to walk home late from work that night, she never would have gotten killed. I didn't know everything that happened, but after Nanny B got settled and started on dinner, I went into the kitchen to speak with her.

"Can I help you with anything?" I asked.

"No. Just have a seat and listen. I feel like venting right about now."

I smiled and took a seat at the kitchen table. "Go ahead; I'm listening."

She sat at the table with me while cutting up vegetables for a salad. "Several weeks ago, Stanley stopped by, but you and Jaylin were gone. I was shocked to see him, and after he told me his purpose, I didn't have it in my heart to turn him away."

"What did he tell you his purpose was?"

"He has cancer. The doctors say he don't have much time to live because they detected it too late. All the man wants to do is make peace with his son before he leaves this earth, and I didn't want to deny Stanley that opportunity."

"I understand, but you of all people know how Jaylin can be. He has a hard time letting things go, and considering what he's been through, I don't think he'll ever forgive his father."

"Maybe you're right," Nanny B said, placing her hand on top of mine. "So, have you decided when you're going to tell Jaylin about the baby?"

"I . . . I was going to tell him soon, but now, I don't know. All of this might be too much for him to swallow."

She gave me a stern look and her voice rose to a higher pitch. "Tell him, Scorpio! If you don't, I will. G'on ahead and get it out of the way so this mess can be over. I know the timing might not be right, but you can not keep putting this off."

"I promise you I'll tell him soon." I stood up. "Do you mind if I go out for a while? I need some time alone to think."

"Go ahead. I'm going to finish up dinner, and if you're not back in time, I'll put your plate aside."

"Thanks. I love you." I leaned down and gave her a hug.

I told Mackenzie I'd be back. Curious to find out where Jaylin was, I left to go find him. Since he'd talked to Nokea earlier, I went to her house first. When I didn't see his car, I headed for Stephon's barbershop in the Central West End.

Jaylin's car was parked behind Stephon's, so I pulled over behind it. When I walked inside, he was in a chair talking to Stephon, who was cutting a customer's hair. Jaylin ignored my presence and continued his conversation with Stephon.

"Anyway, as I was saying before I was rudely interrupted, I can't believe she had you tied up for two damn days."

Stephon nodded. "Ya damn right she did. Fucked my brains out, and I am not lying when I tell you Mona had her shit packed and was gone by the time I made it home."

"That's messed up. But that's how wishy-washy females are. They be pretending like everything cool and saying how much they understand a brotha, but—"

"Well, no woman understands a man who doesn't come home," I said, interrupting. I walked over by Jaylin. "Can we go somewhere and talk? Just you and me, please?"

"Can't you see I'm in the middle of something?"

"Yes, but we really need to talk."

He stood up and stretched his arms. "Man, I'll give you a holla tomorrow. When that fool Shane come out of the bathroom, tell him I'll catch up with him later."

Just then, Shane came out of the bathroom shaking the water off his hands. Stephon quickly tossed him a towel.

"Jay, you gone already?" Shane asked.

"Yeah." Jaylin looked at me. "My woman keeping tabs on me and shit, so you know how that is."

"Hello, Shane," I said. "And I'm not keeping tabs on him. He left without telling anybody where he was going and I got worried."

Jaylin looked at Shane and Stephon. "Now, doesn't that sound like she's trying to keep a brotha on lockdown?"

All the fellas in the shop nodded their heads.

"Whatever," I said. "Let's just go."

Jaylin took my hand and walked me outside. When he asked where I wanted to go, I told him to follow me to Forest Park so we could be alone.

I parked his Porsche, got inside of his Mercedes with him, and in no time, he was all over me. I didn't intend to go to the park and have sex, so I slightly shoved him backward.

"Baby, please, not right now. Later, okay?"

"Here we go with this shit again. I'm telling you now that this rejection bullshit with you ain't going to work for me. There are certain things I expect from my woman, and you know better than anybody that when I want to make love, I expect to make love."

"I don't have a problem with that, but I need to talk to you about something first."

"If it's about my father, I don't want to hear it, Scorpio. You know nothing about my situation with him, so it would be wrong of you to voice your opinion about it."

"Look, I told you once before I'm staying out of it. That's your choice; however, I do want you to apologize to Nanny B. She has been nothing but good to us, and you were wrong for going off like you did."

"Yeah, yeah, yeah . . . I know. Anyway," he said, looking over at me, "what's on your mind?"

I rubbed my hands together. My eyes watered and I lowered my head. "First, I want to tell you how much I love you. You mean everything in the world to me, but I can't go another day with living this lie."

He touched my hands to stop them from trembling. "What lie?" he said. "And don't start all this emotional shit today, please. I'm really not in the mood for it."

"You never are, but that's because you will never understand what I've been going through. I know I'm about to lose you, but try hard to understand that I . . . I had to do what was best for me."

His eyebrows rose. "What are you talking about?"

I kept my head down. "I . . . I had an abortion."

He leaned closer to me, as if he hadn't heard what I said. "Come again?"

"I said that I had an abortion. When I—"

Jaylin snatched my face, squeezing my cheeks with his hands. "You did what?" he yelled. I swore that I saw fire burning in his eyes.

I pulled my face away from his grip. "Just listen, please."

"Are you telling me you killed my fucking child? Is that what you're telling me?"

"No. It wasn't your child! When I was in Denver—"

His fist hit the steering wheel. "Get your ass out of my car!"

"Jaylin, please!"

Furious, he slammed the car door and rushed over to the passenger's side. He pulled the door open and reached for my collar. "Get out!"

"I will do no such thing until you hear me out."

He pulled me out of the car and slammed my back against it. The way he was breathing, I thought he was about to have a heart attack. He poked his pointer finger at my temple.

"Since the day I met your ass, you have done nothing but try to destroy me. You have continuously lied to me, and I have had it, Scorpio. The only reason I haven't let you go is because of Mackenzie. She's the only reason I haven't kicked your ass out of my house. And I can't believe how much money I've lost fucking with you!"

"Don't say that. It's simply not true. We're together because we love each other. I just couldn't stand to have another man's child, and I—"

"Shut the fuck up talking to me!" He let loose my collar then placed his hands in his pockets. He paced back and forth for a minute and then tightly closed his eyes. When he opened them, he looked up at the sky. "Why, man, why?" he yelled. He placed his hand over his face and wiped it.

Trying to comfort him, I stepped up to him and grabbed his other hand. He quickly snatched away.

"Don't touch me!" He pointed his finger at me. "Don't you ever put your damn hands on me again. Do you understand?"

I couldn't say anything. After he got into his car and sped off, I leaned against his Porsche and let out my emotions. All I could do was think about where in the hell I went wrong. All I ever did was love him, and loving him was costing me more hurt than I'd ever imagined.

Nearly thirty minutes later, I calmed down and headed for home. Jaylin's car wasn't there, but I truly hadn't expected it to be. I went inside, and when I heard Nanny B and Mackenzie laughing in the kitchen, I slowly walked in.

Nanny B looked at me and I guess the look on my face said everything she needed to know. She asked Mackenzie to leave the kitchen and then held me tightly in her arms. I held her and lost it.

"It's over," I cried. "He said it was over."

"Don't do this to yourself," she said, rocking me. "You have got to be strong for Mackenzie and never," she commanded, "never let a man cause you this much hurt."

"I know you're right, but he feels so betrayed by me. We've hurt each other so much, and I don't know why we can't stop lying to each other and playing these stupid games. I love him so—"

"Loving him doesn't mean you have to keep putting yourself through this. God has the ultimate say so, and you need to listen to what He's trying to tell you. Yes, you lied, but Jaylin hasn't been no saint either. Just wait until things calm down and decide what's going to be best for you and Mackenzie."

Even Nanny B's encouraging words didn't make me feel better. She didn't understand that all I wanted was for things to be right between Jaylin and me. I went to the bedroom, showered, and lay in bed for hours, waiting for him to come home.

By midnight, he was still a no show. I called his cell phone and got no answer. When I called

Stephon's house, he said he hadn't seen him. I got desperate and even called Nokea to see if she'd heard from him. She sounded sleepy, so I apologized for waking her.

"It's okay, Scorpio, but I haven't seen him. He called earlier and told me about his father, but—"

"Well, if you happen to hear from him, please let me know."

"I will, and trust me, he'll come around. He always do."

"Thanks."

I hung up and waited for my man to come home.


After one whole day without Jaylin, I was dying inside. By day three, I was numb. I hadn't eaten anything and was glued to the bed. Nanny B knew what I was going through, and she took good care of Mackenzie. Mackenzie had come into the room several times and asked me to play with her, but I was completely out of it. I felt bad, but it was something about Jaylin that made me react this way.

The weekend arrived and Jaylin had been gone for five whole days. I was worried like hell and so was Nanny B. She called several places searching for him, and we both pleaded with Stephon to tell us the truth about where he was. Stephon told Nanny B that Jaylin was doing just fine and that he needed time to sort through some things. Feeling as if there was nothing else we could do, we chilled and waited for him to return home.

# 12

## *JAYLIN*

Right about now, I couldn't stand to be in my own damn house. If it wasn't Nanny B sticking her nose where it didn't belong, it was Scorpio with her constant fucking lies that made me stay away. First she lied about being a stripper, then she lied about not seeing anyone while she was in Denver. She couldn't keep her legs closed when it came to my friend Shane, and now, she'd lied about the most important thing a woman could lie to me about—a child. She damn well knew that baby wasn't mine. Yes, I missed being around Mackenzie, but I didn't want her being around all the disrespect I would have had to lay down if I'd gone home.

Of course, I called Nokea's place to see if I could chill with her and LJ for a few days, but insisting that was a bad idea, she begged me to go home. I didn't want to complicate shit between her and Collins more than I'd already done, so I stopped by Daisha's place to chat with her.

We had an interesting conversation, and in so many words, she made it clear to me that she had moved on. She came clean and told me how much I'd hurt her by not being around, and she truly believed, as I did, that everything happened for a reason. Before giving our final good-byes, I asked if I could knock it out for old time's sake, but she stood her ground. I wasn't mad because I always knew Daisha was the type of woman who didn't have a problem doing so.

After a few nights in a suite at the Four Seasons hotel in downtown St. Louis, I called Stephon to let him know my whereabouts. I told him not to let anyone know where I was and to call my cell phone if he needed me.

At first, I spent several nights alone feeling sorry for myself. I even started feeling like the villain, when all these stupid fools in my life had been the ones who failed me.

Pertaining to Stanley, how dare anybody ask me to forgive him? I'd been subjected to an orphanage because he wasn't man enough to take care of me. Hell, I'd been physically abused because he wasn't there for me. Why in the hell would he expect me to embrace him with open arms? And Nanny B, I was so disappointed in her. I thought she knew what I'd been through and understood more than anybody that the last person I wanted in my life again would be him.

As for Scorpio, I didn't know what in the hell I was going to do with her. She had brought nothing but turmoil my way, and every time I turned around, there was a secret being kept in order to "protect" me, according to her. This bitch lived in my house for free, pretended to be pregnant by me, and told me how much love she had for me. Not once did she mention screwing around with another motherfucker while in Denver. I came clean with her about my relationship with Daisha, but not once did she fess up and tell me about her having sex with someone else. Her shit just caught up with her ass. I was surprised she didn't keep the baby and allow me to think it was mine. That kind of shit would have been right up her alley.

Either way, I was furious as hell about everything that had gone down. The truth of the matter was, I didn't owe anybody shit, and from now on, I was done playing Mr. Nice Guy. All this checking in bullshit was gonna stop. All this money-giving shit was coming to a halt. Going forward, that bitch was on her own!

I was tired of spending my money at the casino, and by the fourth night, jacking off just wasn't doing the job anymore. I was horny as fuck, and when I called Mercedes to see if she wanted some company, she invited me over. I showered and changed into a Nike black silk jogging suit I'd picked up earlier while browsing at Union Station.

My drive to Mercedes' place was a long one, and I couldn't stop thinking about my baby Mackenzie. I missed her tremendously and wanted to call the house to speak with her. I dropped the thought because I wasn't in the mood to hear Nanny B or Scorpio's voice. I even thought about the possibility that Scorpio had packed up her shit and left again, but something inside of me knew she wasn't going anywhere any time soon. Besides, where would she run to this time? She had everything she wanted at my place, so what more could she ask for?

I was angry with myself for doing so much for her, only to get stabbed in my back. More than anything, I felt like a complete fool. Being a fool for any woman was a no-no for J. J. Rogers. She was gonna have to pay for her mistakes and for bringing more drama my way.

Mercedes opened the door butt naked—I was beginning to think she was allergic to clothes. When I stepped inside of her house, she closed the door behind me and we both stood in the foyer. I searched her body over, and admittedly, she was put together extremely well.

"Why are you looking at me so suspiciously?" she asked.

"Because I'm impressed by your body, but I have yet to see you with any clothes on. Do you have something against wearing them?"

"No, but like I told you before, I love my body and it is beneficial to my career. I always walk around my house naked, and since I knew you were coming, I didn't feel as if clothes were necessary."

My eyes searched her nearly empty house. It was so empty, that I could hear an echo as we spoke. I could tell she'd just moved in because I noticed plastic still covering several areas of the carpet.

We stood for a moment, but I looked for a quick place to sit. I was about to sit on the stairs, but instead, Mercedes had another suggestion.

"Let's go upstairs to my bedroom," she said, already turning to go up the steps.

I touched her hand to stop her. "But what if I want to chat and get to know you better first?"

She stepped to the bottom stair and faced me. I wrapped my arms around her waist, and she placed her arms on my shoulders. "What is it that you'd like to know about me?" she asked. I stepped up and she took a step backward.

"Are you a good kisser?" I asked.

She placed her lips on mine and we smacked lips for a minute or two.

"Umm," I said, licking my lips. I took another step up and she stepped backward again. "That was pretty good. Now, Mercedes, what in the hell do you do for a living?"

She gazed at me and started to unzip my jogging suit. "I'm a model. Haven't you seen my face before?"

"Uh-uh, but, uh, how old are you?" We stepped up and back again.

"Old enough."

"Where your man at?"

"Not here."

"Are you married?"

"No."

"Any kids?"

"No."

"Do you live alone?"

"Yes," she said, helping me out of my pants. We now stood naked at the top of the stairs. She walked down the hallway to her bedroom and I followed. The upstairs was just as empty as the lower level. The only thing inside of her bedroom was a queen-sized bed against the wall with a bunch of silk pillows on it. The walls were painted white, and a huge framed picture of Mercedes was on one wall.

I sat on the bed and she stood in front of me with her arms resting on my shoulders. "So, do you have any more questions for me?" she asked.

"Yes. As a matter of fact, I do."

"I'm listening."

I slid my fingers between her coochie lips and separated them. "Are you ready to get fucked?"

"I've been ready for quite some time." She sucked her bottom lip as I sunk my finger deep within her. Encouraging me to go deeper, she placed her foot on the bed so I could have easier access.

"Damn, I can tell how ready you are, but how do you want it?" I asked.

"However you're willing to give it to me."

"I can give it to you in many different ways, but I do have a preference."

"Let me take a guess." She pulled my fingers from her insides and got on her hands and knees on the bed. Her head slightly turned so she could look at me. "Are you with me so far?" she asked.

I studied her smooth ass, then placed my hand on my goatee and rubbed it. "No, I'm ahead of you. But, honestly, I think I'd like it so much better if I could, uh, see—"

"See my pussy, right?"

I winked. "You already know me and didn't even have to ask any questions."

Mercedes laughed and scooted back to the edge of the bed. She straddled on her knees and pulled her ass cheeks apart. Her coochie lips smiled at me, and this time, my dick had no problem cooperating.

I strapped up and made my way through the valley. She quickly jerked forward, but I gripped her hips and pulled her back to me.

"Daaaamn, Jaylin," she whined. "It feels like you just ripped my pussy open."

I rubbed her ass all over and pulled her cheeks further apart to alleviate some of the pain. Her walls got so wet that my dick started to easily slip in and out of her. The sex was all right, but the most frustating thing for me was that Mecedes didn't know how to work what she had. I wanted her to throw that ass back to me, but her movements were somewhat . . . slow. She started to come, and the loud hollering and screaming bullshit was working my nerves. I thought she'd lost her damn mind, and when she tightly gripped the sheets, I pulled out of her.

"Come on now, baby. Is all that necessary?"

She fell on her stomach and took deep breaths. "Sorry, I couldn't help it."

I let her recuperate for a moment and then lay on my back so she could ride me. I figured this position was her specialty, but once again, she failed me. She would only go midway down on me, and when I suggested that she put an arch in her back and get busy, she stopped.

"Let me handle this, okay?" she said.

"I wish like hell you would. I'm still waiting."

"For your information, Jaylin, this is not as easy as you may think it is. It's hard for me to move with something like that inside of me."

"Fuck it, then, I'll move."

Mercedes remained on top, but I did most of the work, pumping myself up inside of her. On purpose, I roughly held her hips down and dug deep. The harder I grinded, the more she started to cooperate.

"Now, that's better. Keep throwing that pussy on me and make me feel good about being here."

Mercedes got busy, and in less than five minutes, she came again. I still hadn't gotten my shit off, so I flipped her over sideways, placed one leg high on my shoulder and hardened her clit with the tips of my fingers. I entered her again, speeding up the pace so I could get mine. The harder I pounded, the louder she screamed. She dropped her face into a pillow to silence the noise. There wasn't much for me to scream about, but we eventually released our energy together.

I took a few deep breaths and lay flat on my back next to Mercedes. While looking up at the ceiling, she reached over and lightly backhanded my chest.

"Can I get you some water?" she asked.

"Please," I said.

She left to get my water, and that's when I heard my cell phone ringing. I walked down the hallway to get it out of my pants I'd left on the floor. I saw Shane's name flashing, so I answered.

"What's up?" I said, walking back toward the bed.

"Nothing much, man."

"Then why you bugging me?"

"Look, if you busy, then say so."

"I'm always busy. But what's on your mind?"

"Nothing too urgent, but when you get a moment, we need to chat."

"About what?"

"You said that you were busy, so I would assume you're either fucking, or you're getting ready to."

"Both," I said, looking at Mercedes walking back into the room. She handed me a glass of water and eased herself underneath the covers. When she massaged me, my thang worked its way back up.

"Jaylin!" Shane yelled.

I closed my eyes. "Hmm."

"Would you please give me a call when you have some free time? Trust me, we need to talk."

"Tomorrow," I moaned as Mercedes had my goods in her mouth. My body jerked. "Damn! I'll call you tomorrow."

"Don't forget."

I ended my call with Shane. Mercedes straddled herself on my face, and it was only fair that I returned the favor.


By morning, I was exhausted. Mercedes and I had been at it all night long and my dick was tired. It wasn't like the pussy was all that, because it wasn't. Realistically, it was barely enough to keep my mind off Scorpio, but for the time being, it was something to do. With an ass and body like Mercedes', I thought the sista could throw the fuck down. Her pussy was too, too tight and if I hadn't known better, I would have thought she was a virgin. I should have known better than to judge a book by its cover. Doing so had caused me many disappointments in the past.

Either way, Mercedes' home became a place to lay my head for the next few days. We'd eat, fuck, watch TV, fuck again, sleep, fuck, take a shower, and fuck again. When I realized it was finally time for me to go, I almost hated to leave. Mercedes begged me to stay another night, but I couldn't.

"So, when am I going to hear from you again?" she asked while leaning against the door.

"Soon. And if I forget to call you, you do have my number, right?"

She nodded. Before I jetted, I gave her a long, juicy and memorable kiss.

Before going home, I made a quick stop at a toy store to buy Mackenzie some more Barbies. I must have stood in the Barbie section for nearly an hour, trying to pick out some she didn't already have. I noticed another doll that I thought she'd like even more, and threw a few of those in my cart as well. I knew Mackenzie would have a fit if they didn't have any new clothes to wear, so I picked out some jazzy outfits and headed to the counter.

After all was said and done, I managed to spend eight hundred and seventy dollars on dolls and accessories. The cashier bagged my stuff and I left the toy store shaking my head.

Nanny B had the curtains pulled to the side, and I wasn't sure if she was washing the windows or looking out for me. It was almost 9:00 P.M., so I figured the house cleaning had already been done. She rushed to the door as I grabbed the bags from the trunk and made my way inside.

"We thought you got lost," she said, standing in the doorway.

I cut my eyes and replied with a moody tone. "Nope. Where's Mackenzie?"

"She's upstairs in her room. I don't know if she's asleep or not, but we've missed you around here."

"I'm sure you have."

I walked upstairs to Mackenzie's room. Scorpio must have heard me talking to Nanny B, and as soon as I sat on Mackenzie's bed, Scorpio stepped into the room. Mackenzie was asleep. I gently shook her leg.

"Wake up, sleepyhead," I said.

She rubbed her eyes and sat up in bed. She leaned forward and grabbed me. "Daddy! Where were you?" she yelled.

"I'm fine, baby. I had to go take care of some business."

She pouted. "Why didn't you call me?"

"I don't know. But it doesn't mean I wasn't thinking about you." I reached for the bags and pulled out the dolls. "I was thinking about you so much that I couldn't come home without bringing you something."

Excited, she looked at the dolls and ripped open the boxes. I noticed Scorpio hadn't said a word, so I looked in her direction.

"What's up?" I asked.

"Nothing. I'm just glad you're home."

"Well, do you mind if I talk to Mackenzie for a moment? Alone."

She nodded and left the room. As Mackenzie played with her dolls, I couldn't help but think about losing her. I didn't have much respect left for Scorpio, and the last thing I wanted to do was come between her and Mackenzie. I was on the losing end of this battle, and my stomach turned as I had a feeling the day would come when she would be out of my life for good.

In deep thought, I closed my eyes and held my hands in front of my face. When Mackenzie hopped on my back, I stood up and ran her around the room. She laughed, and I laid her on the bed to tickle her. When she told me to stop because she had to pee-pee, I stopped and she ran to her bathroom. Afterward, she hopped on my back again.

"Whoa . . . wait a minute, baby. Sit down so Daddy can talk to you for a minute, okay?"

Mackenzie moved her long hair away from her face and sat next to me with her pink pajamas on. She clenched her hands together and looked up at me with the prettiest smile. "Thank you for the dolls. I already have most of them, but the other ones are really cute."

"You're welcome. And the ones that you already have, put them on another outfit so they can look different. I'm not going to take them back to the store."

"That's okay. If you don't mind, I'll just give some of them to Megan. She's poor and they don't have a lot of money anyway."

"Mackenzie, that's not something you say about people. Megan's family isn't poor—not living in this neighborhood."

"But she said they were poor because they didn't have a swimming pool, a basketball court, or a movie theater like us. She said her daddy said we're the richest people on the block."

"Yeah, well, that doesn't make them poor, though. We're just blessed . . . how about that?"

"Do you mean like when God blessed me with you? Mama said you're a blessing to us."

"Actually, no, we're a blessing to each other, especially you to me."

"Then why did you leave me? You promised me you'd never leave me again."

"I didn't leave you, Mackenzie. I told you I had some business to take care of. That's why I need you to make me a promise."

"Okay. What is it?"

"I need you to promise me that if you and I are ever separated again, you will always remember how much I love you and know that you will forever stay in my heart."

She wrapped her arms around me. "But I don't want to be separated from you again, Daddy."

"I don't either, but things between your moms and me ain't working out as we'd planned. If she moves out, I can't stop her from taking you with her."

"But I . . . I thought we were supposed to be a family. What about the new baby?"

I hated to go there with her, but she was the kind of kid who wanted answers. "Mackenzie, there is no baby. And as for us being a family, you and I will always be a family."

Mackenzie was silent. I realized how difficult this conversation was for me to have with her, so

I closed my eyes and couldn't go any further. We silently held each other for a while. When I tucked her back in bed, she called my name as I headed toward the door.

"Yes, Mackenzie."

"I love you. Will you sleep with me tonight?"

"I love you too. Just let me go change into my pajamas and I'll be back."

I walked toward my bedroom and wiped the tear that had fallen from my eye. I couldn't deny my feelings about losing her, but what else could I do? Scorpio just wasn't the kind of woman that I thought she was, and I didn't know how much longer I'd be able to put up with her.

When I entered the bedroom, she was in bed, listening to the music on the stereo. I grabbed my pajama pants and took a quick hot shower. Once I was finished, I took a pillow off the bed and headed for the door.

"When are we going to discuss our relationship?" she asked.

I turned at the door, only to cut my eyes at her. She didn't even deserve a response, so I left the room without saying a word.

I got in bed with Mackenzie, and after reading *Cinderella* six times, I was ready to doze off myself. I placed the book on my chest, and Mackenzie rested her head on my shoulder.

Mackenzie was knocked out, but as tired as I was, I still couldn't sleep. I knew there was nothing in the world Scorpio could do or say to make things right between us. She knew how important my children were to me, and not only did I lose out on a baby that wasn't even mine, she also had the power, once again, to take Mackenzie away from me. That was too much power for one woman to have over me, and it bothered me that she'd found a way to tap into a major weakness of mine.

Nanny B tapped my shoulder to wake me. When I asked what time it was, she said it was almost ten o'clock in the morning.

"Wake me up before noon," I said, putting a pillow over my face.

"I wouldn't have woken you up at all, but Shane's waiting downstairs to see you."

"Who?" I said grouchily.

"He said his name was Shane."

"Damn!" I yelled and then pulled back the covers. Mackenzie was still asleep, so I got out of bed and tried not to wake her. I went to my bedroom first and slid on my house shoes, then headed downstairs. I noticed the bed made up, so I figured Scorpio must have already left.

Shane stood in the foyer and gave me a crazy look as I walked slowly down the spiral staircase.

"Didn't I tell you to call me?" he said.

"Yeah, yeah, yeah, but I forgot." I walked into my office and he followed behind me. He took a seat on the sofa, and I leaned against my desk. "So, what's up?"

"I wanted to holla at you about Stephon."

"What about Stephon?"

"Well, I don't want to rush to judgment or nothing, but something with him ain't been quite right lately."

I laughed, making nothing of it. "Mona left his ass. That's what ain't right."

"I know she did, but it's more to it than just that. For instance, the other night, him, Ray-Ray, and me kicked it at his crib for a while. I left to make a phone call, and when I came back, those two fools got to trippin'."

"What do you mean by trippin'?"

"I mean they were acting kind of whack."

"They always act whack, don't they?"

"Yeah, Jay, but this is different."

"Are you trying to say you think the brotha's messing around with that shit?"

"Exactly. Again, I don't want to falsely accuse the brotha or anything, but every time I talk to Stephon, he be talking crazy, man. I can't believe you haven't noticed."

"I noticed a li'l change in him, but I thought the man was hurting because of Mona. Just the other day he told me how much he missed her."

"That could be it too, but just check things out for me. He's a lot closer to you, and if anybody can reach him, I know you can."

Shane stood up, and I thanked him for giving me a heads-up. I walked outside with him and he hopped on his motorcycle.

"You be riding the shit out of this thing, don't you?" I asked.

"This my baby. Whenever you decide to let yours stop collecting dust in the garage, maybe I'll race you one day."

"Bet. And before you leave, I apologize for not returning your calls. I've had so much on my plate that—"

"Don't worry about it." He held out his hand and slapped it against mine. "If you need a brotha to talk to, just holla."

I nodded and he sped off. After all that we'd been through, it felt kind of good to have a friend who had my back.

I was curious to find out what in the hell was going on with Stephon, so I went back inside to put on some clothes. I then rushed into the kitchen to grab my car keys, and saw that Nanny B had breakfast on the table. She handed me a glass of orange juice, and I took a quick sip, then put the glass on the table.

"I gotta make a run. I'll be back shortly," I said.

"Are you sure you're coming back this time?"

"Yes. And you and I will sit down and talk later."

She smiled and I smiled back. Then I gave her a peck on the cheek and jetted.

As I pulled out of the driveway, I saw Scorpio driving down the street. She pulled my Porsche close to my Mercedes and lowered the window.

"I'm in a rush," I said.

"Are you coming back today?"

"Maybe."

"Well, whenever you do, we really need to talk."

"Take a number."

We stared at each other for a few seconds, and then I raised the window and drove off. Listening to her lies was the last damn thing on my mind. I hoped she understood that she was on my time, not hers.

Since Stephon wasn't at his shop, I drove to his house. In addition to his BMW, there were two other cars in his driveway. I knocked on the door, and banged harder when I got no answer. Finally, he opened the door in his red silk boxers, looking beat.

I stepped inside and looked around. "Why you looking all spacy and shit?" I asked.

" 'Cause I'm tired."

"Tired from what?" I said, and then walked over to the couch and took a seat. He sluggishly followed behind me and plopped down in a chair.

"Just tired. I ain't been getting much sleep at all."

"Um, you got company?"

"Yeah, they downstairs."

"Who are they?"

"Gabrielle and Carlotta."

"You've been on this ménage à trois thang for a while, haven't you?"

"You got a problem with it? I can't help it if it takes two to please me."

"No, I don't have a problem with that; however, I do have a problem with you if you're doing drugs."

He cocked his head back. "What?"

"You heard me, nigga. A li'l birdie told me you been messing around with that shit."

"Your li'l birdie can kiss my ass. As a matter of fact, you can tell that nigga Shane I said to kiss my ass, because I know he's the one who told you that shit."

"Are you saying he's a liar?"

"You damn right he's a liar. And he needs to mind his own business. If anything, Jay, you know I don't fuck around like that."

"No, I don't know. Just like I didn't know you

and Ray-Ray smoked weed. You know what that shit did to your mother, so I don't understand why you would even want to touch it."

"That's why I don't. I might smoke a li'l herb every once in a while, but trust me, that's it."

"You wouldn't lie to me, man, would you?"

Stephon looked as serious as serious could get. "Jay, I'm telling you, it ain't my style."

"If you say so. I can only believe what you tell me, and you know how much I hate to be lied to. Please, do not disappoint me."

"Have I ever?" Stephon said, defensively holding out his hands.

"Hell yeah!" I laughed. "Anyway, are you doing okay without Mona? I mean, I know how much you were digging her, and I hope that party wasn't what caused everything to go downhill."

"Naw, it just put the icing on the cake. I tripped, man. You know how sometimes we don't know a good thing until it's gone. But ain't shit I can do about it now. I've moved on, trust me."

"We always do," I said, standing up. I headed for the door and Stephon followed behind me.

"Jay."

"What's up?"

"I was wondering if you had a li'l extra cash. Nigga been kind of dry these days with Mona not helping out anymore, so—"

"Enough said. What you need?"

"A grand, maybe two."

I nodded. "You'll have it in your account by morning."

"Thanks, cuz," he said, giving me a hug. I hugged him back and tightly closed my eyes.

I sat in my car and listened to Miles Davis blow his horn. I now knew, more than anything, that Stephon had lied to me. It was written all over his face. Being partially raised by a crackhead, I could see the monkey on his back. For how long, was the question. I guess it really didn't matter, because once anybody started doing that shit, it was hard to let go. I couldn't understand how or why I hadn't noticed it before. I guess I'd been so tied up with my own mess that I completely ignored it. Now that I looked back, some things with Stephon hadn't been adding up.

I was so frustrated with the lying-ass people in my life that I didn't even feel like going back to my house. I checked in at the Four Seasons again and stayed there for the night. Before going to bed, I called the house to speak to Mackenzie. Nanny B said that she and Scorpio went to Leslie's house and they'd be back later. I told Nanny B to tell Mackenzie I'd see her in the morning, and then shut it down for the rest of the night.

In the morning, I thought about transferring some money into Stephon's account, but I changed my mind. I often said my money would never be spent on drugs, and I meant it. Instead, I moseyed home, only to find Scorpio waiting for me. She looked a wretched mess. Her hair hadn't been combed, and her face was paler than ever. I tried to ignore her while making my way up the steps, but she cursed at me and grabbed my hand. I snatched it away.

"Didn't I tell you not to touch me ever again? Didn't I?" I yelled.

"And didn't I tell you I wanted to talk?"

"About what, Scorpio? Talk about what?"

"About what we need to do with our relationship."

"Damn, do we really need to talk about it? It's obvious, ain't it?" I turned and headed upstairs to Nanny B's room. I was surprised to see her still in bed at nine o'clock in the morning, and when I asked why, she said that she hadn't been getting much sleep because she was worried about me.

"Worried about me for what?" I asked, and then sat down. "Trust me, I'm gon' be all right."

"I don't doubt it, but you got a lot on your plate right now. You need to tackle one issue at a time and deal with it. Ignoring what's going on isn't going to make your issues go away."

"I know, but I just need more time to think things out. As for Stanley, I hate him, Nanny B. Why would you let him into this house?"

"Because I wanted you to prove to him that you're a better man than he is. I was hoping you'd show him, or if not, share with him what a wonderful father you've turned out to be, even though he wasn't there for you. The other day, you allowed him to win. You showed him that you're an angry, bitter, and vengeful person who hasn't been able to move on because of him. Trust me, your reaction was what he expected, and was probably what he wanted."

"Maybe so, but it would have been nice if you had warned me. As close as we are, you could have pulled me aside and told me about him coming over here."

"Jaylin, please. If I had warned you, I would

have never heard the last of it. I handled the situation as best as I could, and I'm not going to apologize for it."

"And I don't want you to. I do, however, owe you an apology."

"If it's from your heart, I'll accept it. Besides, I'm gonna let what you said to me slide this time. If you ever talk to me like that again, boy, I'm gonna get my belt and whip the hell out of you."

I laughed, and so did Nanny B. She got out of bed and put on her cotton housecoat. After she slid on her house shoes, she sat on the edge of her bed.

"So," she said, "now that we've agreed on one thing, what is going on between you and Scorpio? Whatever it is, I don't like it one bit. She's about to lose her mind messing with you."

"And I'm about to lose my mind messing with her. Did she tell you about the baby?"

"Yes."

"You knew?"

"Yes, I knew before you did, but it wasn't my place to tell you."

I shook my head and looked down at the floor. "I'm tired of all the lies. I can't take them anymore. Several months ago, I would have done anything in the world for her. I give her everything, and it still isn't good enough."

"So, are you saying it's over?"

"You're damn right it is. I refuse to be with a woman who constantly lies to me."

"Then tell her. Don't leave her hanging on like she is. She reminds me so much of myself when I was married to your grandfather. He would never tell me how he really felt until it was too late."

"We'll talk, just not right now. I'm still trying to figure out what to do with Mackenzie."

"I've thought about her too. All I'm going to say to you is sometimes we have to give up things that are precious to us. For instance, I had to let go of your mother, your aunt Betty, and your uncle, for my own peace of mind. If I hadn't, your grandfather would have made my life more miserable than it already was. I wish I could have gotten you from that orphanage, but after what he put me through, at the time, I felt it was best for me to leave everything behind me."

I looked at Nanny B with seriousness in my eyes. "I understand, but I don't want to give up Mackenzie. To me, your children are not something you have to decide if you want or don't want. They are yours no matter what."

"I agree. But under these circumstances, Mackenzie comes with a package. So, you need to decide if you're going to keep this package or let it go. This time, if you let it go, you need to let it go for good."

Nanny B and I chatted for at least another hour. When I told her about my speculations with Stephon, she told me Stephon was a grown man, and if that's what path he chose, then there was nothing I could do. I silently disagreed because he meant everything to me. Even though we had our ups and downs, Stephon was like the brother I'd never had. Again, I wasn't going to support what he did, but I was forever going to be there for him. I just hoped that my decision to stick by him wasn't going to come back to haunt me.

# 13

## *NOKEA*

Early Saturday morning, Jaylin was outside ringing the doorbell. I was upset that he felt it was okay for him to show up whenever he wanted to. When I opened the door, the look on my face said it all. He walked right in without being invited.

"Where my son at?"

"In his room. But can you please pick up the phone and call before coming over here?"

"I tried, but the number was busy."

"Quit lying," I said, closing the door.

We headed back to LJ's room. He was already woke, so Jaylin picked him up and sat down in a rocking chair with him. "Man, why you getting so big?" he asked. I stood in the doorway and smiled.

"He is, isn't he?"

"I haven't seen him in a little over a week, and it seems as if he's grown that fast."

"I'm not going to say all that, but he is getting big." Still tired, I yawned. "Would you like some coffee or something to eat?"

"Naw, I'm fine. I just wanted to spend some time with my son since you've been trying to avoid me and everything."

"I have not."

"Yes you have."

"Okay, so maybe I have. But I just don't want you and I to—"

"We won't. We both crossed the line, so forget it, okay?"

"Bet. And while you're enjoying precious moments with your son, I'm taking my butt back to bed."

"Close the door behind you because we might make too much noise."

I closed the door and went back into my room. I lay there for a while, but after listening to LJ and Jaylin play around, I couldn't get back to sleep. An hour later, he came into my room with LJ on his shoulders, and I pretended to be sleeping. Jaylin put LJ on the bed and he crawled his way to me, grabbing my neck. I kissed him several times and placed him on my lap. Jaylin sat on the sofa in my room and propped his feet on the table. When the phone rang, I reached over to answer.

"Good morning," I said, as I already knew it was Collins.

"Good morning, sweetness. So, what time am I picking up the love of my life?"

"You're not picking her up, because she's coming to your place in about an hour or so."

"Now, what would make you think I can wait another hour to see you? I had my clothes on and was on my way over there."

"Well, first of all, Jaylin stopped by not too long

ago to see LJ. I haven't had time to put on any clothes, let alone get any sleep."

"So, you're undressed and Jaylin is there?"

"No," I said and laughed. "I still have on my pajamas, honey, and Jaylin is about to leave."

"Is LJ going with him? I thought he was going to hang out with us today."

"He'll probably go home with Jaylin since he hasn't seen him all week. So, I'll get dressed and hurry right over, okay?"

"See ya soon."

"Love you."

"Me too."

I could see Jaylin had taken in every word I said to Collins. "I'm getting ready to go," I said. "Is it okay if LJ goes home with you?"

"Of course it's okay. I planned on taking him and Mackenzie to see Disney on Ice today anyway."

"Thanks for telling me."

"I was going to tell you, but I've had so much on my mind that I forgot."

This sadness in his eyes was driving me crazy. Definitely something else was wrong. "Are you okay? I know the situation with Stanley is bothersome, and I haven't a clue what's going on with you and Scorpio. Whatever it is, can't the two of you work it out?"

"Not this time."

"What's so different about this time?"

"How about the baby she was carrying wasn't mine?"

I quickly sat up straight. "Jaylin, no. What happened?"

"She met some fool while she was in Denver.

Shit, I don't know. I . . . I thought the baby was mine until she told me the reason why she had an abortion."

"I don't know what to say. I can't imagine how you feel, especially after losing your son."

He let out a deep sigh. "Yeah, it's been crazy. I have all this love to give my children, and there has been nothing but chaos with every damn one of them."

"Please don't harp on the past. You have LJ, and he's not going anywhere. He's yours forever."

He stared at me without a blink. "You too?"

I hesitated for a moment, surprised by his bluntness. I didn't want to get Jaylin's hopes up about us, so I answered his question as best as I could. "I'll always be here for you, if you need to talk."

Jaylin and I continued our conversation, and before I knew it, at least two hours had gone by. I quickly showered, put on some clothes, and walked him and LJ out. I gave my good-byes and headed to Collins' place.

I didn't think he would be that upset with me for being late, but he was. He stood tall, casually dressed in khakis, a striped button-down shirt, and shiny loafers. He pointed his finger at me while I sat on the edge of his bed, listening to him gripe.

"Nokea, I'm not going to sit around and wait while you play house with your ex-boyfriend!" he yelled.

"I wasn't playing house, Collins. I was talking to him about something important."

"Something important like what?"

"Like he's really going through something right now. I at least offered him my support."

"Hey, look, we all go through things. There's not a person on this earth that hasn't been through something. I don't like him leaning on you and coming to you for comfort every time shit don't go his way. If he needs that much help, then that's what a fucking psychiatrist is for. I'm sure his money can buy him plenty of them."

I was taken aback by Collins' tone and quickly stood up. "How dare you come to me like that, Collins? I'm not going to turn my back on the father of my child if he needs me. Now, I don't know where all this is coming from, but no man is going to pick my friends for me. Ex-boyfriend or not, I'm not going to turn my back on anyone if they need me. Sorry, I'm not that kind of person." I walked off, heading for the door.

"Nokea!" Collins yelled.

"What?" I yelled back.

He took a deep breath to calm himself. "Don't go. Please understand where I'm coming from."

"I'm trying, Collins, but I'm not used to you yelling and cursing at me. Trust me, I understand how you feel, but do you remember the reason you said that you love me so much?"

"Yes, I do. I know you're a caring person, Nokea, but when it comes to Jaylin, baby, I don't trust him."

"And I'm not asking you to; however, I'm asking you to trust me. I love you, and Jaylin isn't going to interfere with our relationship."

Collins and I quickly settled our differences and embraced. He knew how much I loved him, and the last thing we wanted was for Jaylin to cause trouble in our relationship. For Collins to be jealous of Jaylin would've been a big mistake. I knew he felt the competition was steep, and when it came to Jaylin, it was hard for Collins to completely trust me alone with him. Collins, however, was a man who felt so confident and sure of himself. I was sure he would do whatever not to let Jaylin get underneath his skin. It was up to me to put Collins at ease, and that was my number one priority.

I rubbed his waves back with my hands and sucked his thick brown lips into mine. As we made love, I couldn't help but think about how I'd had the nerve to ask him to trust me. Just a few weeks ago, I'd known that he couldn't. Feeling guiltier about my feelings for Jaylin during intercourse with Collins, I got emotional.

Collins stopped and looked me in the eyes. "What's wrong, baby?"

"I love you so much, I swear I do. Don't you ever forget how much I love you," I confessed.

"Same here. I feel exactly the same way. I'm sorry for coming to you like I did, and I won't ever talk to you like that again."

Collins and I finished making love, and spent the rest of our day enjoying each other's company. We had lunch at the Macaroni Grill, played a few games of miniature golf, went to the movies, and before the day was over, we went shopping.

I stayed the night at his house and didn't return home until late Sunday night. When I got home, I checked my messages. Jaylin had called, asking if LJ could stay the week with him. He told me if there was a problem to call, but trying to allow them as much time together as possible, I didn't see any need to.

I listened to my other messages and was surprised to get a call from Stanley. He left a number so I could reach him, and begged me to call him back. Having very little to say to him, I decided not to call. However, I was curious to know his purpose, and returned the call later that day.

"Nokea, Nokea, Nokea. How you been, girl?"

"I've been fine, Stanley. How about you?"

"I've been okay. Can't complain after how good God has been to me."

"He is good, but I . . . I'm not quite sure why you called me."

"The reason for my call was to ask you if I could see my grandson. I, uh, know how Jaylin feels, but I was hoping you would let me come see him."

I released a deep sigh, not knowing how to respond to Stanley's request. The last thing I wanted was to come between him and Jaylin. "Stanley, you'll have to talk to Jaylin about that. I don't feel comfort—"

"I have rights to my grandson," he snapped. "I know I wasn't there for my son, but I'd like to have a fresh start with my grandson. I've been diagnosed with cancer, and—"

A part of me didn't believe him, but what if he were telling the truth? "I'm sorry to hear about your cancer, but it's not in my best interest to get involved. Personally, I really don't have a problem with you seeing LJ, and I would love for the two of you to get to know each other. Knowing that

Jaylin would have a problem with it, though, there's no way I can agree to it."

"Would you at least do me a favor and tell Jaylin how much I'd like to be a part of his and LJ's lives? I know I made some mistakes, but I need my family right now."

I shook my head and thought about all of the hurt Jaylin had been through without having his father around. How dare Stanley expect for everyone to jump when he wanted them to? "What about when your family needed you? I don't mean to sound harsh, Stanley, but do you have a clue as to what your son went through without you?"

"I know, Nokea. And I tried to be there, but I couldn't."

"I'd be curious to know what stopped you, but it really doesn't matter. You need to have this conversation with your son, not me. There's nothing I can say to sway him, and you're asking the wrong person to talk to him. If he ever agrees to you seeing LJ, I'll support it, but again, that'll be up to him."

I hung up with no regrets about what I said to Stanley. The more we spoke, the angrier I got, as I thought about how he left Jaylin. To me, Stanley wasn't worth my time.

I tried to give Jaylin a heads-up about Stanley. I called his home phone to speak with him. Scorpio answered, and when I asked if Jaylin was there, she said no.

"Is he still out with the kids?" I asked.

"No, they got back about an hour ago. Shortly after, he left."

"Did he say where he was going?" I asked, irritated because Jaylin was supposed to be spending time with his son, not in the streets.

"Does he ever?"

"I'll try him on his cell phone."

"You do that."

*What an attitude,* I thought and hung up to call Jaylin. I didn't take it personally because I knew what was going on between them.

I waited for Jaylin to answer his phone. When a female answered, I was quite startled and almost had a loss for words.

"Hello," she said again.

"Is this Jaylin Rogers' phone?"

"Yes, it is. May I ask who's calling?"

"Is he there?"

"He's in the shower, but I can get him for you if you'd like."

"No, thank you. I'll call back."

For whatever reason, I was kind of pissed. Now, he came over here pretending to be so hurt and looking pitiful. Then he had the nerve to be shacked up with somebody else? If that was the case, LJ could have stayed here with me. I couldn't stop thinking about how he made me feel sorry for him, until my phone interrupted my thoughts. It was him calling me back.

"Yes," I said dryly.

"Did you call?"

"Yeah."

"What's up?"

"Where are you?"

"I'm over a friend of mine's house."

"I thought you were going to spend some time with your son."

"I did, and I'm going to for the rest of the week."

"Fine, do whatever."

"What's with the attitude?"

"Honestly, you amaze the heck out of me. I don't see how you can keep sleeping around with different women and have no desires to work out matters with the woman in your home."

"Look, I told you I'm at a friend's house. I'll deal with Scorpio when I get ready to, and quite frankly, it's none of your damn business. If you think I'm going to sit at home and cry about what happened, then you got me fucked up. I'm not that kind of man, nor will I ever be. Now, state your business for your call, or say good-bye."

I hung up on his butt. I'm sure his new woman was listening, and I wasn't about to let him go off on me. The thought of going to get my baby crossed my mind, but I knew Nanny B had him well taken care of. I could tell Jaylin was playing with fire, and it was just a matter of time before he got burned.

# 14

## *SCORPIO*

I was going crazy in this house, waiting for Jaylin to come home. The walls felt as if they were closing in on me, and it didn't seem as if he would come around any time soon. By now, I thought all of this would be behind us, but he had made no attempts to reconcile with me.

I was so frustrated that I hadn't been to school in days. I didn't have the energy to go, and even if I did, it would have done me no good. All I could think about was how Jaylin and I kept on hurting each other. I wasn't doing it intentionally, but there were times when things were beyond my control. If he'd never treated me like shit, then I never would have moved to Denver and met Rick. While I was in Denver, Jaylin didn't waste any time meeting people, so why did he expect me to put my life on hold? I knew it was wrong of me not to tell him about the baby, but at the time, I thought it was best. I thought we were having this child together and would soon live happily ever after. But how wrong could I have been? I was going through pure hell, and didn't know what to do to stop my pain.

Jaylin had been gone since he'd gotten back with the kids earlier. As usual, he didn't say where he was going, and at this point, I didn't even ask. I knew he'd had sex with someone else because he damn sure wasn't having it with me. And every time he'd come in late, he'd take a shower, grab a pillow, and head into another room. I offered to give up his bed, but he ignored me and slept wherever he wanted to.

A big part of me wanted to leave, but honestly, I was tired of running. Besides, I didn't have any-where to go, and there was no way I was going to put Mackenzie through this bullshit again. If I even mentioned leaving this house, I knew she wouldn't go. The last thing I wanted to do was force her to leave with me. At the rate things were going, though, maybe I would have to.

When I heard Jaylin coming up the steps, I rolled over and looked at the alarm clock. It showed al-most four o'clock in the morning. Doing the norm, he headed for the bathroom and closed the door. He showered, and as soon as he stepped out of the bathroom, the phone rang. He ignored it, but when I reached over to answer, he wrapped a towel around his waist and walked into the closet.

"Hello," I said in a sleepy voice.

"May I speak to Jaylin?" she asked.

"No, you may not," I snapped. "Who is this?"

"Scorpio, it's Mercedes. Has Jaylin made it home yet?"

My faced scrunched up at the sound of her name. "Yes, he has, but bitch, why are you calling here?"

Jaylin came out of the closet and held out his hand for the phone. "Give it here," he said sharply.

I held the phone in my hand and yelled, "Are you fucking around with this bitch? I know her ass, Jaylin!"

"I don't give a fuck who you know. Now, give me the damn phone."

I slammed the phone in his hand and got out of bed. Not saying anything else to him, I put on some clothes, getting ready to leave. When I reached for the keys on the nightstand, he tightly grabbed my wrist.

"Mercedes, I'll hit you back later." He paused. "Just keep my watch safe and I'll pick it up tomorrow." He snickered. "Yeah, that too. Bye." He hung up and looked at me. "Where do you think you're going?"

"Let go of my wrist. You're hurting me."

He let go. "Don't take my car out at this time of the morning."

"Your car will be just fine."

"I'm sure it will be, especially since it's not moving."

"So, now take the car from me too? What else do you want from me? Haven't you already taken enough?"

"You know what? Take the car. If it's anybody that's been taking shit from the other, Miss Lady, you have worn out your welcome. You sound like a fool standing there telling me what I've taken from you. The only thing that I've taken from you is your pussy, and you offered to give me that. So I don't give a shit where you go, just don't tear up my damn car. If you do, there are going to be repercussions."

He tossed the keys to me and I left.

I didn't have anywhere to go, but I couldn't stand to be around him knowing he was screwing that sleazy ho Mercedes. She knew me and knew me well. She used to be an exotic dancer until she fucked this old-ass rich man who offered her a better future. With his assistance, she began her modeling career. After that, nobody saw her for a while, until we started seeing her face on magazine covers and billboards. She'd been in the newspaper quite often, and I assumed she made pretty decent money.

She and I fell out years ago over Mackenzie's father, Bruce. I didn't know he was seeing both of us at the same time, and when I got pregnant, he left her for me. Soon after, he left me as well and moved to California. I hadn't seen him since then, and quite frankly, didn't want to.

The last time I saw Mercedes, we had a few words. She'd somehow heard about my relationship with Jaylin and teased me about hitting the jackpot. When I told her I wasn't interested in his money, she begged to differ. That's the kind of scandalous tramp she was, and if Jaylin wanted that kind of woman in his life, he could have her.

I was hungry, so I stopped at Denny's to grab a bite to eat. I couldn't stop thinking about Jaylin screwing Mercedes, so I pulled out my cell phone to make a quick call to my girlfriend, Traniece, to see if she had any scoop. It was still early in the morning, but I wanted some answers.

"Girl, do you know what time it is?" she said in a sluggish voice.

"I'm sorry, but I need a favor."

"That's the only time you call. What's up, though?"

"Do you know where Mercedes lives?"

"Yeah, I think so. She not too long ago moved into a house near Eureka. Why?"

"Because I want to talk to her about Jaylin."

"Jaylin? What's going on with her and Jaylin?"

"That's what I want to know. Would you mind giving me her address? I promise you I won't tell her you gave it to me."

"Hold on," Traniece said. She had me on hold for a while and then came back to the phone. She gave me Mercedes' address and directions to her crib. She also asked if I wanted her phone number.

"No, that's okay. Her address is fine."

I thanked Traniece, and after I finished eating and racking my brain about what to do, I headed straight for Mercedes' house. My intentions weren't to cause any trouble. All I wanted to do was find out how serious this relationship was between her and Jaylin. I hated doing shit like this, but I couldn't let her think she had him all to herself, could I?

Traniece must have already given Mercedes a heads-up. When I pulled in her driveway, she stood in the doorway with her arms folded. I could tell she had an attitude by the toot of her lips and the frown on her face. Her hair was pulled back into a neat ponytail, maybe suggesting that she was ready for a fight. I gracefully walked to the door and stood face to face with her.

"Are you screwing Jaylin?" I asked bluntly.

She stepped back and put her hand on her hip. "We're screwing each other. Do you have a problem with that?"

I pointed my finger in her face. "You're damn right I do. Now, I've been through this with you once before, Mercedes, and I'm not going through it again. Why don't you just back off this time?"

"I don't think so. A man like Jaylin can only be an asset to me, and by the way he put it down in the bedroom, I don't think I'm going to give him up that easily."

Her words stung like hell. "So, that's what it's all about for you? Some dick?"

"That's all it's been about for you, hasn't it? He told me how you can't get enough of his ass, about your lies, and how you lied about the baby to keep him. Face it, Scorpio, you fucked up—like you always do." Her neck started to roll. "So don't be coming over here trying to start no shit with me."

Mercedes walked inside, and when she tried to close the door, I pushed on it. The door swung open and hit her in the face. She charged at me, and since I wasn't having it, I grabbed her ponytail and we went at it.

We pounded the hell out of each other. The anger I had as I thought about Jaylin having sex

with her was boiled up inside of me. How dare he
tell her our business? How dare he sleep with a
woman who was major competition for me? She
was really gorgeous, and with each punch to her
face, I intended to mess it up. I had no problem
taking my frustrations out on her. When she got
loose, she struggled to the phone and called the
police.

Foolishly, I didn't have enough sense to get the
hell out of there, so when they came, they arrested me for trespassing and assault. I sat in back
of the police car with handcuffs on and watched
as they towed Jaylin's Porsche away. He, without a
doubt, was going to be livid.

Not wanting to stay one minute in jail, I had to
call him to come bail me out.

"YOU DID WHAT?" he screamed at the top of his
lungs.

"I need for you to come get me," I said softly.

"Where in the fuck is my car at?"

"I . . . I think it's in the tow yard."

"You think, huh? Well, why don't you think
about how you're going to sit in that motherfucking jail for the next several days? I can't believe
your ass!" He hung up.

I didn't even have enough strength to cry. What
in the hell did I expect from him? That son of a
bitch didn't care about me, and I was finally starting to realize it.

I thought about calling Jackson, but I didn't want
it to seem as if I only called him when I wanted
something. Shortly after Jaylin and I had gotten together, I had eliminated many of my friends. It was
times like this I wish I hadn't.

The police told me my bail was $50,000. Ten percent down or not, that was too much money. Now, why would they assume I had that kind of money? I told them the car wasn't mine, but I guess they felt as if they hit the jackpot when Jaylin's information came up. They had no sympathy for me. I guess with acting a damn fool like I did, I couldn't blame them.

I sat back on the cot and thought about all that had happened. When I heard an officer open the gate, I stood to my feet and he told me my time was up. I thought they were being nice by releasing me so soon, but when I walked outside, Jaylin was in his car on the phone. I was so glad to see him and wanted to smile; however, I knew how angry he was so I held back.

"Thank you for coming to get me," I said, closing the car door.

He didn't say one word to me, just looked over and stared while still on the phone. "Yeah, man, I'm gonna stop by there tomorrow. In the meantime, let me deal with this criminal jailbird and I'll call you later."

He ended his call and drove off. Still not saying anything to me, he reached for the volume on the radio, turning it up. I felt as if this was the perfect time for us to talk, so I reached for the knob to turn it off.

"Would you talk to me, please? Don't you see how desperate I'm getting?" I said.

"I don't talk to jailbirds. And I damn sure don't talk to women who feel as if they need to act childish and fight over me either."

"I did what I had to do to defend myself. Besides, she started it."

"I'm sure she did. When it comes to you, the other person is always at fault. So, enough said. Where's my damn car at?"

I reached in my pocket and gave him the card the police had given to me. He drove to the tow yard, and after he dished out more money to get it, he paid one of the fellas there to drive his car home. He insisted I would never drive his car again, and yelled at me like I was a kid or something, all the way home.

I had a serious headache and went upstairs to relax. Jaylin called a taxi to drive the man back to work, and I watched them converse from the upstairs window. The house was quiet because Nanny B, LJ, and Mackenzie were gone. Again, this was another perfect opportunity to talk to Jaylin—or so I thought. But as soon as he came upstairs, our conversation turned into another yelling match.

"You refuse to listen to anything I have to say, so fuck it!" I yelled. I felt grimey from sitting on that cot for hours, and gathered some clothes to take a shower.

"You damn right fuck it," he said, following me into the bathroom. "Why don't you just get your shit and get the hell out of here then?"

"Oh, you would like that, wouldn't you? That way, you could bring your so-called new bitch up in here!"

"I'll bring my new bitch up in here whether you're here or not. I pay the bills here, and if I wanted to, I'll even fuck her in this house with your ass right here."

"Like hell!" I yelled in his face. "If you ever disrespect me like that—"

"You gon' what?" he yelled in my face. "What in the fuck are you gonna do?"

My heart pounded. I was seething with anger. Honestly, there wasn't shit I could do, and I dropped my head in frustration. He grabbed my hair, pulling it back to raise my head. "Don't punk out on me now, Miss Hard-Ass. Tell me, what in the fuck are you gonna do?"

I gritted my teeth and reached for his hair to pull it back. "I swear I hate you. I hate I ever met you, Jaylin!"

He pulled my hair tighter. "I hate your ass too!"

We stood and held each other's hair while angrily staring each other down. My heart was beating fast, and by the way his chest heaved in and out, so was his. The tension was so thick, you could cut it with a knife. Jaylin blinked first, and when he looked at the tears running over my lips, he leaned in to kiss me. I backed away, but he pulled my head forward and covered my mouth with his. His grip in my hair got looser, and so did my grip in his. I closed my eyes and moved my hands throughout his soft, curly hair.

Feeling so relieved, I tore at his clothes and he tore at mine. We stood naked, and he picked me up and sat me on the bathroom counter in front of the mirrors.

I continued to rub through his hair, and he dropped his head against my chest. "Why do we keep on hurting each other like this?" he asked.

"I don't know, but you have to know the hurt

I've caused you was never intentional. I love you, and I would never—"

"Less than a minute ago you said you hated me."

"I hate what you do to me, Jaylin. I hate this hold that you have on me, and I hate the way I feel when you're away from me."

"Me too," he said, touching my breasts. "I be feeling so lost without you."

"Then don't be without me. Who says that you have to?"

I opened my legs wide and wrapped them around Jaylin's waist. I rubbed up and down his muscular back and squeezed his tight ass, as his dick had already found its way inside of me. I'd waited weeks to feel like this, and by the look in his eyes, this moment hadn't come soon enough for him either.

He squatted down in front of me, and I placed my legs on his shoulders while leaning back. He pecked my thighs, and as his tongue licked along the furrows next to my clit, he had me begging for more. I yelled out his name and encouraged him to fuck me well.

For the next hour or so, Jaylin provided what I'd asked for. I rode him backwards while he sat on the edge of the Jacuzzi tub. I knew my performance was to his satisfaction when he filled up my insides with one creamy, heavy load.

I wasn't done with Jaylin just yet. I got on the floor, inviting him in between my legs. He enjoyed watching me play with myself, so I inserted my finger and moaned as I rubbed my swollen clit. I imagined that he was touching me, but he sat on the sidelines and continued to watch. It didn't take long for him to join me on the floor, putting his mouth to work. I entertained him on one end, and in a sixty-nine position, he entertained me on the other. His perfected finger-fucking abilities caused my juices to run between the cheeks of my ass. I trembled all over and tried hard to concentrate on what I was doing to him.

Eventually, he backed out of my mouth and put his hardness where it belonged. He was rough, and pounded the hell out of me on the floor.

I slightly pushed his hips back and scooted back a bit. "Jaylin, slow down. Take your time, baby, okay?"

His rhythm slowed as he whispered in my ear, licking it. "I want a baby. I want you to have my baby, soon."

"I want that more than anything in the world. So however long we've got to go at this, I'm game."

I could barely keep up with Jaylin. We worked on our baby for what seemed to be hours. Nanny B and the kids had even come home, but we were so into it that we just closed the door and continued.

By the time we crossed the finish line, there wasn't anywhere else in the bathroom to explore. We looked at each other and laughed as he lay on top of me in the bathroom's linen closet.

"Are we finally finished?" I asked while taking deep breaths. "I don't think I can go any longer."

Jaylin rolled on his back and put me on top of him. "Yes, I'm finished. But we still need to clean up, right?"

I looked at my handsome man lying on the floor and smiled. "Yeah," I said. "Then let's go to the tub and clean up."

Jaylin massaged my breasts together, and when he noticed my nipples swell, he slightly lifted me from his lap and went inside me again. I had no energy left and couldn't even move. He squeezed my sweaty backside and guided my movements on top of him. I couldn't believe my pussy had the nerve to tingle.

"This is your last one. I . . . I don't understand how . . . why I keep coming like this."

Maybe I didn't know, but Jaylin did. He had mastered every single spot on my body, and the way he provoked my insides was no exception.

I fell forward on his chest, and he rubbed my back to comfort me. "You think you are so good, don't you?" I said.

"I am."

"Says who?"

"Says your pussy every time I dive into it. Didn't you hear the way it just spoke to me?"

"Trust me, it don't know any better."

"Oh, it knows. And its owner, she knows better too."

"The only thing its owner knows is she got some potent stuff too. And since she knows that, you better not think about fucking Mercedes again or else I'm cutting it off."

"Are you giving me an ultimatum?"

"Take it however you want, but she and I got some bad blood between us. I'm not about to compete with her again."

"What happened between y'all?"

"It's a long story. I'll tell you about it while we're in the tub."

Jaylin ran our water, and I hurried to check on Nanny B and the kids. She was downstairs doing the laundry while the kids watched *Finding Nemo*. Seeing that everything was cool, I headed back upstairs. Jaylin was singing in the tub, and I put my ass in his face to shush him.

He cleared his throat. "Do you know the gap between your legs is about the same width as my dick?"

"No, I didn't," I said, easing down in the water. "But thanks for noticing. I'm sure it didn't get there on its own."

"You had that gap before I met you."

"I did not."

"Yes, you did. It was one of the first things I noticed about you."

"If I did have one, trust me, it wasn't as big as it is now."

"I agree. And I've had the pleasure of making it grow."

"You are so silly. Is that all you think about?"

"No, but, uh, tell me what's up with you and Mercedes."

Jaylin lathered our bodies with soap and water while I gave him the scoop about Mercedes and me. When I told him she used to mess around with Mackenzie's daddy, he couldn't believe it.

"It's a small, small world. You can't even lie about fucking around these days. That's why nine times out of ten, I'm always honest about my shit."

"Okay, Mr. Honest Man, who else have you been screwing besides Mercedes?"

He cocked his head back. "What?"

"You heard me. I know you've been messing around with somebody else, haven't you?"

"Nope. As a matter of fact, I kept it simple this time around."

"Ain't nothing about that tramp simple. Why'd you have to go sleep with her? Of all the women in St. Louis, why her?"

"Why not? Baby got back, and she—"

I put my hand over his mouth. "Don't even go there. If that's the case, I got back and plenty of it."

"But not like—"

"Jaylin, don't. Please don't compare us."

"I'm not, so don't go getting all bent out of shape. And even though baby girl might have back, she ain't got no front to back it up like my baby do."

My throat ached, and his words stung like hell. "I don't appreciate you comparing the two of us like that. You gotta know how much that shit hurts."

"That's because I wanted it to. I was just so angry at your ass, Scorpio, that you left me no other alternative. I'm not going to even say that I'm sorry, because a huge part of me ain't."

"Fine, then remain angry with me for lying to you, but don't make me continue to pay for it. Can you at least promise me that this vengefulness of yours is over?"

"Oh, it's over. As long as you can promise never to lie to me again."

"After what I went through, I promise that from now on, I will be open and honest with you about everything. But you gotta promise me that you will never have sex with Mercedes again. Remember how you felt about Shane and me? That's the way I feel about you and her. I need to hear you say that you will never go back there again."

He playfully stuttered. "I–I—"

"Jaylin."

"Okay, I promise."

"And what is it that you're promising me?"

"I promise you I will never go to her place again."

"Don't take me for a fool, Jaylin. Tell me you'll never fuck her again. I don't care where it is: her house, your house, her car, your car, wherever. Tell me it will never happen."

"Okay, damn. I will never fuck Mercedes again. That is, of course, as long as you keep your word about not lying and we remain together."

"That's still not good enough. I don't care if we're together or not; I want her out of your life."

He huffed, pretending as if he really hated to make me a promise. "Done deal. Now, let's talk about something else."

"Something else like what?"

"Like how much sex it's going to take for us to make this baby."

"Oh, Lord. I knew that was coming."

"So, are you saying you don't want to?"

"I enjoy having sex with you, but I don't want our relationship to be based on that alone."

"Do you think that's all it's based on?"

I shrugged my shoulders. "Sometimes I do. Sex

always seems to work out our problems, and that's not good. I don't want to get into the habit of relying on it to work things out for us."

"Having passionate sex with your woman is the most relaxing and stress-relieving solution to any man's problems. Mad at your ass or not, it always works for me. Pussy be so good, sometimes I forget why I was mad at you to begin with."

"But we need to rely on our communication, talking things out instead of avoiding them. Being honest is another problem. Sometimes I feel as if I'm afraid to be honest with you because of your anger. I shouldn't have to feel that way."

"And going forward, don't. From now on, I won't get angry. I'll listen to you first, and then kick your ass later, okay?"

"See, Jaylin, you're playing and I'm serious."

"I'm serious too. But my dick is getting real hard right about now, and I'm anxious to make this baby with you. Besides, we got all night to talk."

"And we got all night to fuck."

"Then we'd better get started."

As usual, having his way, we wound up having sex again. Nanny B and the kids had fallen asleep, and for the first time in weeks, Jaylin was passed out in his own bed. He even had the nerve to snore, which was something I rarely heard him do. I guess he was glad to finally be back in his own bed, and I was truly glad to have him sharing it with me once again. I only hoped our reconciliation efforts would last.

# 15

## JAYLIN

Now that things were pretty cool on the home front again, I had a little more time to deal with Stephon and his problem. He'd been calling the house like crazy, trying to find out why I hadn't deposited the money I'd promised. Until I knew what was really up, I wasn't giving him shit. This is the same stuff that went down with Aunt Betty and me, and she soon found out I wasn't playing. Give or take, she used Stephon to get money from me, but I wasn't going to play the fool this time around.

I called Shane to speak with him further about the situation, and he agreed to meet me for a game of golf. I hadn't played since retirement, so it was quite relaxing. Shane didn't know how to play at all, so I got a kick out of watching his balls go into the water and trees.

"This is bullshit, man," he said. "I for damn sure ain't no Tiger Woods."

"Not even when he was three," I joked. We both

laughed and hopped into the golf cart to go to the next hole.

"So, have you had a chance to talk to Stephon or what?" Shane asked.

"Momentarily. In so many words, he said you're a liar."

"Never have been, and never will I be. All I'm saying is something isn't right with the brotha. I can only speculate, but you be the judge."          .

"I have been, and I'd say you were right. I'm gonna bring it to his attention one more time, and if he lies to me again, he's on his own. You know I love my cousin to death, but a drug addict is somebody I can't tolerate."

"I hear you."

Shane and I stayed on the green for several hours. He even started to get the hang of things. He almost came close to beating me, but when the ball slipped away from him at the last hole, he fell to his knees.

"Damn it!" he yelled. "Now, why didn't that sucker just go in there?"

"Seems to me like you need to learn how to work your *holes* a little better, like I do."

"Trust me, I work my *holes* pretty damn good," he said, getting off the ground.

"Who you shaking down these days? You never talk about one specific person."

"That's 'cause women play too many games. I don't have time for that shit. I keep one or two who I can kick it with every now and then. Other than that, there's nobody in my life on a regular basis."

"Sometimes it gotta be like that, and I don't

blame you not one bit. Relationships, marriages . . . all that shit can take up too much of a brotha's time. When I was sticking and moving, I was definitely better off."

Shane slapped his hand against mine and we headed to the barbershop to see Stephon. One of the barbers said he and some other fellas had gone to a strip club, so not having anything else to do, Shane and I headed to the East Side.

The club was stuffy as hell, and I could barely see from the dimmed lighting. I scanned the room hard, looking for Stephon. When I noticed him in a circular booth with some other brotha, I tapped Shane on the shoulder to get his attention.

We both looked quite casual—me in my Nike shirt, hat, and shorts, and Shane in his khaki shorts and polo shirt. My appearance wasn't a factor, as I truly was there to see what the hell was up with Stephon. He saw us coming, and before he could slide out of the booth, I slid in next to him.

"What's up, cousin? You weren't getting ready to leave, were you?" I asked.

The other dude got out of the booth and Shane slid in on the other side.

"As a matter of fact, cousin," Stephon said, "I was on my way out."

"Look, Stephon," Shane said, not beating around the bush, "say whatever you want, but I'm a brotha who's concerned about you. The—"

Stephon quickly jumped on the defensive. "Man, I don't need you to be concerned about me. Y'all the ones tripping. I can't believe y'all would even think I would do something like that. Jay, especially you. Shane don't know no damn better, but you should know what time it is."

"I don't know shit. I know what you're saying, but shit ain't been right with you, man. Either you're more hurt by Mona leaving your ass, or something else is going on with you. I don't know what it is, so I can only assume."

His tone lowered. "Maybe I am more upset about losing my woman than I show. But let me get through this how I want to get through it. When you're going through something, I don't go around thinking you're a damn crackhead, do I?"

"Hey, fine. If you say you're cool, then I trust you. I'm not going to interfere again, and neither is Shane. But if you need me, you know I'm here."

"Me too," Shane said.

Stephon looked at both of us and grinned. When this half naked chick danced on the table in front of us, he leaned back and looked up at her. After she worked the table, she turned around and squatted her ass directly in our faces. I reached in my back pocket and pulled out the envelope that had Stephon's two grand in it. I slammed the envelope in his hand.

"You can do better than this. Don't spend it all in one night," I said, sliding out of the booth.

He pounded his chest with his fist. "Thanks, bro, and trust."

"Let's hope so." I looked at Shane, as he seemed to be mesmerized by the chick on the table. "Are you leaving with me or not?" I asked.

He waved me off. "Uh-uh, not right now. Stephon, you don't mind if I stay, do you?"

"Not at all. After all, what are friends for?"

I wasn't in the mood to stay, so I told both of those fools goodnight and headed home. I wanted so badly to believe Stephon, but I couldn't. I had my doubts, and the only person I felt could clear shit up for me was Mona.

On Saturday morning, Mercedes had been calling me like crazy, so I made arrangements to go see her after I stopped by Daisha's crib to see Mona. Mona was hesitant at first, but when I told her how important it was that we talked, she agreed.

I told Nokea to pick LJ up early, and asked Scorpio to stay there until Nokea got there. Sometimes I felt like Nanny B had too much on her, but when I brought it to her attention, she disagreed and reminded me how much joy the children had brought to her life. I didn't want to argue with her, but I talked to Scorpio about us going out with the kids more often to give Nanny B a break. Scorpio agreed, and said that after Nokea left, Mackenzie and her would vamp for a while. She knew about me going to see Mona, but I didn't tell her about going to see Mercedes. I knew she'd start tripping, and I wasn't up to hearing her gripe.

Daisha acted kind of snobby toward me, so I took a seat in the living room and waited for Mona to come. I was alone for a while, and after Daisha ended her phone conversation with whomever, she finally came into the living room to join me. She sat far across the room, like I was a pit-bull ready to bite.

"Why you way over there?" I asked.

"Because this chair is comfortable, that's why," she snapped.

"Fine, but are you mad at me about something? The last time we spoke, I thought everything was cool."

"It is cool, Jaylin."

"Then what's up with your funky attitude?"

"I don't have an attitude. Don't get mad at me because I chose to disassociate myself with a man like you."

"Don't be so bitter, baby. You look quite ugly when you act that way. And just when I thought you had—"

"Well, you thought wrong. I am so tired of men like you and Stephon going around stomping on people's hearts. God does not like ugly, and one day, the two of you are going to regret everything you've done."

"Then back off and let God be my judge, damn it! You need to step off the cross and let him take care of me. He's the Almighty One, and not you. Whether you believe it or not, I pay for my mistakes all the time. He makes sure of that, so there ain't nothing bad you or anybody else can wish upon me."

The doorbell saved Daisha and me from going any further. When Mona came in, Daisha gave her a hug, walked upstairs, and slammed her door. Mona sat in the living room with me, and before she tried to take God's place, I quickly cut her off.

"Look, I know you're still upset about what

happened between you and Stephon, but I didn't ask you to come here for that. I don't know the details of what went down between y'all, and it really ain't none of my business."

"Then what is it that you want from me, Jaylin?"

"All I want to know is if you've ever seen Stephon doing drugs."

"Is this an attempt of his to get back with me? I thought you had something serious to discuss."

"No, no, honestly, it's not an attempt. He's been acting kind of different lately. Something's up with him."

"Well, I don't know. You know what kind of drugs he uses, don't you?"

"Not really. I saw him smoking some weed a few times, but that's it."

"Jaylin, please. Why are you sitting there lying?"

"Trust me, I'm not lying to you. If he's doing anything other than smoking weed, I don't know about it."

She folded her arms and crossed her legs. Then she looked at me suspiciously. "Are you telling me you didn't know Stephon's been snorting cocaine for let's say . . . a little over a year now?"

"Honestly, I didn't know. I asked him about it, but he continues to deny it."

"Don't drug addicts always lie? My decision to leave him was not solely because of his obsession with women. It had a lot to do with his drug abuse. He promised me he would stop, but that just never happened. Now, I admit we fired up many joints together, but Stephon took shit too far with the cocaine. It became an everyday habit, and I couldn't get with that."

I was in disbelief. Even though I knew something was up, the news was hard for me to accept. "Why in the fuck didn't I see it? I'm always over at his place and at the barbershop."

"The evidence was there. When you came around, he never hid anything, so that's why I thought you knew. He also told me he got the money from you, so I thought you were cool with it."

"No way. Not after what our family has been through because of that shit. I can't believe him. Damn!"

"Please don't tell him I told you. If there's anything I can do to help, let me know. I got a feeling, though, that you're gonna have to let him sweat this one out."

"We'll see," I said, standing to leave. "We definitely will see."

I thanked Mona for her time and jetted. Again, I felt as if I was fighting a battle with Stephon that couldn't be won. How could he lie to my face like that? Didn't he understand we were in this shit together? I couldn't understand what would make him turn to drugs when he could have had anything he wanted. All he had to do was ask and there it was.

His excuse of being under pressure didn't suffice. I felt pressure every single day of my life. He wasn't under any more pressure than I was. And if he was, he knew all he had to do was pick up the damn phone. I was mad as hell just thinking about the shit, and really didn't know what I would do, if anything.

I called Mercedes and told her I was on my way.

I wasn't in no mood for fucking, and since I'd promised Scorpio I wouldn't do it, I planned on keeping my word. My reason for going to see her was to talk her into dropping the charges against Scorpio and to somehow call it quits. If she dropped the charges, getting my money back was also a plus.

However, when she came to the door with an ocean blue lace negligee on, I was encouraged to change my mind.

"So, you do have *some* clothes, huh?" I said, wrapping my arms around her.

"Very skimpy clothes. I thought you'd like to see me in something other than my birthday suit."

"The birthday suit is fine, but it does help to be creative sometimes too."

Mercedes and I smacked lips for a while, and she reached for the buttons on my shirt to undo them. I pecked her lips and grabbed her hand. "Baby," I said, "I need you to do me a favor."

"Anything."

I pecked her lips again. "Um, I like that. But are you certain that I can have anything I want?"

"Anything your heart desires."

"I hope so. But, uh, I need you to drop the charges against Scorpio."

"Anything but that."

I moved my head back. "Why not?"

"Because she is not going to get away with what she did to me. I lost a very important job because I had an ugly scratch on my face."

"I understand how you feel, but just drop the charges, okay?"

"I don't know, Jaylin. She deserves whatever she's got coming."

"That's fair, but do it for me, please. You don't have to do it for her; just do it for me."

Mercedes took her arms off my shoulders and walked over by the huge picture window. She placed her hands on her hips and sighed. Persuading her was going to be a lot tougher than I thought, so I walked up from behind, squeezing her waist.

"Baby, please. You don't need the hassle and neither does she. The only reason I'm asking you to drop the charges is so I can get my damn bond money back. I hate throwing away my money on something so ridiculous."

"Then you should have left her ass in there. Why did you bail her out anyway?"

"If it wasn't for Mackenzie, I wouldn't have. Scorpio and I talked, and she's looking for another place to live. This will all be over with sooner than you think."

"Listen, I'll do it, but only because of you. You'd better keep her away from me, Jaylin, or next time, I'm going to hurt her."

"That's my girl," I said, kissing her cheek. "But there won't be no next time."

Even though I was not up to having sex with Mercedes, I did it anyway. I felt kind of bad lying to her, but I really didn't want Scorpio to have to stand before no judge because of me. It wasn't even about the money, because I couldn't care less. There simply was no other way out of this mess other than for Mercedes to drop the charges.

As for ending it with her, doing it today would

have been a big mistake on my part, especially when I had her in the palm of my hand. I decided to wait until Scorpio was completely off the hook, and then I would break the news to Mercedes.

It was getting late, and Mercedes asked if I would stay the night. I told her LJ was at the house and I didn't want Nanny B to be up all night with him. I found myself telling her one lie after another. This definitely wasn't my style.

I was surprised to see that I made it home before Scorpio and Mackenzie. Nanny B said they were spending the night at Leslie's house. Just the thought of them sleeping there gave me the creeps, but I was glad I didn't have any explaining to do. While I was at Mercedes' place, Scorpio had called a few times, but I didn't answer my phone. I waited until I was in bed and on my way to sleep before I returned her call.

"So you didn't want to sleep with me tonight, huh?" I asked.

"I did, but you took too long to get home. I called your phone several times, but you didn't answer. Where were you?"

"I left my phone in the car while I talked to Mona. After I left her place, I stopped to get a bite to eat. This shit with Stephon was heavy on my mind, so I didn't feel like talking to anyone."

"So what did you find out? Is he really messing around with that stuff or what?"

"I'm afraid so. Mona confirmed everything for me."

"I'm sorry to hear that. I know you were hoping to hear something different."

"Yeah, I was. Tomorrow I'm gonna make plans to talk to him again. Just straight talk between me and him, nobody else."

"I hope it works out. In the meantime, if you want me to come home, I will. Mackenzie and I wanted to spend some time with Leslie and her kids because they've been kind of going through some things too."

"Naw, I'll be all right. I need to get some rest anyway."

"Are you saying you can't rest with me there?"

"That's exactly what I'm saying. With your body lying next to mine, woman, I can't stay focused on getting any sleep."

"Same here. I'm gonna miss you tonight, though. If you get too lonely, grab my body pillow and hold it as if you're holding me."

"Trust me, it's not the same. Just hurry back."

"Can't wait. I love you."

"Ditto."

Nanny B touched my shoulder and startled me. I had dreamt about telling my sperm donor what a wonderful man I'd become without him in my life. When I quickly jumped up, she stepped back.

"Are you all right?" she asked.

I stretched. "Yeah, I'm fine. Stanley was just starting to take credit for what he didn't do, that's all."

"Now, that sounds just like him. And I guess I

don't have to ask if you've made plans to speak to him."

"No, you don't have to worry about that, because I don't think that's going to happen any time soon."

"I did all I could do, so I'm out of it."

"Thank you for agreeing not to interfere anymore. I'll deal with Stanley in my own way."

Nanny B nodded and sat on my bed. "Listen, on Friday I need to go take care of something, if you don't mind."

"That's fine. Scorpio and I can handle things around here for one day."

"I know, but I'll be gone for two weeks."

"Two weeks? What are you going to be doing for two weeks?"

"My sister and I are going on a vacation."

"That's nice. I'm glad you're doing something for yourself. Take as long as you need, and we'll do our best to manage."

"You need to take a vacation too."

"Yeah, but I got so much shit going on here that I can't find the time to leave."

"That's because you're starting to make too many other people's problems yours. You're only one man, Jaylin. You can't take care of everybody and you can't make everybody happy."

"I agree. And I'm not trying to."

"I hope not. Whatever it is that's going on with Stephon, you need to let it go. Out of everything that's happened with you, I got a feeling about this one. History repeats itself, and I don't want to see you get hurt in the process."

"My guards are up this time. Stephon's problems will not consume me or affect my life in any way."

"I hope not. Just be careful, okay?"

"You have my word."

I didn't care what nobody said; Nanny B was the love of my life. I've never had anybody care for me and love me as much as she did. Bottom line, she was the bomb!


I didn't waste any time calling Stephon. It was eight o'clock in the morning and I told him I'd be right over.

"Man, I'm trying to get some rest before I go to the shop. Why don't you stop by the shop and holla at me later?" he said.

"Because I need to see you now. I'm on my way."

Within the hour, I was at Stephon's door. He frowned about me coming over so early, but I didn't give a damn. He walked down the hallway to his room and plopped his naked ass down on the bed. He covered his face with a pillow and placed his hand on his thang. I scanned his room for drugs as I sat down on a beanbag chair. I did notice two blunts in an ashtray lying on the floor.

"Wake up, nigga!" I said.

"Jay, I'm tired. You be getting up too damn early for me."

"Only when I got something heavy on my mind."

Stephon took the pillow off his face and laid it next to him. He realized that I wasn't going anywhere, so he finally sat up and scooted back against the headboard. "Speak," he said.

"I'm not gonna beat around the bush, so I'm here to tell you that I know you've been snorting 'caine. If you need help, go get it. I don't want you to wind up like your mother, and I'm prepared to do everything to make sure that doesn't happen."

Stephon had a blank expression on his face as he moved his head from side to side. "I can't believe you still trippin' with me—"

"Stop the motherfucking lying, nigga. I've had too many people tell me what's up, and they have no damn reason to lie on you."

"Punk, don't yell at me! You ain't my daddy. I told your ass, I ain't doing that shit. If you don't believe me, then fuck you."

"Nigga, fuck you. And I got your punk," I said, standing up. Stephon hopped up, and we stood face to face.

"What you want, nigga?" he yelled.

"I need for you to get your pussy ass together. If you don't want to, then fuck you. Don't call me when you fall flat on your face, and I mean that shit."

Trying to avoid a fight, I left his room, heading for the front door. Stephon yelled at me from down the hall.

"You don't understand me, fool! You don't understand nothing about me! If you did, then you'd know why I do what I do. You act like you're so much better than everybody, and you don't know shit about a struggle."

I slammed the door and turned to look at him. "DON'T HATE ON ME, NIGGA!" I yelled, swinging my fist. "That's your problem now! I have had it harder than any damn body in our family. You sorry sons of bitches had your mama, your daddy, and each other. I had nobody! Now, a long time ago I had a choice: either I was going to sit back and feel sorry for myself like you and your conniving-ass brothers, or I was going to make a way for my damn self. Don't blame me if your ass got left behind."

"You damn right you didn't get left behind. Nanny B made sure of that, didn't she? She, like everybody else, always got to protect Jaylin. Jaylin this, and Jaylin that. Let's all make sure Jaylin don't get his fucking feelings hurt. Fuck that shit, man. You have had support from people all around you. I have had nothing. And if I want to get high to relax my damn mind, then who in the fuck are you to come in here and look down on me?"

"I'm nobody," I said, casually walking down the hallway. "If you haven't felt my love for you, I'm sorry. There ain't nothing I can do about it. You have always had me, Stephon, and you know it. Don't stand there and point the finger at me because you're not man enough to work out your own damn problems. If you are bitter about what Nanny B did, go talk to her about it, not me."

"All I'm saying is she didn't have to leave me out like that. And you had many opportunities to tell me who she really was, but you didn't. Can't you understand how excluded I felt?"

"She and I made a promise not to tell anyone that Grandpa left the money to her and she gave most of it to me. But please don't make this about money. If Nanny B's decision to give me the money is the reason you're doing drugs, then I'll go to the bank right now and split my account down the middle with you. It ain't about that, Stephon, and you know it. 'Fess up and take responsibility for your own actions. Again, I'm here, but if you continue with your bullshit, you will soon stand alone."

I walked off and Stephon followed behind me, calming his tone. "My drug usage ain't as bad as you think it is. I've only snorted that shit a few times, so don't go thinking it's more than what it is. It's not that severe where I need to go get help."

"I hear differently. And ain't it a coincidence that your mother used to tell us the same damn thing?"

Stephon walked past me and sat on the arm of the couch. Feeling as if we were finally getting something accomplished, I leaned against the wall next to the window.

"What you want me to do, Jay?"

"I would like for you to get some help, but it's all about what you want to do. I would also like for you to chill out with these threesomes you keep having. Every time I come over here you're with different women, and I got a feeling that having sex ain't all y'all been doing. You need to be careful about the company you keep."

He laughed. "Man, I be using condoms. You know how it is; I like to have fun. And we don't always do drugs."

"I don't believe you. When I spoke to Mona yesterday, she said you were obsessed with sex and that the reason she left you was more about you doing drugs than you cheating."

"Obsessed? Please. I don't get no more pussy than you get. If I'm obsessed, you're overly obsessed."

"But I get my pussy from the same person. Yes, I'm obsessed with her pussy, but that's a good thing."

"Nigga, please. You've had sex with more than just Scorpio this year. I can't believe you're standing there pretending—"

Stephon had a point. Sometimes it was hard for me to see things for what they truly were. Even though he didn't recognize my change, I had done so—a little. Still, I defended my situation and changed the subject. After all, this wasn't about me. "You're right; I have had sex with someone other than just Scorpio, but drugs aren't on the menu. Now, getting back to your obsession, how many women have you slept with this year?"

Stephon placed his finger on his temple. "Let's see . . . it's mid-year now, so—" He counted his fingers and looked up as if he were thinking. "Between forty and forty-five. Now, how many have you slept with?"

"Damn! It for damn sure ain't been nowhere near that many. Actually, it's only been four, three of which wouldn't have happened if Scorpio hadn't been tripping."

"Well, I'm just trying to keep up with the old Jaylin. This new one kind of flaky and shit."

"Whatever, nigga. Sometimes change is good."

Stephon and me talked for a while. He said he would lay low with the drugs, and assured me he didn't need any help. I couldn't do nothing but go with the flow. I hoped everything would be cool, but only time would tell.

When I asked how he found out about Nanny B, he claimed that he figured it out shortly after she had broken the news to me. He also showed me a picture of Nanny B in her wedding dress, standing next to Grandpa, Aunt Betty, and Mama. When I asked where he got it from, he said he found it in his mother's belongings she'd left behind. He also showed me a letter from Aunt Betty that confirmed Nanny B as being our stepgrandmother. I understood his frustrations about her not giving him any money, but to me, that was a good thing. Stephon didn't seem to really take ownership of his problem, and that only meant trouble.

# 16

## *NOKEA*

Stanley drove me crazy about seeing LJ. I asked if he'd talked to Jaylin about it, and he insisted talking to Jaylin was a lost cause. I hadn't spoken to Jaylin in a little over a week. He seemed so preoccupied every time I called, so I wasn't trying to interfere with whatever was going on between him and Scorpio. I was also trying to keep my own relationship on the right track. Collins was very uncomfortable with Jaylin and me being friends, so maybe it was time for me to leave well enough alone. The last thing I needed was for Collins to feel as if he couldn't trust me, because without trust, I knew it would be hard for this relationship to work.

For whatever reason, I conceded and agreed to let Stanley come by my place to see LJ. I wanted LJ to know who his grandfather was, and since Stanley was ill, I at least wanted some pictures to show LJ, just in case something happened. The first time Stanley came, everything was cool. He

played with LJ all day long, I took pictures of
them together, and I let Stanley take LJ around
the corner to get some ice cream. I was a little
worried, but when they came back and I saw the
smiles on their faces, I felt at ease.

My problem didn't occur until the second time
he came for LJ. It was a Friday morning and he
asked if he could take LJ to the circus. I saw no
harm in letting LJ go to the circus with his grandfather, but when I hadn't heard from Stanley all
day, I started to get worried. He left a cell phone
number for me to call him, but when I called, he
didn't answer.

When six o'clock rolled around, I panicked. Jaylin was supposed to pick up LJ for the weekend at
eight, and Collins and I had dinner plans at nine.
I must have called Stanley's cell phone a million
times within the hour, and he still hadn't answered.

I called Collins in a serious panic, and he said
that he'd be right over. When he arrived at my
place, I couldn't stop crying.

"Baby, calm down. Everything is going to be
fine," he said.

Tears streamed down my face as I looked to
Collins for answers. Of course, he didn't have
them. All he could do was hold me in his arms.
"Where is my baby, Collins? Do you think he—"

"No, no, just calm down. If he's not back by the
time Jaylin gets here, we'll call the police."

"But I can't tell Jaylin. He's going to kill me. I
had no right to let his father take LJ, Collins."

"Yes, you did. You thought you were doing what
was best. Now, have a seat and let me make some
phone calls."

I sat on the couch. I couldn't get myself together. Every time I'd hear a car, I'd rush to the window, but there was no Stanley. The hour moved quickly, and I watched Collins pace back and forth on the phone and Internet, trying to come up with an address for Stanley. When he told someone to hold on, he clicked over, and said it was Jaylin.

I shook my head. "I . . . I can't talk to him, please. Tell him I'll call him back."

"Baby, you have to. He's not going to want to hear it from me."

I silently prayed for the safe return of my son before I put the phone up to my ear and sniffled.

Jaylin quickly inquired. "Nokea? What's wrong, baby?"

"Would you come over here, please?"

"I was calling to tell you I'm on my way. But are you okay? Where's LJ?"

"Just come, okay?"

"I'm coming! What's up? You haven't been fighting with your man, have you?"

"No," I said in a shaky voice.

"I was getting ready to say . . . I didn't want to come over there and bust nobody's head open."

"Jaylin, LJ is gone. He's not here."

There was nearly ten seconds of silence. "Gone? What do you mean by gone?"

"Your father took him—"

"Wha—wait a minute. You allowed my father to take him?"

"He wanted to take LJ to the circus. I didn't think he would be gone—"

"Nokea," he said, "if my son ain't at your house

by the time I get there, I'm gonna break your fucking neck. Simple as that. Why in the hell—!" He got louder. "Why in the hell would you let LJ go anywhere with him? I have got to be fucking with the most ignorant-ass bitches in St. Louis." The phone went dead.

I covered my face, and Collins sat down on the couch and comforted me. I knew things were about to get ugly, so I called the police before Jaylin came.

They arrived first, and shortly after, Jaylin came storming through the door. He yelled at everybody, and one of the officers asked him to calm down.

"Fuck that! You calm down. If it were your damn child, you wouldn't be calm either."

"I understand, sir. But this is your father we're talking about, right?"

"Hell, no! He is a stranger to me, and should have never been allowed to leave this fucking house with my son."

The officer looked at me as Collins held my trembling body. "Is there any known address for him? Something or anything we can go on other than his cell phone? You must have gotten something."

"She too damn stupid to think like that. How you gon' let your child run off with somebody you know very little about?" Jaylin yelled.

"Man, that's enough," Collins said. "I know you're upset, but I'm not going to let you stand there and disrespect my woman. Now, we're all in this together. Being angry with each other isn't going to help us find LJ."

"He's right," the officer said, looking at Jaylin. "Maybe you can help us find him. Do you have any idea where your father might live?"

"He's not my father. My nanny is the only source I have that might know. She's on her way out of town for two weeks, though. She left this morning, and I'm hoping that she'll call me soon. There's no guarantee she'll know his address, but it's all I can think of."

"Do you have a number where you can reach her?" I asked Jaylin in a soft voice.

He pointed his finger at me. "Don't you say one damn word to me. After I get my son back, I'm gonna do everything in my power to take him away from your ass."

"Jaylin," Collins said, "that's not even necessary. I'm asking you to chill and stop disrespecting my wom—"

"You got one more damn time to interfere before I'm gonna tell you about your so-called-ass woman!" He turned to me with rage in his eyes. "You'd better get him. Quick!"

Collins continued to take up for me, and Jaylin wasted no time in blurting out what was on his mind.

"If she your damn woman, Collins, then why she still fucking me? Huh?" He pounded his chest. "Tell me that, nigga."

My heart dropped to my stomach. Collins released me from his arms. I fell back in the chair and covered my face with my hands. Collins pulled one of my hands away from my face so he could look at me.

"You . . . you aren't, are you?" he asked.

I could see the hurt in his eyes. I shook my head. "No, I'm—"

"You're a damn liar," Jaylin yelled. "I can tell you when, where, and how, if you want details. And I will, if my damn son don't show up soon."

The police asked everybody to calm down. After they got Jaylin to chill with the yelling, Collins grabbed his suit jacket from the back of the chair. He placed the back of his hand against my cheek and rubbed it.

"I hope everything works out for you," he said in a calm voice.

I held his hand. "Don't go. Please don't leave me," I cried.

"You'll be okay. Trust me, you will." He lowered his hand, ignoring Jaylin, who stood by the doorway, and walked out.

"Get out!" I yelled at Jaylin. "Get the hell out of my house!"

He looked around as if I were talking to someone else, then pointed to his chest. "Are you talking to me?" he asked.

"You're damn right I'm talking to you. Get out!"

"Woman, you got me all fucked up. I'm not leaving this house until my son gets here. After that, you will never have to worry about seeing me again. I'm sorry your man is gone, but that's what you get for dealing with a chump. I'm not about to walk out that easily."

I asked the officer if he would make Jaylin leave, and he did. Jaylin got in his car and parked it right across the street from my house.

The police stayed outside and talked to him for a while, and before they left, they came back inside to talk to me again.

"We're gonna keep an eye on things for a while, but we're really not supposed to do much until the child is missing for more than twenty-four hours. We can issue an Amber Alert, but with the child being with his sick grandfather, who knows what could have gone wrong? Hopefully your son will return home safely and we can all put this behind us."

"Thank you, officer. It's almost eleven o'clock now, so if he's—" I was choked up and couldn't stop crying.

"We're gonna check with you throughout the night. If you hear anything, let us know. By morning, we'll start a search for him."

"Okay, and thanks again."

"Ms. Brooks, I do have to ask you this before I leave: Do you think this might have anything to do with money? Your ex-boyfriend seems to be a wealthy young fella, so you just never know people's motives."

"I hope it doesn't. If that was the case, he would have called by now, don't you think?"

"I don't want to scare you, but sometimes the longer people wait to contact you, the more anxious they know you'll get. Let's hope that's not the case."

"I hope not," I said, walking him to the door. I looked at Jaylin. He had his head leaned against the driver's side window. I couldn't see his face, but I could only imagine.

\*   \*   \*

About one-thirty in the morning, Jaylin knocked at the door. I was on the couch slowly drifting into another world. Not having the strength to argue with him, I opened the door and walked away.

"Put on some shoes and let's go," he ordered.

"I don't want to go anywhere. Not until my baby comes home."

"Fine, stay here then. Nanny B just called and gave me Stanley's address."

After hearing that, I put on my shoes and grabbed my purse. Jaylin and I drove quietly in the car to where Stanley lived. When he pulled in front of a two-family flat on the south side of St. Louis, he looked at the paper and verified the address with the numbers on the house.

"That's the car he was in," I said, pointing to a Ford Focus.

When we got out of the car, we looked in the back seat of Stanley's car. LJ's car seat was still there.

My stomach was rumbling and I could barely walk up the steps. Jaylin rang the doorbell, and when I stepped onto the porch, he gave me a peculiar look, as if he knew something wasn't right. We stood outside for a while, and after a few more knocks, Jaylin kicked the door. It was loud. Every time he kicked it, my heart jumped.

Finally, the door cracked off the hinges and we both cautiously stepped inside. We looked up the dark staircase, and unable to see where we were going, Jaylin pulled out a pistol and took my hand. I was shaking like a leaf, following closely behind him. The steps loudly creaked, and when we made it to the top, Jaylin turned on the light switch. He let go of my hand. When we heard LJ's cries, we ran to where he was. He was on the kitchen floor in a pile of mess. I hurried to pick him up and cradled him tightly in my arms.

Jaylin kissed the top of his forehead. "Damn, I'm so happy to see you." He looked at me. "Stay right here. I'm going to check the other rooms."

I stood embracing LJ and rocking him in my arms. I heard Jaylin yell something, and I rushed to where he was. I stood in the doorway and saw him kneeled down next to a bed. I could see Stanley's legs and knew what time it was.

"Don't come over here," Jaylin said in a low voice. "Go call nine-one-one."

I rushed in the other room to call 911, and when I heard Jaylin cry, I sat on the couch and lost it.

"Why did you do this?" I heard him yell. "I was coming to tell you how much I didn't need you, and how much I hated you for leaving me. But you had to punk out, didn't you?" He continued to yell. "Didn't you! You always punking out on me, man. What did I ever do to you? Huh?"

I felt every bit of his pain and went to his side. He held Stanley by the collar, but it was too late for him to hear anything Jaylin had to say. I took Jaylin by his arm and tried to lift him.

"Come on, baby. Please don't do this to yourself. Let him go . . . please," I begged.

I had seen Jaylin cry before, but never this hard. He looked up at me with tears pouring down his face. "Why me?" he said. "I'm on a roll, ain't I?"

"It be like this sometimes. It'll get better, though. Trust me, it will."

Jaylin slowly got up and stumbled away from Stanley. We all went into the living room, and while I changed LJ's diaper, Jaylin sat stone-faced on the couch. I was so worried about him. As soon as I finished with LJ, I sat next to him, clenching his hand with mine. "I love you, and I'm so sorry about this," were the only words that came from my mouth. He didn't respond.

While the paramedics were there, Jaylin still sat motionless on the couch and didn't say a word. Knowing very little about Stanley, I answered as many questions as I could for the police. The paramedics said by the looks of things he died from a heart attack. They took his body away. This day, without a doubt, was one of the saddest days of my life. I prayed for things to get better for Jaylin, and as he cried on my shoulder, I was willing to do anything in my power to make sure his life was peaceful.

# 17

## *SCORPIO*

I felt extremely bad for my baby. He tried to be his usual self, but he couldn't. Several times, I noticed him looking spaced out, and when I asked what was on his mind, he refused to talk about it.

At first, I was so angry with Nokea when he told me what she'd done, but I guess it all worked out for the best. I guess a part of her must have known Stanley wouldn't be around for long, and allowing him time with his grandson was the best thing she could have done. I didn't know if Jaylin was still mad at her, but they hadn't talked much after going through such a big ordeal.

Nanny B heard about the news, and she got back from wherever she was in a flash. She talked to Jaylin in her room with the door closed, and it seemed as if he found more comfort in her than he did with me. By all means, I wasn't mad. I was glad he had someone else to lean on as well.

What we all found out about Stanley was that he liked to keep to himself. He didn't have many friends, but he did have a daughter and another son. Jaylin knew nothing about them, and when he found out they were all close in age, and that they'd had a relationship with Stanley, he seemed so disappointed.

The day of Stanley's funeral, Jaylin refused to go. He stayed in his bed and watched TV all day long. Nanny B, Mackenzie and I went to pay our last respects, and we were surprised to see Nokea and LJ there as well. Even Stephon showed up, but Jaylin stood his ground.

On the drive back home, Nanny B and I had an interesting conversation. She said that she was tired of what was going on, and it was time to do something about it. When I asked what she meant, she didn't elaborate, but I could tell she had something up her sleeves. Her attachment to Jaylin puzzled the hell out of me. For someone who had only known him for a few years, she was overly protective, kind of like a mother to him. When I asked Jaylin if he had any connection to her, he insisted she was only the nanny. Nothing more, nothing less.

We returned from the funeral, and Jaylin didn't say much to anybody. He didn't ask anything about the funeral, and I knew that talking about it would only make matters worse. If he wanted to know, I was sure he'd ask. Until then, I kept quiet. I got in bed with him, and he laid his head on my chest and fell asleep.


Loud music and a thumping noise were coming from the basement. I squinted at the alarm clock. It was six o'clock in the morning. Jaylin was out of bed, so I grabbed my purple silk robe, and then headed for the basement. The music came from his workout room, so I leaned against the doorway and watched him pound the hell out of a punching bag. Sam Cooke's "Change Is Gonna Come" was playing. When Jaylin saw me, he turned down the music and sat on his weight bench. I had the pleasure of watching his six-pack go to work while he was doing his sit-ups. His body dripped with sweat, and the black Nike stretch shorts he wore nicely hugged his ass.

I walked further into the room to turn off the radio. Jaylin successfully continued with his sit-ups, and once he reached two hundred and fifty, he called it quits. He took deeps breaths, lying flat on his back.

"Now, I know you can give me more than that," I said.

"Not today," he said as he continued to breathe hard. "This is what happens when I stop working out."

He dropped to the floor and I squatted on top of him, straddling his midsection. He then sat up and wrapped his arms around me.

"Are you gonna be okay?" I asked. "I'm worried about you."

"Yep. I'm going to be fine."

"Are you sure?"

"Positive. So go upstairs and put on some clothes so we can go."

"Where are we going?"

"I'm going to finish my workout. After that, I want to go look for another car."

"What's wrong with the ones you got?"

"It's time for something new."

"Okay, but first, I'm going upstairs to change so I can work out with you."

"You do that."

I went upstairs to change. I slid into my pink-and-gray stretch workout suit and tennis shoes. My hair was in a sleek ponytail, and I added a little gloss to shine my lips. Jaylin worked the punching bag again, and when he saw me, he stopped.

"Don't you look all cute and everythang," he said.

"Don't I always?"

"I don't know now. Lately . . ."

"Whatever," I said, punching his arm.

"You know, you really need to learn how to fight. Those punches you be throwing be pretty damn weak."

"That one I gave you at Daisha's house wasn't weak."

"Okay, with the exception of that one, the rest sucked."

He stood behind the punching bag and held it steady. "Come on, give it your best shot."

I put up my fists, and when I threw a punch, I missed the bag and hit Jaylin right in his eye.

"Damn!" he said, squeezing his eye together.

I covered my mouth and laughed. "I'm sorry, I—"

"You think that shit funny, don't you?"

I was still laughing. "It was an accident."

He rushed me, and we fell back on the mat. He sat on top of me and held my hands together. I could barely breathe with his weight on top of me. Just for the fun of it, we playfully wrestled.

Our workout allowed us to spend quality time together that our relationship had been missing. I thought we'd get through our workout without having sex, but that didn't happen. He was back in action, and I was one sista who was eagerly waiting.

By noon, we got dressed to go look for a new car. Mackenzie and I dressed alike in our purple linen sundresses and satin sandals. She carried a white purse filled with Barbies, and wore sunglasses trimmed in white. My purse was white too, but I decided to do without the glasses. I put her hair in a ponytail like mine, and we patiently waited downstairs for Jaylin to get ready.

It seemed like it took all day for Jaylin to get dressed, and when he finally came downstairs, he was casually dressed in some black linen pants and a crisp royal blue button-down shirt. His Rolex was visible on his wrist, and he had shaved his goatee to perfection. By the looks of him, you could tell he had money. He slid his sunglasses over his eyes, and we were ready to go and enjoy our day.

At the first car dealership, which sold Lamborghinis, Jaylin didn't seem interested. We then checked out the Bentley dealership and six other places, but he still wasn't satisfied. I suggested going home to search for a car on the Internet, but he wasn't going home until he found what he wanted.

We finally made it to the Jaguar dealer, and I'm happy to say that we stayed for a while. Not for him, though, but for Nanny B. He called and asked if she wanted a new car. He tried to coax her into getting one, and after she turned him down, we left again.

"Baby, what is it that you're looking for?" I asked while he drove to the next place.

"I don't know. I like Escalades, but too many people have them. Besides, that punk Collins got one, and I don't want to be like him."

"I thought you and Collins were cool. Why he a punk all of a sudden?"

"Because he is, that's why."

"Well, why don't you just go look at the Escalades? They're really nice, and if you load it up with options, you can make it quite different from everybody else's."

Jaylin drove to the Cadillac dealership, and surprisingly, he had a smile on his face. We must have looked at every Escalade on display before he decided anything. And just when the salesman got all hyped up about Jaylin buying the truck, Jaylin changed his mind and we left again.

"Where are you going to now?" I pouted.

"I'm getting tired, Daddy," Mackenzie complained.

"Just be patient, all right? These kinds of things take time."

We drove to the Lincoln dealership, and after being toured around the whole lot full of Navigators, Jaylin was about to cut another deal. We skipped right over the finance manager and sat in the "Big Man's" office. Jaylin told him he was paying cash.

Before he heard the grand total, Jaylin looked

over at Mackenzie. "Which one do you like the best? The Escalade or Navigator?" Jaylin asked.

The owner compared the two, but Jaylin ignored him. He continued to wait for Mackenzie to answer.

"I think they're both nice, Daddy. Really, I can't decide."

Jaylin sat silently for a while, and then looked at the owner behind his desk. "I don't like those rims," Jaylin said arrogantly. "I need twenty-four-inch chrome rims, heated seats, televisions in the front and back, a CD player and DVD integrated navigation, satellite radio, a digital map, sun roof, front and back seat airbags, power everything, and a nicer grill for the front." He went on and on, trying to make this Navigator different from everybody else's. The owner pulled out books and more books, showing Jaylin how he could accessorize his Navigator. When it was all said and done, he agreed to have Jaylin's silver Navigator delivered in less than a week.

"That was torture," I said, walking back to his car. "Are you happy now?"

"Not quite," he said, getting into the car.

We drove back to the Cadillac dealer and pretty much the same thing went down. He added so much mess to the truck, and the grand total blew me away. I sat with my mouth wide open.

"Baby, what are you trying to prove?" I asked.

"Nothing. I needed a new car. You know how I am when I can't decide."

"I know how you are with your women when you can't decide, but I didn't think you would be the same way about a car."

"Well, sorry, I am. Had Mackenzie decided for me, we wouldn't even be here."

I looked at Mackenzie in the chair next to him with her hands pressed against her face like she was bored. I rolled my eyes and asked Jaylin to hurry it up.

"Please don't rush me." He smiled. "We got one more stop to make and then we'll go home."

I huffed. "You are not going back to the Jaguar dealer, are you? Take me home if you do, please."

He laughed. "Don't go giving me no ideas. I was talking about dinner. I want to take you and Mackenzie to an extravagant restaurant."

I was so relieved that we weren't going to another dealership. Jaylin ordered the final touches for his SUV and was promised delivery in one week. The whole place sucked up to him like he was God almighty, and I was so sure that pumped up his ego even more.

We went to *his* favorite restaurant, Morton's of Chicago. We enjoyed a wonderful dinner together, stopped by the mall to do some shopping, then we headed home. I had fallen asleep in the car and so had Mackenzie. It had been a long day and we were exhausted.

I felt as if I couldn't even make it up the stairs. After Mackenzie ran up them, Jaylin tossed me over his shoulder and ran up the steps with me.

"Your ass is getting heavy," he said, laying me down on the bed. He lay on top of me. "You ain't pregnant, are you? Please tell me that you are. That would just make my day."

I shook my head. "Not yet. But we can work on our baby whenever you'd like."

He kissed me, then rose up and went into the closet to change clothes. I got Mackenzie ready for bed and then went back into our bedroom. Jaylin had gone downstairs to get something.

The phone rang, I looked at the caller ID and saw that it was that tramp Mercedes. I wasn't going to answer because it was just like the devil to try to ruin a good day, but I couldn't help myself.

"What?" I said in a nasty tone.

"This doesn't sound like Jaylin. Is he there?"

"He's busy. And why do you keep calling here?"

"Because he hasn't asked me to stop. The question is, what are you still doing at his house?"

My eyes connected with Jaylin's as he came through the door. He whispered, asking who it was. By the tone of my voice and discouraged look on my face, he could instantly tell it was a female.

"Hang up," he said. Mercedes and I continued to have our dispute over the phone. "I said hang up!" he yelled.

I held the phone in my hand. "Do you want to talk to her?" I asked.

He snatched the phone and hung up on Mercedes. "When I tell you to do something, just do it, all right!"

The phone rang again.

"No, it's not all right. But this is your house, and you pay the bills, right?"

"You learn something new every day, don't you?"

I threw my hands in the air. I didn't even feel like arguing with him. How a nice day like this one turned out to be so shitty, I didn't know. One minute he was cool, and just that fast, the bastard had an attitude. Not because of anything I did, but because his bitch wouldn't stop calling the house. I promised myself, if this mess didn't stop, I would soon show him that two could play his game.

# 18

## *JAYLIN*

My trucks were right, tight, and on time. I felt like a new man as I sat in my black set-the-fuck-out Escalade. And when I hopped in my silver Navigator, I knew I was in a class all by myself. Only a few of us could go there, and I was glad to be one of them.

There was no doubt about it; it was simply time to make some changes. Life was too short, and I was tired of all the let-downs and lies from those around me.

For whatever reason, my stepbrother and sister had been on my mind. I wanted to find out more about them and put closure to my feelings about Stanley. Thing is, I just wasn't ready yet; but from what Nanny B had said, they were anxious to meet me.

Also, I decided to let Stephon do whatever the hell he was going to do, and made him agree not to ask me for nothing until he got some help. To this day, he still insisted everything was cool, but when I talked to Shane the other night, he said the brotha was tripping again. He told me about a fight they'd almost gotten into at Stephon's house. Shane said he wasn't going to his place anymore until Stephon got himself together. I couldn't blame Shane, and encouraged him not to have any regrets.

As for Nokea, I guess she was still upset with me about Collins. I kind of felt bad about their relationship, but when I told her how angry I was, she just didn't understand. There wasn't nothing I could say or do to fix her problem with Collins, so I left well enough alone. She'd been kind of tripping with me seeing LJ, and when I confronted her about it, she apologized and said it was hard for her to let him out of her sight after what happened. I knew how protective she'd gotten, so I tried to allow her some space.

That was hard for me to do because I'd been thinking about her a whole lot. Through my difficult times, she'd always been there for me. I felt so connected to her at Stanley's place, the way she held me in her arms and cried with me just . . . did something to me.

Scorpio, well, she was being her usual self. I know she wanted to be there for a brotha, but she still hadn't put her ring back on, which left me kind of skeptical about her. That was a tiny problem for me, and if I felt as if I couldn't trust my woman, who knows what would happen? Several times, I commented about her putting it back on, but she made excuses about still not being able to trust me. Honestly, for now, I was cool on the pussy thang. She was backing it up correctly, so I didn't have no reason to trip. I know she thought there was still something going on with Mercedes and me, but really, there wasn't. I mean, she'd called several times, but I told her how I felt about losing my father and she backed off. And when I saw a letter addressed to Scorpio about the charges being dropped, I knew my mission had been accomplished.

Now, though, I had to work on getting her phone calls to stop. Scorpio was having a fit. It was causing a bit of turmoil in my relationship, so I decided to go to Mercedes' place and end it.

As usual, it was hard going to see her because she was one sexy woman. Her naked body instantly stiffened me, but there was a purpose for my visit. I called it off as we stood in her kitchen.

"I just need to back off this relationship for a while," I said.

"Fine. What do you want me to say? If that's how you feel, then I can't do anything about it."

"No, you can't," I said, backing away. "And, uh, good luck with your modeling."

"Yeah, whatever." She followed me to the door, and when I stopped for a hug, she stepped back. "Don't bother."

I shrugged my shoulders and then went on my way to Nokea's house to get LJ. As soon as I hit Highway 270, Mercedes' number flashed across my cell phone.

"Yes," I said, feeling as if that breakup was too easy.

"You used me, didn't you?"

"What? Baby, I didn't use you. I told you I'm just going through something right now."

"Something like trying to work out things with Scorpio?"

"Yeah, that too, but don't take it too personal."

"I'm not going to sweat you like these other sistas probably do, but there's a cost for going around and stepping on people's hearts. You'll pay for what you done to me."

"I guess I should consider that a threat and watch my back, huh?"

"More than a threat."

"Good," I said, having no fear. I didn't know Mercedes that well, but I had been threatened by many women in the past. Just like the others, I let her comment roll off my back. "Stand in line, Mercedes, and remember, there are plenty of women waiting before you." I hung up on Mercedes and turned up my booming-ass system.

When I got to Nokea's house, she was outside washing her car. She looked delightful with her li'l blue jean shorts and white half T-shirt, which revealed her nicely cut midriff. She displayed one of the prettiest smiles I'd ever seen on her face, and it made me feel good that she was happy to see me. I walked up to her as she squeezed water from a towel and moved her bangs aside to wipe the sweat from her forehead.

"Your son is not here," she said.

"What? You let him out of your sight?"

"Yeah, after my daddy yelled at me about not seeing him." She looked at my truck. "Is that new?"

"Yep. You wanna go for a ride?"

"Sure." She grinned. "Let me turn off the water and lock my door."

Nokea went inside to get her purse. I couldn't

help but take a good glimpse at her butt when she got in my truck. Trying hard to keep my comments to myself, I got in without saying a word.

We drove around, talking and laughing about everything and everyone. I wanted to apologize for breaking up her and Collins, so I parked at a nearby park. She followed me to an old wooden bench under a willow tree and we both took a seat.

"Are you still mad at me?" I asked, clenching her hand with mine.

"A tiny bit. I know you were angry that day, but I never expected you to put my business out there like you did."

"Yeah, well, I didn't either. How are things with you and Collins, though? Have you talked to him?"

"I've called him, but he told me he needs time. I feel so bad, and I hate he found out about us sleeping together the way he did."

I rubbed Nokea's leg. "I'm sorry, but I lost it when I found out about LJ. There are many times that I don't think about shit before I do it. I wasn't trying to mess up your relationship, but Collins was working me with that 'my woman' bullshit."

"Well, there isn't much I can do about it now. I'm allowing him time to cool off, and we'll talk soon."

"I know you don't believe this, but if there's anything I can do, let me know."

"You've already done enough. Besides, I don't think Collins ever wants to see your face again. If there's anything you can do, you can tell him you lied."

"Now, that I won't do. That would make me look stupid, and I'm not going there. If you have any other suggestions, let me know. In the meantime, you might consider telling the truth. That's the only way you're going to be able to put this behind you."

"Maybe so. I hope he'll forgive me."

"Please. How is he going to forgive you for still loving me?"

Nokea smiled and cut her eyes at me. "What makes you think I still love you?"

"Because the feeling is mutual." I hopped down off the bench. Nokea looked shocked and appeared to be tongue-tied. I kept quiet too and picked up some rocks, throwing them into the lake. Just as I was about to throw another one, Nokea took my hand, holding it with hers.

"What about Scorpio?" she asked.

I moved my hand from hers, tossed the rock, and spoke the truth. "I love her too. Both of you complete me, and as selfish as I am, I want you both. I know it doesn't make sense to you, but you don't know or understand what I'm feeling inside. It's like one minute I want you, LJ, and me to be a family so badly, and the next minute, I see Scorpio as my wife and having my children."

Nokea reached up and touched my face. "It's tough being torn between two, isn't it? I'm in the same predicament. After all these years, I can't believe how much I still love you. When I met Collins, I thought my love for you was well behind me. The day we made love confirmed that I'd been fooling myself all along. Thing is, baby, I don't know what to do. I love Collins dearly, but there are times I can't stop thinking about being with you."

Nokea's eyes filled with water and I held her in my arms. I knew what she was going through, as I'd been fighting the same battle for a very long time. I wanted to be with her, but I wasn't ready to let go of my relationship with Scorpio either. Trying to have both of them would mean nothing but trouble, but if I could have my cake and eat it too, I would. Nokea being with Collins made it easier for me to get along without her. I kept telling myself that she was with another man and I had to move on. Now, with knowing how she truly felt about me, I wasn't sure how I'd be able to do it.

"What are we gonna do?" she asked.

"I don't know. Seriously, I don't know which way to turn."

I placed her head against my chest and held her for as long as I could.

Before leaving the park, Nokea hopped on my back for a horseback ride. She was light as a feather, and I had no problem carrying her. As we got to my truck, Leslie got out of her station wagon with her kids. Nokea, not knowing who Leslie was, slid off my back while Leslie looked at us like we were crazy. I opened the door for Nokea to get inside the truck and quickly closed it.

"You out playing house again, Jaylin?" Leslie said with her hand on her hip.

"It ain't none of your business what I'm doing,

so tend to your kids and mind your own business."

Her neck started to roll. "Uh-huh. I got my cell phone right here, and we'll see whose business it is."

"Whew, I'm shaking like a leaf," I said, laughing as I got inside of my truck.

I grinned at her and sped off. Nokea tooted her lips and folded her arms in front of her.

"Who was that?"

"Scorpio's ole whack-ass sister."

"Sister? They don't even look alike. I mean, she's a pretty girl, but—"

"They half sisters. Same mama, different daddy."

"Oh. But what if she calls Scorpio?"

"And?"

"And I was all on your back, laughing and hugging on you like you were my man."

"Everything will be cool. I don't have problems like you have."

"So in other words, you don't think she's going to trip?"

"Yeah, she gon' trip. But she knows I got her all taken care of."

"Jaylin, you're a mess. You need to stop using your goodies to get you out of trouble."

I winked. "It works all the time, doesn't it?"

"Not with me. When we get back toget—" She paused.

"Go ahead. Finish what you were about to say."

"I said when . . . when we get back to my house, I need to finish washing my car."

"No. You were about to say when we get back

together, throwing my dick on you ain't gonna work. So when we gon' hook up again?"

"We're not."

"But I thought someday we might."

"Well, you thought wrong."

"Maybe I did, but . . ." My phone vibrated. The number was coming from my house. I knew it was Scorpio, so I answered.

"What's up, baby?" I said.

"Who are you with?"

"Nokea."

"What are you doing at the park with Nokea?"

"Talking."

"Talking about what?"

"I'll tell you when I get home."

"Well, what's this I hear about her on your back?"

"I gave her a horseback ride. It was totally innocent. Would you like to ask her how innocent it was? She's right here."

"No, I do not want to talk to Nokea. Just hurry it up home."

"Why, 'cause you got something good waiting for me?"

"How about a good ass-kicking?"

"Can't wait."

I hung up. Nokea sat shaking her head.

"I have to give it to you, my brotha. You got the game and g'on with it. That's exactly how you used to do me. That's the kind of stuff that every time I think I want to be with you again, something slaps me back to reality and says I'd better not."

I laughed. "It's not a game. I can spend time with the mother of my child if I want to. It's important for my son to stay in a happy environment, and if you're happy, he's happy. If I want to take a day out of my busy schedule to make you happy, then I can."

"Save it. You don't have to convince me; you have to convince her."

I drove Nokea back to her house, and when I got out of my truck to go inside with her, she pushed me away from the door.

"Please, go home and make sure your woman is cool."

"I am. Can I at least get a glass of water, lemonade . . . or something before I go?"

She rolled her eyes and let me inside. I followed her into the kitchen, and as she reached inside of the refrigerator for a pitcher of Kool-aid, I stood closely from behind and whispered in her ear, "I'm dying to make love to you."

She breathed in, then closed her eyes without turning around to look at me. Speechless, she reached up and rubbed the back of my head. I pecked down the side of her neck and reached down to unbutton her shorts. I reached my hand inside of them and separated her lips to feel her wetness. My finger inched further in and Nokea took a deep breath. I quickly released my finger from her grip, zipped her shorts and backed away from her. She turned around.

"Don't play games with me, Jaylin."

"I'm not. But, I'm going home. Tonight, though, meet me at the park around ten o'clock."

"And what makes you think I'll be there?"

"Because you don't want to deprive your pussy like that, do you?"

I kissed Nokea on the forehead and jetted.

Making love to Nokea was heavy on my mind. I knew Scorpio would be mad, and it was obvious that one of us would wind up in the guestroom tonight. My intentions were not to hurt her, but after what Nokea revealed to me today, I couldn't hold back my feelings for her. I wanted her relationship with Collins to end, and I would do my best to shake up things between them. If I was forced to choose between her and Scorpio, so be it. Whenever the time came, I'd weigh my options and be willing to take my loss. Since Stanley's death, I realized that tomorrow was never promised to any of us. I was living for today, and if I wanted to make love to Nokea, then without any hesitation, I was going to do it.

Scorpio was in the kitchen, running her mouth on the phone. When I walked in, she told whoever it was she'd call them back. Her snappy tone led me to believe that it was her sister she'd been talking to. I didn't say a word until Scorpio yelled about me carrying Nokea on my back.

"I can't believe you're tripping over something as simple as a horseback ride."

"Really? Well, let me go cock my legs open on Shane or Stephon's back and let's see how you feel."

I conceded to her point and took a seat next to her in the kitchen chair. "Okay, so I'd be mad. I didn't look at it that way. We were just playing around and she hopped on my back. I carried her to my truck because we joked about how light she was."

She rolled her eyes. "Well, whatever was going on, I don't like it."

"You never do. You act like I can't have any female friends at all. You can't keep me in this house forever, baby."

"I'm not trying to. I'm just tired of all these other women, Jaylin. Once you get rid of one, here comes another. And Nokea? She will never go away. I'm sure Collins would be upset if he knew she had her legs straddled on your damn back."

I knew that continuing this argument with Scorpio was going to last way into the night. That's just how she was; she wasn't satisfied until she got me upset and made me go off on her. I wasn't about to do either, especially since I was so excited about meeting Nokea. "Look, this is petty. I'm going to bed. I've had enough headache for one day."

"And so have I, but you bring it on your damn self. You act as if no explanation is needed for your actions, and I really get tired of this nonchalant attitude of yours."

I defensively held out my hands. "What do you want me to say? I'm sorry, okay? I said it, so let's be done with it."

I left the kitchen and headed upstairs to my room. After I showered, I put on my silk pajamas and got in bed. I flipped through a *GQ* magazine and looked at the alarm clock on my nightstand. It was already nine o'clock. Fifteen minutes later, Scorpio came into the room, grabbing pillows off the bed.

"Am I sleeping alone tonight?" I asked, as she was already headed for the door.

"Get used to it for a while."

As soon as she walked out, I got up, slid into my jeans and a white button-down shirt. I hid my motion lotion in my back pocket and grabbed my keys to go. I stopped by the guestroom where Scorpio was to let her know I was leaving.

"I'll be back. I need to go clear my head for a minute," I said.

"Which head? Just tell her I said hello, and if it's that bitch Mercedes, tell her she can have you."

"Assumption is a motherfucker, Scorpio. And one day, it's going to cost you big time."

I left and headed for the park to meet Nokea. I wasn't sure if she would come, but I hoped that she would.

When I got there, her car was nowhere in sight. I looked at my watch. It was five minutes to ten. I walked over to the wooden bench we'd sat on earlier today, gripping my hands together while waiting for her to show.

By ten fifteen, I felt disappointed. I knew she had her doubts, but I seriously thought she would show. As I was beginning to think maybe it was a good idea she hadn't shown, I heard some branches crack from behind me. I quickly turned and there she stood, smiling, with a blanket in her hands.

"Where's your car?" I asked.

"Parked way over there." She pointed to where it was. "I didn't want anyone to see it. Have you been waiting long?"

"Long enough."

I pulled her to me and we instantly locked lips. I couldn't wait to feel her again. Once I spread the blanket on the ground, we kneeled in front of each other. I leaned in for another kiss, but she placed her finger on my lips to stop me.

"I have to be honest with you about something, Jaylin."

"What?"

"I'm planning on working things out with Collins."

"Good. And I'm planning on working things out with Scorpio. But for now, we're here, and that's all that matters."

Nokea eased out of her oversized shirt and laid her naked body on the blanket. I removed my clothes too, and while lying next to her, I explored her body by massaging every part of it with the cherry-flavored motion lotion. Nokea sat up on her elbows and moaned as she felt my hands go to work. She had been there and done this with me before, and had already widened her legs so I could dive in.

I separated her insides with the tips of my fingers and squeezed a few drops of the lotion over her hardened clitoris. With the tip of my tongue, I licked her clit in a circular motion, covering it with my mouth to make it vibrate. Like always, Nokea tasted damn good. When I inserted my fingers to assist me, I watched as her sweaty, flat stomach trembled and heaved in and out. She started to take deeper breaths and was seconds away from releasing her juices in my mouth.

"I miss this so, so darn much," she admitted, holding my head tightly in place.

I removed her grip from my hair and wiped my mouth. Her taste was what I'd been dying for, but there was so much more about her that I admired.

I politely asked that she turn on her stomach, and with no hesitation, she turned and laid her head on her hands. I separated her legs, kneeling in between them. Using my strength to hold myself over her, I licked down her back and circled my tongue on her curvy ass. She let out soft sounds of pleasure, and when I made my way through the valley, she got tense. I eased up a bit, working her at a slow pace from side to side. She caught onto my rhythm. The realization of being inside of her again gave me a feeling I hadn't had in a long, long time.

Nokea got on her hands and knees, which allowed me to manuever in farther. I held her petite waistline from behind, and while enjoying the feel of her, I rubbed her ass, reaching my hand around front to tickle her cherry drop.

She dropped her head in defeat, then spoke in a soft tone. "Why does this feel so good when we're doing this?"

"Because it's just meant to feel this way."

"Do you even feel what I'm feeling?"

"Yes, baby, I feel the love."

Before I came, I quickly pulled out, wanting our moment to last. I couldn't get enough of sucking her pussy, and my tongue brought her to climax again. She couldn't get enough either, and reached back for another round of my dick. I held back big time on coming, until she sat on top of me and leaned back on her hands for leverage.

She worked me over like a pro, and ready to explode, I sat up, grabbing her waist tightly. My eyes closed, and all I could think about was how much love I had for this woman.

We sat quietly for a moment, embracing each other. All I could hear was the wind blowing, the water flowing in the lake, and crickets chirping. I enjoyed the mood while Nokea lightly scratched up and down my back with her nails. I moved her off my lap and we lay face to face on the blanket.

"This seems like a dream." She looked at the dark sky and shining stars. "My journal can't hold what I'd like to write in it tonight."

"You won't be writing it tonight."

"Yes, I will, because we'd better get going. Just in case you forgot, I still have a job I must go to."

"You know you don't have to work. As much as I pay you in child support, you could sit back for the rest of your life."

"Then that would mean I'd be depending on you to take care of me. Sorry, that's not my style. I've always had my own things and always will. I'm not trying to go there with you and Scorpio, but I truly believe that's where the downfall is in your relationship. As long as she allows you to provide for her, she can't say a darn thing about what you do."

"Maybe, or maybe not. But she's trying to do some things on her own, though."

"Trying to do them and actually doing them are two different things. I know she's going to school, but she has taken so many steps backward because of her fallouts with you. One day she's there and the next day she's not. When you're trying to accomplish something, you can't let no one or nothing stand in your way. You're making it too easy for her, Jaylin, and you know it."

"I have my reasons, but can we not talk about Scorpio right now? I'd like to enjoy my time with you before you work things out with your man."

"I'm working it out with him now, aren't I?"

Nokea gave me a kiss. We lay there for at least another hour talking, then we got back into our clothes and left. I followed her to make sure she made it home safely. I knew this was a turning point for me, but the next move, if any, had to come from Nokea.

# 19

## *NOKEA*

Since LJ was still at my parents' house, I called Collins while I was at work to see if we could talk later. Finally, he agreed to it, and I told him I'd be there no later than six o'clock that evening.

I felt guilty. How dare I try to reconcile with him when I was confused once again? I closed my eyes and sat at my desk for hours, fading in and out of a trance, as I thought about making love to Jaylin last night. I could still feel him inside of me; the tenderness between my legs wouldn't allow me to forget. My secretary, Marty, had even buzzed in a few times and I didn't hear her. She was forced to get out of her seat and come into my office just to make sure everything was okay.

"Marty, I'm fine," I said, snapping out of it. "Did Pat call yet? We're supposed to have lunch today."

"Yes, she called earlier, while you were on the phone. She said she'd be here by noon and said if your plans changed before then to call her."

"Thanks. Now, would you mind closing my door?"

Marty closed my door and I went back to day-dreaming again. The thought of Jaylin's hands touching me, his licks between my legs, and whispers in my ear gave me chills. I chuckled as I thought about our conversation, and nibbled on my nails when I thought about what I had done to Collins.

Realizing that I should have been thinking about my real future, Collins, I desperately tried to drop my thoughts of Jaylin. I turned to my computer, and when I received an instant message, I clicked on it. It was a card sent from Collins: *After all, I still love you.* My eyes watered and I emailed him back, telling him I loved him too.

Pat waited for me in the lobby. Already in downtown St. Louis, we went to the Old Spaghetti Factory on Laclede's Landing. Not really hungry, I kept it simple and ordered a salad. Pat ordered spaghetti with meatballs and a salad as well.

"Are you eating for two or three?" I asked.

"Uh-huh."

My eyes widened. "Are you pregnant?"

"You asked if I was eating for two. I'm eating for my stomach and me. I didn't say anything about being pregnant. You must have a baby on your mind."

"Girl, please. LJ is enough for me. Besides, I don't even have a man to have no baby with."

"Not having a man doesn't mean you ain't still fucking. I'm sure you and Collins have been at it since y'all broke up."

"No, we haven't. He isn't playing with me, girl.

He is mad. I don't know what I'm gonna have to do to get him back."

"Bend over. It works for me every time."

I laughed. "You sound like Jaylin."

"I'm sure I do. Have you seen him lately? I hope you haven't, especially after how he played you by telling Collins."

I lowered my head and didn't give Pat eye contact. "Yeah, I've seen him. We talked about what happened and he apologized."

"With his mouth or with his dick? Which one?"

Thinking about it, I put on the biggest smile. I couldn't resist telling Pat the truth. "Both," I whispered. "Sorry, I couldn't help it."

"See! I told you! I knew it would happen again. All he gotta do is start slapping that thing around, and after that, your mind is gone. It seems as if his dick is a powerful thing that'll make you lose your job, forget about your friends, say to hell with your kids, and have you doing shit that you never thought you'd do. I'm so glad I haven't been cursed with that kind of power, and you should not let it have that much control over you like it does."

"Pat, Jaylin's penis does not make me do any of the things you mentioned. And trust me, it's not all about the sex either. When you said that I still loved Jaylin, you were right. I'm also in love with Collins. And believe it or not, I want Collins' and my relationship to work out."

"I believe that you do. But while you and Jaylin still doing all this screwing, where in the hell is Scorpio at? Is he still with her or not?"

"Yes, they're still together. He told me he loves

her, but that doesn't bother me because I know he still loves me too. If you think I'm interfering, I'm not. She's going to destroy their relationship on her own."

"I don't care if you're interfering or not. I have no sympathy for a woman like her. A few years back, she stepped on the scene and trampled all over your relationship with Jaylin. She knew he was seeing someone else, but she was determined to have him all to herself. In case you forgot, she moved her and her child in with him and treated you like you didn't exist when you came to his house. Don't let me remind you about her smirking when you busted the two of them in the shower." Pat snapped her finger. "On your birthday, I recall. Not once did that bitch think about what you were going through. It's gon' kill her ass when she finds out how much he still loves you, but that's what women like her get."

"I remember the hurt she caused me, but Jaylin caused me more hurt. If I can forgive him, why not forgive her? I feel for Scorpio. She has probably been through more stuff in these past few years than I ever did, being with him for almost ten years. I've never lived with him. I can only imagine what it must be like."

"Just be careful. Try hard to rekindle your relationship with Collins and go from there."

"You can count on that."

Pat and I finished up lunch. Before we left, I told her about my amazing night with Jaylin. Again, she told me to be careful trusting him again. I had every intention of doing so.

* * *

I got to Collins' place early because I was anxious to see him. He was in his office on the phone and looked pissed. He had a frown I'd rarely seen before, and his voice had much authority. He yelled at somebody about what had gone down in Detroit with his business, so I wasn't sure if my visit would be successful.

As I waited, I walked around his office and picked through some of the educational books on his bookshelves. I didn't want to show impatience, so I sat in a chair and thumbed through, *Do You* by Russell Simmons. Several times, I peeked at Collins and thought about the damage I'd done and was continuing to do to our relationship. He was easily every woman's dream, and I had the nerve to be tripping.

When he stood up, I checked him out in his tailored beige suit, shiny brown leather shoes, and silk shirt that was unbuttoned. As he caught me checking him out, he finally smiled to show his pearly whites. Moments later, he ended his call. He wiped down his face with his big, strong hands and sighed. I could see the stress on his face and hated that I had brought him more.

I closed the book and walked over by him. "Is everything going to work out with the business?" I asked.

"Yeah. My partners and I are trying to figure out how we're going to make up for some of these losses. Do you know those fools swindled over a hundred thousand dollars from us?"

"Are you kidding me? That's a shame. How did they get away with it?"

"Trust. We trusted the fools to deliver and sell our products, but they were stealing merchandise and selling it on the streets for half price." Collins lowered his head. "Seems like I can't trust no damn body these days."

I wanted to say he could trust me, but I didn't want to set myself up like that. Instead, I rubbed his wavy hair. "Baby, everything is going to work out. If you'd like for me to invest in your business, I will. I'll do anything I can to help."

"When it comes to money, Nokea, we're not suffering. If anything we need to cut back on the bonuses for the year. That's all."

"I see. But again, if you need me, I'm here."

He gazed at me but didn't smile. "So, what's up with you and Pretty Boy? And please don't lie to me. I've been lied to enough."

"Collins, there's nothing up with Jaylin and me. We've been intimate one time since you and I have been together and that's it. Jaylin made it seem as if we were screwing every chance we got, and that's not so."

He rubbed his chin, thinking about what I'd implied. "One time, huh? Well, tell me about this one time."

"What do you want to know about it? I really don't want to go into details."

"If this intimate moment took place in the beginning of our relationship, maybe I would understand. I know you had a hard time letting him go, but if it was recent, it's gonna be tough for me to swallow. We've developed something intriguing over the last several months. Time and effort have been put into this relationship, and I'll be disappointed if you've allowed Jaylin, or any man, to take that away from us."

Not wanting to answer Collins' question, I slowly walked back over to a chair and sat down. I crossed my legs and rubbed my hands together. Thinking hard, I folded my arms and looked at him. "What can I say other than I messed up? I'm not going to say I'm sorry, because you believe that saying you're sorry only means trouble in a relationship. There isn't trouble in my relationship, and there won't be any trouble. All I can ask is for you to give me another chance. I love you and I promise I will never hurt you again."

"Promises are made to be broken. I know that, and so do you. Your intentions might not be to hurt me, but when you get caught up in shit like that, you have very little consideration for the other person's feelings. I've been there before, Nokea. I love you too, but I'm not going to cry about it, I'm not going to lose my mind over it, and I'm not going to be as forgiving as you want me to."

My eyes watered as I looked at him. "So, are you saying this is over? People make mistakes, Collins. Baby, I didn't know what to do."

He walked over by me. He got on his knees in front of me and held my hands with his. "Whether it's over or not, that's up to you. I'm not rushing back into this until I know it's over between Jaylin and you for good. I'm not going to allow him to make love to my woman when he wants to. My woman is my woman. And when she knows she's only my woman, that's when we'll talk about working this out."

"But I want to work this out today. I don't want to be without you any longer. I'm afraid I'm going to lose you to someone else. What if you meet someone else during our separation?"

"I'm in the midst of loving somebody, Nokea. I don't have time for games, and I'm not interested in meeting anyone else. Temptation is around us every day. Your situation isn't any different from mine. If I love you enough to turn temptation away, I want the same in return. No ifs, ands, or buts about it."

A tear rolled down my face. "So, I just go home—"

"Go home and think about it. Don't call me until you've thought long and hard about it. When you're in the mood to laugh, think about who you want to laugh with. When you cry, think about who you want to hold you and wipe your tears. When you want to make love, think about who you want loving you. If the answer is only me, then I'm here."

Collins stood and pulled me to him. He gave me a squeezing hug and kissed my forehead. I felt horrible, but I couldn't be mad at him for standing his ground. He was simply that kind of man. I just had to find myself and figure out who or what I really needed versus what I wanted.

# 20

## *SCORPIO*

Things were looking up for Jay Baby and me. He gave me the lowdown on Mercedes, and since she'd stop calling the house, I knew something had happened. He also told me about her dropping the charges against me. I wasn't sure what he had to do to get her to agree to it, and I really didn't want to know.

After our disagreement the other day about Nokea, I thought about how innocent a horseback ride really was. I knew him and Nokea kidded around with each other a lot, and since Nokea and Collins' relationship was going strong, I figured she wasn't thinking about Jaylin.

Of course, that was just a thought. When Jaylin slipped the other day and said Nokea and Collins had broken up, I started to get a bit worried. I knew she wasn't the type of woman to intrude on somebody else's territory, but when it came to Jaylin, I also knew anything was possible. They had been on the phone more than usual, and it seemed as if he was spending more time at her house as well. I tried not to trip, but since she didn't have a man in her life, I damn sure thought Jaylin was trying to fill that void.

So, being the curious and investigative woman that I was, I watched this one play itself out. I listened in closely to their conversations, and whenever Jaylin went to pick up LJ, I asked to go with him. He didn't seem to trip, but Nokea seemed a little bothered by seeing me all the time. When I asked if everything was cool, she insisted it was and put on a fake smile. I questioned Jaylin about her demeanor, but he said he thought she was upset about her relationship not working out. I also inquired about what happened between Collins and Nokea, but Jaylin said she wouldn't tell him. I didn't believe that for one minute, but I would put some money on it that he had something to do with it.

Late Saturday night, Jaylin asked if I was in the mood to go out to a nightclub. Having nothing else to do, I agreed. I hadn't been out in a long time, and I wanted to show him how well I could throw down on the dance floor.

While he was in the shower, I went into the closet to look for an outfit. I had so many clothes, but I searched for something extremely sexy with a touch of class. I found a black satin jumpsuit I bought months ago at Saks Fifth Avenue that still had the price tag on it. The top part was a halter that only covered a portion of my breasts. My back was exposed, and the pantlegs flared out with nearly a two-inch cuff at the bottom. It was perfect for the night, and I couldn't wait for Jaylin to see me in it.

He took forever in the bathroom, so I went to another one to shower and change. I arched my brows, put on my M.A.C. makeup, and styled my hair. After I slid into my clothes, I looked in the mirror. The jumpsuit perfectly clung to the curves in my body. I couldn't decide if I wanted my hair up or down, so I kept styling it many different ways. I knew Jaylin liked it half-and-half, so I put most of it up and let the rest dangle down my back. When I heard him yell that he was ready to go, I put on my accessories, slid on some "Oh Baby" lip-gloss, a dash of perfume, and headed downstairs.

As I walked down the steps, Jaylin had his back turned. He was talking to Shane on the phone, and told him to meet us at the club. When he turned around and saw me, he stared, appearing to be frozen in time. His conversation came to a halt, but as soon as he blinked, he turned his back, continuing to talk.

By the look in his eyes, I could tell he was pleased. I stood at the bottom of the steps and waited for him to end his call. He called Stephon, too, then finally walked up to me and sniffed.

"What's that you're wearing?" he asked.

"Dolce and Gabbana."

"You smell delicious."

"And you?"

"Issey Miyake."

"You smell workable."

He leaned forward and kissed me, then backed up to give me another look. He shook his head. "Turn around," he asked whiled stroking his goatee.

I grinned and turned around. "Hmm. I'm not sure if this is a good idea."

"Why?" I asked. "What's wrong?"

"You kind of look better than me. Plus, I'm not prepared for any fights tonight."

"Jaylin? Sounding insecure? I don't think so. Besides, if any fighting goes on tonight, you'll have your boys with you, won't you?"

"Yeah, but I'd rather have my girl for backup any day of the week." He put his arms around me and squeezed my butt. "We making my baby tonight. As soon as we step foot in this door, Miss Lady, your ass is mine."

"So, I guess you're feeling my outfit, huh?"

"Woman," he shouted and shook his body, "you make me wanna scream. The outfit is banging, but I'm thinking about what's underneath it."

I smiled and lightly pushed his shoulder. "It ain't like you haven't been here and done this before. So where are we going?"

"Looking like that, you need to be on the red carpet in Hollywood, but we're going to a new club in North County tonight. Maybe to the East Side afterward, but we'll see."

"I'm ready whenever you are."

Since we both had on black, Jaylin drove the black Escalade to match. He was dressed a bit more laid back than I was, and had on his Armani wide-legged white pants and gray silk button-down shirt that did justice for his eyes. He looked good in anything he wore, so it didn't take much effort on his part.

While driving to the club, we got along well, but as soon as we got to the club, it was on. Actually, the trouble started outside with the police officers checking me out from head to toe. And when we got inside, many men approached me as if Jaylin wasn't even there. At first he didn't trip not one bit, until this one brotha took my hand and boldly kissed it.

"She cool," Jaylin said loudly. The brotha smiled at me and slowly walked away.

I laughed as Jaylin took a napkin and wiped my hand where the brotha had placed his lips. "Go to the bathroom and wash that shit off," he said angrily.

"You can't be serious. Washing my hand—"

"Go do it!" he yelled.

I stepped back and let go of his hand. Refusing to get my clown on and embarrass both of us, I walked away to mingle. I noticed him watching me, and that's when I took a detour to the bathroom. While in the bathroom, I damn sure didn't wash my hands. I put on some more lip-gloss and chatted with this chick named Chelsea I knew from school.

I finished my quick conversation with her, and when I came out of the bathroom, I looked for Jaylin. I was quite surprised to see him on the dance floor.

The chick he danced with didn't have nothing on me, so he was really tripping if he thought I'd be intimidated. She was a bit on the thick side, and had thick lips that I'm sure caused him to wonder.

T.I.'s latest hit was thumping loudly through the speakers. The chick turned around and swayed her ass against Jaylin's frontside. He gazed down at her working him, holding his arms in the air. There was no breathing room between them; she definitely made sure of that. He touched her hips and had the nerve to wrap his arm around her waist.

Now, the night was going to get interesting if we weren't going to show each other respect. I walked to the bar, got myself a drink, and changed my attitude. All I had to do was find a dance partner, and that was quite easy. I had already been asked many times if I wanted to dance, but I had to find a dance partner who Jaylin would see as competition.

A sexy, fine bald brotha, who could have been Tyson Beckford himself, stepped my way. He stared me down, and I didn't waste no time in escorting him to the dance floor. I didn't even go nearby where Jaylin danced because that would have been too easy. Instead, I went to the other side of the dance floor. The DJ kicked down "Slow Motion," and that indeed described my rhythm.

It wasn't long before the Long Island Iced Tea took effect, and when I turned to face Mr. Sexy, he greeted me with a satisfying smile. "What's your name?" he whispered.

"Sugar," I said, closing my eyes.

"You are definitely something sweet." He rubbed my hips while we danced, and when he placed his thick lips on my neck, I tilted my head to the side.

"Where your man at?"

I slowly opened my eyes and saw Jaylin looking at me from just a few feet away. He rubbed his goatee, not looking too happy. I smiled and motioned my finger for him to come to me. He did, and stood face to face with me.

"This is my man right here," I said. "Isn't he gorgeous?"

Mr. Sexy looked at Jaylin, grinned, and walked away. I put my arms on Jaylin's shoulders and we danced. "Why you so uptight?" I asked.

"Because I don't like nobody touching on you like that."

"What? Do you want me to go wash my neck now? Or would you rather I take off my outfit and go wash my body? Which one?"

"Neither. Just be cool, all right? And please don't drink anything else tonight."

When the song was over, Jaylin and I got off the floor. We held hands as we eased our way through the crowd to find a seat. I was furious with all the women staring him down, whispering, and touching him like he was a celebrity. When this chick jumped in his face and offered him her panties, I released his hand and walked away. I saw Shane, Stephon, Ray-Ray, and some other fellas they were with standing near the doorway. I walked up to them.

"Hi, guys," I said. Stephon didn't say anything. He just stood there staring at me without a single blink.

Shane leaned forward and gave me a hug. "Hey, Scorpio. How you been doing?"

"I'm doing fine. How about you?"

"Couldn't be better." He turned around to the fellas behind him. "You know Jeff, Clarence, and Andrew from the shop, don't you?"

"Yeah, I've seen them before," I said, and then spoke to them as well.

"Where my boy at?" Shane asked.

I shrugged. "Somewhere. I don't know."

Shane looked over my shoulder and Jaylin walked up, slamming handshakes with everybody. There wasn't any place to sit, so we all stood close by the doorway. While they were conversing about something that went down between Shane and Stephon, I tuned them out. Jaylin had his arm wrapped around me, and rubbed my stomach every once in a while. When I moved my body to the music as a signal that I wanted to dance, he ignored me and continued to talk to his friends. I didn't trip because I blocked the females from getting to him. They glanced over my shoulders and tried hard to make contact with him. Many rolled their eyes at me, but I proudly stood in front of him because this man was mine.

I did my best not to get upset, especially since many men were attempting to get at me. Mr. Sexy himself had a napkin and pen in his hand, and mouthed from across the floor for me to give him my phone number. Not wanting to be disrespectful, I smiled and shook my head. He put his hands together, imploring me. I shook my head again, and when I turned my head and blushed, that's when I saw Stephon eyeballing me. I tried to play it off by smiling, but he had a lustful look in his eyes and didn't crack a smile. He wet his lips, which made me very uncomfortable. I immediately interrupted Jaylin's conversation with Shane and told him I wanted to dance.

"In a few minutes, baby. Do you want something else to drink? Why don't you get something else to drink?"

I flagged down a waiter and ordered another drink. After he brought it to me, Jaylin paid for it and kept on running his mouth. Just when I thought the night couldn't get any more interesting, Felicia came through the door. Now, that sure as hell got the crew's attention. Stephon, Jaylin, and Shane had all been there and done that before. She strutted in with one of her girlfriends like she was Cinderella. Her hair was in micro braids that hung midway down her back. The outfit she had on was very revealing, but I admit, it was kind of cute. It was a gray lace short skirt and had a jazzy gray silk blouse to match. Her cleavage showed just a bit, but as for her backside, it was clearly visible to the naked eye. I liked how well she matched the outfit with her high-heeled gray-strapped shoes and silver accessories. I had no problem giving credit where credit was due, and the men had no problem showing their approval either. The ones standing nearby checked her out, and when she got closer to us, she couldn't help but notice me. Her eyes scanned my outfit as she reached over me to tap Jaylin on his shoulder.

"Hey, you," she said. He spoke to her and took his arm from around me to give her a hug. After he did, he put his arm around me again. She spoke to Stephon, Shane, and Ray-Ray too, and hugged them as well.

Before she walked away, she tooted her lips and rolled her eyes at me. I can honestly say that I have never hated anyone as much as I hated Felicia. Jaylin should have known better than to say one word to her, especially since she was good for nothing but opening up her legs to his friends. She and I never got along, and from day one, I could tell she was trouble. She was always jealous of me, and I was so sure she was still upset that Jaylin had put an end to their relationship because of me.

Stephon and Shane leaned forward to look at her ass, and when I turned to see if Jaylin looked, he turned his head the other way.

"You know you want to look," I said.

"What?" he said, smiling. "I ain't thinking about Felicia."

"Shit, I am," Stephon said, continuing to look at her while holding his dick. "I don't know about y'all, but my shit is thumping."

Shane laughed and had the nerve to give Stephon five. Not even trying to hear them give that bitch props, I told Jaylin I saw a friend of mine and stepped away.

As I stood nearby talking to a friend of mine from school, Felicia quickly made her way back over to the fellas. She and several other females that couldn't wait for me to walk away were all over Jaylin. Shane and Stephon had their share of prospects as well. It was unbelievable to see so many females trying to get attention. In the meantime, two men had gotten me a drink when I didn't even ask, and both had given me their phone numbers. Jaylin hadn't been paying much attention to me, so instead of being rude and not accepting the numbers, I put them in my purse. Afterward, I walked back to where Jaylin was because I couldn't even see him anymore through the crowd.

"Excuse me," I said, forcing my way up to him. This one chick's lips touched his ear as she whispered in it. He nodded his head, seeming to be tuned in. I reached for his hand and snatched him away.

"Come on, let's dance," I said.

"I was waiting on you," he replied.

"Confessions" played, so I followed Jaylin to the dimly lit dance floor.

"What's your name?" he said, pretending as if he didn't know me.

"What do you want it to be?"

"Mrs. Jaylin Jerome Rogers."

"That's a tough woman to be. I don't know if I'm ready for that title yet."

"Ah, you ready. More ready than anybody I know."

"I wish I were. But as you can see with your own eyes, there's a little too much that comes with the territory."

"That's fair, but I know you can handle it. Nobody . . . no woman in here can compete with you, and I don't want you to make me wait too long, all right?"

"Never."

Jaylin hugged me tighter and we continued to dance. I saw Stephon walk to the dance floor with Felicia, and they danced closely by us. I could only imagine where the night was headed with those two, and the thought of that tramp disgusted me.

Shane came on the dance floor with his partner, and I couldn't help but think how lucky she was. He really had it going on, and any woman capable of landing him was truly blessed. At that moment, I closed my eyes and thought about my love for Jaylin. It wasn't that I didn't want to marry him, but we still had so many problems. I didn't trust him to save my soul, and there was no way I wanted to feel that way about a man I intended to spend the rest of my life with. If things didn't go as planned right now, I could always just pick up and walk away. If I married him and things didn't work out, I had so much to lose. He'd already mentioned a prenuptial, and he always said if we ever got divorced, I would be left without. I hadn't brought much of nothing to our relationship, and I took him at his word. For now, it was in my best interest to hold out until I knew for sure that he was going to be the faithful man I wanted and needed him to be.

My thoughts continued as I lay my head on Jaylin's shoulder. When I opened my eyes, Stephon was looking over Felicia's shoulder while gazing at me again. His stares made me uncomfortable, and I was surprised that Jaylin hadn't said anything. I ignored Stephon and lifted my head from Jaylin's shoulder.

"You didn't go to sleep, did you?" he asked.

"No, I was just thinking."

"About what?"

"About how many positions you're going to put me in tonight."

"Damn, what a coincidence. I was thinking about the same thing."

"How many positions did you come up with?"

"Uh, at least twelve so far."

"Twelve? Is that all you can think of? You're gonna have to get a bit more creative, aren't you?"

Jaylin slid his hands down, cupping my ass. "Talk like that is liable to get you hurt, messing with me. When I start getting more creative, I don't want to hear your mouth, okay?"

"That's fine with me. I'm game for whatever you are."

We pecked lips, and when the DJ kicked up the music, Jaylin and I left the dance floor. I felt my hair sliding down, so I went to the bathroom to fix it,\ and to wipe the sweat from my forehead.

As I looked in the mirror and tried to style my hair, it was no surprise when Felicia came in after me. She stood right next to me, looking in the mirror as well. Another chick in the bathroom complimented my jumpsuit, and that, of course, sparked a conversation I didn't want to have.

"Thank you," I said.

"Do you mind telling me where you got it?" she asked.

"I bought it at Saks Fifth Avenue. It's been a while, so I doubt that they'll have any more."

Felicia snickered and then interrupted. "You mean Jaylin bought it, right?" She looked at the chick who'd paid me the compliment. "He's the, uh, the brotha out there with the movie star effect. And girl, he is loaded with money. Unfortunately, a lot of his money is spent on trash."

The chick looked at Felicia and me, then walked out of the bathroom. We seemed to have the attention of everyone in the bathroom.

I gave her a dirty look that could kill. "You know, Felicia, I had hoped to avoid you tonight. Why, every time I see you, must you show your ass?"

"You mean the same ass your man can't keep his eyes off of tonight?"

"Him and every other damn man up in here that you've opened up your legs to. You need to grow up and chill out."

"You ain't exactly no saint now, bitch. From what I hear, when it comes to your relationship, you're hanging on by threads. So look around you tonight. You just might see your replacement up in here. And from all the attention Jaylin's getting, you'd better get him home before he slips away. You and I both know how easy he can get away from you, right?"

"I don't worry about tramps like you, Felicia. You or any of these other women up in here that keep staring at me,"—I looked around, as I knew I had some haters—"y'all will never have what I have. And even after four years with him, he never gave his heart to you, so get over it and keep on fucking his friends like you do so well."

Feeling the drama about to go down, I walked out. I searched for Jaylin and found him leaned up against the wall, talking to this very attractive chick who looked too much like Nokea. I walked up and told him I was ready to go.

"In a minute," he said. She grabbed his hand and pulled him toward her.

I snatched his hand away from hers. "I'm ready to go now!" I yelled. "If you want to stay, go ahead and stay. I'll see you at home."

He yelled right back at me. "I said in a minute! Now, cool out!"

I stormed away from Jaylin and headed for the

door. Mr. Sexy jumped in front of me and halted my steps.

"Are you leaving?" he asked.

"Yes."

"Can I go with you?"

"No, but you can take me home."

"My pleasure."

We walked out, and no sooner than he had turned on the chirper to unlock the doors to his Lexus, Jaylin came outside looking for me. When he saw me, I was just about ready to get in the car.

"Where in the fuck are you going?" he yelled.

"I told you I'm going home."

"You got two seconds to step away from his car, or I will kick your ass all over this parking lot."

I couldn't help but laugh to myself at how jealous he was. I looked at Mr. Sexy and thanked him for the offer.

"Any time." He smiled then got into his car and slowly drove off.

I got into Jaylin's truck. He glared at me like I was the one who had done something wrong.

"You was seriously about to get hurt," he said, closing the door for me, then entering on the driver's side.

"I told you I was ready to go, but you were too busy trying to find a replacement for me."

He cocked his head back. "What? I knew her from the shop."

I folded my arms and put my neck in action. "Whatever. I know I'm getting sick and tired of confrontations with your women. Everywhere I go, it's always something. And that bitch Felicia, I could just kill her ass. How could you even in-volve yourself with a woman so . . . so stupid?"

"I often ask myself the same question." He laughed and drove off the parking lot. "But don't let her get to you like that. You know what you got, and I ain't trying to be too confident, but that's just how it is being with a man like me. You gotta let a lot of that shit roll off your back."

"Just like you let the men who confronted me roll off your back, right?"

"Hey, I wasn't tripping. I knew one thing: you came to this motherfucker with me, and you were leaving with me. I didn't give a shit about who looked at you, bought you a drink, touched you, felt your ass, or licked your neck."

"Yes, you did. If that were the case, you wouldn't have tripped when that brotha kissed my hand, or when that one touched my backside. And if I had not asked you to come dance, that brotha was seconds away from being laid out on the floor."

He laughed, then put a frown on his face. "Who felt your ass in there? Nobody better not had touched your ass."

"Well, sorry you missed it. But I know for a fact the brotha I was going to leave with didn't stand a chance. I saw you looking at him like you wanted to mess him up."

"You got that shit right. I was about to fuck both of y'all up. Letting that nigga touch all on you like that. Had your eyes closed and every-thing, like you was thinking about him fucking you. I was gon' make sure you saw the light when you opened your eyes."

"Please. Just like you were going to kick my ass all over the parking lot too. You know you be talking more shit than anybody I know."

"Trust me, I ain't talking no shit. If I ever catch anybody tampering with my pussy, I'm killing his ass and your ass too."

We laughed and decided never to go clubbing together again. For some reason, he couldn't believe all the attention I got, and I never imagined it would be so crazy going out with him. The women simply didn't care if he was there with me. I could only imagine what would have happened if I wasn't there.

Jaylin hurried home. I barely made it to the door before he removed my jumpsuit from around my neck. We were still outside, my back against the door and my breasts in his mouth while he sucked them.

"Can't we go inside?" I said, squirming against the door.

He ignored me and continued sucking and massaging my breasts. My nipples were at full attention, and my body tingled all over. Jaylin placed his hand behind my head, pulling it toward him. He sucked my lips into his while rubbing his hands through my hair as we kissed. We smacked lips for what seemed like forever, and when he started in on my breasts again, I couldn't handle his touch. He could tell how anxious I was for him.

"Is my pussy wet yet?" he asked.

I nodded. "Dripping wet." I reached back and unzipped the lower part of my jumpsuit. It dropped to the ground, and I placed Jaylin's hand between my legs. "Is that wet enough for you?"

Jaylin closed his eyes and nodded as he touched deeply inside of me. "Let's go make this baby. I got a feeling he's coming tonight."

"She. Not he."

"Then I'll shoot for twins. How 'bout that?"

"Sounds like a plan to me."

Not being able to make it to his bedroom, we worked on our baby in the middle of the foyer. Eventually, we made it to his bedroom and worked even harder. Sex with Jaylin, without any doubt, was off the chain. Every time I thought our sex life couldn't get any better, it did. He came up with every possible position he could think of that night. It was never the same ole thing with him, and I admired a man who always stepped outside of the box, adding something new.

As for the baby, or babies, I couldn't believe I hadn't gotten pregnant yet. The doctor said everything was fine, but I couldn't understand why, after all of our efforts, there still was no baby. I wanted his child so badly, and I hoped more than anything the day would come for me to break the good news.

# 21

## *JAYLIN*

My life seemed to be back in order. And even though Nokea told me we couldn't go there again, I didn't take it personally because I knew she was trying to work out things with Collins. Still, I missed her, and the thoughts of what happened that day stayed on my mind.

As for the fellas, we were pretty tight again too. Stephon and Shane settled their differences, and I started to trust Stephon when he said he'd cooled out with the drugs. Ray-Ray said he wasn't cooling out for nobody, so he and I really didn't hang out as much as we used to. I wasn't trying to run his life, but I was concerned about him as well.

I tried to give Nanny B a break from the kids, so she and I spent the entire day together. I took her to Frances Day Spa in Clayton, bought her some items at Frontenac Plaza, we had dinner at Tony's on Market Street, and afterward, we went to the movies. Since she cut her vacation short to come back and see about me, she had another one planned already. She wouldn't tell me where she was going, but said she'd be gone for another two weeks. I made her promise to call us every day, and she promised she would.

After I dropped off Nanny B at the airport, I stopped by Mackenzie's school to see how she was doing. She was in kindergarten already, and looked like such a big girl as I watched her through the door. I didn't want to go in and interfere because the teacher seemed as if she had everything under control. Instead, I thought about how much happiness Mackenize had brought to my life. Since she had been a part of it, it had definitely changed. I visualized LJ's first day of school, wondering if he would grow up to be anything like me, praying that he would.

My thoughts quickly turned to Scorpio and me making a baby. It just wasn't happening. It puzzled the hell out of me that she could go to Denver for three months, have sex with another brotha, and get pregnant by him in an instant. Here I was, pumping all kinds of juices inside of her, and wasn't a damn thing happening. If I hadn't gotten Daisha pregnant, I would have thought something was wrong with me. Scorpio had been back and forth to the doctor and he said everything was fine. Maybe it just wasn't meant for us to have a child together. I wasn't sure, but something or somebody didn't want it to happen.

In the meantime, I enjoyed every doggone moment we spent trying to make our baby. Scorpio was every man's dream come true. She knew how to please a man way beyond his expectations. I'd never had a woman as good as her, pertaining to sex, and probably never would. It was just something about her insides that made a brotha like me go crazy. I was hooked like it wasn't funny, and there wasn't nothing she could do to make me feel any differently about her.

There had been times, though, that I wanted to kick her ass to the curb, but after a few days, or maybe even a few weeks, my ass got back to reality. And the reality of the situation was, I was pussy-whipped by her just as much as she was dick-whipped by me. Our love for one another played a big part as well, but my sexual desire for her overpowered everything. I couldn't speak for her, but that's simply how it was for a man like me.

Shane invited me over to check out his pad, so not having much to do, I stopped by. When I got there, I was shocked to see Felicia sitting on his couch. I asked if I should come back, but he insisted she was on her way out. She stood up and addressed me.

"Sorry I can't stay, but you could at least walk me to my car, can't you?" she said.

"Now, why would I want to walk you to your car?"

"Because I asked you nicely and I want to mention something to you."

I told Shane I'd be right back. I walked with Felicia downstairs to the parking garage. When we got to her car, she leaned against it. "Jaylin, I have to know something," she said, folding her arms.

"What's that?"

"Do you ever think about me?"

"All the time, Felicia."

"I mean in a good way."

"No."

"Not even a little bit?"

"No."

"So, you didn't think about me after you saw me at the club the other night?"

I rubbed my goatee, pretending to be in deep thought. "As a matter of fact, I did. I gazed at your ass several times and said now, that's a nice piece of ass right there."

She smiled. "And then what?"

"Oh, and then I said to myself that's the same plump, juicy ass that's been fucked by my cousin, one of my closest friends, and only Lord knows who else."

She shrugged. "So. You got a reputation too, you know? Besides, what does my being with other men have to do with us?"

"Nothing at all," I said, placing my hands in my pockets. "But I'm not at my best when I'm sexing a woman that my cousin has been with. I've made one exception, and I don't think it's in my best interest to make another one."

"So, are you saying we will never get a chance to sweat together like we used to?"

I thought about my previous sex sessions with Felicia and nodded. "We did used to work up a sweat, didn't we? So, who knows? Maybe in another lifetime."

"Maybe so," she said. She reached out for a hug and then jetted.

I went back upstairs to Shane's place. He was laid back on the couch, looking at TV. He quickly hopped up and stood next to me.

"Let me give you a quick overview of my place," he said, pointing his finger in several directions. "That's the kitchen. Right next to it is the dining room. My bedroom is in the middle of the floor, the bathroom is behind those bookshelves over there, and we're standing in the living room. And, oh yeah," he said, tapping my shoulder. "My art studio is behind those shelves over there too."

I observed the mid-size studio with approval. His place wasn't all that bad. It was a little too cramped for my taste, but I dug some of his contemporary furniture. "You cool, bro. You doing a whole lot better than I thought you would be."

"Where's the faith, man? Damn."

"I got it. But I don't know if I'm gonna keep it if you keep messing around with Felicia."

Shane sat on the couch and so did I. "Man, it ain't even like that. Felicia came over here right before you called. She wanted to tell me about this business she wants to start, and asked if I would be her partner."

"What kind of business?"

"Some type of architectural firm. You know she already works for one, and I guess she's trying to venture out on her own. Knowing how much I love art and design, she asked if I would be interested."

"If there's anything decent I can say about her ass, she is a woman who knows how to handle her business and make money."

"Yeah, I know. That's why I'm thinking it might not be a bad idea."

"You're right. It might not be."

"My only problem is I don't want to get involved with her again."

"Why not?"

"'Cause, Jay, she ain't nothing but trouble. You know she still fucking Stephon every once in a while, don't you?"

"No, I didn't know. I thought he was done with her."

"I thought he was too—until the other night. He took that ass home and plowed it."

"How do you know what he did with it?"

Shane sat up and cleared his throat. "'Cause I was in the other room doing my thang. I could hear what was going on."

"Whatever happened to a man's privacy? You motherfuckers are wild. I thought I was bad, but—"

"But my ass, Jay. If it wasn't for Scorpio, you would've been right along with us."

"Maybe so, but why everybody always got to fuck at Stephon's crib? Your place is nice enough for the ladies to come to."

"Only ladies who are special to me come up in here. Frankly, I don't like for everybody to know where I live."

I looked at Shane's bed and thought about his short time with Scorpio. "So, I guess Scorpio was kind of special to you, huh?"

I had caught Shane off guard. He paused and swallowed. "No offense, but I kind of liked her ass, man. You really got yourself an amazing woman. If you don't mind me saying, I momentarily checked her out the other night. Nobody fazed her but you. You could see the love in her eyes. And as for the sistas in there, there were some fine ones, but they couldn't touch her with a ten-foot pole. That had to make you feel good."

"What can I say other than I expect the best? Maybe she too bad for me, though, or maybe even too good."

"You lost me. What do you mean?"

Thinking about Nokea, I stood up and paced the floor. I had been very confused about my feelings for Scorpio and Nokea, and wasn't exactly sure which route to take. I leaned against Shane's bookshelf and put my hands in my pockets. "I don't know what's up with me, man. One minute I'm feeling for Nokea, and the next minute Scorpio is the best thing that ever happened to me. I'm confused, dog."

"I can't help you with that one because Nokea is a magnificent woman too. I'd love to be caught up with two women like them."

"And if you were, what would you do? If something inside nagged the fuck out of you about settling down for good, what would you consider?"

"I'd give myself six months without the two of them. No contact, no pussy, no dates, nothing. After that, whichever one of them I couldn't get out of my system, then that would be the one for me."

"That would never work for me. I couldn't even imagine being without either of them for six months, especially with the kids and everything."

"Hey, you asked what I would do, and I told you. You're the kind of person who will do whatever he wants, so—"

"You're right. So let's pop the Remy and drink to me making the right decision."

"Bet."

Shane and me kicked it at his place until nine o'clock that night. We ordered pizza and played a few hands of poker. He was an all right fella, and I was kind of glad I had someone else to kick it with since Stephon seemed to be choosing another path. When I called his house to see if he wanted to come by Shane's place, he said he had something else to do. He sounded kind of bitter about something, but I really didn't trip.

Before leaving Shane's crib, I called Scorpio to let her know I was on my way home. She said Mackenzie, her, and LJ had been out all day long and they were about to lay back and watch some movies. We exchanged the love, and I promised her I'd hurry home.

Late Monday night, Nokea stopped by to pick up LJ. I was downstairs working out. I rushed her out, as going to see my sister and brother in the morning was on my agenda. Nokea had gotten my sister's address and phone number at Stanley's funeral, and she gave it to me, so I called Delores to let her know I'd be stopping by in the morning. Up until recently, I was afraid of finding out more about Stanley, but it was either now or never.

In the morning, Scorpio and Mackenzie headed for school, and I headed out as well. We missed having Nanny B around; especially me, since I wasn't getting any home-cooked meals. Scorpio did her best to whip something together, but honestly, the shit she cooked made me want to throw up. When it came to Nanny B's cooking, I was spoiled and couldn't wait for her to come home.

My first stop was at my sister Delores' house. Again, I called to let her know I was on my way, hoping she'd tell me she had something to do. It was just my luck that she happily told me to come over, stressing how anxious she was to meet me. She said that she worked from home as an interior decorator. She was three years older than I was, so I knew if anybody had answers to my questions about Stanley, she would.

On the drive to her place, it puzzled me as to why I couldn't let the situation go. I thought after Stanley died I'd be able to put behind my concerns about him leaving me, but I couldn't. I'd even dreamed about him a few times, but in my dreams, we got along just fine.

When I arrived at Delores' house, an older lady smelling like gin and juice, whose hair was wrapped in a bun, answered the door. I knew Delores was younger, had gray eyes like mine, and had a darker complexion, so I asked for her.

"Come on in, Jaylin," the woman said. "Delores is expecting you. Have a seat on the couch and I'll go get her for you."

I sat down, and as I waited for Delores, I looked around the muggy and distastefully decorated room. I noticed two pictures of Stanley hanging on the wall and a whole bunch of other pictures crookedly hung as well. For Delores to be an interior decorator, I found the room to be quite old fashioned and tacky. The couch was made out of an itchy-feeling plaid fabric. Two old-timey leather recliners with rips in them were next to the couch, and an old floor model TV was in the far corner. Figurines cluttered the place, and the green fuzzy carpet didn't match a damn thing.

Delores came in covering her mouth. She got emotional as she held out her arms for a hug. I hugged her, but I guess I was not as excited as she was, so I quickly let go.

"Jaylin Rogers," she said, staring at me. "Boy, you know you look a lot like our father."

I took a seat and so did she. "I've been told that I look a lot like my mother. What I can remember, I think I look like my mother."

"Well, we only have one picture of your mother. You do look like her, but Stanley made you."

Still disagreeing, I kept quiet.

"So, tell me something about yourself," she said, giddy as ever. "At Daddy's funeral, I met your girlfriend, your son, your daughter, and your son's mother. My niece and nephew are some of the cutest children I have ever seen."

"Thanks, but, uh, there really isn't much to know about me. I don't work, I don't really like to do anything, and I love my kids."

"Well, I barely work, I'm not married, I don't have any kids, and I love my family. That was my mother who answered the door. I guess you know that her and Stanley was never married either."

"Actually, no, I didn't know. You see, I'm trying to find out how or where did all y'all fit in? I never even knew I had a brother and sister until he died. Did y'all know about me?"

"Yes, we did. But I'm gon' call Mama in here to

talk to you." She turned around and yelled, "Mama! Come here for a minute." Her mother came in and stood in the doorway. "First of all, would you tell Jaylin how much he looks like Stanley?"

Her mother walked further into the room and sat in one of the raggedy recliners. She stared at me, taking a sip from her mug. "Yes, honey, you sholl look like the Stanley I remember. He was a fine young man, but I'll be the first to tell you that y'all's daddy wasn't worth a damn!"

"Mama, don't go telling Jaylin any bad stuff about Stanley. From what I can tell, he didn't seem to like him that much."

"It's not that I didn't like him," I said in my defense. "It's that I really didn't know him like I thought I did. I never understood why he walked out on my moms and left me."

"Jaylin, my name is Ursula. Ursula Blackstone. Stanley walked out on you and your mother like he walked out on me and my two babies 'cause he was a punk!"

Delores defended Stanley again and cut her eyes at Ursula. "Mama, don't be talking about Daddy like that. You know he had issues."

"We all had issues, chile! I always tell it like it is, and if don't nobody like it, to hell wit' 'em. I never understood why you always took up for that fool, especially after how he treated us." She looked back at me, and I could tell the alcohol was brewing. "Jaylin, I met yo' daddy first. When I got pregnant with Delores, he ran off and got with yo' mama. They got married, and then you came along. That fool ran back and forth between the both of us. I got pregnant again, and he did what he knew best—ran out! When yo' mama got killed, we got back together, and two months later, his butt was gone again, this time for good. Nobody had heard from him in years."

I was interested in what Ursula had to say. I sat up while clutching my hands together. "Did anybody know where he went? I mean . . . at my mother's funeral, he told me that everything would be cool. He said we'd still be a family, even with Mama being gone. I believed him, but next thing I knew, I was in an orphanage."

"Baby, you for damn sure were in a better place than us. If somebody had taken my babies and me in, I would've let 'em. At the time, we didn't have a pot to piss in or a window to throw it out of. This one right here," she said, pointing to Delores, "almost died on me one day from being so hungry. I didn't have no money, and Stanley promised me the world. I quit school to be with him, and without an education, who in the hell was gon' hire me? It was pitiful!

"Your brother, Jeffrey, he suffered the most. He wanted his father in his life so bad, but there wasn't nothing I could do. Then, I guess about five or six years ago, Stanley decided to show up. Show up for what? That's what I wanted to know. My kids were grown and didn't nobody need him. Delores kept in touch with him, but Jeffrey refused to fool with Stanley after what he did to us."

Delores turned to me and held my hand with hers. "What Mama really trying to say, Jaylin, is stop blaming yourself for what Stanley did. Jeffrey blamed himself for a long time too, but I know deep in my heart that us being born wasn't the reason Daddy walked away. I spoke to him personally about it, and he said he just didn't know how to be a man. He was afraid of his responsibilities and he didn't have enough money to take care of y'all's household and ours.

"I thank God for giving me the strength to make peace with him, but I understand how you and Jeffrey feel too. If you really think about it, Jaylin, you were better off than all of us were."

"You damn right he was!" Ursula said, wiping her tears. "I never understood how one man could cause all these people so much hurt. I'm telling you that man was the devil, and I hope he's gone straight to hell."

"Mama, don't go getting all upset about this—and you shouldn't say mean things like that. It's in the past now, and it's just time for all of us to forgive Stanley and move on."

I couldn't believe that I had found someone else who obviously hated Stanley more than me. "I agree about moving on," I said, standing up.

"You're not getting ready to go already, are you?" Delores asked.

"Yeah. I don't want to take up any more of your time. I appreciate both of y'all taking the time to talk to me."

"There will be no such thing as you leaving so soon," Ursula said, standing up. "Take off your shoes and relax. That's if your feet don't stink. Let me cook y'all something to eat. I apologize for letting that fool upset me."

I laughed and looked down at my shoes. "No, really, I can't stay."

"Why? 'Cause your feet stink? With a sharp pair of shoes like those, they betta not be stinking."

"Mama, cool out," Delores said. "Come on and stay, Jaylin. We have so much more to talk about, other than Stanley."

I hesitated for another moment and sat back down. "Okay, but just for a little while."

Ursula Blackstone was my kind of woman. She cracked me the fuck up. I wound up staying a lot longer than I'd anticipated, and we all talked for hours about our families, friends, careers, and even more about Stanley. I didn't know I had so many other relatives. I laughed at the many pictures they'd shown me of some of the ugliest people I'd ever seen.

By five o'clock, I did kick off my shoes. And instead of us going over to Jeffrey's place, he came over with his wife and daughter. At first, we didn't say much to each other, but when Ursula told the same story about how Stanley abandoned everybody, Jeffrey definitely had something to say. He was just as bitter as I was, and the hurt of not having a father around showed on his face.

Thing is, though, they really did have it a lot tougher than me. I couldn't imagine some of the things they had gone through, and I realized that everything had worked out for the best.

As eight o'clock neared, I decided to call it a night. Ursula got out her camera to take pictures of us. We all resembled each other in many ways, but the one thing that stood out the most was everybody's gray eyes and thick eyebrows. They called me a white boy since I was the lightest and both of them were a chocolate brown.

I asked Ursula to send me a photo in the mail so I could show it off. I promised to keep in touch and encouraged them to do the same. Before I left, Jeffrey offered to walk me out to my car.

"This is nice, Jaylin," he said, touching the hood of my Navigator.

"Yeah, I just got it not too long ago."

He nodded and reached out his hand. "It was good seeing you, my brotha. We've been strangers for too long, so be sure to keep in touch."

"Will do," I said, reaching for his hand to grab it.

He gave me a hug and pat on my back. "Love you," he said.

He caught me completely off guard, and after I hesitated for a moment, I responded. "I love you too."

Jeffrey watched as I got in my truck and drove off.

I must have smiled the entire way home as I thought about the Blackstone family. They were some of the most genuine, funny, and caring people I'd ever met. During the whole time with them, I felt the love. It proved to me that with Stanley being in our lives or not, his three children turned out to be just fine.

# 22

## *NOKEA*

Collins and I slowly but surely worked our way back to each other. He'd taken me to dinner the other night, and afterward, we went to his house and made love. I was so happy to be back in his arms, and this time, Mr. Jaylin was not going to interfere. I'd been playing him off like crazy. I wasn't trying to be mean or anything, but we both really needed to move on with our lives.

Jaylin called the other day and told me about his newly found family. I was really happy for him. When he asked if I would meet them, I told him I'd already done so at Stanley's funeral. Jaylin wanted more, but I felt as if I didn't want to intrude on Scorpio's territory. Since she planned on being his wife, she was the one who needed to know his family. Besides, I didn't want Collins tripping with me. He wasn't cool with Jaylin coming to the house to get LJ, he wasn't cool with me going to Jaylin's house to pick him up, and he sure in the heck wasn't cool with us spending hours on the telephone.

Jaylin wasn't too happy about my sudden distance, but I wanted to make sure I wasn't going to be left behind. I truly felt as if the day was near for him to break the news about Scorpio and him getting married. On occasion, I even talked to her, and she couldn't stop talking about how they were putting forth every effort to make a baby. Under the circumstances, my feelings were hurt. I knew the times he and I shared together were coming to an end—if they hadn't already.

Early Sunday morning, I sent Mama to Jaylin's house to get LJ so he could go to church with her and Daddy. Right after they left, Jaylin rang my phone. I already knew what his gripe was about because we'd argued about Mama picking up LJ the night before.

"So, are you going to avoid me for the rest of your life?" he asked.

"No. I told you I'm trying to work out things with Collins. Can't you understand?"

"Yeah, I understand. I understand that he's running shit over there. It doesn't make sense that you're refusing to come to my house because he's insecure."

"Wouldn't you be? I'm not saying I'm never coming over there again. All I'm saying is right now it's not a good idea."

"What about my family?"

"What about your family, Jaylin?"

"I'd like for you to get to know them. Our family

reunion is coming up, and I'd like for you and LJ to go."

"LJ can go, but I can't. Besides, isn't Scorpio going?"

"Yes."

"Then why do you need me to go?"

"Because you're the mother of my child and I want you to be there."

"But I'm not family, Jaylin. If I were going to be your wife, then yes, I would love to go. That position is already taken, so cool out, all right?"

"Nokea, you and I have always been there for each other, no matter what. Don't let anyone take that away from us, okay? All I'm saying is think about it. Scorpio doesn't mind. I already told her you were going. Clear the shit up with your man and let me know.

"This is not about you and me, baby. This is about LJ getting to know his relatives. Some day, if I'm not around, I want you and him to be close to my family. Now, is there anything wrong with that?"

"I guess not, but we'll see. Let me think about it."

"Think hard," he said, and then hung up.

Once again, I was in a tough situation. I wanted to do this for LJ and Jaylin's sake, but there was no way Collins would agree. He'd be uncomfortable with the whole thing, and I didn't want him to feel that way. If I didn't tell him about my desire to go, then I stood the chance of him finding out that I'd gone behind his back. Honesty was so important to him, so I decided to mention it to Collins later on at his place.

I arrived at Collins' place around four o'clock. He whipped up a pot of spaghetti and leaned over to give me a kiss while he stirred. I asked if I could help, and when he insisted he didn't want my help, I sat at the kitchen table, watching my adorable man in an apron. He poured two glasses of Moët and sat next to me with a glass in his hand.

"Let's drink to new beginnings," he said. Our glasses clinked and I took a few sips from mine.

"I'm so happy we worked this out. You have no idea how much I've missed this," I confirmed.

"Oh, yes, I do," he said, standing up. He walked back over to the stove, continuing to prepare our food. I got up and wrapped my arms around his chest. I laid my head against his back, closing my eyes in deep thought.

After Collins finished dinner, he set the table for two, dimmed the lights, and lit two tall vanilla candles. He held my hands from across the table and we looked at each other through the flames.

"I want you to be with me forever," he said. "With everything that's going on in Detroit, my partners decided that one of us should be there on a regular basis. I haven't made a decision yet, but there's a possibility it's going to be me. If so, I want you to move with me."

There was silence. I didn't know what to say about his sudden news. "But . . . but you said months ago that you wasn't going to move. St. Louis is home for me, Collins, and I can't make you any promises right now."

"Then don't. I'm just telling you if I decide to go, it'll be soon."

"How soon?"

"Two months, or maybe three. I'd love to stay here, baby, but my partners and I came too far to let our business go down the drain."

"Well, why can't one of them go?"

"Curtis, his wife has cancer and she's getting her treatments here. And Kenny, he's got three young kids that go to school here, and a wife who loves her job. Me, I wouldn't have to make as many sacrifices if I decide to move."

"What about LJ and me? Are you willing to lose us?"

"Not in a million years. That's why I want you to come with me. You can always come back to St. Louis to visit."

"Collins, it's not that easy. I can't walk away from my family like that. And my job? Lord knows I'll never find a job making as much money as I make right now. I recently got another promotion and I'm happy with it."

"Your parents can visit us, and you can always come back to visit them. As for your job, baby, I have plenty of money to take care of us. It isn't important for you to make a lot of money. You can get a part-time job, if that makes you happy. Hell, stay at home and tend to LJ for all I care. I just want you with me, that's all."

Thinking about it, I closed my eyes and rubbed my temples. I didn't want to move away, but I loved Collins too much to let him go alone. I opened my eyes and rubbed my hair back. "How long are you going to give me to decide?"

"How long do you need?"

"I don't know," I said, standing up. I wasn't

hungry anymore, because something else had come to mind. I leaned against the counter and folded my arms. "Baby, all I can think about is that darn agreement I gave to Jaylin months ago. Do you remember what it said?"

"Yes. It said if you left St. Louis within the next five to ten years, he'd get custody of LJ."

"That's right. And I'm not going to give up my child to him that easily."

"You don't have to. Trust me, my lawyer would make sure that didn't happen."

"I don't want any lawyers getting involved. There has to be a better way."

Collins walked over to me, as he saw how upset I got. "Calm down, baby. We'll come up with something, okay?" He gave me a hug and kissed my forehead.

After his news, I wasn't in the mood to do anything but go home and sort through my feelings. There I was thinking about this darn family reunion, and I was now faced with a decision like this. I didn't want to let Collins go alone, but what was I going to do about LJ? Collins knew I'd never leave my son behind, and battling this out in court would mean hell for everyone. All Jaylin had was a stupid notarized letter signed by him and me, and witnessed by our attorneys. I wasn't sure if that would even hold up in court, but I didn't want to take any chances. Still, I promised Collins I'd give my attorney a call in the morning. Before I did anything else, I wanted to find out if Jaylin even remembered me making such a stupid agreement. I knew it would come back to haunt me, but what could I do about it now?

On Monday, I took an extended lunch break to go see Jaylin. I called to tell him I was coming over, and when I got there, he was chilling around back by the swimming pool. He wore a white wifebeater, some blue jean shorts, and dark sunglasses. He flipped through a magazine and tossed a ball to Barbie so she could catch it.

When I asked where everybody was, he said Mackenzie and Scorpio were at school, and Nanny B had gone to the grocery store. He invited me in, but since it was so beautiful outside, I sat next to him on one of the plush lawn chairs.

"You look nice," he said, checking me out in my soft pink pantsuit.

"Thanks." I squinted at the sun shining in my face. "Is this what retirement allows you to do all day long?"

"Yep. And when I got something on my mind, I like to come out here and chill."

"What's on your mind?"

"It doesn't matter, but why are you here?"

"I came to tell you I'm not going to your family reunion. Again, if you want to take LJ, feel free. I think you know as well as I do that I have no business going with you."

Jaylin laid the magazine on the ground and avoided looking at me. He scooted back on the lawn chair and placed his hands behind his head. "That's cool. I figured you wouldn't go."

"Please don't be mad at me. I just need time to work on my relationship first."

"I thought you and Collins had already worked things out."

"I thought we did too, but Collins wants to move

to Detroit. I'm not sure if I'm going with him or not."

Jaylin was silent as he stroked his goatee. He whistled for Barbie to come to him, and threw the ball again. He leaned back in the lawn chair and cleared his throat. "When you move, make sure you bring LJ to me," he said casually.

"Who says I'm moving?"

"Your man says so. He's got you under his wing right now, making you feel all guilty and shit about having sex with me, so you'll go. And I don't care if you go. Just know that according to our agreement, my son stays right here with me."

"I said that I haven't decided anything. And don't be so nonchalant about this. I remember what our agreement said."

He removed his sunglasses and looked straight in my eyes. "Good. I hope you do remember; that way I don't have to look like the villain when you don't have your child."

His words stung and angered me. I cut my eyes at him and snapped, "That's not going to happen and you know it."

"Yes, it is. And you want to know why, Nokea?" I looked down to fidget with my nails. "You're going to lose out on everything because Collins is playing you for a fool. His decision to move to Detroit all of a sudden is to get you as far away from me as possible. It is a weak move on his part, and I can't believe you've fallen for his bullshit."

"That's not what this is about. His business is in turmoil and he has to go take care of it."

Jaylin gave me a hard stare. "Don't be no fool, okay? Now, if you don't mind, I'd like to continue with my thoughts—alone. It's been almost two weeks since I had to disrespect anybody, so please don't be the one to break my record."

I stood up. Just as I got ready to leave, Scorpio slid the patio door open and walked over by us. After she gave me a shitty hello, she leaned down, giving Jaylin a mouthwatering kiss.

"Hey, baby," she said, ignoring me. "Guess what I got today?"

"What?" he said. His whole attitude had changed that fast.

Excited, she opened a small bag and pulled out a pregnancy test. "My period is three days late and we might have ourselves something in the oven."

"Now, that's what I'm trying to hear." He pecked Scorpio on the lips and looked at me. "Do you mind?"

"No, I was just leaving."

I said good-bye to Scorpio and left.

See, that was the kind of mess that made me want to move as far away from him as possible. One minute he was on, and the next minute he was off. If his plans were to have a baby with Scorpio and marry her, then why couldn't he just allow my son and me to move on and do our thing? Sometimes I hated that he was LJ's father. He was too darn controlling and always had to have everything his way. This time, if I decided to go to Detroit with Collins, I was going to put up a fight!

# 23

## *SCORPIO*

My pregnancy test showed a big fat negative. I was truly disappointed, and so was Jaylin. He was pissed about me getting him all hyped up, but with the nauseated feeling inside of my stomach and my delayed period, I thought this time was it. I thought the test might have been wrong, but it proved not to be when I got my period five days later. Again, I hadn't a clue what was wrong, but as I lay in bed with my head resting on Jaylin's shoulder, I suggested maybe something was wrong with him. Of course, he corrected me.

"Ain't a damn thing wrong with me," he said, holding me as we watched TV.

"How do you know?"

"Because I just know. Simone, Nokea, or Daisha didn't have no problems."

"I know they didn't, but how do you really know Daisha's baby was yours? You'd only known her for a short time, so what made you trust her when she said the baby was yours?"

"I don't know. I just did. Besides, when I saw my son, I knew he was mine. There was no denying him."

Frustrated, I got up and walked outside on the balcony. I looked up at the sky and silently prayed for a baby. Shortly after, Jaylin came out on the balcony with me. He stood with his hands in his pockets and looked up at the sky as well.

"I guess that's all we can do is pray, huh? If it's meant to be, then I guess it'll happen," he said.

"I hope it will. I know how much you want a baby, and I feel so bad that for whatever reason, I can't give you one."

"Don't stress yourself about it, okay? Believe it or not, I'm more concerned about you putting your ring back on. Seems like ever since you took it off, we've had a streak of bad luck in our relationship. Why don't you put it back on and let's try to start this all over."

I smiled and wrapped my arms around his waist. I laid my head against his chest and rubbed it. "Go get my ring so I can proudly wear it. This time, I promise you, no more lies, no more secrets, no more anything. I want this to work out between us, and I'm not going to give up on us having a baby."

Jaylin and I went back into the bedroom. He pulled the ring out of a drawer and placed it back on my finger. I vowed that things would get better between us, and so did he.

That promise was short-lived because the next day, things started to get heated. Mackenzie was at school and Jaylin had taken Nanny B to get to know Delores and Ursula. I was offended because he hadn't even offered to take me, but I got tired of griping about every single thing. Not saying that my gripes weren't legitimate, but I knew Jaylin would figure out a way to make my concerns invalid. Either way, Nanny B was just the nanny, so why was it so important for her to get to know his family better? I wasn't trying to hate, but it seemed that my competition was right in this house.

I felt foolish for comparing myself to an old woman like Nanny B, but it was hard not to. She had control over him; he listened to her, and he rarely ever raised his voice at her. He showed her more love than he did anyone. I didn't like it one bit, but again, it was something I just had to live with.

Instead of having a pity party, I decided to whip up dinner for everyone. I didn't have any classes, so I thought about helping Nanny B out so she didn't have to cook. I put on her apron, and opened the fridge to see what was inside. I pulled out some pork chops and placed them on the counter. Then I opened the cabinet and saw some macaroni. I went back to the fridge to see if we had some cheese. We did, so I removed the cheese from the fridge, along with some collard greens and crescent dinner rolls.

As soon as I put the macaroni on the stove to boil, the doorbell rang. I saw Stephon on the porch, and immediately opened the door.

"Hey, Stephon," I said. He spoke back and walked in without being invited. He wore a blue striped shirt that was unbuttoned and showed his white T-shirt underneath. It was neatly tucked into his well-pressed jeans that fit his muscular body well. His hazelnut eyes searched the room.

"Is Jaylin here?" he asked.

"No, but he should be back soon," I said, moseying back into the kitchen. He followed.

I sat at the table, picking the collard greens. While watching me, Stephon leaned against the kitchen's doorway and lightly rubbed his bald head.

"Do you know where he is?" he asked.

"Him, Nanny B, and Mackenzie went over to his sister's place."

"You say soon, but how soon will they be coming back?"

I shrugged. "Maybe by four o'clock. You can wait if you'd like."

Stephon pulled back a chair and sat at the table with me. We really didn't have much to talk about, and I was uncomfortable again with the way he lustfully looked at me.

"Can I get you anything to eat or drink while you wait?" I asked.

"I'd like something to *eat*, but, uh, if there are any sodas in the fridge, I'll take one."

I got up to get Stephon a Pepsi and set it on the table in front of him. Knowing that he never had a problem going into the fridge to get it himself, I reminded him that this house was just like his house.

"I know, and Jaylin has always made it clear that what's his is mine. I just wanted to check out a li'l something from behind," he said, grinning.

I swallowed the huge lump in my throat. I could tell where this conversation was going. Still, I wanted to know where Stephon was coming from. It was always good to know when I had to watch my back. "Check out something like what?" I inquired.

He leaned back in the chair and placed his hand over the hump in his pants. "Something like . . . do you mind if I tell you how your body turns me the fuck on?"

"I'm really sorry that it does, because there's nothing I can do about it. From now on, please keep your comments to yourself. Maybe Jaylin doesn't mind, but I do."

"You're right, because he doesn't mind. He told me to have at it any time I wanted to."

"Well, I don't care what he said. I'm not going to be put on display by him or anybody else. Now, if you don't mind, either you can change the subject, or I'll have to ask you to leave. "

Stephon defensively held out his hands. "Hey, subject changed. In the meantime, I was wondering how things were going with you and Nokea."

My tone was dry. Stephon had definitely pissed me off. "Everything is fine with Nokea and me. Why do you ask?"

"I mean, are you still cool with Jaylin having sex with her? They've been tight for a real long time, and I wasn't sure if—"

I huffed and laid the greens on the table. "Stephon, why don't you leave? I don't know what kind of trouble you're trying to cause, but your lies will get you nowhere with me."

"Lies? Who says I'm lying? You can ask Jaylin for yourself. He won't lie to you because he's not the kind of man who would lie. And if he does, which you know is rare, you'd instantly know it. He'll cock his head back and say, *what?* And pretend that he doesn't hear you."

I rolled my eyes, ready for Stephon to leave. "Thanks for your advice. Now, is there anything else? I'd like to have dinner ready before he comes home."

"Yes, there's one more thing." He stood up and placed his hand on the side of my face. "For the record, Jaylin still loves Nokea. I, on the other hand, am digging the shit out of you. I keep visualizing myself fucking the shit out of you, and you, pretty lady, are settling for less when you don't give me the opportunity. If you ever need me, and I do mean ever, you know where to find me."

I moved his hand away from my face and stood up. "Not interested—at all."

He winked and walked out of the kitchen. When I heard the front door close, I took a deep breath and dropped back in the chair. Stephon knew better than to come to me like that. I didn't care what anybody said; that brotha had it out for my baby. Every time I'd mention to Jaylin that I didn't like Stephon's comments, he'd tell me Stephon was just playing. When I reminded him about Nokea, then Jaylin would say, "Stephon knows better and would never cross the line again." To me, it didn't seem as if he knew better. Had I dropped my panties, he would have torn into me. Still, I didn't want to stir up any trouble between them, so I decided not to tell Jaylin. Besides, he'd blow it off anyway. He was so happy about his "new family" and I didn't want to do anything to disrupt the wonderful behavior he'd been displaying lately.

When Mackenzie came rushing through the kitchen door with her backpack on, I was putting the finishing touches on dinner. She picked up Barbie and reached for a dinner roll on the table.

"Go wash your hands first," I yelled. She put the roll in her mouth and ran out of the kitchen. Nanny B and Jaylin came in, talking loudly about his folks. When they saw dinner on the table, both of them quickly shushed. Nanny B walked around the table and smiled as she looked at the food. Jaylin stood, rubbing his goatee with an unsure look on his face.

"Can I get a thank you?" I said.

"We–well, it looks good," Nanny B stuttered. "It looks to me as if you did a remarkable job."

"Thank you," I said, and then turned to look at Jaylin. "So, are you going to just stand there or what?"

"It ain't gon' jump out at me if I sit down, is it?" he said.

"Let's hope not," I said.

We all sat down, and when Mackenzie came back, Nanny B blessed the food and we got busy. Everything tasted fine to me, but when I looked up, I saw that after biting into a pork chop, everybody's eyes were roaming. When Jaylin bit into one, he closed his eyes; Mackenzie frowned at the food, and Nanny B cleared her throat. Jaylin scooped up a spoonful of macaroni and cheese, and after taking one scoop, I guess that was enough for him. He spat it into a napkin, wiped his mouth, and stood up.

"That's it for me. I'm going to White Castle. Anybody else want something?"

"Baby, quit playing. It is not that bad," I said.

"Like hell! I'm sorry, baby, but this shit will kill us. What did you do?"

I looked at Nanny B. "Is it that bad, Nanny B? Please be honest."

"Well, chile," she said, beating around the bush. "It's kind of got a little—"

"It's horrible and too salty," Mackenzie said. She lowered her plate. When Barbie ran up to it, Jaylin yelled.

"Mackenzie! Don't you give Barbie that food. She'll be laid out if you do."

They all laughed. Finding nothing funny, I sat with my arms folded.

"Come on, y'all," I said. "I can't believe my cooking is that bad. Now, I admit, it doesn't taste like Nanny B's cooking, but it ain't as bad as y'all say it is either."

Jaylin ignored me. "Like I said before, does anybody want some White Castle?"

"Why get White Castle when I cooked this food?" I stood up, walked over to the refrigerator, and took out the German chocolate cake I'd baked. "I even baked a cake. I know this is the bomb, so y'all better at least eat this."

Mackenzie got all hyped up, but before she could dive into it, Jaylin stopped her.

"Please let me be the brave one here. I don't want you to hurt yourself," he said to Mackenzie. He took a fork and cut into it. When he put it into his mouth, he closed his eyes and chewed. Seconds later, he slowly opened them. "You should be ashamed of yourself. Please get me a glass of water before I choke on this."

"But—"

"But my ass!" he yelled with the cake in his mouth. He gagged. "Get me some water!"

Nanny B rushed to get him some water, and after he spat the cake in the trashcan, he wiped his mouth, eyeballing me. "Are you trying to kill us or something?"

"Jaylin, there is nothing wrong with this cake." I took a bite, and after I spat it in the trashcan, I smiled. "Okay, so I messed up the cake."

"You messed up the whole damn dinner." He laughed. "But the thought was sweet of you."

"Really, it was," Nanny B said. "Next time, though, you and I can do it together so I can figure out what you're doing wrong."

"Hopefully there won't be no next time," Jaylin said. "Scorpio should be banned from the kitchen cooking like that."

"More like thrown in jail," Nanny B said, adding her two cents. We all laughed, and when Jaylin suggested going to pick up dinner at Sweetie Pie's on West Florissant Avenue, I offered to go with him. Nanny B stayed and cleaned up the kitchen with Mackenzie's help.

I changed clothes, Jaylin grabbed the keys to his Navigator, and we jetted. No sooner than we got inside, he was all over me about an empty 7-Up can I left in the cup holder.

"All I'm saying is throw the damn can away once you're finished with it. What purpose does it serve in the holder if it's empty?"

"None. But is it going to kill you by being there?"

"Yes. And so are those scuff marks from your shoes all on the edge over there. I spent too much money on this truck for it to be messed up."

"Damn, Jaylin! How is an empty can and one little black scuff mark going to mess up this truck?"

"One soda can could turn into two or three cans. One mark can turn into more marks. If you gon' drive my shit, just take care of it, all right? The only thing that needs to be in here is your ass in that seat. That's it."

"Whatever. Just drive the damn thing and get your food. Haven't you picked on me enough already?"

"I wasn't picking on you. I thanked you for cooking, thanked you for the effort, and thanked you for not killing us."

"You're welcome. And before I forget to tell you, Stephon stopped by earlier to see you."

"I told that fool I wasn't going to be there. What did he want?"

"He didn't say."

"That's cool. I'll give him a call later."

I was quiet for a moment, as I tried to lead up to asking him about Nokea. I waited until after we left Sweetie Pie's with three bags of food before I asked him.

"Say, have you heard from Nokea lately?" I asked.

"Nope."

"So, she hasn't said anything else about the family reunion?"

"Nope."

"Hmm." I paused. "Well, when she came by the house the other day, what did she want?"

"She wanted to tell me about her plans to move to Detroit."

I widened my eyes in shock. "What? She's moving to Detroit?"

"She might."

"What about LJ?"

"What about him?"

"I'm sure he's moving with her."

"Not in a trillion years."

"So, I guess in so many words, that's what you told her?"

Jaylin reached over and patted my lap. "I love the way you read my mind. Had she only done that before she came over, she could have saved both of us some time."

"You and her have really been through a lot. After all y'all been through, it amazes me that y'all can still be such good friends."

"Yep."

"Or am I missing something? You aren't still sexually involved with her, are you?"

He took his eyes off the road and cocked his head back. "*What?*" he said, as if he didn't hear me.

"I said the two of you aren't still intimately involved, are you?"

"Nope. It's been a very long time since we've been down that road."

"Your idea of a very long time and my idea are two different things. So, when's the last time you had sex with Nokea?"

He immediately got defensive. "What's with all the questions, Scorpio? I'm not in no mood to discuss Nokea."

"Hey, I just asked. Don't get all bent out of shape about it."

"Then case closed. Trust me, there's nothing for you to worry about."

I left the situation alone because I already had my answer. This bastard was still fucking around with Nokea! After all we'd been through, he was still running back to her for sex. I couldn't believe it. And I had Stephon to thank for telling me the truth. I didn't say anything else to Jaylin that night. When we got home, I felt sick to my stomach and couldn't even eat. Instead, I went downstairs and thought hard about making some changes in our relationship.

# 24

## *JAYLIN*

Having three important appointments, I left the house around eight-thirty in the morning. My first stop was to go see my attorney, Mr. Frick, about this bullshit with LJ. I had a feeling Nokea and Collins' stupid asses were up to no good, so it was in my best interest to get a move on things.

Collins was what I called a straight-up punk-ass, weak brotha. He couldn't even stay here and fight for his own damn woman because he was afraid of losing her to me. What he didn't know was if I truly wanted to, I'd take Nokea away from him in a heartbeat. There was no doubt in my mind she would leave him to be with me, but I wasn't trying to go there. Now, though, I wasn't sure what the hell I would do. I wasn't as worried about LJ, because at the end of the day, I knew he wasn't going anywhere.

After sitting with Frick for hours, he pretty much gave me all the confirmation I needed. He told me that as soon as they made a move, be sure to let him know. I intended to do just that, as well as let that punk, Collins, know how I felt about the whole damn thing. He'd called me on my shit before by coming to my office that day with Nokea, so it was only fair I called him on his shit.

I had another stop to make before going to see him. Apparently, Stanley had a life insurance policy. I'd gotten a letter from his attorney the other day, asking me to come to his office. When I got there, I had a long wait. Being the impatient brotha that I am, I was about to leave when he came out of his office and invited me in.

Stanley's attorney was an older black man, kind of on the chubby side, bald, and couldn't even talk right. He rambled on and on about Stanley. Really not trying to hear all the mumbo jumbo, I suggested he get to the point. He gave me a letter. I opened it and read:

> *My son, if you're reading this, I guess you know I'm gone. It's not by choice, but as usual, God had his way. I wanted to tell you that even though we never had a father and son relationship, you were always in my prayers. There wasn't a day that went by I didn't think about you.*
>
> *After your mama died, I was lost, man. I didn't have much to offer you, or anybody for that matter, so I thought it would be best if I just went away. I knew you'd do all right for yourself because you were that kind of kid. You used to always take charge and stand up for yourself when you felt something wasn't*

*right. Standing up might have gotten your butt spanked several times, but I admired you for having the courage to do so.*

*Courage, you see, is something I never had. I didn't know how to fight for what was mine, or for what I wanted. I bailed out, son, just as I did on everybody else. You have every right to hate me, because I deserve it. But hating me isn't going to give you the peace of mind you deserve.*

*I hope by now you're starting to see the picture. I loved you, Delores, and Jeffrey, but I know my way of loving you all wasn't nearly enough. It was, however, at the time, the best I could give. As for the money, it was the least I could do. I don't even know if you're going to accept it, because that's the kind of man I know you are. If you decide to take it, please put it to good use. I chose you because, out of all my children, I always felt as if you had it the worst, being without a mother and a father. It wasn't even your choice, but you've grown to be a wonderful man, an outstanding father, and the son I always dreamed you would be. Whenever you make your way up here to Heaven, don't forget to say hello.*

*Love, Stanley*
*(I hope that's not asking too much.)*

I folded the letter and held it in my hands. I looked at his attorney and spoke calmly, "I don't want the money. Split it between my brother and sister and be done with it."

"But it's five hundred thousand dollars we're talking about here."

"I don't care if it's five million dollars. Just do it."

"Ya see, I can't. Once everything is settled, I have to give it to you. After that, you can do whatever it is you want to do with it."

"That's cool," I said, standing to leave. "Is there anything else?"

"No, that's pretty much it. But you don't seem too excited about the money. Most people would be in here jumping for joy."

"Well, money doesn't excite me. Having my father in my life would have, though. No matter how bad things were."

"I understand, young fella, and I'll be in touch."

"Thanks for your time," I said, shaking his hand.

On my way over to Collins' house, I thought about what Stanley said in his letter. To me, it still didn't make much sense. I had so many friends and knew so many brothas who struggled every day to take care of their children. Some had four and five, maybe six kids, and they didn't go off and abandon them. At the time, he only had Delores and me. What was so hard about taking care of two damn kids? And with the help of Mama and Ursula? I couldn't figure the shit out, and really didn't give too much of a fuck about it anymore.

As for the money, what was I supposed to do with it? I don't want to seem ungrateful, but was I supposed to take a trip or something, use it for my education, buy a house—what? I was already a completely established man, and at this point, there wasn't nothing Stanley could do to enhance my life. I'm sure Delores and Jeffrey were going to feel differently, but they could most certainly have every dime of it.

I knew exactly where Collins lived because I had to pick up LJ a few times. When I rang the doorbell, I could hear him yelling at someone on the phone. I didn't even think the wimp had it in him to get loud, but knowing his ass, he probably put up a front every time I came around.

"Who is it?" he yelled.

"Your nightmare," I yelled back.

He opened the door and quickly ended his call. "Come in," he snapped with an attitude. I stepped in and stood in the foyer. "Would you like to take a seat, or do you prefer to stand there?" he asked.

"No seat. I won't be long."

"Good, because I'm busy. So what's on your mind?"

"My son. I'm sure you know Nokea told me about your plans, and I wish you all the luck in the world. I do, however, want to let you know some serious shit is going to go down if you and Nokea think my son is going with you, because he's not."

Collins sighed and shook his head from side to side. "Jaylin, why won't you allow Nokea to be happy? You have done nothing but turn her world upside down since you've known her. And the moment she finds true love, bam. What do you do? You step right in and try to take it away. If you love her like you claim you do, then step back, my brotha. Trust me, she and I are going to work this out, and when we do, man, I feel sorry for you."

"Collins, you are living in a fantasy world. You

need to feel sorry for yourself and not me. And to think I used to have so much respect for you. You know damn well the reason you want to leave St. Louis is because you're afraid of losing Nokea to me.

"If you think you're the true love of her life, then why do you feel threatened by me? I'll be more than happy to answer that for you: it's because every time you look at her, you get a vision of me being right next to her. When you're making love to her, you feel my presence. It's as if I'm right there with you. When she closes her eyes, you know who she sees.

"All I'm saying is don't fool yourself. Taking her many miles away ain't gon' make her love for me go away. She's still going to feel the same way and you know it. So man up and face reality, punk."

He opened the door, asking me to exit. "Grow up and prepare yourself for a major loss," he said. "We'll soon see which way Nokea turns, won't we? And when she chooses the better man, because she already has, I'll be sure to send you a postcard, thanking you for fucking her over so badly so I could love her like she deserves to be loved. Now, get the fuck out of my house and don't come back over here unless I ask you to."

"There's no need for me to come back, Collins. You have nothing I want, or for that matter, nothing I can't have. So adios, my brotha. Good luck to you on your move to Detroit, and try not to stay away too long this time. The last time you left, you failed to handle your business here, so I had to do it for you. Nokea didn't mind, and like always, the pleasure was all mine."

I walked out and Collins slammed the door behind me. I laughed at the shit. Since I knew he would call Nokea to tell her about my visit, I waited for her to call. I had the phone in my hand, and no sooner than I hit Highway 40 going back to my house in Chesterfield, she called.

"What are you trying to do to me?" she asked with a raised voice.

"I'm trying to prevent you from fucking up your life. I stopped you once before, but this time I don't know if I can save you."

"You don't have what it takes to save me. I wish you would just back off, Jaylin. You continue to make things difficult for Collins and me, and I'm sick of it."

"Now, how did I make shit difficult for y'all by telling him my son wasn't going with you?"

"That's not all you told him and you know it. So what, you and I had sex. Do you have to keep throwing it up in his face?"

"You and I didn't have sex; we made love, and Collins needs to know that. Especially since he thinks he's going to run off with my damn son."

"Just like Scorpio needs to know it too, right? How would you like it if I told her what in the hell's been really going on? She's so darn excited about having your freaking baby, so how would you feel if I shattered her world?"

"It wouldn't bother me one bit because she already knows what she got. She ain't tripping off of me fucking another woman."

"Fucking another woman, maybe not. Loving one, hell yes. Now, stay out of my business before I start making trouble for you."

Before I could say another word, her li'l sassy ass hung up on me. Again, I didn't trip because I knew what time it was.

When I got home, there wasn't nothing but peace and quiet. Everybody was gone, so I went into my office and called Stephon.

"What's up?" I said. "Did you stop by to see me?"

"Yeah, man. I kind of need a favor."

"I guess I already know where this conversation's going."

"Damn, why you gotta be all like that?"

"What's the favor, Stephon?"

"Man, with the economy being so bad, things getting kind of tight. The shop ain't doing too good, and I'm two months behind on my rent. As for my bills, shit, I don't even want to talk about those."

"What did you do with the money I gave you?"

"Jay, you know two thousand dollars ain't no money. I blew some of it at the club that night, tried to get caught up on some bills, and you know gas ain't no joke. I wouldn't even be in this predicament had I not paid almost ten grand for Mona's engagement ring. I've been trying to get it back so I can pawn that motherfucker, but she refuses to give it to me."

"Well, right now, I can't help you. All my money is tied up in investments. Check back with me in a month or so."

"Man, come on. All the money you got ain't tied up in investments. Don't even play me like that. I know you think this about some drugs, but it ain't."

"I never said it was. All I said is I ain't got it."

"Not even five grand?"

"Stephon, look, last month I gave you exactly seven thousand two hundred fifteen dollars and twenty cents. That's down to the penny. What in the hell you did with it, I don't know. I'm not going to continue to waste my money like that. If you need some more money, I suggest that you seek another profession."

"See, I bet you don't tell your bitch that. Sorry that I'm a man and I can't fuck you like she do, but you wrong, Jay. How you gon' do something for another motherfucker and I'm your damn cousin?"

My brows scrunched in. "Man, I don't know what's gotten into you, but something straight up got you tripping. Don't you worry about what the fuck I do with my money. I ain't giving your ass nothing. I'm tired of taking care of your grown ass, Stephon. Your banking institution has shut down."

There was a long pause before Stephon said anything. "You selfish son of a bitch. You gon' need me one day. Fuck you and your money."

Stephon hung up on me. Two hang-up calls in one day and I was getting pretty pissed. Nokea and her bullshit was on my mind, and so was Stephon. I'd been doing just fine, and hadn't had to go off on anybody in weeks, but these damn fools were itching to get scratched.

By the time Scorpio came home, I headed out to get some shit off my chest. She asked where I was going, and I told her I'd be right back. I gave her a kiss and jetted.

I drove to Nokea's house. She opened the door with an attitude.

"I'm not too thrilled to see you either," I said after I walked in.

"What is it, Jaylin? If you came all this way to argue, I don't feel like it. If you came to see your son, he's taking a nap."

"Then good. He don't have to see me put my foot in your ass for hanging up on me."

Nokea walked over to the couch and plopped down. She crossed her legs and calmly spoke to me. "Stop being so vulgar and come sit down so we can talk."

"Okay, that's better." I walked over and sat next to her on the couch.

"Jaylin, I don't know about you, but I'm getting tired of going through this stuff with you. Why can't you move on with your life and I move on with mine?"

"We are moving on, Nokea. Look, you can't expect for me to be happy about you moving away. I have too much to lose if you do. It's as simple as that."

"You're not going to lose your son, okay? I've already decided I'm not moving to Detroit. I told Collins that earlier, and now the ball is in his court."

"Good. Then I don't have to take this conversation any further. I can go kiss my son right now and leave."

I went into LJ's room and gave him a kiss. Before I got ready to leave, Nokea called my name.

"What's up?" I asked.

"So?"

"So, what? You wanna have sex before I go?"

She smiled. "No, silly. Is Scorpio pregnant or not?"

"Aw, that." I walked back over to the couch and sat down. "Naw, not yet. She thought she was, but we got a little bit more work to do."

"Well, I'll be glad when she gets pregnant so you can cut LJ some slack."

I motioned with my finger."Come here," I said. She came around the couch and stood in front of me. I grabbed her waist and tossed her on the couch. I lay on top of her and playfully kissed her cheeks, tickling her. "I am never going to cut my son any slack. You understand?"

She laughed and tried to bite my face. I turned my head from side to side, then stopped to lick her face. She tried to wipe her face with her hands, but I held them above her head. She struggled to get away from my grip and laughed when she couldn't. I licked her cheek again, but she kept turning her face from side to side.

When my cell phone rang, we stopped playfully tussling, but I continued to hold her hands together. A blank stare came over my face and I stared into Nokea's eyes. My dick was on the rise, and Nokea widened her legs so she could feel it. Our lips met up and we started to kiss.

My phone continued to ring back to back, so I stopped kissing Nokea and reached for it, clipped to my jeans. It was Scorpio's cell phone number, and fearing that something was wrong because of the numerous calls, I was forced to answer.

"This better be good," I said while still lying on top of Nokea.

"Jaylin Jerome Rogers, if you kiss her one more fucking time, I'm going to drive your Escalade right through her damn window! Get the hell off her and bring your ass outside!"

I swallowed and looked up at the window. I saw headlights, so I eased off Nokea. "We just playing. Damn. Why you tripping?"

"You wanna play, huh? Okay, we're definitely gonna start playing."

I made my way to the door. Once I heard my truck skid, I yelled for Nokea to move. She had no idea what was going on, so she jumped off the couch and stood behind me. When I didn't hear the truck anymore, I called Scorpio's name.

"Oh, I'm here. But listen to you protecting her and making sure she doesn't get hurt. You must really love her, don't you?"

"Baby, it ain't even like that. I'm on my way home, so meet me there in a few, all right?"

"Uh-uh. Your smooth-ass talking ain't gonna work this time. The only thing you can do at this point is tell me what it's going to take to end this with you. Please tell me what must I do, Jaylin."

"You don't want to end this, and neither do I."

"Of course you wouldn't want to. You're having your cake and eating it too. Like you've always done."

"Scorpio, look, I'm not playing around with you anymore. I know you're upset, but you'd better not do anything stupid."

Nokea tugged on my shirt and tried to find out what was going on. Starting to feel as if something wasn't right, I ignored Nokea and continued to listen to Scorpio on the phone.

"You really don't think I'm going to kill myself over you, do you?" she said.

"I hope that you wouldn't."

"Jaylin, please. But I will tell you this: after tonight, you and I are over, baby. We are over!"

"Why are you saying that?"

"I figured if you could still love Nokea for betraying you when it came to your son and for fucking your cousin, then maybe you'd love me more if I stabbed you in the back. I mean, she planned a life with Stephon and they were about to get married and raise your child together, weren't they? But what do you do? Not a damn thing. To this day, you continue to love her. You continue to make love to her and treat her like she's a fucking queen or something."

I closed my eyes and thought about Stephon's and my conversation earlier. He would love an opportunity to comfort Scorpio right about now. "So, what are you saying?" I said calmly. "You know how much I love you, and if you think Stephon is the answer, you're sadly mistaken. Like I said, I was just playing with Nokea. She already has a man. Why don't you calm down and go home so we can talk about this when I get there? I'm on my way."

"Too late. I'm on my way to see the boss. He's the real head Negro in charge. Everybody else goes to him when they're in need, so why shouldn't I?" She hung up.

I called her phone back several times, but she didn't answer. Nokea kept bugging me about what was going on. Trying to keep myself under control, I told her I'd call her later and then jetted.

I hopped in my truck and called Stephon's house. When I didn't get an answer, I called his cell phone.

"Damn! Will somebody answer the phone?" I yelled out loudly. I called Scorpio's phone again; still no answer. I was going back and forth between her and Stephon's phones, and got no response. I laid my phone down and sped up to get to his place.

By the time I reached the highway, it was crammed. It was down to one lane because of a car accident. "Well, I'll be damned!" I yelled, as my truck couldn't go anywhere. Furious, I picked up my cell phone and looked at it. I called Scorpio's cell phone and politely spoke to her voice-mail.

"Look, I know you're probably upset with what you saw, but it ain't what you think. Please, please don't have sex with my cousin. You don't want this to be over with, baby, and neither do I. We've come too far to go out like this, and I know you wouldn't do this to me. As soon as you get this message, call me."

Traffic moved, but not fast enough for me. My stomach turned in knots. Finally my phone rang. It was Scorpio.

"Hello," I said. I didn't hear anything, so I said hello again. When I heard her ask Stephon to fuck her, I wasn't sure if she was playing with me. Either way, I yelled into the phone. "Scorpio, don't do it!" Finally, I heard Stephon say something, but I couldn't make it out. I now knew she wasn't playing and was very well in his presence.

I spoke calmly, already feeling defeated. "Did you hear what I said?"

The phone went dead. It was evident that she had called me personally so I could hear the shit go down. I was so pissed that I managed to maneuver my truck over to the shoulder and ride it. Many horns sounded off, but I didn't give a fuck. Just when I had nothing but open driving lanes in front of me, a cop that was parked on the shoulder stopped me. It took everything I had not to drive off.

He slowly walked to my truck. "Sir, are you in a rush to get somewhere?" he asked.

I spoke anxiously. "Yes, I am. I have an emergency, officer. I know that no explanation is a good one, so I'm not going to defend myself for driving on the shoulder."

"Well, I'm sure that car mangled over there probably had an emergency too. He's in critical condition. Why don't you just take your time and hopefully you'll get to where you're going without causing yourself or any other motorist any harm?"

"I will, sir."

I thought I was off the hook, until he asked for my driver's license and registration. That took up more time. When he came back to me, he returned my items, encouraging me to have a safe day. He stopped another car from passing and allowed me to go by. I thanked him, but as soon as he was out of my sight, I was on a roll again. I called Scorpio's number again; still no answer. Stephon's place, no answer. When I called Shane to see if Stephon told him about our conversation, he told me he'd spoken to him earlier.

"What did he say?" I asked.

Shane laughed. "He said he don't fuck with your ass no mo'."

"No, seriously. Is that what he said?"

"Those were his exact words. When I asked what happened, he talked a bunch of bullshit, man. I told him he needed to get his shit together and he hung up on me. Anyway, what's up? You sound kind of—".

"Shane, I feel myself about to lose it. Scorpio's at his house right now playing games."

"What kind of games?"

"She's angry with me about some silly shit, and threatened to have sex with Stephon. I can't believe she would think of doing something so stupid. I don't think she's going to go through with it, but I don't trust that nigga Stephon. I'm about ten minutes away from his crib, and I don't have a good feeling about what's about to go down. I love her ass, man, and if she allows that fool to fuck her, I don't know what I'm gonna do."

"Just chill, Jay. I'm on my way over there too."

I hung up and tried to prepare myself for the worst. I could hear the hurt in Scorpio's voice, and I had a feeling she wasn't playing with me this time. A part of me felt bad for not sharing with her my feelings for Nokea, but it was too late to think about what I could or should have done better. I knew damn well Stephon couldn't be trusted alone with Scorpio, and many, many times in the past, he'd made it clear how badly he wanted her. Even though he knew how much love I had for her, Stephon was the kind of person who did whatever he wanted, however he wanted, and to whomever he wanted.

When I pulled in front of Stephon's place, it was obvious that she wasn't playing. My Escalade was parked next to his BMW, causing me to rush out of my truck. I'm sure the door was purposely left cracked for me.

As I stepped inside, I knew that I was already too late. I heard the headboard banging against the wall, and Scorpio's moans I'd know anywhere. Stephon even had the nerve to turn on some music and darken the house. Hurt like hell, my mind was gone as I paced down the hallway to his bedroom. I picked up a wooden chair that sat by his other bedroom's door and carried it on the way.

When I pushed the door open, it squeaked, but they couldn't hear it over the music. I saw with my own eyes: Scorpio straddled on Stephon's shoulders. He held her up against the wall and was going to town, licking her pussy. Her hair hung down over her face, and her moans implied that she was enjoying herself.

I picked up the chair and slammed it across his back. The chair cracked into pieces, and he immediately shouted out in pain, holding his back. Scorpio tumbled to the bed, and I grabbed her ankles, pulling her toward me.

She kicked and started to scream. "Stop! Jaylin, don't! Let me go!"

I ignored her and yanked her ass forward as hard as I could. She fell hard on the floor, and managed to kick her legs away from me. She scooted backward and backed into the corner. "I will call the police," she screamed. "I swear if you touch me, I will have you arrested."

"You gotta make it to the damn phone first, stupid ass!" I grabbed her hair tightly and looked at Stephon rolling back and forth on the bed. "What does her high yellow ass say, nigga? In case she forgot to tell you." I pulled Scorpio off the floor and shoved her on the bed next to him. She cried and demanded that I let go of her hair. I was in a rage, and with each word she spoke, my grip got tighter. I turned her over and pointed to my name tattooed on her ass.

"This ass says Jaylin, and Jaylin only! Where in the hell does it say Stephon?" I yelled.

He looked at me, and was brave enough to snicker like the shit was funny. "Man, it ain't nothing but some pussy. You . . . you fucked up my back over some pussy?"

"You stupid, basehead fucking fool! I told you I had love for this . . . this—get your ass off his bed!" I yelled. I pulled Scorpio off the bed and shoved her toward the door. "I'm coming back for your ass in a minute," I said to Stephon.

I dragged Scorpio down the hallway by her hair and tried to break her damn neck. She continued to kick and scream, and I could hear Stephon yelling his bullshit too. I was zoned out, focusing my anger on Scorpio.

When we got to the living room, I slammed her naked ass on the couch. Having no sympathy for her tears, I straddled her as she swung wildly, demanding that I get off her. My hand turned red from the tight grip on her hair, and that's when she had the nerve to scream that she was sorry.

"Bitch, you ain't sorry! You would have fucked him anyway!" I backslapped her ass so hard that my fingers burned.

When Shane came rushing in, he tried to save her.

He pulled me back and grabbed my arm. "That's enough, man! It ain't yo' style, Jay. Just let her go, please," he said.

She tried to get bad after Shane showed up, and kicked me on my legs, also smacking my face. When she spit on me, I broke loose from Shane and wore her ass out! During the process, Stephon limped into the living room with a gun in his hand. He aimed it directly at me.

"How you gon' trip with me over some pussy? Get your punk ass out of my house," he ordered.

I backed off Scorpio, walking right up to him. "You wanna kill me, nigga?" I yelled. Having nothing to lose, I placed the gun on my chest. "Shoot me, motherfucker! Go ahead and shoot me!"

"No! Please!" Scorpio yelled. "Don't shoot him! I'm sorry, baby! I'm so sorry!"

Shane hurried over and stood between us. "Stephon and Jay," he said calmly, "come on, now. Stephon, man, put the gun down."

"Don't encourage the nigga, Shane. Pump it into me, cuz. Let's get it the fuck over with. This what you want, ain't it? You hate me so damn much, so get it over with."

Stephon pushed Shane back and held the gun close to my chest with a devious look in his eyes.

Not even giving a fuck, I yelled again for him to pull the trigger. Scorpio screamed repeatedly for him not to do it, and when she came over by us, I shoved her away. I saw that Stephon didn't have the courage to follow through with his plan, so I smacked the gun away from my chest and punched him so hard that he fell backward.

He tried to sit up on his elbows, but in pain, he spat a gush of blood from his mouth. He gave me a hard stare, and then rushed to get up. When he did, he grabbed my waist and we both fell backward on the floor. Shane tried to separate us, and when he got punched in his face, he yelled out loudly for us to break it up. As mad as I was, all I could think about was picking up the nearest object and busting Stephon's head open.

We went at it for a while, and his living room was turning into a disaster area. Once I slammed him on the floor, he took deep breaths while rolling to his side. He grabbed his back and yelled out as if he were in dying pain. Blood dripped from his mouth and from mine as well. I heavily breathed in and out, maneuvering myself to a chair on one knee. I touched underneath my eye, and when I looked at my fingers, blood was on them too.

Scorpio eased her way over to me, trying to wipe the blood from my mouth with her hand. I shoved her away again.

"Shane, please get this bitch away from me before I kill her."

"Come on, Scorpio," he said, helping her off the floor. She sat on the couch and placed her hands over her face.

"Baby, I never meant for this to happen. I swear I didn't. I'm sorry," she sobbed.

I wiped the blood from my mouth and furiously looked at her. "What in the fuck did you think was going to happen, you stupid ass?"

"Let's go, Jay," Shane said, as I was about to go fuck her up again. He walked over and helped me stand up. I stood in front of her. "Give me my damn keys."

"No," she said, shaking her head. "This is not over, and—"

"Give me my keys, bitch!" Before I knew it, I backslapped her ass again. Shane grabbed my hand, and unable to control myself, I landed a punch on his jaw. He stumbled back and tightened his fist.

"The keys are on Stephon's dresser," Scorpio yelled, as she knew Shane and me were about to go at it.

Shane frowned and his forehead lined with thick wrinkles. He pointed his finger at me. "I know you're mad, but once I get your keys, we are out of here. If I have to fight your ass to get you out of this house, I have no problem doing it."

"Bring it on then, nigga!"

Shane stood for a moment, and then walked off. He came back with the keys in his hand. "Let's go. I'm driving your Escalade home, so let's go."

I stepped over Stephon, as he was still laid on the floor, holding his back. He insisted that he couldn't move, and yelled for Shane to help him. Shane ignored him.

On my way out, Scorpio begged me not to leave her. "Don't do this to me," she sobbed, barely able to get the words out of her mouth. She ran up to me. "I've been through so much with you, and I didn't know what to do when I saw you with Nokea. Can't you understand how I felt?"

I was too damn mad to understand anything, and as she pleaded for me to forgive her, I put my fist through the wall next to her face. "Fuck you, Scorpio! You got what you wanted. Now, leave me the hell alone."

Shane saw me get hyped again, so he pulled me outside. He asked Scorpio to put on her clothes and said he'd come back for her.

I couldn't even think or see straight on my way home. My eye was swollen and my entire body throbbed with pain. By the time we made it to my house, Shane had to help me get out of the car. I was stiff as a board. As soon as he opened the door for us to go inside, Nanny B came out of the kitchen. She wiped her hands on an apron, and then put her hands on her hips.

"What in the hell happened?" she asked with a disturbed look on her face. Shane walked me to the couch and sat me down.

I reached up, feeling my swollen jaw. "Me and Stephon had a fight."

"A fight?" she said, raising her voice. "Jaylin, y'all should know better. This doesn't make any sense." She went back into the kitchen, and came back with a wet towel, an ice pack, and some bandages. She sat on the table in front of me, and when I cut my eyes at her, she moved over to the couch. "At least you still got your sense of humor. Now, lean back," she said. She placed the ice pack on my eye and wiped the dried blood from underneath my eye and lips.

"That's a nasty cut on your face." She looked at Shane with frustration. "Why were the two of them fighting?"

"I don't know all the details, but—"

"Over a stupid-ass bitch," I said with my eyes closed. "And some damn cocaine and money."

Nanny B continued to doctor me up. After she wrapped my right hand with a bandage, she offered to take Shane back to his car. I apologized for punching him, and then thanked him for helping me. Before they left, I warned them not to bring Scorpio back to my crib.

They left, and I slowly made my way upstairs to my bedroom. I was glad Mackenzie was asleep because I wasn't up for any questions. I struggled to make it to the bathroom and dropped my head after I saw my face in the mirror. It was pretty much fucked up, and I was mad as hell. I punched the mirror and glass shattered everywhere. When I saw blood coming through the bandage on my hand, I made my way to the shower, turning it on. Fully clothed, I slid down against the glass doors and closed my eyes. I was hurt like hell, and sat motionless as the hot and steamy water poured on me.

# 25

# *SCORPIO*

By the time Shane made it back, Stephon needed way more help than I did. I asked Stephon if he wanted me to call an ambulance, but he said he didn't want the police at his house. Luckily, Nanny B was with Shane, so I got in the car with her, and Shane took Stephon to the hospital.

Nanny B didn't waste any time tearing into me. Already feeling bad about what had happened, I really didn't have much to say.

"This shit has got to stop!" she yelled. "I'm fed up with you and Jaylin's mess, and this is the last straw!"

I leaned my head against the window and held a towel with ice in it against my mouth. "Just take me home, Nanny B," I mumbled. "I want to go home."

"I am not taking you back to that house tonight. I'm too old to be keeping two idiots apart, and I'm not about to kill myself trying to do so."

"We'll work it out. Please, just take me home."

Nanny B ignored me and drove downtown to the Hampton Inn. She parked the car and got out to go inside. I stayed in the car, and when she came back, she opened the passenger's side door.

"Stay here for a few days and allow things to cool down. I don't want Mackenzie caught up in all this mess, and I'm sure you don't either."

"But I want to go home," I said, covering my face. "Jaylin and I need to talk."

Nanny B kneeled down and touched my hand. "Scorpio, you need to stop doing this to yourself. Sometimes things don't work out for a reason. Now, I don't know exactly what happened, but you and Jaylin need to be as far away from each other as possible right now. So please, go inside. Get some rest and I'll come back and check on you in the morning."

I sat for a moment, and then got out of the car. Nanny B walked with me to my room and stayed for about an hour. Before leaving, she asked if I would be okay, and I told her that I would be. She gave me a squeezing hug and told me she loved me.

Feeling numb, I tore off my clothes and went into the shower to wash off Stephon's scent. I rubbed my hair back and let the water stream out on my face. The tears just kept on flowing because no matter how hard I tried to convince myself that having sex with him was the right thing to do, I realized just how wrong I was. Even if Jaylin was still having sex with Nokea, I should have known there was a better way to handle this. I always knew a part of him still loved Nokea, but deep down, I knew he loved me more. That's why

I couldn't believe I stooped so low, even after I knew I'd be the last woman standing.

Now, though, there was no telling what would happen. We'd made it through tough times before, but I wasn't sure about this time. As usual, I wasn't going to give up without a fight. To me, Jaylin and I were meant to be together, and that's simply how it was going to be.

I finished my shower, wrapped a towel around me, and got in the bed. I pulled the covers over me, and called home. He answered in a low voice. "Jaylin," I said softly. He didn't respond. "Baby, are you there?" He still didn't say anything. "Well, if you're listening—"

"I'm not," he said, and then hung up.

I called back, but he wouldn't answer. After a while, he took the phone off the hook. When I tried his cell phone, he turned that off as well. I must have played the entire day in my mind at least a million times. Over and over again, I listened to the message he'd left earlier as he was on his way over to Stephon's house. He was hurt bad. As much as he said he'd kick my ass for messing around on him, I thought he was just playing. I'd never seen him so angry before, and when Stephon put the gun to his chest, I could see in Jaylin's eyes that he cared nothing about dying. What if Stephon had pulled the trigger? I was so wrong for creating such a mess, but I had no problem putting the blame on Nokea. Why couldn't she just leave us alone? I hated her so much. After this, I knew she'd find a way to give Jaylin the comfort he needed.

By morning, I still hadn't had any sleep. When

I heard a knock at the door, I lay there until I remembered Nanny B saying she'd be back to check on me. I opened the door and was glad to see her. She had a bag in her hand and a plate covered with aluminum foil. She came in and put the plate and bag on the table. Before she sat down, she pulled my robe from the bag.

"Here," she said, reaching to give it to me. "I knew you didn't have anything to put on, so I brought a few things for you to change into."

"Thank you," I said, putting on the robe. I sat back on the bed and pulled the cover over me. "Did Mackenzie make it to school okay?"

"Yes. I dropped her off and then came here."

"Where's Jaylin?'

"When I left he was still asleep. We stayed up late last night and talked about what happened. I believe in being fair, and I know there are two sides to every story, so I'd like to hear yours—if you don't mind."

"I'm too ashamed of myself to tell you what I did. Whatever he told you was probably the truth."

"I know he told me the truth because he had no reason to lie to me. When he told me how much he loved you, I believed him. And when he said he would have killed Stephon over you, I believed that too."

"Did he tell you how much he loves Nokea? This wouldn't have ever happened if I hadn't seen the two of them about to have sex."

"Yes, he told me he loves Nokea too. But he didn't tell me he was about to have sex with her. Through your eyes, though, maybe they were about to get intimate. I'd let you be the judge of that because I wasn't there."

"Well, yes, through my eyes they were. And he knows damn well that they were too."

"But, baby, whether they were or weren't, you had no business going over there. If you can't find it in your heart to trust him, then you don't need him. I'm not saying that Jaylin is a trustworthy man, because we both know that he's not. All I'm saying is if it's gotten to the point where you have to follow him around and have sex with Stephon for revenge, then you have to know it's time to move on."

"No, I just think we're going through something right now. Soon, all of this will be behind us and everything will be back to normal. You know how we are, Nanny B."

"And just what do you call normal? It is not normal for a man to have control over you the way Jaylin does. It is not normal for him to have sex with any woman he wants to, or for you to pat him on the back as if it doesn't matter. It is not normal for him to love another woman and for you to act as if it's okay. It is not normal for you to have sex with his cousin and think everything is going to be fine, and, my dear, it is not normal for you to get pregnant by another man, lie about it, and think that he's forgiven you.

"Everything I can think of about y'all's relationship is abnormal, if you ask me. But if you think that some miracle is going to happen for the two of you, then you go right ahead."

"Well, I'm a firm believer that love can conquer anything. Any obstacle, any—"

Nanny B got angry and snapped at me. "I want you to leave the house, Scorpio. In a few days, I want you to come to the house, pack up your things, and go."

"I will do no such thing," I said, sitting up. "Now, I know how much Jaylin means to you, but he means more to me. I need him just as much as he needs me. We've been down this road before, and our love for one another always brings us back together. I don't give up that easily, and you should know that."

"Chile, you are so blind. When Jaylin and I talked last night, I asked if he could find it in his heart to forgive you. He said there wasn't a chance in hell, and I believed him. He also said if you came back to that house, he wouldn't throw you out, but he would make it so bad for you that you'd want to run out. I believed that too. I'm trying to save you from a life of nothing but heartache. I will give you five hundred thousand dollars of Mackenzie's money, to use for you and her, if you leave the house in a couple of days."

"Mackenzie doesn't have five hundred thousand dollars."

"Yes, she does. She's not supposed to have access to it until she's eighteen, but I'm getting desperate. I want Mackenzie to be happy, I want you to be happy, and more than anything, I want Jaylin to be at peace. So take the money and do as I asked."

"Nanny B, you can't buy me out of Jaylin's life. I told you, I'm in this relationship for the long haul, and I mean it. We're going to work this out and soon."

She stood up, putting her purse on her shoulder. "If I only had somebody to talk some sense into me when I was going through my ups and downs in my marriage. Please, think about what I said. It's time for this relationship to come to an end, and everyone needs to focus on their own future. Don't you think so?"

She headed for the door and walked out.

Everybody was going to focus on their future. Nanny B just didn't understand what type of bond Jaylin and I had. I'd known couples that went through what we did every day and still prevailed in their relationships. If anything, she needed to mind her own freaking business. She was so caught up and obsessed with Jaylin that it seriously drove me crazy. I knew how much she cared for him, but damn! She was poking her nose where it didn't belong, and I was furious about it.

Not wanting to stay cooped up in the room all week, I took my butt to school. Normally, when Jaylin and I had our ups and downs, I'd stay home. This time, I wasn't going to do that. Even though I'd been going to school here and there, I was still considered a full-time student. I'd even taken up a theater class, and the instructor was quite impressed with my playwriting.

During my English Literature class, I couldn't stay focused. The instructor assigned students to read their papers in front of the class, and by the time he called on me, I was in another world. He skipped over me.

I stayed after to apologize. I told him I had some personal problems, but when he told me I at least had a C-plus in his class, I was cool with that. I left, heading for my theatrical class, where I remained focused for the rest of the day.

On the bus ride back to the hotel, I thought about Mackenzie and Jaylin once again. When I was a kid, I watched my mother go through so much, and wondered if Mackenzie even noticed why one day I was there and the next day I wasn't. I didn't want to call the house because I hated to lie to her about where I was.

As for Jaylin, I hoped by now he was ready to talk this out with me. Since I knew him so well, I decided to wait a few more days before I called him.

Early Saturday morning, I finally called. He answered sounding a little more upbeat.

"Hi," I said. There was no response. "Okay, if you don't want to talk to me, can I at least come home?"

"Any time." He hung up.

Anxious to see him and Mackenzie, I gathered my things and left the hotel. I didn't even care that I didn't have a ride home. I did have money for a taxi, so I called a dispatcher and a taxi came for me.

Needless to say, I was so glad to be home. I didn't expect things to be perfect, but I knew Jaylin would eventually come around and we'd discuss what happened. But when I stuck my key in the door, the lock wouldn't turn. I tried harder to turn it, but the key bent. I rang the doorbell, and that's when Nanny B came to the door and opened it. There was no smile on her face as she took the bag of clothes from my hand.

"I'll go wash this stuff for you. Have you had anything to eat?" she asked.

"No, but have the locks been changed? My key wouldn't work."

"And neither does mine," she whispered. "So, are you hungry?"

"Not really. Where are Jaylin and Mackenzie?"

"They're all out back by the swimming pool. Megan spent the night, and Nokea brought LJ over."

"Oh, I see." I walked over by the window and looked out at them. Megan and Mackenzie were in the swimming pool, while LJ sat on Jaylin's lap and played with his sunglasses. I turned and looked at Nanny B. "Has he said anything else about what happened?"

"Nope. Actually, he hasn't said much at all. He hasn't returned any of his phone calls and has kind of been to himself."

I nodded and went upstairs to his room. I stood in the doorway and stared because it was spotless. The marble surrounding the fireplace was sparkling, the plush carpet was vacuumed, and the windows were so clean, they looked as if they didn't exist. New satin Gucci sheets were on the bed, and the pillows on the sofa in the sitting room were in neat rows. As for the closet, it didn't make any sense. Like always, his suits were neatly hung, but not one shoe was out of place. Other items were neatly folded or put on hangers. Even my things were in order. Jaylin was the only person who could clean his room like this, so I was careful not to mess up anything.

I quickly changed into my black bikini. It didn't

reveal too much; I didn't want to look too sexy with the kids being around. It was, however, sexy enough and had a fishnet wrap to match. I tied the wrap around my waist, put my hair in a pony-tail, and headed out back to join them.

I slid the patio door aside and walked out. The sun shone so brightly that I placed my hand above my eyes to see. Jaylin sat on the far side of the swimming pool in a lawn chair, and I couldn't tell if he saw me or not through his dark sunglasses. I sure as hell saw his fine ass, with his shirt off and dark, tanned body. LJ had some sunglasses on too, and they looked so adorable with their match-ing red swimming trunks.

When Mackenzie hopped out of the pool, she ran up to give me a hug. Megan followed and hugged me as well.

"If I'm going to be shown this much love, I might just stay away a little more often," I said.

"Mommy, why did you and Leslie go on vaca-tion without telling me? I wanted to go too."

I looked at Jaylin, and then looked back at Mackenzie. "Maybe next time, okay? I promise you next time you can go."

"Okay," she said, kissing me on the cheek and then jumping back into the pool. Megan jumped in after her. I watched them for a while, then headed to where Jaylin and LJ were.

I removed my wrap and sat back on the lawn chair next to him. He didn't say one word to me. Trying to break the ice, I reached for LJ, who had already reached out for me. I sat up and put him between my legs. There was something in his curly hair, so I picked through it to remove it. He started playing with me, and took off his glasses to put them over my eyes. When I kissed his cheeks and tickled him, he cracked up. Jaylin still wasn't saying anything, and when LJ called me Mama, Jaylin got up and walked into the house.

Shortly after, he came back outside with a glass of iced tea in his hand. He stood by the patio door and drank it, then went to the other side of the pool to sit down. I knew he was trying to avoid me, so I continued to play with LJ. Moments later, I got up and held LJ's hands as we walked slowly up to Jaylin. I put LJ on Jaylin's lap and headed for the diving board to dive into the pool. I swam around with Mackenzie and Megan, then we went for the slide. The girls had so much fun, but I was tired. I rested by the edge of the pool, then got out of the water to dry off.

Still, Jaylin hadn't said anything to me, so I lay on my stomach next to him on a lounge chair. I saw him take quick peeks at my body, but that was it. He turned up his iPod and tuned me out completely.

Later in the day, Nanny B called us inside because dinner was ready. I wanted some privacy with Jaylin, so I took LJ off Jaylin's lap and walked back into the house with Mackenzie and Megan. They all sat down to eat, and I went back outside and stood next to the Jacuzzi, where Jaylin had moved to. He still had his sunglasses on, but by looking at him from the side, I could see that his eyes were closed. He was leaned back, listening to some music. When I got into the Jacuzzi with him, he felt my leg touch his and sat up. He glared at me, closed his eyes again, and continued to lean back.

This was the closest I'd been to him all day. I noticed some stitches on his hand, which were still a bit bruised. I leaned in to examine his face and saw a bruise underneath his eye behind his sunglasses.

I felt bad because all I had was a sore head from him pulling my hair so hard, and a busted lip that had already healed. My thighs were a bit bruised too, but I knew he held back on beating the shit out of me like he really wanted to. If he hadn't, I would have looked like Stephon. From what I could remember, he was way more messed up than Jaylin was.

I sat feeling so sorry about what had happened, and when Jaylin mumbled something with his eyes closed, I didn't even hear him.

"What did you say?" I asked.

He sat up and placed the iPod behind him. "I said what in the fuck do you keep looking at?"

"I can't help it. I didn't know you were hurt this badly. Are your hands still hurting?"

"Yes, I'm hurting very badly. It's ranked second to the most pain I've ever had in my entire life. So, to answer your question if it still hurts, it's a hurt that I'm not going to get over any time soon. As for the marks and bruises you see, those will fade away in no time. Maybe in a week or two they'll be gone. I'm hoping you'll be gone by then too."

"It's not that easy for me, Jaylin. I'm not going anywhere."

"Do what you please, Scorpio. You are free to do anything you want to do." He got out of the Jacuzzi, wiped himself off, and went inside.

I stayed outside and thought hard about everything that had happened. There was no way Jaylin would get rid of me that easily. I was prepared to handle anything he could throw my way. Besides, I had been through it all anyway, so nothing he could do to me now could piss me off any more than I'd already been. More than that, I loved him with everything I had. I really didn't have any place to go, and this was the life I'd become accustomed to. Like always, we were going to someway or somehow work this out. Yes, I felt bad for running to Stephon, but I had to get Jaylin to see that him loving Nokea, without telling me so, is what drove me to Stephon. That in itself was going to be a difficult thing to do.

After Megan and Mackenzie got settled in for bed, so did Jaylin. I asked if he wanted to be alone. He told me to sleep wherever I wanted to, so I chose to sleep with him.

We got in bed naked, but he immediately turned away from me. I eased over close to him, and he gave me a look that could kill. That being my cue, I waited until he was asleep before I challenged him again.

While Jaylin was in a deep sleep, I made my move. I lowered myself to suck him, and was surprised to see his dick turn hard. I wasted no time putting him inside of me, and carefully went for a ride. He grinned and slowly opened his eyes. He stared at me for a moment, and before I could get in another good stroke on top of him, he quickly sat up. I thought he wanted to take control, but when I felt him deflate inside of me, I knew the party was over. He tightly held my hair back with his hands and gritted his teeth.

"This isn't a game I'm playing with you, Scorpio. Get the fuck off me, and do not touch me again. Do you understand?"

My feelings were hurt because we'd never gotten to this point in our relationship. "Please don't do this to us," I whispered. "Let me make it up to—"

He pulled my hair tighter. "Do you understand what I just said?"

"I understand what you said, but your dick said something else."

"My dick was in a dream with somebody else."

"Let me guess: Nokea, right?"

He winked. "Nobody else. Now, if you're going to lay with me, don't be over here breathing down my neck. Scoot over and chill the fuck out."

Not even trying to sweat him over no dick, I eased off him. I turned my back, hoping that he'd eventually come around. The one thing I knew about Jaylin was that he couldn't lay in this bed for long without making love to me. I was sure I wouldn't have to wait too long for him to get himself together and forgive me for something that was his fault too.

# 26

## *NOKEA*

Jaylin really didn't talk much about what happened, but I couldn't believe he and Stephon had been at it again. This time, though, was nothing like the fight they'd had at my house. Jaylin was messed up, and when I called Stephon's house to check on him, some chick answered and told me he was in the hospital.

When Jaylin left that day, I knew something was about to go down. If anything, I was more surprised I hadn't heard from Scorpio. Jaylin said she saw us about to have sex, and being the type of woman she was, I expected her to confront me.

I couldn't even imagine what Jaylin was going through, but I had my own problems to worry about. After I told Collins I wasn't moving to Detroit, he'd become kind of distant. When I'd call, he'd cut our conversations short. When I'd go by his house, he'd pretend he was too busy and didn't have time for me. I simply told him to make up his mind as to what he anticipated on doing with our relationship.

By all means, I was more in love with Collins than I'd ever been. But the truth of the matter was, I knew his attempt to move me to Detroit was so that I could be as far away from Jaylin as possible. Not only that, but I was getting tired of kissing his butt. I made a mistake, I owned up to it, and there was nothing I could do to change it. Either he was going to forgive me and move on, or say the hell with our relationship altogether.

While at work on Friday morning, Collins called and asked if we could have dinner. I was surprised to hear from him, and I could tell in his voice he was anxious to see me. Probably he was more anxious to have sex with me, since he'd asked me to meet him at the Ritz Carlton hotel before dinner.

I knew that the Ritz was an extravagant hotel, so I left work early and went home to change. I didn't overdo it, but I put on a red spaghetti-strapped short dress and accessorized it with silver. I raked my layered hair and spiked the front. Before I left the house, I left Jaylin a message, asking him to pick up LJ at my parents' house around eight, instead of at my house. Once I dropped off LJ, I headed to the Ritz to see Collins.

When I got there, I couldn't remember what room number he'd told me earlier to meet him in, so I called his cell phone to find out where he was. He directed me to one of the ballrooms, and since I didn't have a clue as to where they were, I asked a bellhop for assistance. He walked me to the room, and when I opened the door, my heart dropped straight to my stomach, causing me to hold it.

Collins sat at a beautifully decorated round table all by his lonesome self. He wore a black tuxedo, and when he saw me, he stood, inviting me to join him. Unable to resist, I walked up and embraced him. At that moment, I knew there was no other place in the world I wanted to be.

Collins pulled the chair back for me to take a seat. I smiled and looked up at the beautiful chandeliers that gave the room a dimmed lighting. Three waiters stood close by, and a few musicians played some relaxing music. Collins gave notice to the waiters, and one of them immediately brought over a bottle of wine, filling the wine glasses. After the waiter stepped away, Collins moved his chair close to mine and held up his glass. I lifted mine as well and asked, "What shall we drink to this time around?"

"Let's drink to me finally realizing that everyone is entitled to mistakes. I've made them before, and I don't want to go another day without the woman I love. Let's just move on, okay? I don't care if it's in St. Louis, Detroit, Alabama, Mississippi . . . wherever. As long as I'm with you."

I was relieved to hear those words come from his mouth. "Then let's drink to staying together."

"Always," he said, leaning in for a kiss.

Collins and I drank more wine and talked intensively about our relationship. During dinner, I felt like the luckiest woman in the world. He was, by far, the best man any woman could hope for. There wasn't anything about him I didn't love.

And even though I still had feelings for Jaylin, being with him never made me feel as safe and secure as I did when I was with Collins.

Dinner was over and the waiters moved the table so we could have the entire floor to ourselves. I wanted so badly to make love to my man, and if the others weren't around, the moment seemed so appropriate. The musicians played "One in a Million You" by Larry Graham. Collins held me tightly in his arms as we slow danced.

I closed my eyes, placing my head against his chest.

"Do you know what I did today?" he said.

"No. What did you do today?"

"I had a very interesting conversation with someone."

"Oh, yeah? And who might that be?"

"Your mother."

I pulled my head away from his chest and looked up at him. "My mother? What did you talk to my mother about?"

"The usual. I figured she knows you better than anybody, so I asked her what really makes you happy."

I smiled. "And what did she say?"

"She said the simple things in life, nothing fancy or extravagant. Just knowing that you're loved, she said, means more to you than anything."

"What else did she say?"

"She didn't say much else, but what your father said is what kind of threw me for a loop."

Knowing Daddy better than anyone, I backed away from Collins. "What did he say?"

"He said that his baby girl deserves nothing but

the best. Said you'd been through a lot and he hoped more than anything you'd find happiness. When he told me he'd kill me, I got kind of scared."

I was confused. "Kill you? For what?"

"He said he'd kill me if I didn't live up to his expectations as his son-in-law."

Collins smiled and got down on one knee. I trembled all over, my fingers unable to stay still. He reached in his pocket, and before he could even put the ring on my finger, I screamed out, "Yes!"

He stood up and lifted me with joy.

"Baby," I said in tears after he put me down, "I don't want to wait. I don't want a big wedding because I don't care about all that stuff. I just . . . I just want to do this as soon as possible."

Collins looked shocked. "Like when? How soon are we talking?"

"Soon. Today, or tomorrow, the next day . . . I don't care."

"Okay, then let's make arrangements to leave for Vegas tonight, and by tomorrow we'll be done with it."

"I love you so much," I said, kissing him over and over again.

We parted ways and hurried home to pack. Mama and Daddy had called, trying to find out if I'd accepted Collins' proposal. I informed them that I had, but cut our conversation short because of time. When I thought about calling Pat to tell her, I changed my mind because I knew she would keep me on the phone forever with questions about Jaylin. As for him, I didn't even want to think about how he would feel about the news. For now, I wasn't going to tell him anything. Our plane's departure was at ten fifty-five tonight, and we were going to be on it.

I packed my suitcase and called Collins to tell him I was on my way, but when I made it to the front door, I saw headlights from a truck that pulled into my driveway. I looked at my watch. It was almost eight o'clock. It was obvious that Jaylin didn't get my message about picking up LJ at my parents' house, because it was him.

Panicking, I slid my suitcase by the side of the couch to hide it. I straightened my dress and looked in the mirror beside the door to wipe the dried-up tears from my face. I opened the door and put on a pleasant smile.

"What are you grinning for?" he asked, and then stepped inside.

"No reason. But LJ is with my parents. They had something at church this evening and wanted to take him with them."

"You made me drive all the way over here for nothing? Why didn't you call and tell me to pick him up over there?"

"I did call you. I guess you didn't get my message." I stood close by the door, continuing to hold it open.

His eyes seached me over. "You look nice. Why you all dressed up?"

"I'm having a late dinner with Collins. I was on my way out."

"Dinner, huh?" he said, placing his hands in his pockets and moving toward the living room. I hoped that he wouldn't see my suitcase, so I quickly closed the door and walked toward the kitchen so he would follow me.

"Yeah, dinner," I said, entering the kitchen. "Would you like something to drink?"

"No," he yelled, staying in the living room.

As I stood by the doorway, my heart raced. I thought of many ways to rush him out, but when I opened the kitchen door, he eyes were glued to my suitcase.

"Are you going somewhere?" he asked.

I wasn't good at lying to Jaylin, and getting him to believe me was going to be hard. I placed my hand on my hip and massaged my forehead. "That's, uh, I . . . I packed that when I thought I was going to Detroit."

"You wouldn't happen to be going to Detroit tonight, would you?"

"Look, I told you I wasn't going to Detroit. Now, would you please leave so I can meet Collins for dinner? I'm already late."

Jaylin lifted the suitcase, placing it on the couch. He tried to open it, but it was locked.

"Give me the key," he said, holding out his hand.

"For what?" I snapped.

"Give me the damn key!"

I rushed up to him, reaching for my suitcase. "No! Now, again, would you please leave so I can go?"

"I'm not going anywhere until I see what's in this suitcase. Since you forgot to tell me about the engagement ring on your finger, I know there better not be any of LJ's fucking clothes in this suitcase."

I completely forgot about the ring. "Look," I said, unlocking the suitcase, "there is nothing in here that belongs to LJ. See?"

Jaylin picked through my clothes and then looked at me. "So, when's the wedding? Since you got all this negligee in your suitcase, I assume it's soon."

"I don't know," I said, closing the suitcase, unable to make eye contact.

"You gon' do this to me again, aren't you?"

"Do what, Jaylin?"

"I can't believe that here we go again."

"What are you talking about?"

That look of hurt that I hated to see in his eyes was there. "Nokea, don't play me like no damn fool! You're going to marry this fool, aren't you?"

"No, I am not going to marry a fool! I'm planning on marrying Collins if I can get the hell out of here. But it's just like you to stand here and try to take this opportunity away from me."

"I'm not taking anything away from you. I find it odd, though, that something brought me over here just in the nick of time. And I was going to call and tell you I'd pick up LJ tomorrow because I wasn't feeling well." He turned my shoulders so I could face him. "Nokea, don't do something that you know for a fact you're going to regret."

"I don't regret loving Collins, Jaylin. I won't regret being happy for the rest of my life. I do, however, regret letting this . . . this fuck thing continue with us. It is over and you're going to have to move on now." I took my suitcase off the couch and carried it to the door. Jaylin rushed after me, grabbing my suitcase.

"Fuck thing? You know this ain't no fuck thing

between us, Nokea. Don't do this to me. Please don't leave me like this. I need you. I've always needed you. Marrying Collins is a mistake, baby, and you know it."

I did my best to convince myself that it wasn't. "No, it's not."

"Yes, it is," he fired back.

He snatched the suitcase away from me. I pulled it back, and as we tugged back and forth, it fell open and my clothes fell out. I looked at my watch. It was already eight-thirty. I kneeled down and quickly tried to throw everything back inside of the suitcase. Jaylin wasn't about to let me leave, so he lifted the suitcase, making everything fall out again.

"You're not going to do this to me," he said casually.

"Stop it!" I yelled and covered my face. "Would you please just go?"

He grabbed me by my arms and made me face him again. The hurting child that I remembered seeing in the orphanage stared at me. The one that I'd watched suffer so much over the years because of his mother's death was pleading for me not to do this. The one who had my heart, but had somehow managed to lose it yet again, was before me. This time, however, my mind was made up.

"Do you want me to go be miserable?" he asked. "I've been there and done that. I'm not in a hurry to go do that again."

"Fine, then," I said, moving away from him. "Stay here. I gotta go."

I left my suitcase and rushed to my car. I looked at him standing on my porch and quickly drove off. By the time I was less than a mile down the road, I thought about going back, but I couldn't. Something inside wouldn't allow me to. That didn't stop me from pulling over to the side of the road to release my emotions, but I didn't turn around.

I made it to Collins' house around nine-fifteen and we headed for the airport. Having plenty of time, we embraced each other as we waited for our plane's departure. I visualized Jaylin's expression on my porch, but my thoughts of marrying Collins helped to ease my pain.

I was even more at ease when the plane took off for Vegas, and I was calm by the time it arrived. We got a room for the night, woke up early the next morning to take care of business, and by late evening, I became Mrs. Collins Lorenzo Jefferson.

I was so glad to put my love for Jaylin behind me. For some reason, after I told Collins what had happened at my house, he didn't think I would go through with our marriage. I reminded him about how much I loved him, and stressed how important it was for me to live a peaceful life. Knowing that I didn't have to worry about Collins loving me one moment and then not loving me the next, like Jaylin would have done, my decision was not a difficult one.

# 27

## *JAYLIN*

I was sick to my stomach. I stayed at Nokea's house for at least another hour, and when she didn't come back, I locked her place up and left. I couldn't believe that fool Collins had smoothed her over and taken her in an instant, just like that. My heart ached as I thought about him being the victor, and I figured he was on cloud nine about Nokea's decision. Still, a tiny part of me had faith that Nokea wasn't going to go through with it.

I left her place and drove around for a while, thinking hard about our relationship. Majic 104.9 put daggers in my heart when they played Brian McKnight's "Shoulda, Woulda, Coulda." Maybe I should have been a better man. If it was too late for me, then I had no one else to blame but myself. I had messed over Nokea for years, so why did I expect her to sit around and wait for me to get my shit together? My eyes welled with tears, so I pulled over to the side of the road and chilled. I couldn't believe that my thoughts of her being married to someone else had caused me so much hurt, and I hoped she'd call me soon.

I sat in my truck for hours, thinking about my mistakes. I didn't want to go home because Scorpio was the last person I wanted to see. She made me so sick, but my hands were tied because of Mackenzie. I knew I was about to lose her, and I couldn't understand how I managed to travel back down this road again. The stress was too much for me, so I got a room for the night and did what I knew best—got drunk.

By morning, my head spun and I was laid out on the floor with the covers wrapped around me. The last thing I remembered was taking a shower and getting my dick sucked. Thing is, I didn't remember by who.

There was a knock on the door. When somebody called out housekeeping, last night's events entered my memory. I opened the door and saw the same chick from housekeeping that came to my room last night to bring me some extra pillows. Jennifer, she said her name was. I moved away from the door to let her in. She was a plain-Jane kind of white gal, had nice breasts, straight long blonde hair, and blue eyes. Her ass was nothing to brag about, but right about now, I didn't care what she looked like. All I wanted to do was roll over and die.

"Did you get enough rest?" she asked.

"No," I said in a dry tone as I sat on the bed. "What time is it?"

"Almost noon. Before I clocked out, I wanted to stop in and check on you. Last night, you seemed so—"

"Look, I'm fine. I just need some more rest, so if you don't mind."

She walked toward the door, then turned to face me. "Say, Jaylin?"

"What's up?"

"Do you mind if I call you some time so we can go out? I mean, you . . . you really seem like a nice person."

I stood up and made my way to the door. Before saying anything, I kissed Jennifer's forehead. "Do yourself a favor and forget about last night. By the time I leave this room today, I will have no recollection of what happend. Do you understand what I'm saying?"

She gave me a fake grin and nodded. After she left, I showered, put on my clothes, and jetted.

When I got home, Nanny B was on her knees, scrubbing the hell out of the kitchen floor. I stood in the doorway and shook my head.

"You don't have to clean the floor like that. I know my floor ain't that dirty, is it?"

She squeezed the wet sponge in the bucket and stood up. "I'm trying to keep myself busy. Why didn't you come home last night?"

"Because I had something to do. Where are Scorpio and Mackenzie? And did anybody call?"

"Why ya asking? You don't return anybody's calls anyway. And Scorpio took Mackenzie to dance class."

"Did Nokea call?"

"No, she hasn't. But everybody else has. Shane and Ray-Ray said call them when you get a chance; a few of your lady friends called, but I'm not relaying any names to you. And Delores and Jeffrey called. They wanted to know if you still planned on going to the family reunion. If so, they said for you to call them."

I put my hands in my pockets and looked down. "No, I'm not going. I'm not in the mood."

"Well, suit yourself. What's wrong with you anyway? Why the long face?"

I looked at Nanny B, as the look of hurt was still fresh in my eyes. "She bailed out on me."

"Who?"

"Nokea. I think she married Collins."

Nanny B took a deep breath and reached for my hand to hold it with hers. "Just let her be, Jaylin. If that's what she wants, then there's nothing you can do."

"I know. But, I thought—"

"Well, you thought wrong. You can plan your life out all you want to, but the Man upstairs has the final say so." She lifted my chin and looked at me with sympathy in her eyes. "Move on, Jaylin. If there's anything I can do, let me know."

"There's not much that anyone can do right now. I'm just praying for some kind of miracle."

Nanny B crossed her fingers and I headed upstairs to my bedroom. I got more irritated when I saw the bed hadn't been made up, Scorpio's shoes weren't in the closet where they belonged, and her nightgown was laid across the chaise. In the bathroom, she left her makeup on the counter and a towel was lying in the middle of the floor. I snatched it up and tossed it in the hamper where it belonged.

As soon as she got home, I inquired about Mackenzie. Scorpio had dropped her off at Megan's house, so that gave me a moment to address my concerns.

"If you're going to continue to live here, please pick up after yourself. I'm not your fucking maid and neither is Nanny B."

"I didn't have time to make up the bed because Mackenzie ran late for her dance class. As for the towel, maybe I should have picked it up. The shoes and the nightgown—don't be so petty."

"I find it quite odd that when I don't come home, you always find little shit like your uncleanliness to tick me off. Stop playing games with me, okay? The next time you leave my room in this condition, I might not be so nice."

She put her hand on her hip and rolled her neck around. "And the next time you decide to stay out all night long, I might not be so nice either. Anyway, where were you? You could have called to let me know you weren't coming home."

"Call to tell you that I was at a hotel getting my dick sucked? I thought that might be a bit disrespectful, but since we don't mind going there, I'm telling you where I was now. "

"I hope it was good. But since you came home to me, maybe not, huh?"

I wasn't up to arguing with her today, and it certainly wasn't on my list of priorities. Instead, I went downstairs to my office to use the phone. I called Shane and listened to him gripe about me not returning his calls.

"So, that's how a brotha get played? No returned phone calls, no nothing, huh?" he said.

"Man, I've been living in another world. I don't know if I'm coming or going."

"So I take it things haven't gotten any better."

"No, actually, they've gotten worse. But I'm not going to sit here and cry about it. What's been up with you? Everything cool?"

"Real cool. Things been kind of looking up. You remember that investment I told you about with Felicia?"

"Yeah, I remember."

"Well, that's going along pretty smooth. She . . . I wanted to talk to you about investing or being a part of this, but that's totally up to you."

"I don't know, man, but don't hold your breath. I got enough shit going on as it is."

"Making more money never hurts anybody. I can fill you in on what we're doing, but why don't you call her too? She's got some good ideas, and I think you might be interested."

"I might. If anything, though, I might just give a li'l donation since you got your hands in it."

"Now, I'd appreciate that too. But again, that's up to you."

"Cool. Now, is there anything else you want to bug me about?"

"Yep. Have you talked to Stephon?"

"Nope."

"Well, I was hoping that we—"

"Shane, I'm not going there with you."

"I know you don't want to hear it, but he said—"

"I don't want to know what he said. If you're going to be a friend of mine, then be one. When it comes to Stephon and my brothaship, it's done. Don't interfere anymore, okay?"

"Cool. I'm done with it."

"Good. Again, if there's nothing else, I'll call you later."

"Peace," he said, and then hung up.

I stayed in my office for a while and then picked up the phone to call Felicia. When she answered, I wasted no time getting to the point.

"So, tell me about this new business you're trying to start," I said.

"Why don't you come over so I can tell you all about it?"

I hesitated to respond because I knew Felicia had other things on her mind. I did too, so I told her I'd be right over.

I changed clothes and grabbed my keys to go. Of course, Scorpio stopped me on my way out.

"Do you mind telling me where you're going?" she asked.

"Do you really want to know?"

"Yes."

"I'm going to see Felicia."

"Felicia! For what?" she yelled.

"Business and pleasure."

"Don't lower your standards and start messing with her again."

"My standards are already low if I keep fucking with you, so what's the difference?"

"Don't you dare compare me to that bitch. We have nothing in common and you know it."

"He's called the boss man, baby, or the head Negro in charge. Remember Stephon? Every woman goes to see him in her time of trouble."

She couldn't say nothing, so I winked and walked out.

*  *  *

When I got to Felicia's house, she was on the phone with Shane. She told him I was there to talk business, and when she gave the phone to me, he laughed.

"When you mean business, you really mean business, don't you?" he said.

"Yeah, something like that," I said, sitting back on the couch. I glanced at Felicia, who was already kneeled in front of me, unzipping my pants. "Tell me something, Shane, and I want the truth."

"What's up?"

"Have you had sex with Felicia lately?"

"Naw, dog. It's strictly business for me. You can ask her for yourself."

Felicia removed her panties and I reached into my pocket, handing her a condom. She slid it on me and admired my growth.

"Shane, how about I let you take care of the new business, and for now, I take care of some personal business?"

"Jay, it's whatever you want to do. Just learn a li'l something about what she's trying to do with the business, a'ight?"

Felicia straddled my lap, putting my dick inside of her. She had always been a good rider, and rode me like she had something to prove. I held the phone up to my ear with my shoulder and massaged her ass. Shane cleared his throat.

"Did you hear what I said?" he asked.

"Aw . . . yeah, I agree. Let's talk tomorrow."

"Will do," he said, and then hung up.

I let the phone drop and continued to let Felicia

work me until she got tired. That took a while, and by then, I felt angry about being there again, about Nokea and Collins, and about my messed-up relationship with Scorpio. I took my frustrations out on Felicia, and fucked her as hard as I could. Being the freak that she was, she allowed me to put her in every position I could imagine. We ended the session with her bending over the couch and me smacking her insides from behind.

"Come with me," I demanded while watching her ass jiggle. "Back it up, baby girl, and come with me."

I took deep strokes inside of her, and right after I exploded, she did. I leaned over her body feeling drained.

She reached her hand back and rubbed my ass. "Jaylin, that was so, so good. I've missed this. We've got to make up for our lost time."

"We will—later," I said, easing myself out of her. I went to the bathroom and quickly wiped up.

When I returned, Felicia was on the couch with her robe on. I sat next to her, rubbing her leg. "So, are you ready to talk business or what?"

"I'd rather be doing something else, but we got all night for that, right?"

"Of course, but, uh, tell me what's the plan. I think you have potential as a businesswoman/entrepreneur, so I'd like to hear some of your ideas."

Felicia hipped me to the partnership she and Shane were trying to create. I really wasn't interested in being a partner, so I told her I'd make a generous donation. I didn't say how much it would be, but I did tell her I'd talk to Shane about it and give the money to him.

It wound up being a long night at Felicia's house. I didn't head home until three o'clock in the morning, and Scorpio had the nerve to be up in bed waiting for me. She wanted to argue, but I did the usual: took a shower, climbed into bed, and ignored her. I turned out the lamp, and she reached over, turning it back on.

"You had sex with her tonight, didn't you?" she asked.

"Yep." I pulled the covers over my head.

She yanked the covers back and got out of bed. She snatched her body pillow, and I knew she was headed to one of the guestrooms. I cleared my throat and spoke calmly to her. "I want you out of my house, Scorpio. The sooner you leave, the better."

"Never," she said, and then stormed out.

She was dying from my ill treatment. But she had no idea how vicious I could get. I guess she thought I was playing with her, so maybe it was time for her to see with her own eyes that I wasn't.

On Monday, I took things to another level. I knew Felicia would be hounding me after fucking her so well, and that she was. She called while Scorpio was at school, and I asked her to come over. Of course, she was proud to show her face at my crib again. It was just the ammunition I needed.

After she arrived, we went to my basement and I showed her the updates I'd made to it. I poured both of us a drink and we sat at the bar talking.

Felicia got tipsy, and so did I. She was all over me, ready for me to stick it to her again.

I knew that Scorpio was coming home soon, so I undressed Felicia and walked her over to my couch. I lay back, and she straddled me like I was a horse. She opened my robe and began to massage my chest.

"Did I ever tell you how much you mean to me?" She smiled.

"Not recently, but I'm glad to have made such an impact."

Felicia leaned down for a lengthy kiss, and that's when I heard the alarm chime when someone opened the front door .

"Who is that?" Felicia whispered.

"Probably my nanny. Don't worry; she won't come down here."

We got back to kissing, and just as Felicia was stroking me down below, we heard footsteps on the stairs. Felicia turned her head to the side and my hands went up to cuff her ass. I massaged it, and her attention turned back to me.

"Jaylin, who—?"

I looked over Felicia's shoulder. Scorpio stood at the bottom of the stairs. Her arms were folded, her eyebrows showed a high arch. Seeing Felicia's backside had obviously angered her.

"Can't you see I'm busy?" I said with a calm voice.

Felicia looked behind her and smiled. She did not remove herself from on top of me, and instead of getting up, she pulled at my boxers to remove them. My hard dick plopped out. That's when Scorpio had seen enough. She rushed over to us, and when Felicia backed away, Scorpio slapped the shit out of me.

"You bastard!" she yelled and punched my chest. "I hate you! I swear to God that I hate every single thing about you."

I sat up and spoke calmly to Scorpio again. "I said it before, and I'll say it again: I want you out of my house—soon. If you hate me so much, then leaving here shouldn't be no problem."

When she tightened her fist to punch me again, I hurried to grab it. "I'm not going to fight with you, Scorpio. Just do us both a favor and get out of here."

Scorpio snatched her wrist away from me with a gang of smoke coming from her ears. Her face was beet red and her eyes were stabbing me like sharp knives. Even Felicia saw what I did, but she had already backed away from the madness. I stood to remove my robe, and after I tossed it to Felicia to cover up, Scorpio slapped me again. This time, I'd had enough. I pushed her back on the couch and pressed my knee against her stomach so she wouldn't move.

"This is payback for spitting in my damn face at Stephon's house. Now, stop all the drama and get the fuck out of my house before I hurt you even more."

I removed my knee from her midsection, but she was trying like hell to provoke me. She tried to damage my goods with her feet, so I grabbed her ankle and twisted it. "Do you want me to hurt you?" I said, slightly turning it. The pain was becoming unbearable, and she yelled for me to let go. I did, and then turned my attention to Felicia, who seemed to be getting a kick out of the whole damn thing.

"Put your clothes on," I ordered.

Felicia rolled her eyes, and as she walked over to the bar to get her clothes, Scorpio got up too. She headed in Felicia's direction, but I stood between them.

"Move, Jaylin," Felicia yelled. "If that bitch want some of me, I'll be willing to give her something to remember."

Scorpio reached over me to take a swipe at Felicia, but missed. I shoved her backward and yelled for her to get out once again.

"The two of you deserve each other." She chuckled. "How . . . how could I have been such a fool?" She moved her head from side to side, wiped her tears, and hurried up the stairs. I was glad because I knew she was on her way out.

"She was about to get hurt up in here," Felicia said while putting on her clothes.

"I apologize for getting you involved. I'll call you later, all right?"

Felicia was hot as we walked upstairs together. I opened the front door and smacked her ass on the way out.

"You are a mean brotha," she said. "You knew she was on her way home, didn't you?"

I shrugged my shoulders. "A man gotta do what he gotta do, baby."

"I guess so," she said, then leaned in for a kiss. "Call me," she said, and jetted.

I hurried upstairs to see if the "love of my life" was gathering her things to go. Surprisingly, she was. I sat on the bed, propped up my feet with a pillow, and watched. I even threw in a few whistles here and there to piss her off. She didn't like my calm attitude, and picked up a shoe to throw it at me.

"Bastard!" she yelled.

"I got a few names for you, too, but I won't go there. Just keep packing, all right?"

She rolled her eyes, and my whistles continued. I had this day planned out in my mind, so I made sure Nanny B and Mackenzie were gone for the entire day. So far, everything was falling into place.

"I can't believe this shit," she fussed while slamming her clothes on the bed. "Why did you ever come into my life? I shouldn't have ever moved into this damn house with you. It was truly a big, big mistake!" She went back into the closet.

"I agree."

She pointed her finger at me. "Don't say nothing to me! When I leave here, don't you come looking for me, or for Mackenzie. We never want to see your face again."

"Speak for yourself. And Mackenzie's not leaving here until I say she leaves. Just in case you forgot, I have custody of her too."

"Well, she's not going to live with you. She's going to live with me, whether you like it or not."

"Don't be so angry, baby. Why your face turning red? I'm not going to keep Mackenzie from you. She's your daughter. So, if it makes you happy, you're not the only one losing out. I'm going to lose out big time, but that's just how it's got to be."

She didn't have nothing else to say. She gave

me crazy looks, and when I boldly talked on the phone to Yolanda, a young lady I met the other day, Scorpio threw one of her three-inch heels at me. I ducked, but it hit my expensive lamp, knocking it to the ground.

"Yo-Yo, let me call you back," I said, ending the call and standing to my feet. "Hurry up and get your crazy ass out of here," I yelled at Scorpio. "As a matter of fact,"—I walked into the closet—"you ain't moving fast enough for me. Let me help you get your shit. Everything's already nice and neat for you, so it shouldn't take you this damn long."

When I started to help, she stood with her arms folded. She couldn't stop telling me how much she hated me, and when she tried to strike me again, I pushed her to the ground.

"If you hate me so much then leave!" I rushed over to the phone and picked it up. "It's either the police or a taxi. Which one do I call? Your choice."

She threw a bottle of perfume at me this time, and to prevent myself from picking up an assault charge, I dialed 911.

On my way downstairs to open the door for the police, she continued to curse at me. I explained to the police that I had an irate bitch upstairs, and made it clear that I wanted her to leave. They walked upstairs with me to my bedroom.

"Ma'am," one of the officers said, "if you're not on the deed or occupancy permit to this house, you'll have to leave."

"Neither," I said, with both papers in my hands. I quickly handed them over to the officer. He looked at them and told Scorpio she had ten minutes to get the rest of her things and go.

Taking her time, she managed to occupy thirty more minutes of my time. Even so, she was on her way out. She called her sister Leslie to come get her, and when she couldn't reach Leslie, she called the taxi that I had offered to call for her earlier.

After Scorpio and the officers left, I closed the door and sat in the middle of the stairs. Finally, I felt closure. A sense of relief came over me, but I also knew the road ahead would be tough. I had less than one month left with Mackenzie, and after that, I was going to let her go for good. There was no other way for this to work itself out. I knew if I kept a hold on her, I'd have to keep Scorpio in my life. Without a single doubt and no more questions asked, that was something I had no desire to do.

That night, I called Nokea to see if she'd made it back home. I still didn't know if she went through with the marriage, and I truly hoped that she hadn't. I had faith in what we still shared, and hoped more than anything she still had faith in us as well. Getting no answer, I left a message for her to call me the moment she got in.

# 28

## *SCORPIO*

I could have killed Jaylin for the way he treated me. And then, to bring that bitch Felicia to the house and fuck her was the worst thing he could have ever done. I truly thought we would work out our differences, but any kind of reconciliation between us was out of the question now.

It puzzled me why he was so angry with me for having sex with Stephon. He didn't trip with Nokea for doing so, or Felicia. Why the hell was he being so hard on me? It didn't make sense. I could see if Stephon and I had been at it multiple times. Actually, we'd only had sex for about ten minutes before Jaylin came in.

He was always bragging about *his* pussy and *his* ass. Well, he should have taken care of his pussy and ass, instead of running to Nokea's house, taking care of hers. I was furious about the whole thing, and wanted to kill him for what he'd done. Then, to call the police on me like I was some kind of threat to him really pissed me off.

How dare he treat me this way, especially after all the crap I put up with from him?

At this point, all I wanted was my child, and for him to stay the fuck out of our lives. He'd asked for one month with her, but I was only giving him two weeks. After that, he'd have to adjust without her. The only reason I allowed him two weeks was because I knew how Mackenzie felt about him. She was going to be devastated, and it was up to him to tell her why things didn't work out.

I paced the floor at Leslie's house. Damn, I was mad! I was mad at myself for not moving on sooner, mad at myself for allowing him to get away with all the crap he did, and certainly mad at myself for not planning for a future without him.

If anything, I should have listened to Nanny B a long time ago. She warned me, but stupid me, yakking on and on about how much we loved each other and how in the end, we'd still be together. He knew damn well he always wanted Nokea, but didn't have the guts to say it. What a waste of his time and money, continuing this charade with me. Even trying to have a baby with me was ridiculous, especially since he'd known about his feelings for Nokea. He was one confused motherfucker, and I didn't care if I ever saw his high yellow butt again.

I stayed up all night, thinking about what had happened. I had already cried so much I couldn't even allow one more tear to fall. What good was all this crying going to do me anyway? I wasn't doing nothing but hurting myself, because he for damn sure was moving on with his life, and moving on fast.

The next morning, I got up early and went to school. School was the only thing I had going for me, so it didn't make sense to allow the hurt from my relationship to hold me back. I stayed focused in my classes, and not even thinking about Jaylin, I started to feel like I was getting something accomplished.

In my theatrical class, my instructor, Mr. Betts, asked me to stay after class so we could talk. I thought it was in reference to my absences, but he told me how much he enjoyed reading my scripts. He asked if he could use one to create a play, and I was more than happy to let him do so.

For the next several days, Mr. Betts and I worked hard at reworking my script, and still, Jaylin was far from my mind. It wasn't until my fourth day away from him that things started to get rough. Mackenzie had been heavy on my mind too, but I didn't want to be the one to break the news to her about things not working out between Jaylin and me. She hated coming to Leslie's house, and I knew it was up to me to find a place for us soon.

I was curious to find out if somebody had already taken my place. Not being able to go another day without hearing from Jaylin or Mackenzie, I called Jaylin's house. Nanny B answered.

"Hello," I greeted. "I know Mackenzie isn't home yet, but is Jaylin there?"

"Yes."

"Can I talk to him?"

"Scorpio, he has company. But I'm glad you called, because I want to talk to you."

My throat ached, but I wasn't surprised. "About what?"

"About what I mentioned to you at the hotel. The offer still stands, and I'd really like for Mackenzie and you to have the money."

"Why, Nanny B? Why are you still trying to help me when you know I don't deserve it? I should have listened to you and tried to help myself."

"Yes, you should have, but you didn't. You can, however, take the money and plan for a better life for you and Mackenzie's future."

"I appreciate it, but why . . . why us?"

"Because I love Mackenzie, Scorpio. More so, I love Jaylin, and I know how much it's going to hurt him to lose her. The only way he's going to be able to part with her is if he knows for a fact she's going to be well taken care of. I want to make sure that happens. I'm offering you the money because I know he's going to make you an offer as well. I want you to be woman enough and turn him down. If you have to, tell him to go to hell with his money because you don't need it. If you accept it, he's going to feel as if you'll always need him, or you can't make it without him. This will be our secret, and I promise you he will never know anything about it."

"Based on what has happened, my decision has changed. It was easy for me to decline your offer before, but I now know that Jaylin and I have no future together. I shouldn't have depended on him, but I did. Thank you so much for helping me out of this messed-up situation. I'll be forever grateful."

Nanny B asked me to give Jaylin and her a month with Mackenzie. After what she'd done for me, how could I refuse? It puzzled me as to where she got the money from, but I didn't even want to know. She had to be more to Jaylin than just his nanny, but at this point, it didn't even matter. She had come through for me, and her generosity was right on time.

Before ending our conversation, I asked Nanny B if she would tell me who was at the house with Jaylin. She wouldn't tell me, but she did say it was somebody she or I didn't know. That, of course, kicked out my suspicions of it being Nokea or Felicia. Jaylin had already had a new bitch occupying his time. He was known for not wasting any time.

The weekend came and was almost gone. I lay downstairs on a bed in Leslie's basement in deep thought about what could have been. By this time, yes, I was miserable. Nobody understood how badly I felt about losing Jaylin. As much as I tried to say that what I'd done was justified, I knew that putting myself out there for Stephon was the stupidest thing I could have ever done. I said I wanted it over between us, and I'll be damned if Jaylin didn't give me what I wanted.

As I lay there in misery, I was surprised when Leslie brought the phone to me and told me it was Jaylin. Anxious to talk, I took a deep breath before placing the phone on my ear.

"Hello," I said softly.

"I called to speak to you about Mackenzie."

"What about her, Jaylin?"

"Nanny B's going to bring her to you at the end of next week. There's no need to prolong my misery, and I'm tired of lying to her about why you're not around."

"That's fine with me. I just wanted to allow you all the time you needed."

"I'll be fine. She's getting older, and she understands more things than we give her credit for. I had a long talk with her last night, and I think she understands why two people who love each other simply can't be together."

"No, I guess we can't. But it's nice to hear that you still love me."

"I love you from a distance, though. There's a difference."

"There's no difference. Love is love, no matter how you look at it."

"Well, I'm looking at it from here, and you're looking at it from over there. As long as you stay there, we'll be cool."

I laughed. It felt so good to hear his voice. "I really fucked this up, didn't I? Having sex with Stephon was the ultimate betrayal, wasn't it?"

Jaylin was silent for a while, and then he responded, "Let's not talk about this, okay?"

"No, it's not okay. I need to know why my having sex with him hurt you so badly when other women in your life have done the same thing."

"Scorpio, you just don't get it, do you?" His voice got loud. I didn't intend for us to go there, but I wanted to know why.

"No, I don't get it. I mean you . . . you had every right to be mad at me, and you still have every right, but it was only ten minutes with somebody I had no love for."

"And for me, that ten minutes cost us a lifetime of happiness. Why? Because you were the one thing I had and loved that Stephon couldn't take away from me. Since day one, he wanted you so badly, but I promised myself he would never have you.

"During the time he slept with Nokea, we were not together. She was free to do whatever she wanted to do, and with whomever she wanted to do it. The nine years that we were together, not once did she betray me. In spite of all my bullshit, she remained faithful to me. After we broke up, Stephon moved in for the kill. She was vulnerable and she gave in. I couldn't be mad at her for moving on when I had moved on myself.

"As for LJ, now, that's a different story. She was wrong, and so was Stephon. But it was another attempt of his to take something else away from me.

"Bottom line is, you and I were together, baby. You were engaged to me, and something like that should have never happened."

I still tried to defend myself. "But I was angry about seeing you with Nokea."

"So, did it make sense for you to go fuck my cousin? Hell naw! If anything you should have demanded some answers from me and called me on my shit like you always did before. If you had asked why I was at Nokea's place, I would have told you the truth. If you had asked if I was about to make love to her, I would have told you the truth again. Whether you wanted to hear the truth or not, you knew I would have been honest. I always allowed you to make choices and often laid my true feelings on the line. Either you were going to accept me, or you weren't. And if you weren't, then you should have been woman enough to walk out of this house on your own free will and leave my ass alone."

"That's easy for you to say now. I made many attempts to talk to you about your feelings for Nokea. You weren't honest with me about your feelings for her, because you weren't being true to yourself. Either way, nothing's going to help me fix this mess I've gotten us into. I do appreciate you telling me how you feel now. You never really opened up to me like this before. Since you're doing it now, I would like to know, do you still love Nokea? And were you about to have sex with her that day?"

He cleared his throat. "Yes, and possibly. I do still very much love Nokea, and if she would have allowed me to, I would have had sex with her that day."

His words stung and my eyes welled with tears. "How can you still love her after all we've been through? You don't know how much it hurts to hear you say that. Did you even love me as much as you loved her?"

"Trust me, I'm not trying to hurt your feelings. I can be blamed for our failed relationship too. This ain't all on you. Don't be so hard on yourself, okay?"

"I'll try not to be, but you didn't answer my question about who you loved more."

"There were many times that I thought I loved

you more, but times that I realized I didn't. When I asked you to marry me, it wasn't no game. I wanted you to be my wife because there was nobody that I loved in this world more than you. But then all the lies started, and I didn't know how to deal with it, baby. We worked it out by having sex, but honestly, the hurt never did go away. Eventually, I turned to other women, and sometimes had no regrets for doing so. That was a signal for me that something was wrong."

"Damn, Jaylin, we know where we made our mistakes. Why does this have to end? I can't take back what I did with Stephon, but I promise you it will never happen again. If I ever get angry with you, I will call you on your shit and demand some answers from you. Please don't end our relationship like this. Take time to think about it before you call this completely off with me."

"I have thought about it. I'm making myself sick thinking about it. To me, we've hurt each other enough and the final verdict is in: it's time to move on. The reason I called was to offer you some money for you and Mackenzie. I want my child to be well taken care of, and you'll have to find a better place to live. As you know, Mackenzie has money already due to her when she turns eighteen, but that's a long way down the road. For now, I want you to get on your feet and provide for her like you've never provided for anybody in your life. I don't want to know where you decide to move, I don't want no phone number, and I definitely don't want a key. Just take what I'm offering you and go be happy."

"But there's no way we're going to be happy without you."

"Yes, you will. It might take some time, but one day you will be."

"I can't take the money, Jaylin. I've got to stand on my own. I've taken enough handouts from you, and I don't want any more. Just please support my decision. I promise you that Mackenzie will be fine."

"Are you sure? I know you're a good mother, but can you provide—"

"You have my word."

"And I'm going to hold you to it. Now, can I please get off this phone? I'm not a phone person, and I don't like talking to anybody this long."

I smiled because I knew he was giving me special treatment. "Before you go, can I ask you one more question?"

"What?"

"Are you going to marry Nokea?"

He paused again. "Right now, I'm approaching life one day at a time. I need to be by myself for a while, and as for Nokea, I'm gon' sit back to see what happens. She could very well be a married woman as we speak. The last time we spoke, she was on her way to becoming one."

That was music to my ears. "Are you serious?"

"Very."

"I know you don't want to hear this, but maybe her getting married is a sign that we need to do the same."

"And what is getting married going to do for us? Is a piece of paper going to stop all of the lying and deceiving one another? Is it going to allow us to put everything that's happened between us in the past? I don't think so, baby, and I'm not about to live in a fantasy world."

I nearly choked on my spit. This was reality, and I very well had to face it. "Thanks for talking to me. I love you, and I always will, no matter who you're with."

"I know. Now, I gotta go," he said.

He hung up and I held the phone in my hand. A little "I love you too" would have been nice, but I guess I expected too much from him.

Of course, I couldn't sleep a wink thinking about Jaylin. What if Nokea did get married? Wouldn't that at least crack the door again for us? I took in everything he said about this being over, but nobody could blame me for still wanting to hang on like I did. Jaylin left one hell of an impression on me, and I hoped that our final chapter hadn't been written.

# 29

# *NOKEA*

Collins and I finally made it back from Vegas. I had the time of my life and so did he. We'd stayed cooped up in a hotel suite for almost two weeks, and when we got back home, the honeymoon still wasn't over. We stopped by my parents' place to check on them and LJ. After seeing that everything was fine, we went back to Collins' place and continued our honeymoon for at least another week.

Collins wined and dined me the entire time. He bought me dozens and dozens of roses, and we had candlelit dinners almost every night. He even picked out the lingerie he wanted me in for the day, and had rose petals spread throughout his entire bedroom. The only people who entered the house were the masseuses who came to give us massages. Tense from all of the excitement, I enjoyed every bit of it. Being with him was like a dream come true, and my husband was responsible for making me happier than I'd ever imagined.


By Monday morning, it was back to business for me. I told Collins there was no way I was quitting my job, and he didn't try to persuade me. We did, however, want to live together, so I called a real estate agent to help sell my house. I made an appointment to meet her at my house at seven. Before doing anything else, I had to return Jaylin's numerous calls. He left me fourteen messages, and I at least owed him the truth. He wasn't only angry with me about my decision to marry Collins, but also, he was furious because LJ had been at my parents' house for almost three weeks and he hadn't seen him.

When I called to speak to him, even Nanny B was upset with me. She said she'd missed LJ as well, and said it was wrong for me not to let them know what was going on. I wanted to tell her to get over it, but that wouldn't have been appropriate. Either way, she continued with her attitude, and I expected the same from Jaylin. When he got on the phone, all I could do was hope and pray that I didn't have to listen to this mess for the rest of my life.

"All I'm saying is you could have at least called. If you didn't want to talk to me, cool. But you could have called Nanny B and said something to her."

"Jaylin, I was very busy. I'm sorry, but I didn't have time to go back and forth with you and my parents about LJ. When I left, he was in a safe place, and in the same safe place when I got back."

"So he ain't safe when he's over here? Is that what you're telling me?"

"I'm not saying that. I didn't want to have to worry about him, that's all."

"That's bullshit and you know it. If anything, you didn't want to listen to me tell you how foolish it would be for you to get married. Not only that, but you didn't want to have to call my house with Collins around."

"All I wanted was peace and quiet. That's what I got, and that's all there is to it."

"So what else did you get? Did you just happen to get a husband while you were away?"

Over the phone was not how I wanted to break the news to him. "Come by my house later on today, okay?"

"I'll be busy later on," he said, yelling through the phone. "Yes or no? Did you or didn't you get married?"

"I said come by later so we can talk."

"You did, didn't you?"

"I want to see you la—"

"Damn you, Nokea," he said softly. "Damn you." He hung up.

I knew this wasn't going to be easy for him, and feeling hurt myself, I dropped my head on my desk. A few tears had the nerve to fall, but when it came to the bond we shared, that's just how things were. Whenever he hurt, I hurt. Whenever I hurt, he hurt. It was so sad that we couldn't work things out, but he had to know that this day was destined to come.

At the end of the day, I gathered my things to leave. Collins had some flowers delivered to me today, and the enclosed card asked for his new bride to hurry home. I was so proud to be his wife, and quickly left to meet the agent so I could get to Collins soon.

When I got home, Jaylin was parked in front of my house. A part of me knew he would be there, so I had already prepared myself for his visit.

I got out of my car and pulled my briefcase and folders from my trunk. Jaylin leaned against his truck with his hands in his pockets and watched. Looking awfully gorgeous in his well-pressed khakis, dark shades, and peach button-down Polo shirt that hugged every muscle in his arms, it was kind of hard to ignore him, but I did.

I closed the trunk, and he followed me inside. Not saying a word to each other, I laid my things on the floor. He grabbed my arm, swinging me around to face him. He removed his sunglasses so I could once again look into his hurting eyes. I tried to pull myself away from his grip, but he grabbed my arm tighter.

"How could you do this to us?" he said, swallowing hard. I couldn't stand to look into his eyes, so I lowered my head, looking down at the floor. "Look at me, damn it! How in the fuck could you go marry this fool, knowing how much we love each other?"

I looked up and saw a tear roll down his handsome face. "Jaylin, I love Collins—"

He shook me by my arms. "Bullshit, Nokea! You know damn well you don't love his ass. Did you think marrying him would destroy your feelings for me? It's right here, baby." He pounded his chest with his fist. "Stop fooling yourself. You know damn well who you're in love with."

I didn't want to confess my feelings for him, and started to cry as well. I pounded his chest and screamed out, "Why won't you let this go? Why can't you just leave me alone? Please, Jaylin, just leave me alone."

"I can't because I love you." He put my arms around his waist, and then wrapped his around mine. I leaned my head against his chest, and we stood full of emotions. Jaylin pulled me back, held my shoulders, and looked face to face with me. "Your marriage to Collins means nothing to me. All you have is a piece of paper that I'm going to do everything in my power to destroy. Don't make me go to the extreme. Accept this for what it is and do something about it."

He leaned forward to kiss me, and I'll be damned if my tongue didn't have the pleasure of dancing with his. It was a very intense moment, and when his hands lowered to raise my skirt, I was supposed to stop him, but didn't. I reached for his zipper, but that's when he stopped me. He cradled my face in his hands and wiped my tears with his thumbs.

"I refuse to make love to a married woman. Correct this mess so we can be together. I'll wait to hear from you—soon." He pecked my forehead and left.

Feeling as confused as I was, I wished that I was dreaming. I couldn't believe how badly I wanted him. My mind had been made up, and that's all there was to it! For God's sake, I was a married woman now. I had a husband whom I loved, and there was no reason for me to correct anything. So what, the feelings I still had for Jaylin didn't go away? Now what? Eventually they would disappear, and everything was bound to work itself out—I hoped.

The agent finally showed up and we talked for hours about what we needed to do to get started on selling my house. It sounded pretty simple to me, so we made plans to put my house on the market the following week. After she left, I called Collins and told him I was on my way.

When I got there, as usual, he was on a roll. Dinner was on the table, the candles were lit, soft music played, and my lingerie for the night was laid across the chaise in the living room. I was full of emotions about what had happened earlier, and could barely look into the eyes of my own husband. He questioned my demeanor, but I told him I had some issues at work and was a bit sad about selling the home I'd lived in for years. I felt bad for already lying to him, and that made the night even worse. If anything, I knew one lie would always lead to another.

Either way, I made it through the night without letting my thoughts of Jaylin completely ruin it for me. Collins and I didn't make love, but just the thought of him holding me in his arms for the rest of our lives was all that I could wish for.

# 30

## *JAYLIN*

Drinking and fucking, fucking and drinking, were all that I could do these days. Nanny B left with Mackenzie on Friday, and after seeing Nokea the following Monday, I seriously had no purpose for living. Just about everyone that I loved had slipped right through my fingers. I couldn't do nothing about either situation, and there was something that bugged the hell out of me about not being in control.

The night Mackenzie and Barbie left, I had to stay away from the house. I didn't return home until Saturday morning, and by then, she was gone. Thing is, I didn't have the guts to tell her that she was never coming back. I talked to her the night before and told her I'd be away for months on business and didn't know when I'd return. She cried hard and made me promise to come get her when I got back. I promised her I would, but there was no way for me to keep that promise.

I stayed in her room for the entire day, torturing myself as I looked at the little things she'd left behind: a few Barbie dolls, her hair brush, and the *Cinderella* book she'd made me read to her at least a million times. I placed it on my chest, and when Nanny B came in and found me, I was a mess. Even she cried with me, but she always gave me the strength and encouragement to move on.

Just when I thought things couldn't get any worse, Nokea hit me with her news. I was so hopeful that she'd come home and say she wanted to work things out with me, but what a fool I'd been again. This time, though, she went all the way. The thought of her having another man's name and making love to him tore me up inside. She was supposed to be Mrs. Jaylin Jerome Rogers. How dare she settle for anything less?

Thing is, though, I never imagined losing Mackenzie or Nokea would be this difficult for me. And crying? Now, that was something that I wasn't supposed to do. I felt like a punk because Nanny B had walked in on me several times when I was in the midst of having one of my moments. She tried to lift my spirits, but there was no way that she or anybody understood what I'd lost. Just last night, Nanny B tried to pull me off the floor. I was stretched out in the kitchen, drunk as hell. I resisted and wound up sleeping there for the entire night.

At times like this, I wasn't being too particular with the women in my life. My dick was anxious for Nokea, but we already know why I wasn't going there. I had some cravings for Scorpio, too, but my heart just wasn't in it. The only thing I could do was continue my freaky-ass fucking with Felicia. I had even brought Mercedes back into the picture, and Yolanda was my newest twang. She was a bit on the thick side, but had a booty that could bounce like a ball.

If anything, though, I knew I would never have a problem going back to any woman I'd been with before. Laying down good pipe like I did had great benefits, and all the women in my past were well within my reach. That, of course, was with the exception of Daisha. Good dick or not, she wasn't having it. When I called to see if she'd shake a brotha down, she straight hung up on my ass and told me I needed Jesus. I agreed, for there was no way for me to get through this without Him.

Once again, I passed out naked on the floor beside my bed. Nanny B came in and hit me across my bare back with a wet towel.

"Why you tripping?" I said, slowly getting off the floor to sit on the bed. My head banged and my body was aching all over. I had one rough night with Mercedes. Her loving was getting better and better each time.

"Is this how you're going to live the rest of your life?" Nanny B asked with a frown on her face.

I rubbed my temples. "Nope."

"Then get your butt up and go do something constructive."

"Look, I got a headache. I don't feel like going anywhere."

She picked up the two empty cans of beer and the Remy bottle on my nightstand. "This isn't the Jaylin I know. You'd better find him and fast."

"And if I don't, what's gonna happen? You gon' leave me too?"

"I just might do that. I'm too old to be babysitting a grown-ass man, Jaylin. Now, go put on some clothes and get your butt out of here. I suggest you not go meet any more women because this damn phone is driving me crazy." She tossed the towel over her shoulder and walked out.

She was a sassy, bossy li'l something, but I knew I'd better get my butt up before she walked out on me too. Then I'd really be fucked.

I took a hot shower and called Shane to see what he was up to. He suggested we go for a ride on our motorcycles, and since I hadn't been on mine this year, I agreed to it. It was scorching hot outside, so I put on my Levi's and a dark blue wifebeater. I slid into my black leather motorcycle boots and reached for my helmet that was hidden away in the closet.

Nanny B was pleased to hear I was going with Shane. I advised her not to wait up for me, covered my eyes with shades, and jetted.

I tore up Highway 70, maneuvering in and out of lanes. When I got to Shane's place, he was already outside waiting for me. He wore his black Levi's, black boots, black T-shirt, and had a black and white bandana tied around his head. I pulled my bike beside his and removed my helmet.

"Are you ready?" I yelled over the loud sounds of our bikes.

"Ready as I'll ever be. Just follow behind the Knight Rider. You just might learn something."

Shane put his helmet on and took off. I followed, but by the time we reached the highway, he straight-up left my ass. He was moving fast, and in order to catch up, I had to crank it up past 100 miles per hour.

We circled the highways in St. Louis about three times before stopping. We parked our bikes on the riverfront and sat on the steps near the Gateway Arch. I pulled off my helmet to stretch, and so did Shane.

"Now, that's what I'm talking 'bout," I said, giving Shane five.

"Me too. I live for days like this, man. That's why I tried to get you and Stephon to—"

"Man, I told you don't bring that cocksucker's name up around me."

"I know what you said, but can't y'all squash that shit? I thought things may have cooled down by now."

"Well, you thought wrong. Stephon cost me some serious losses this time."

"Was it that upsetting to you that he had sex with Scorpio? I mean, I came close to it and you didn't trip as much with me. Can't you and him get past it?"

"I don't know about him, but I can't. I wish Stephon all the luck in the world, but I don't want no dealings with him anymore. Scorpio belonged to me, and I told you fools that time and time again. He wasn't trying to hear it, though. When she went to his place that day, he should have thrown her ass out of his house and called me so I could come kick her ass for being so stupid. But that was asking too much of him."

"Yeah, I feel you. And I'm not trying to put ownership on a woman's pussy, because it goes wherever it wants to, but Felicia was my pussy when you snatched that up from me. If I can put it in the past, why can't you?"

"Would you stop referring to Felicia all the time? All I want to know is, did you love her at the time? If you did, then I was wrong. However, you never said y'all relationship was that serious."

"That's because I didn't want y'all to know. Actually, yes, I was crazy about her. I was troubled by her ending our relationship to be with you."

I placed my hand on Shane's shoulder and spoke with sincerity. "Hey, I'm sorry, dog. I didn't know how much you cared about her. And what about now? You know I've been dipping into that again, don't you?"

"Yeah, I know. I'm a li'l bothered, but I don't have feelings for her like I used to. We're trying to work out this business thing, and that's pretty much it."

"Listen, enough said. I won't ever touch her again. Actually, she kind of working my damn nerves already. And as a friend, you should have told me how you felt. By holding shit back, you're creating another Stephon, and I don't need that in my life again."

"I'll never be like Stephon, but you're right."

"That's cool, but tell me something and be honest."

"I don't have a problem with being honest."

I nodded, knowing that I could trust Shane to tell me the truth. "Okay. If Scorpio came to your place that day and asked you to fuck her, would you have done it?"

"Whew," Shane said, leaning back on the steps. "That's a tough one. She's a badass woman, Jay. But since the opportunity presented itself before, I can honestly say that I wouldn't have. If anything, I would have hurt myself more by doing so because of her love for you. In addition to that, something about your name tattooed on her ass just ruins it for me."

We laughed and bumped our fists together. When I looked up, four females in a red convertible BMW pulled over to the curb and asked for our names.

"My name or his name?" Shane said, pointing to me.

"Both. Y'all both fine," the driver said. The other three sat in the car picking and choosing. We stood up and walked over to the car to get a better look. From a distance, they looked kind of young, but I definitely had to check further into it.

We stood close to the car, quickly noticing that all four of the sistas had it going on, which was quite unusual. Debating on what to do with all this fineness, Shane and I looked at each other, and instantly had a solution.

"What's your names?" I asked, referring to the two in the back.

"We asked first," the driver said.

"This is Knight Rider," I said, pointing to Shane, "and I'm the Cherry Popper."

They laughed. I for damn sure had their attention.

"Cherry Popper," the one in the back said, "can I take a ride with you?"

"I'd like to ride with Knight Rider," another said. "I love me a brotha with twisties, and you, my dear, are wearing them well."

Shane and I glanced at each other again. "Why don't y'all get out of the car?" he said. They grinned and all of them got out. Immediately, our eyes dropped to their backsides, as that would be a true determining factor as to who was working with what tonight. "Okay, give us some names and ages," Shane said.

The driver responded. "I'm Toni, and I'm twenty-five. Ebony and Alisha are twenty-six, and Vicki is twenty-seven. Now, are we old enough to get a ride from you brothas or what?"

Shane turned to me. "Jay, you up to taking these females for a ride?"

"I'm actually up for them giving me a ride," I said, looking at Ebony. "But since we don't have any extra helmets, the police might trip. If we can exchange some phone numbers, though, maybe we can make arrangements to give them a ride later on."

Ebony had already caught my drift and wrote her number on a piece of paper. Toni and Vicki seemed to be Shane's kind of gals, and immediately connecting, he made conversation with them. Alisha wasn't left out. After conversating with her and Ebony, I found myself digging her better than Ebony. I still didn't believe how old they were, so they showed me their driver's licenses. I then promised them a call later so we could kick it.

"Cherry Popper, don't play," Ebony said, squeezing my arm. "You are too fine, and I really want to see you again. Tonight, if possible."

Loving the attention, I watched as she walked her sexy self back to the car. She had lighter skin than Alisha, who was a darker chocolate. Ebony wore the hell out of a pair of cargo pants that hung low on her hips. Her midriff was bare and revealed the muscles in her abs and her belly ring. What attracted me most to her was her wild and curly brown hair and her catlike gray eyes like mine. It was hard to get my mind out of the gutter.

"I'm serious about calling. I'm a man of my words, and I said I would."

Alisha stood close by and held my hand before she got into the car. "If you call one of us, you got to call both of us."

Since she was braless, I looked at her nipples poking through the tightly fitted strapless pink halter that went well with her chocolate skin. Her hair was combed back in a sleek, shiny ponytail, and her buttered brown lips had my imagination going wild. "That won't be no problem either," I said, taking a glimpse at her backside as she got into the car. It wasn't a big ass, but it was nicely fitted into a pair of blue jean capris.

I looked at Shane as he opened the car door for Toni to get in. "Man, get me out of here before I get myself in trouble," I said.

"How I'm gon' save you and I'm trying to save my damn self?"

The ladies gave their good-byes, and after we agreed to hook up later, they jetted.

I hopped back on my bike and so did Shane.

"So, where to now?" I asked.

"Man, I'm going home so I can get ready to delve

into some pussy. It's been a while, and I told them I'd call them within the hour."

I lowered my helmet, a bit frustrated that we were done with riding. "Are you serious?"

"Negro, I ain't joking. I haven't had sex in about two months. I be having these dry spells and then bam! Women like that come along and my mind goes astray."

I laughed. "You are serious, aren't you?"

"Hell yeah! And don't tell me you're not going to have the pleasure of knocking off those other two. I know damn well the thought crossed your mind."

"It did, but—"

"But what?"

"I already got plans tonight."

"With who?"

Trying to figure out what I was in the mood for, I pulled out my cell phone and called my new gal, Yo-Yo, to tell her I was on my way. Quickly changing my mind when I thought about one of Mercedes' back rubs, I called to see if she was at home. She answered.

"Mercedes," I said.

"Who is this?" she asked.

"It's the Cherry Popper, baby."

"Oooooh, what do you want, Mr. Cherry Popper?"

"A nice warm set of hands rubbing all over my back, maybe even occasionally stroking my dick."

"Is that it?"

"Some pussy would be nice, too, and a li'l oral sex. Maybe up against the wall, in the shower, on the floor, from the back, in the kitchen, on the steps . . ."

"Whew, it sounds as if I have an eventful night ahead of me. And just when I was getting bored."

"Thanks to my call, things are starting to look up. I'll be there in about an hour. If you'd gather some things for me to take a shower, I promise I'll throw in a li'l something extra tonight."

"Damn, can't wait."

I hung up and looked at Shane. He shook his head from side to side.

"What's with the Cherry Popper bullshit, man? You know you be killing me."

"Always hate the playa, Knight Rider, and while you're at it, hate the game. So many do, so let's get the hell out of here and go take care of business."

Shane agreed and we jetted.

I rode back to his place with him, and before I left, I gave him a check for $50,000 to help out with his new business with Felicia. He thanked me repeatedly and said he'd repay the money as soon as things popped off. I wasn't worried about it, because I knew he was the kind of brotha who stood behind his words, just like me. I also told him to relay a message to the ladies about me not making it tonight, and that I'd make every effort to call them soon.

I took care of business at Mercedes' crib, and when I got home, the house was clean and quiet. Nanny B left a note and said she'd be back in a couple of days. Having nothing to do, I did what I knew best—got blissfully drunk.

I was fucked up as I lay on the floor in the theater room watching *Scarface* again. My mind wandered about Nokea, LJ, Scorpio, and Mackenzie. While I was at Mercedes' place, Nokea left a message about my plans to pick up LJ. She sounded as if she had to whisper to say that, so I was in no mood to return her call. Besides, if she wasn't talking what I wanted to hear, then fuck her. Scorpio and Mackenzie, I hadn't heard from them at all. I, of course, wasn't going to call Mackenzie, because I didn't want to listen to her cry about me not being there. Deep down, I was miserable and couldn't figure out a way to make it end. All the pussy in the world couldn't save me now— but it did have a way of helping me forget about some memories I wanted so desperately to forget.

# 31

## *SCORPIO*

Finally, I was on a roll and wasn't leaving any grass underneath my feet. When it came to handling my business, my *I*'s had been dotted and my *T*'s had been crossed.

When Nanny B dropped Mackenzie off that Friday evening, she also gave me some money to help me get things going. The rest she said she'd have deposited into my account, and the day after, it was surely there.

On Saturday, I went to purchase a car. Splurging just a little, I paid cash for a black Thunderbird, and then I drove around all day looking for a place to stay. When I found a beautiful split level condominium in Lake St. Louis, I couldn't help but go for it. I completed the application right then and there, and made arrangements to move in the following weekend. I was dying to get out of Leslie's house because there was so much chaos going on that Mackenzie and I were about to go crazy.

I thought about calling Jaylin many nights, but I couldn't. Calling him would put me right back where I started, and I wasn't prepared to do that. I was so much better off not knowing what he was doing and who he was doing it with. I'd talked to my girlfriend, Traniece, and she told me Jaylin and Mercedes had been seeing each other again. I was beyond devastated, and lost many hours of sleep that night, thinking about the promise he made me about never seeing her again. At this point, though, there wasn't anything that I could say or do about it.

Mr. Betts and I put the finishing touches on the play I'd written. Finally, I had something to be proud of. I couldn't wait for everyone to come out and see it. I still had a while to go before graduating, but for me, I felt as if I'd overcome a huge obstacle in my life. I'd sent Nanny B and Jaylin an invitation to come, and when I talked to her, she said she'd be there no matter what. When I asked about Jaylin, she said that he wasn't in his right state of mind to see Mackenzie, and the further he stayed away from her, the better. I agreed because I knew how much drama it would bring about if she knew he was back from his so-called "business trip" and didn't call her. She'd been asking me almost every day about him, and when we finally moved into our new place, I guess she kind of knew that we were there to stay.

The day of the play, I was a nervous wreck. I wanted everything to be perfect, and I definitely had to be the sharpest sista there. I'd shopped for hours, and when I picked out an eggshell white Jones of New York pantsuit, I knew it was the one for me.

Before the play started, I was on cloud nine, as everything seemed to be going perfect. I looked at Leslie and Mackenzie as they sat close by, waving at me. When I saw Nanny B come in, it finally hit me that somebody was missing. That, of course, was Jaylin. He'd been the one who encouraged me to do this to begin with. He'd given me the money to further my education, even when I fucked it up and failed miserably in my classes. I thought about how none of this would have been possible without him, and he wasn't even there to share my success with me.

I smiled at Nanny B as she made her way over to Mackenzie and Leslie. When I read Mackenzie's lips as she asked Nanny B where Jaylin was, I felt sad. I dropped my head, held my hands tightly together, and prayed for him to come.

Occasionally throughout the play I turned around, glancing at the auditorium doors in hopes that Jaylin would come through them. He never did, and when Mr. Betts called my name to introduce me as the writer of the play, I stood and nearly lost it. The audience gave their approval with thunderous applause and whistles, but still, there was no Jaylin. I didn't know if my tears were because he didn't show, or because I was happy about my accomplishment. I do know, however, that having him there with me would have made every bit of the difference.

Afterward, I exchanged hugs with Mr. Betts, the cast, and many people from the audience who were overwhelmingly pleased. For the first time, I think Mackenzie was kind of proud of me. Even Nanny B's tight hug and tears in her eyes showed that she was, but when Leslie said it, I was surprised. When I reached over to give her a hug, I looked over her shoulder and saw Jaylin standing far back near the double doors. Our eyes connected, and it seemed as if all of the pressure had been lifted off me. He opened his arms as if to ask where was his hug, so I let go of Leslie. I asked Nanny B to take Mackenzie outside so she wouldn't see him, and made my way up to him.

He had to be the most gorgeous man I'd ever seen. His suit was dark blue and he wore a baby blue shirt underneath. A few buttons were undone, showing his chest that I admired so much. Never leaving home without them, his tinted blue sunglasses covered his to-die-for eyes. All I could think of was why did we ever mess up things between us?

Anxious to feel him in my arms again, I walked up and wrapped my arms around his waist. He squeezed me tightly, tenderly kissing my forehead.

"Congratulations," he said.

I leaned back and looked up at him. "Thank you so much for coming. How long have you been here?"

"Long enough to know that you have talent. I must say, the play was awesome and I'm really proud of you. I sat in the far back because I didn't want Mackenzie to see me. As I watched you, though, you didn't seem too happy."

"I wasn't, but I'm happy now that you're here."

"You should have been happy before. Never let me steal your joy, okay?" he said.

I nodded.

"So, are you going to let me take you to dinner tonight?" he asked.

"Of course."

"Where would you like to go?"

"I don't know. I'll have to think of one of my favorite restaurants."

"Then Morton's it is."

"That's your favorite restaurant."

"So?"

"So I'll meet you there around eight?"

"I'll see ya then."

We let go of each other, and happier than I'd been in a long time, I turned to walk away. Since I wore off-white pants, I had a thong on, and was sure Jaylin could see right through my pants. I worked my hips from side to side to make sure he watched. When I stopped and turned my head slightly to the side, I saw that he was all into it. He winked at me and I turned around, continuing to strut my stuff.

I ran behind schedule because Leslie was late picking up Mackenzie. I was anxious to see Jaylin, so I hurried to make it to Morton's by eight. When I arrived, he appeared to be patient as he talked to one of the waiters by the door.

One waiter escorted us to a table, and right after we sat down, he showed us the steak display so we could later choose which one we wanted. Jaylin already knew what he wanted, and I sat for a moment trying to decide.

"I . . . I'm really not in the mood for a steak," I admitted.

"Well, they got other things you can order." He looked at the waiter. "Would you mind?"

"No, I don't think you understand." I looked at the waiter with tears in my eyes and touched the diamond engagement ring on my finger. "I . . . I want my man back. If there's any chance you can serve me at least three orgasms in one hour, touch me where it sends chills throughout my entire body, lick my insides until I can't take it anymore, and give me a baby that I so desperately want, then I'll allow you to serve me. No offense, but I don't think you can." I looked at Jaylin. "There's only one man who serves me like that, and I hope he's willing to do it tonight. Please, baby, can we go somewhere for you to serve me?"

The waiter looked at Jaylin and smiled. He hesitated for a minute and then stood up. He shook the waiter's hand and laid a hundred-dollar bill on the table. "Until next time," he said.

I took a deep breath, stood up, and followed behind him as we made our way to the exit. We walked outside and he turned to face me. "I don't want to go back to—"

"We won't," I rushed to say. "I will not call you, I will not force you to be with me, and I will never come to your house unless you ask me to. Just make love to me tonight. I need to feel you, please."

Jaylin stalled. "Scorpio, it's not that simp—"

I quickly pulled his face to mine and kissed him. I hadn't touched his soft lips in a while, and it didn't surprise me how good they felt against mine. He welcomed my kiss, then backed away.

"Listen," he said. "If we do this I don't want no questions asked, I don't want no crying, nor do I want any talk about us getting back together. Basically, all I want is silence."

"Anything . . . anything you want."

Jaylin took my hand and walked with me to my car. He said that riding together would only bring on a deep conversation between us, and he wasn't up for it. He asked me to follow him to the Four Seasons hotel, so I did.

Jaylin paid for a room, and dying to get him out of his suit, I damn near ripped it off at the door. We were barely inside as he reached for my clothes to take them off as well. By the time we made it to the bed, the moment was tense and our clothes were history.

I lay back, and noticing a little hesitation on his part, I opened my legs, rubbing between them. I then dropped my head back and moaned his name. Clearly seeing my juices starting to flow, he got on the bed and put his face between my legs. He worked my slit better than he had ever done before, and I came fast. As he wiped my juices from his lips, he stared deeply at me without saying a word. His dick entered me and instantly hit another home run. I trembled all over, watching as he kept his eyes closed. I massaged his ass, and as his strokes felt amazingly good to me, I kept sucking in my bottom lip.

Jaylin's eyes had been closed the entire time. I wanted to know what was on his mind, so I held his face in my hands and asked him.

"Shhh," he whispered. "Don't ask me any questions right now."

"I'm sorry. I don't like it when you're this quiet. Tell me what you're thinking."

He opened his eyes, gazed at me, and then closed his eyes again. He continued to work me, but surprisingly, not at his best. My body still tingled all over, and I was about to come again. I talked nasty to him and stressed how much I still wanted to have his baby. He did not respond, and on the verge of my next explosion, he dropped his head on my chest.

"I can't do this," he said, slamming his fist into the pillow. "Damn! I can't do this."

"Baby, please don't stop. We can do this. We're going to do this together."

He gave me a few more strokes before stopping again, a look of hurt on his face. "I'm sorry, baby, but I can't. The thought of you giving yourself to *him* is killing me."

"Then don't think about it," I said in a soft voice. "Think about us . . . me, being inside of me." I made my way on top of him. Knowing how much he admired my ass, I straddled him backward and used the floor for leverage to ride him. I gave him everything I had, as he massaged my ass tightly with his hands. I kept him occupied for a short while. He momentarily talked about how turned on he was by watching my juices ooze out on his dick. When he stopped talking and rolled me over, that's when I got worried.

He seemed to get frustrated and roughly slammed into me from behind. My insides couldn't handle this pain, and I stopped my motion.

"Baby, you're hurting me," I said.

"I can't help it." His strokes came to a halt and his head moved from side to side. "You just don't understand."

"If being with me is that painful for you, then don't do it. I can't make you love me anymore."

Jaylin closed his eyes. It wasn't until that moment that I realized how much damage I'd done to him by having sex with Stephon. When I felt him deflate inside of me without coming, I remained on my stomach and let him rest his head against my back. Sadly, I had a feeling this was the last time he would ever come my way again.

I turned around, attempting to talk to him about his feelings, but when he said that he didn't want to talk about anything, he meant it. When I brought up him being with Mercedes again, he put his clothes back on and pecked me on the cheek.

"Jaylin," I said with a huge lump in my throat.

"What?"

I nervously pulled the ring off my finger and reached out to give it to him. "I guess I should face the fact that this is really over, huh?"

He took a hard swallow and stood motionless as he stared at me. His eyes watered, and not wanting me to see his emotion, he turned his head and walked toward the door. He hesitated to open it and dropped his head. "Keep it. I never wanted anyone else to have it but you."

He opened the door, and as soon as I heard it close, I immediately burst into tears. I held back the entire time he was there, but I knew the only man I had ever loved had just walked out of my life for good.

I stayed at the Four Seasons for three days, trying to cope with my pain. I finally got up enough strength to get out of bed and go home. I wanted to call Jaylin, but I didn't want him to know how badly I was doing without him. Every time I started to feel better, Mackenzie would bring up his name, or talk about our time together, and then I'd be right back where I started. I prayed many nights for God to remove the feelings I had, but I knew there was no way for my feelings to vanish overnight. With Him being in control, I at least looked forward to the day my hurt would all be over. There was no doubt that my prayers would someday be answered. I just hoped it would be soon.

# 32

## *JAYLIN*

What a mess, I thought, while slumped over on the couch in the bonus room. Nanny B was so furious with me that she couldn't even stand to be around me. I'd seen her roll her eyes at me several times, and I guess after she cleaned up my vomit, that was enough for her. I told her she didn't have to do it, but she accused me of being lazy. Now, that was a new word for me. A playa? Yes. A ho? Maybe. A womanizer? Maybe that too. But lazy? I don't think so.

After my encounter with Scorpio the other night, I lost it. I'd been fucked up ever since then, and didn't know where to turn. I'd known having sex with her wasn't going to work out, even though I tried like hell to keep my mind off Stephon. Scorpio looked so beautiful that day, and I thought that after I saw her, maybe there was still a chance for us. It turned out, though, that the feelings I had for her were no longer there. That fire burning inside of me that I used to get

when I went inside of her was gone. I hated like
hell that she allowed Stephon to take that from
me, and there was no way for me to forgive her.

To this day, I still ached like hell because I loved
her as best as I could. To lose her and Mackenzie
over a cousin who betrayed me was like dying a
slow death for me.

The least I could say was I was still proud of
Scorpio for pursuing her dreams. I hoped more
than anything that she and Mackenzie had a happy
and wonderful life together. I, of course, made
sure of that. Whether it was Nanny B's money or my
money that Scorpio refused to accept, Mackenzie
and her were well off. What she didn't know was
that Nanny B and me were in this together. We
both wanted the best for them, and with the half
million–dollar deposit Nanny B gave, the best they
would forever have.

I felt somewhat the same way about Nokea. Al-
though she'd stopped calling, I knew it was because of Collins. He was threatened by me, and
the more I stayed out of their lives, the better off
they all would be. I wished her well, and had no
intentions to beg her again to be with me.

In my condition, I didn't want LJ being around
me anyway. I knew I'd take off with him in a heartbeat, and would probably wind up in jail for kid-
napping. I left everybody alone and chilled out in
my house with my dedicated, loving nanny.

Nanny B had been away for several days, and I
was quite lonely. She called to check on me, insisting she and her sister would be back from vacation in a few days. How much vacation did
somebody need? If anything, I knew she was upset

with me because of the way I'd been acting, and she needed a break. I wanted to get myself together, but when I thought about Collins making love to Nokea, I couldn't do anything but take a drink. I thought about how happy they were with my son, and couldn't stop tearing up over the bullshit.

Trying to avoid my crazy thoughts of killing somebody, I poured a few shots of Tequila and sat up in bed, feeling sorry for myself. The house was quiet. No Mackenzie's curious questions, no LJ's cries, no Nokea's squeaky li'l voice, and the best pussy I'd ever had was taken away from me by my cousin. If there was anybody I'd kill, he'd be the one.

I tightly closed my eyes and rubbed my chest as I thought about all that Stephon had done to me. Why he hated me so much, I would never understand. At this point, though, I didn't give a shit. I hoped like hell that he suffered for what he put me through.

I picked up the phone to call Ebony and Alisha. Mercedes, Yo-Yo, and even Felicia had been sweating me about coming to see them, but today, I was in the mood for a li'l something different. I chatted with Ebony for at least an hour, and after I gave her directions to my crib, she said she and Alisha would be there by seven o'clock that night. It was only two o'clock in the afternoon, so I finished up my drinking and passed out again.

The loud ringing of the phone awakened me, and I was pissed at the caller for interrupting my dream. Nokea and I were in the midst of making love, and that punk Collins had just walked in on us. When I looked at the caller ID, I saw that it was Shane. I hit the intercom button.

"What is it?" I yelled.

"What a fucking greeting," he said. "You can't respond no better than that?"

I sat my naked body up in bed, rubbing my eyes. "Okay, what's up?"

"I heard you're having company tonight."

"Damn, good news travels fast, don't it?"

Shane laughed. "Yeah, it does. But that's not the purpose for my call. I kind of wanted to talk to you about Stephon."

"Shane, man, how many times am I gonna have to tell you I don't want to talk about that fool?"

"I know, but he really needs you, Jay. I talked to the brotha moments ago and he's sorry for everything that's happened. He admitted that those drugs made him do crazy things, and said what happened between y'all confirmed he needed help."

"You damn right he needs help, but what in the hell do you want me to do? I no longer want anything to do with him and that's final. I have been backstabbed by him too many times, and I'm not going to subject myself to it anymore."

"I understand, but this is difficult for me because I'm caught in the middle. I understand what he's going through, and I understand your position as well. I just hope he doesn't disappoint me like he's disappointed you."

"Well, prepare yourself; it's bound to happen. Stephon needs to learn how to stop being a hater. Since I'm not there for him, he's going to lean on you a lot. I appreciate you being a friend to him, because he's definitely going to need one. If he starts depending on you for money, let me know. I'll give it to you, but not to support his habit. Make sure the brotha gets the help he needs, and do not allow his barbershop to close. I invested too much money in that place, and I'd hate to see it go under. If you got to run it yourself, please do it."

"I don't care what anybody say about you, Jay, but you're all right with me. There's not many brothas who would do that, and again, I'm grateful to have your friendship."

"Then be grateful enough to let me take my ass back to sleep. I'm trying to get rid of this hangover before the ladies come over."

"So you kicking down a threesome tonight, huh?"

"I haven't decided yet. Believe it or not, I haven't gotten down like that since college. I'm not sure if I still have it in me."

"Negro, please. Whatever you do, though, make sure you're strapped. Vicki and Toni were wild. I'm sure those other two are just as *creative*."

"I hope so. I guess I'd better prepare myself for a long night, huh?"

"I'm afraid so. We kicked it that night, but you know I'm a man who likes to stick and move if the feeling ain't there. Ever since that night, they've been calling me every day and it's driving me crazy. I ain't looking for no relationships, and pussy is not my priority over here. I got other shit I'm working on, and I gotta stay focused on my business."

"I feel ya. And trust me when I say pussy should not be the priority. It'll mess you up like me, and you don't want to feel how I'm feeling right now."

"You'll be all right, Jay. We all have setbacks, but you know how to bounce back and stand tall. That's why I admire your punk ass so much."

"I'm glad you see it that way, but listen; if I don't get a chance to holla back at you tonight, I'll give you a holla tomorrow."

"Peace," Shane said, and then hung up.


When the doorbell rang, I was still in bed naked. I'd gotten a new security system on the doors because of my breakup with Scorpio, so I picked up the remote. I turned the TV to the outside cameras and saw Ebony and Alisha on the porch. I buzzed them in and directed them to my bedroom through the intercom.

"Hello, ladies," I said as they came through my bedroom doors.

They spoke back, and I asked them to have a seat on the chaise in my sitting room. I got up to pour us some drinks and handed the glasses to them.

"Thanks, Jaylin. And if you don't mind me saying this, you have one of the nicest butts I've ever seen," Ebony said, touching it.

"No, it's the front that's got my vote." Alisha laughed and clinked her glass with Ebony's. "And what's up with your crib, Jaylin? You didn't tell us you had it going on like this. Are you a baller?"

"No, but what difference does it make? We still gon' get down tonight, right?"

Alisha and Ebony looked at each other. "What do you mean by getting down?" Ebony asked.

I dimmed the lights, and then set my glass of

Moët on the fireplace mantle. I gave both of them a serious look and touched their prize for the night.

"Don't ask any question you already know the answer to. Y'all know what's on my mind, and I'm not in the mood for a bunch of chit-chatting. So drink up and decide quickly where we go from here."

Ebony placed her drink on the table and stood up. She put her hand on her hip. "Well, don't hold back, Jaylin. And don't talk to us like we're amateurs, because we're not." She reached inside her purse and tossed a condom to me. "Strap up, my brotha. You'll soon be in the mood."

I caught the condom, looked at the package, and then tossed it back to her. "Too small. I got that part all taken care of."

I went to my closet to get a condom, and watched as the ladies got naked. I then sat on the bed and contemplated how I was going to invite them into Jaylin's World. Ebony's well-shaped, light-skinned ass kind of reminded me of Scorpio, so tagging that was the first option on my mind. Alisha, though, her meaty breasts were dying to get sucked, and I couldn't wait to get inside of her pussy that was trimmed so well. Without a doubt, both of them were some badass women, so I couldn't go wrong either way.

I decided to lay back and let them have at it— and that, they did. They sucked me well, and before I let my explosion go to waste, I rose up and gave them a healthy taste of me. The excitement kept me hard as ever, and when I put my goods in Ebony while fingering Alisha, they cut up. I slid on another condom and reversed my actions so they both could be fulfilled.

They were both going crazy and allowed me to have my way with them. We wound up in the shower together, washing each other from head to toe. Again, the pleasure was all mine as I watched Alisha lick me from the front and Ebony lick me from the back.

I closed my eyes and thought about Stephon, wondering if his threesomes had been this successful. Nokea being with Collins was fresh in my mind, and when I thought about not being able to perform with Scorpio that day, my dick finally calmed down. When the thought of LJ and Mackenzie crossed my mind, I hurried to wrap it up.

My bedroom was a mess, so I pulled the stained sheets off my bed. Ebony and Alisha helped me put on some new ones and climbed in the bed with me. I used the remote to turn on the TV, and kicked up some music that played throughout the house.

"Can we stay the night?" Ebony asked while rubbing her feet against my leg underneath the sheets.

"Maybe . . . just one night. After that, don't y'all be bugging the shit out of me."

They laughed. "You know you had a good time too," Alisha said. "So stop frontin' like you didn't."

"I never said I didn't. Actually, I had a superb time. How about y'all?'

"It was off the hook! I can tell you do this all the time by the way you just manhandled both of us."

"Any man would love to do this all the time;

however, I don't. Reason being, I like to take my time with pussy. With both of y'all, I was worried about somebody getting neglected."

Alisha looked at Ebony. "Girl, are you feeling neglected? 'Cause I'm not."

"Hell no. This time, no, I'm not."

"So, y'all the ones who get down all the time like this, not me."

They laughed again. "Believe it or not, it only happened once. And the brotha we did get down with had nothing on you," Alisha said.

"Sorry to hear that, but what made it so different with me?"

"The difference was how your strength played a major part to that going down like it did. How did you balance yourself like that and keep on stroking? That takes talent. And,"—Alisha cleared her throat and sized up my dick with her hand—"the thickness and length of your dick was a major plus. You know how to work it. I'm still feeling you inside me. That's when you know a dick was good to you."

They laughed and reached over me to high five each other. Ebony added her two cents. "In addition to that, how does your tongue and mouth vibrate like that? That was wild. I couldn't keep myself from coming after being worked like that."

"It's my ancient Chinese secret and can never be revealed. And I'm glad you ladies enjoyed yourself. I aim to please, and I'm always delighted to hear when I do."

They snickered.

"Where's your woman at, Jaylin? I know you have one," Ebony asked.

"I got plenty in my world, but nothing on a regular basis. Now, if y'all gon' stay, don't start asking me any questions about my personal life."

"Hey, no questions asked," Ebony said, reaching for her purse. She pulled out a small bag of cocaine, and after passing it to Alisha, she offered it to me.

As stressed as I was, I thought about it. Then I thought about how Stephon must have gotten hooked on the shit. That prompted me to give Ebony one of the hardest looks she'd probably ever seen. "Don't do that shit in my house. Your drugs are not welcome, and I will throw your ass out of here with that—"

"It's just—"

"Did you hear what the fuck I said? I don't want no excuses. If you don't like my rules then get the fuck out!"

"Sorry. Damn." She reached over and laid the bag on my nightstand. "Do you mind if I go get some water, though? I'm kind of thirsty."

"The kitchen is downstairs. Don't be wandering around my house. I can see you on my cameras."

She put her hand on her hip. "All I want is some water. Would you like for me to get you some too?"

"Yes, and thank you."

Alisha yelled for Ebony to bring her some too as she left the room.

"Why didn't you go with her?" I asked. Giving me a hint, she pulled back the sheets and displayed another condom. I made my way on top of her and rubbed her messed-up ponytail back with my hands. I stared into her light brown eyes and she stared back.

"You are so damn fine, Jaylin," she said. "I bet you can have just about any woman you want. Is there anything I can do to make you mine?"

"Nothing. But when you think about me for the next few days, other than my dick being inside of you, I want you to think about how much damage you're doing to yourself by doing drugs. You're too beautiful, baby, and I know a woman who has potential when I see one. You understand what I'm saying?"

She nodded.

I opened Alisha's legs and inched my way back inside of her. Her legs were high on my shoulders, and she complained about the pain. I backed out a li'l bit and she gave me the go-ahead to continue. I could tell she wasn't as experienced as she claimed to be because her rhythm wasn't right and her pussy was too tight. The thing that I did like about hers, better than Ebony's, was the juiciness of it. Not only that, but it was tasty, and the minimal hair that covered it was smooth against my lips. By all means, Ebony's wasn't bad, but I preferred Alisha's. Hands down, though, Ebony was the best at giving a head job.

Since Ebony took all day with the water, I had time to focus on Alisha like I wanted to. She squirmed around and tightly held my hips.

"You're too tense. Just relax, and when I put you on top of me, take your time," I whispered in her ear.

Alisha got on top of me and refused to take in all of me. I widened her ass cheeks with my hands and pumped myself into her. Ebony had finally came back into the room, and I'll be damned if Nanny B didn't come in behind her. My eyes widened and my motion stopped.

Alisha quickly turned her head, and not knowing who Nanny B was, she eased off me. Ebony got in bed too and pulled the sheets over her. We were all embarrassed. The look of disgust was written all over Nanny B's face.

She looked at the cocaine on the nightstand, gave me a hard stare, and rolled her eyes. "I came home early to check on you because you didn't sound too well over the phone. If I could, I would throw you out of your own damn house, but finish up, and we'll talk in the morning." She walked out and closed the door behind her.

"Who was that?" Ebony asked.

"Don't worry about it."

"Do we have to leave?"

"No, and I said don't worry about it." I looked over at Alisha. "Would you like to finish?"

"Of course," she said, and then eased on top of me.

Alisha and me picked up where we left off, and shortly after, Ebony joined in again. We damn near kicked down an all-nighter, and by morning, I was beat. Ebony and Alisha woke me to tell me they were leaving. I was so tired that I could barely keep my eyes open or walk them to the door.


Later that day, I felt someone looking over me in my sleep. When I opened my eyes, Nanny B startled me. She had something in her hand. I looked at it and saw that it was a broom and some Lysol. I quickly sat up, advising her that it wouldn't be wise to hit me with a broom. She looked at me like I was the worst thing she'd ever seen and spoke sternly.

"I don't believe in abuse, and the broom is to sweep the bathroom floor. The Lysol is to kill the germs in this house. and I'm sure there are plenty of them in this room." She sprayed a dash of Lysol on me. "Now, get your butt up, and after I sweep the floor, we're leaving."

"Leaving? I ain't going nowhere."

"Yes, you are, so come on." She tried to pull me off the bed.

I struggled to get up, but couldn't. "Damn. Where are we going? I'm still tired."

"Just put on some clothes and look nice."

"Don't I always look nice?"

"Not when you got two naked women in bed with you, you don't. It's the most inappropriate and disgusting thing I've ever seen. And I hope like hell you aren't doing drugs."

"No, I'm not doing drugs. They brought that mess over here and I asked them to put it away. The only thing I'm guilty of is having fun. You want me to have fun, don't you?"

She pointed her finger at me. "Don't make me disrespect you. That kind of fun will get you in trouble. Now, go trim your beard because it looks a bit fuzzy. I've never seen it look like that."

I slowly walked to the bathroom and looked in the mirror. My beard was a little scruffy, so after I took a shower, I shaved and put on a sweat suit.

Nanny B was downstairs waiting for me. "Hurry it up now. We gon' be late," she yelled.

"Late for what? For the last time, where in the hell are we going?"

"Don't worry about it. Just come on."

"Well, am I driving or you?"

"I'll drive."

We got in her car and left. When she drove to Lambert Airport, I was puzzled. She parked the car, and that caused me to put up a big fuss.

"Nanny B, I ain't up for going on no trip. I'm not in the mood. Damn!"

"Just shut your mouth, Jaylin. You're getting on my nerves!" she yelled.

I didn't say another word, but as we walked through the airport, I had a serious attitude. When we got on a private plane, I didn't know what the hell was going on. By then, I was fuming, and tried to prevent myself from going off on Nanny B.

We were on the plane for a few hours. When it landed, we were in Miami, Florida. I waited for Nanny B to get her mess together as she looked around for someone. When this tall African man came over and asked if I had any luggage, I looked at him like he was crazy. Nanny B told me his name was Ebay, and she told him we didn't have time to pack anything. She pulled him aside to whisper something else to him, then said we were ready to go.

We got into a run-down Ford truck. Ebay drove extremely fast, and I damn near flew out of my seat. I asked him to slow down, but he talked some funny shit that I couldn't understand. In so many words, he ignored me. I didn't care how beautiful Florida was; I simply was not in the mood for a vacation. I told Nanny B how much I hated to be forced into doing something, and again, she told me to shut my mouth.

By the time we reached our destination, it was almost dark outside. The signs said we were in Palm Beach. Ebay pulled in front of what looked to be a beautiful resort. It had palm trees in front of it and the blue ocean was several feet away. White sand surrounded the place, and it was extremely quiet. The only thing you could hear were the waves splashing against the rocks. Nanny B smiled and I smiled back.

"Okay, so it's a nice place. I'm only staying for one week and that's it."

She nodded and we both got out of the truck. After that, she tipped Ebay and he sped off. Not knowing what else she had up her sleeve, I followed behind her as we walked to the tall double wooden doors. She searched for her keys. When we walked inside, I was at a loss for words.

"Whose place is this?" I asked with a puzzled look on my face. It was off the chain. I had never seen anything like it.

"It's a friend of mine's. When I need to relax, I come here to get away. When I took my vacation, this is where I was."

"You should have brought me with you then," I said, looking around. The place was sparkling clean, and the tall architectural columns really set it off. The floors were a shiny dark wood, and most of the furniture inside was tropical wicker. There were very few doors and windows, and you could see right outside to the sandy beach and ocean.

"Come on," Nanny B said. "Let me show you around."

We walked into the master bedroom. It was to die for. The king-sized bed sat high off the floor, draped with sheer white material. It was covered with a quilted white blanket and had white silk pillows all over it. On one side of the bed was a huge palm tree that nearly touched the sky-view glass ceiling. Near the other side of the bed were wooden double doors that led to a patio.

I stood outside and looked at the awesome and peacefully quiet scenery. I was mesmerized, until Nanny B yelled for me to come see the master bathroom. Knowing that it couldn't possibly be better than my bathroom back at home, I was in disbelief once again. The Jacuzzi tub was twice the size of mine, had pearly white marble that surrounded it, and had waterfall faucets on both sides. Next to it was a stand-up round glass shower made with the same pearly white marble floor. What caught my attention was the television that rose up at the touch of a button, and a double-sided fireplace with a view into the bedroom.

Nanny B took me to the other bedrooms, which had lofts above them and were just as fabulous as the master bedroom. The kitchen was a chef's dream come true. After I saw the rest of the place, I had to sit down to catch my breath.

Nanny B gave me some water as we both sat back on the plush wicker chaises in the living room, underneath four tropical ceiling fans that blew cool air on us.

"So, do you like it?" she asked.

"Shit, who wouldn't? This place is . . . there really ain't no words to describe it. I've only seen places like this in the movies. It makes my house look like I've been on welfare. I don't know what to say about it."

"How about you calling it home?"

I cocked my head back, looking at Nanny B. "Whose home?"

"Your home." She took my hand and placed the keys in it. "That's if you want it."

"I thought you said this was somebody else's house."

"I said a friend of mine, and that friend just happens to be you."

"But I can't live here, Nanny B. It's too far away from everything. And what about my house? You know I ain't giving up my house. It's not like this, but—"

"Jaylin, you paid a little over one million dollars for that house. I had an appraiser look at it a few weeks ago and it now appraises for almost two million. If you sell it, you have nothing to lose. When things started to take a turn for the worse, I had to look out for us. I knew what the outcome would be, but you didn't see it coming.

"This place had been on the market for a long time, partially because there weren't too many people who could afford it; but the sellers wanted somebody special to have it. When I came down and met them a few months ago, they said this place brought nothing but happiness to their lives.

"I won't always be around, and I don't want to live the rest of my life in turmoil. I want to be right here with you, or maybe someday your wife and children. That's not too much to ask for, is it? If anything, when I get to heaven, I want your mother to look at me and say, 'Bertha, what a wonderful job you've done in such a short period of time.'

"If you stay where you are, baby, you're going to destroy yourself, and I don't want that to happen. Seeing you with those women last night was the last straw, and if you stay, it's only going to get worse."

I stood up, placed my hands in my pockets, and paced the room. "I know things haven't been great. Living here sounds all good and everything, but I got so much to lose if I move here."

"What do you have to lose? And don't give me no woman's name, because women will come and go. You've learned that the hard way, and I know you're not going to let any of them hold you back."

"But what about LJ? Mackenzie? Moving here might mean I'll never see them again."

"LJ can always visit you here. And you can always go back to St. Louis. As for Mackenzie, you have got to let her go. She'll be all right, Jaylin. Allow yourself a fresh start, and don't bring any of that mess here with you. Someday, you might meet yourself a wonderful woman here. Nokea and Scorpio have moved on with their lives, and it's time that you do the same."

I sat back down, gripping my hands together. "I don't know what I'd do without you in my life. How soon, or when is this transition supposed to take place?"

"The place is already yours. Either you can stay here and I'll go back and wrap up everything, or we can go together."

"How long is it going to take to wrap up everything? You know my birthday is right around the corner, and I'd like to be settled by then."

"I'd like to be back here by then as well. I've planned this out for months, so it won't take long to go back and do what I gotta do. The only problem I'm going to have is getting those movers to move all of your darn suits out of that closet."

"I didn't even look at the closets here. Is there enough room? You know I gotta have room for my suits, Nanny B."

"And where are you going to wear them to? On the beach? Chile, you don't need all that stuff. Mostly everything in that house can stay, or either be given away to charity. There's no way you can bring all of it here."

"I know, but this wicker stuff ain't my style. It's nice, but I'd have to customize this place to my liking. So I do need to go back with you. There's some personal things I need to get, and I got one last thing I need to take care of."

"And what's that?"

"Delores and Jeffrey. You remember that money I told you about that Stanley left?"

"Yes."

"I want to make sure they get it."

Nanny B nodded and told me that after one night in this place, I'd be hooked. She didn't lie, because after I stayed for one night, I had changed my mind about going back. I slept like a baby, and by the end of the week, I decided to stay and let

Nanny B and her "hook-ups" tie up everything at home. She'd been on the phone all week, taking care of mostly everything, because she was afraid I'd get cold feet.

"Are you sure you don't want to go with me?" she asked on her way out.

"I'm positive. It's only going to take a few phone calls to take care of things for Delores and Jeffrey, and I'll be done with it. When you get back to the house, you already know what to do, don't you?"

"Yes," she said, giving me a hug. "Stay by the phone, though, just in case I need you."

"I will."

Nanny B jetted with Ebay again, and I sat outside for a while and checked out my new place. Later on, I went for a relaxing jog along the beach and got a bigger view of the unbelievable scenery. There were several houses along the beach, and everybody who lived there had nothing but privacy. I saw just a few people lying on the beach, here and there, and had noticed one couple outside making love.

Once I got finished with my two-mile run, I sat down close by the water. I pulled my T-shirt off and placed my towel around my neck. I leaned back and looked up at the clear blue sky. I thanked God for my peace of mind, and told Mama how much I missed her. I even gave Stanley a shout-out too. I was finally able to tell him that I'd forgiven him.

Thinking about Delores and Jeffrey, I got up and jogged back to the house to call them. I hated that I didn't get a chance to say good-bye, but I was afraid that if I went back with Nanny B, I would have changed my mind and stayed.

I called Delores first, and when I broke the news to her about the money, she couldn't stop crying. I told her I'd make arrangements for her and Jeffrey to get the money as soon as possible, and she thanked me over and over again. Before we ended our call, she asked where I was. Not wanting anyone to know, I declined to tell her. I did, however, tell her I loved her and wished her and Jeffrey the best.

By late evening, the phone rang off the hook. I was outside resting on a hammock, as the thought of LJ was heavy on my mind. I wanted to call Nokea, but I just couldn't. Instead, I ran to answer the phone, since I knew it was Nanny B.

"What took you so long to answer the phone?" she asked.

"I was outside resting."

"Well, it's about twenty-five darn people in this house helping me get things together. I got three men working on your room, and this closet just doesn't make any sense. Do you really need all of this stuff?"

"Yes. I need everything that's in there. My suits, jeans, ties, hats, shirts, cuff links, shoes, jewelry, fur and cashmere coats, and watches. Please don't forget my Rolexes. And my pictures, don't forget my pictures, especially the ones over the fireplace."

"Okay, I'll make sure they pack them. Is there anything else you can think of?"

I tried to think about what was in every room

of the house, but it was hard. "Yes, there are a few more things. Please have somebody go get them for me right now."

"What is it, Jaylin?" Nanny B sounded frustrated.

"Send somebody to Mackenzie's room to get her hair brush, those two Barbie dolls she left, and her *Cinderella* book."

"Okay. Now, is there anything else?"

"Tell them to get it now, Nanny B. I don't want them to forget it."

She put me on hold and asked somebody to go get it. When it sounded like something broke, I heard her yell. I could only imagine what the house looked like, but I knew she had everything under control.

She came back to the phone. "Tomorrow the house goes up for sale. The furniture stays, so the agent said you're going to get even more than what you're asking for. Now, isn't that a blessing?"

"You know what, though? I kind of like the chair in my office. Do you think—?"

"Hell no! Buy you a new one. Jaylin, I'm not going to stay here and go through all this stuff now."

"Fine, but there's also a cedar chest in the basement with pictures—"

"They already got it."

"Cool then."

"I'll see you in a few days."

"Yes, you will, and thank you. I love you."

Nanny B hung up and I went back outside to lay on the hammock. I dozed off because the cool breeze felt so relaxing. When I woke up, it was almost one o'clock in the morning. I went inside and lay across the bed. Thinking about LJ, I picked up the phone, only to put it right back down. I knew calling Collins' house this time of the morning would be a crime, and I was in no mood to listen to Nokea chew me out for calling. My thoughts of Mackenzie wouldn't go away either, but it was in my best interest to put the past behind me. I was glad I didn't have Scorpio's number because I probably would have called and asked them to come here with me.

I knew that Nanny B planned to have the house phone disconnected tomorrow, so I called to check my messages. I hadn't checked them in a little over a week, and the recorder said I had forty-nine messages waiting. My usual lady friends had called several times, and even though I told Ebony and Alisha not to bug me, they did. Alisha called way more times than Ebony and demanded some alone time with me. She went on and on about how she couldn't get that night out of her mind. I deleted her messages. Mercedes even tried to get an attitude about me not calling her, and threatened not to have sex with me again if I didn't return her call. Whoop-dee-doo. It wasn't like the sex was all that, so I deleted her messages as well.

I continued to listen to my other messages. Shane bugged me, Delores and Jeffrey had both called to check in on me, and even Scorpio had called several times to say that she loved me. When I heard Stephon's voice, I instantly pushed the delete button because I didn't want to hear anything he had to say.

As for Nokea, she left the majority of messages. She was furious with me since I hadn't called to see about LJ. She even cried and begged me to call, just to let her know I was okay. The last message, which she'd left earlier today, said she'd see me at Café Lapadero for my birthday next Tuesday. She apologized for being so distant and tried to explain herself by saying how much she wanted her marriage to work. She wrapped up her message by telling me how happy she was with him, and then told me how much LJ missed me. After hearing that, I deleted the message. If anything, it validated that moving away was the best thing I could have done. Finally, her words gave me closure. There was no telling when I would ever see her again.

# 33

## *NOKEA*

I was a nervous wreck not hearing from Jaylin. He hadn't called to see about LJ or anything. I'd called his house several times and got no answer. I'd even been by there, and still no one was there. Even Nanny B was nowhere to be found. I put one and two together, figuring they all must have taken a vacation or something. Maybe they were at his family reunion and he was angry with me for not going. Hell, maybe he and Scorpio decided to take off and go get married. With him being so angry with me, it was right up his alley to pull a stunt like this, so I tried to relax and get him off my mind.

Collins and I were doing pretty well. He could tell how uptight I was about LJ not being with Jaylin, and he tried to get me to relax. LJ and I lived with Collins now, and I was happy that we were all finally together as a family. His parents had even come into town to congratulate the "happy couple," and when they were here, I invited my parents over to finally meet them. They all got along so well, and it seemed this was the way it was supposed to be all along.

Even Pat and Chad came over for dinner a few times, and I'd finally gotten a chance to meet Collins' partners' wives. When I mentioned something about Curtis' wife having cancer, they all looked at me like I was crazy.

After they left that day, I asked Collins if he lied to me about her condition just so he could get me to move to Detroit with him, and he admitted that he had. At the time, he admitted to being threatened by Jaylin, and explained how desperate he was to keep me. I wasn't mad at him for lying because I'd had my share of secrets too. He didn't know I planned on meeting Jaylin for his birthday at Café Lapedero, and when he asked if I had made any plans for LJ's birthday on the same day, I told him that I hadn't.

The morning of LJ and Jaylin's birthday, I was overly excited. First, because my baby was finally two years old, and second, because we were finally going to see Jaylin today.

As usual, I got up early. Collins was already out of bed, and when I walked into the kitchen, he was cooking breakfast. I leaned in, giving him a smack on the lips and then grabbing a piece of bacon.

"Is the birthday boy up yet?" he asked.

"Nope. He's still asleep."

"Then maybe we can get a li'l down and dirty in the kitchen before he wakes up."

"We already got a li'l down and dirty last night, didn't we?"

"That was just an appetizer," he said, wrapping his arms around me.

As soon as Collins and I were about to get busy, LJ started yakking.

"Excuse me," I said, gathering my robe in the front. "The king awaits me."

Collins laughed and I headed to LJ's room. He had a huge smile on his face, but when I sang "Happy Birthday" to him, he started to cry. I went into my bedroom, pulled out a picture of Jaylin from my wallet, and put it in front of LJ. He grabbed the picture and when I sang again, he giggled. I carried him into the kitchen and we sat down at the table to eat.

"So, you're not going to do anything for his birthday today?" Collins asked.

"No, not today. I might take him somewhere over the weekend, but I'm not sure where. Around noon, I'm meeting Mama at the mall, and we'll probably do a little shopping, that's all. How about you? What do you have planned for today?"

"Nothing. I'm going to hang around here and do some work. If you don't mind, maybe LJ and I can go somewhere together and hang out later."

"That's fine. If you want to, you can hang out with Mama and me at the mall."

"No, thank you."

I laughed, and after we ate breakfast, I cleaned the kitchen and did a little more tidying around the house. It got close to eleven o'clock, so I gave LJ a bath and put a blue Nike jogging suit on him. Since Jaylin always tried to dress like him, I put on my Nike jogging suit as well.

By quarter to twelve, I was on my way out. I stopped by Collins' office to say good-bye, but he was on the phone. Instead of interrupting him, I blew him a kiss and whispered to him that I'd see him later.

Having a little time to spare, since we usually didn't meet up until one o'clock on Jaylin's birthday, I stopped at the store and bought Jaylin a birthday card. I let LJ pick it out; I knew Jaylin would like it.

When we got to Café Lapadero, the waiter sat us outside. He brought over some rolls and tea for me, and gave LJ a coloring book and crayons. LJ was growing up fast, and every time I looked at him, I couldn't help but see Jaylin's face. I couldn't stop kissing him on his cheeks, and he gave me a smile that nearly melted my heart.

After a while, I started to get worried because it was already one o'clock. I took a deep breath and sat back in the chair. The hand on my watch ticked away. Jaylin was already thirty minutes late. I reached for my cell phone to call his house, but the operator said the phone had been disconnected. Thinking that I had dialed the wrong number, I dialed out again. I got the same response, so I called his cell phone. That was still on, so I left a message, telling him that LJ and I were waiting for him.

Feeling as if something wasn't right, I flagged down the waiter and asked if anyone had called for me. When he said no, I continued to sit there and wait. By two o'clock, I was disappointed. Jaylin wouldn't forget about meeting us for anything in the world. And with it being LJ's birthday, I was positive that he would have called by now, or at least shown up.

I hung around a little while longer and ordered LJ's and my food. By the time that came, it was going on two forty-five. I wanted to cry, and my stomach ached badly. I picked through my salad and had no desire to eat. I dialed Jaylin's number again. When I felt someone touch the back of my chair, I discontinued the call and turned around. It was Collins.

"Hey," I said, shocked to see him.

"Hi." He sat across the table from me and crossed his legs. He then picked up a menu. "Have you ordered yet, or is the salad enough?"

"I . . . I just wanted a salad. I'm not really that hungry."

He looked at the menu and then called for the waiter. "I'll have the chicken marsala, but light on the sauce, please."

"Will there be anything else?" the waiter asked.

"Baby, are you sure you don't want anything else?" Collins asked.

"No, really, I'm fine."

The waiter walked away to get Collins' food. LJ stayed occupied with coloring, and Collins reached over and rubbed his head. He then looked across the table at me.

"So, why didn't you tell me you were coming here?"

"Because I didn't know I was coming."

"Yes, you did. You mentioned to me before that you always meet Jaylin here on his birthday. Question is, why did you lie about it?"

"Who says that I'm meeting Jaylin here, Collins?"

"So, you're not?"

"No, I'm not. I came here to have lunch with my son."

"Well, what's the purpose for the flowers and the teddy bear?"

"What flowers and teddy bear are you talking about?"

"You didn't get them? Let me get them for you." Collins called for the waiter again, and when he nodded, I turned around as the waiter headed my way with a dozen long-stemmed red roses in a beautiful crystal vase. He also held the shirtless teddy bear in his hands.

"Ma'am, I'm sorry. These came for you a little while ago. I didn't know—"

"That's okay," I said, looking at the flowers and the bear. I pulled the card out of the opened envelope and read it:

> *Sorry I couldn't make it, but as you can see, I must be tied up. Kiss my son for me, tell him I said happy birthday, and make sure he knows that Daddy loves him. As for the teddy bear, I removed the shirt that said "Yours Forever, Nokea," since you no longer belong to me. Gotta go, and give Collins my best.*

"So," Collins said, "why didn't you tell me you were supposed to meet him today?"

"Because I didn't want you to get upset with me, that's why."

"You're damn right I'm upset. I have a serious problem with my wife secretly conspiring to meet her ex-boyfriend for lunch on his birthday. More so, him sending her flowers and a teddy bear."

"It's just lunch, Collins, and I knew you wouldn't understand. I told you that Jaylin and I meet here on his birthday. For God's sake, I have his son, and I can't keep them apart forever."

He leaned closer to me and raised his voice. "I remembered you telling me, but when I asked what you were doing today, you said nothing about coming here. As for keeping him and LJ apart, I never asked you to do that. All I ever asked was for you to be honest with me and to be true to yourself. But you just keep on lying about shit, Nokea, and I'm nobody's fool."

"Would you mind keeping your voice down? I'm not going to sit here and let you embarrass me. We can go home and talk about this, but now is not the time or the place."

"Then you tell me when the time is appropriate," he yelled. "You will never convince me that you don't love him anymore if you keep on doing shit like this behind my back. I don't feel as if I can trust you. Do you have any idea where trust ranks in a marriage?"

The waiter brought Collins his food, but being so livid with me, he didn't even stay around to eat it. I felt bad about getting caught up in another lie, so I left the restaurant to go home and work this out with him. When I got there, his car was gone, so I knew he'd taken another detour. Where? I hadn't a clue.

Since he wasn't home, I drove by Jaylin's house to see if I could catch up with him. This time, his house looked quite different. His cars were no longer in the driveway, and his house looked somewhat deserted. When I got out of my car, that's when I noticed a padlock on the door. I looked at the window and saw a FOR SALE sign taped to it. What in the hell was going on? Where was he?

I panicked and rushed back to my car. I called everyone that I could think of who knew him, and nobody knew where he was. I was sure Stephon would know, but he swore up and down that he hadn't talked to Jaylin in months. When he suggested that I call Shane, I called his house to speak with him.

"Please tell me and don't lie. Do you have any idea where he is?"

"No, honestly, I don't. I talked to him about a week ago and he wished me well and said he was doing fine."

"Was Scorpio with him? I mean . . . did he say they were together?"

"I'm sorry, but again, I don't know. If I did, I would surely tell you."

"Thanks," I said, and then hung up.

I sat outside for a moment, and when I saw a car park in my rearview mirror, I hurried to it. I carried LJ on my hip and walked up to the lady who got out of her car.

"Mrs. Bedford, I'm sorry I'm late, but have you had a chance to look around yet?" she asked.

"No. I mean I . . . I looked through the window, but—"

"Well, wait until you see the inside. It's the nicest house in the neighborhood, and the price is worth every dime."

I followed behind the lady, and when she took the lock off the door, I walked inside.

"Isn't it lovely?" she said, smiling as we stood in the foyer.

"Yes, it's very beautiful."

"And if you'd like, all of the furniture stays. It's up to you. I'm sure the owners will negotiate a price."

"I see," I said. "Do you mind if I go upstairs?"

"Not at all. Take your time and look around. And there's a surprise waiting for you downstairs."

I rushed upstairs to Jaylin's bedroom and saw that everything was gone. My stomach turned in knots and I damn near lost it. The closets were empty, and the room no longer carried his scent. I gasped for air and quickly ran downstairs.

"Where are the owners?" I said, barely able to hold back my emotions.

"They moved, honey."

"Do you know where? I mean, this is such a beautiful house, and I can't imagine anyone wanting to give up something like this."

"I don't know. I think they moved to Florida. If you're worried about them coming back, they're not."

I stormed out of the front door. The lady called after me and asked if I wanted to continue the tour. I couldn't believe Jaylin had left without saying a word to anyone, especially to me. I broke down in the car and could barely get myself together when I got back home. How Jaylin could jump up and leave his son without saying a word puzzled the hell out of me. He hated his father for doing the exact same thing, and then to turn around and do it to LJ was too hurtful for me to understand.

Before I went into the house, I called Jaylin's cell phone again. I cursed him out and told him what a shitty father he'd been. I wished him and Scorpio a happy fucking life together, and called her a few names while I was at it. My purpose for saying such cruel things to him was so he'd get angry with me for what I said and call back.

Almost a week later, that phone call still hadn't happened. And neither did a conversation between Collins and me. I was zoned out, and felt as if I lived in another world without Jaylin. Collins could tell something was wrong with me, but he didn't bother to ask. When he found me downstairs on the couch snuggled up in some covers, crying and listening to Alicia Keys' "If I Ain't Got You," that's when he insisted we talk.

"What is wrong with you?" he said, shaking me.

Not being able to hold back any longer, I grabbed him around his neck, sobbing on his shoulder about losing the man I truly loved. "He's gone, Collins!" I yelled. "I'm sorry, but Jaylin's gone for good!"

# 34

## *JAYLIN*

Now, this was the life. No headaches, no arguing, no fussing and cussing, and no sex. I hadn't had no pussy in quite a long time, and it really didn't even bother me. I'd been keeping myself busy by taking late-night jogs on the beach, reading, and relaxing. Nanny B would go jogging with me sometimes too, but when she did, I had to walk slowly with her. I often chilled outside on the hammock, or rode around for a while with Ebay to check out my new city.

I didn't think things would go as smoothly as they were, but I couldn't complain. I had my middle of the night setbacks, thinking about the past, but under the circumstances, I couldn't help it. When I thought about Shane's advice a while back, to take months away from everybody to see who or what I really wanted, that advice was the best advice he could have given me.

Eventually, I was able to put the memories of Scorpio's and my relationship to rest. Letting go of my thoughts of her wasn't easy, but I needed so much more from a woman than some good pussy. I had no regrets for what we shared, but my way of loving her would've never been enough. A few more years of us being together would have brought about much turmoil, and that was something neither one of us needed.

As for Daisha, Brashaney, Felicia, Heather, Mercedes, Alisha, Ebony, Yo-Yo, and the many whose names I failed to get, the thought of being with them again never, ever crossed my mind. Sad to say, they were convenient at the time, and other than Daisha, the relationships had very little value to them.

Nokea, however, she stayed with me. I slept with the thoughts of her at night, and woke up with the same thoughts of her in the morning. I'd gotten her messages, but the last time we spoke, she begged me to allow her to be happy. If being with Collins was making her happy, then that's where I wanted her to stay.

The day of LJ's and my birthday was difficult for me to get through. I visualized Nokea at Café Lapadero with LJ, and wished I could be there with them. At the time, all I could do was send flowers. I wasn't sure how she'd feel about the teddy bear, but it was time to give him up too.

Nanny B had tried to cheer me up that day, but seeing that she couldn't, she suggested I go hit the water with our neighbors on their yacht. That was pretty cool, and it kept my mind off Nokea for hours; however, when I returned home that evening, I stayed up the entire night and let my emotions get the best of me. Nanny B said many encouraging words to me, but at that moment, all I wanted was to personally wish my son a happy birthday and see the woman I loved.

Each day, though, continued to get a little easier for me. I hoped that one day I'd be free of her, and when that day came, then I'd be able to cope with seeing LJ. If I made attempts to do it now, it was going to hurt me even more knowing that Collins and her were still together. The less I knew about their situation, the better off I was.

Ebay drove me to the grocery store to get a few things. Nanny B planned dinner and invited our neighbors over to join us. The Nelsons were an old white couple that had lived near the beach for years. They were some of the nicest people I'd ever met, and we all had become good friends. Mrs. Nelson claimed that I was too handsome to be alone, and offered to introduce me to her daughter. I declined because meeting somebody new wasn't on my agenda. I hadn't seen Nokea for almost three months now, and my heart still ached for her.

I stood in line, waiting to pay for my groceries. That's when I noticed this chick who resembled Nokea from behind. My heart raced, as I thought it was her. When I reached out to touch her shoulder, the woman quickly turned around.

"Yes?" she said.

"I'm sorry. I thought you were someone I knew."

"No, but I'm sorry that I'm not who you were looking for."

\*   \*   \*

When I got back home, I told Nanny B about what had happened. She suggested that I go lay down until dinner was ready. I lay in bed, closed my eyes, and couldn't stop thinking about Nokea. Listening to the ocean always helped calm me, so I took off my shirt and walked along the beach in my jeans.

It puzzled me how much Nokea was on my mind. The couples on the beach made me think of her even more. I took a deep breath and sat down close by the water. I did sit-ups and stopped when I reached two hundred. When I looked up at the sky, the dark clouds rolled in and the rain started to pour. A cool breeze kicked up, and I got drenched as I made my way back home. Almost out of breath from running, I hopped over the balcony to go inside.

When I opened the double doors to my bedroom, my eyes played tricks on me again. I wiped the rain from my face with my hands and looked at my bed. I thought I saw Nokea lying there, and I couldn't take another step. The room was dark, but when the lightening flashed to light it up again, I saw that she was still there. I stood somewhat afraid that I had lost my mind, and kept blinking my eyes. If anything, I thought I was dreaming. I was known for having hallucinations when I felt under pressure.

The sheer white curtains blew gracefully around the bed and the leaves trembled on the palm tree. Could I have died and gone to heaven?

Nokea must have noticed how out of it I was, so she placed the teddy bear on her lap and sat up on her elbows. She smiled. "We came to get our shirt back. What took you so long?" she said softly.

I hesitated to answer, fearing I would be talking to myself. "So . . . so I'm not dreaming? Baby, is it really you?"

"Why don't you come pinch me? And not on my behind."

I still didn't believe it was her, so I stepped up to the bed. She pulled the covers back and exposed her naked body. I reached out my hand and pinched her butt.

"Now, that ass was real." I smiled, so damn happy to see her.

We stared at each other and couldn't keep the smiles off our faces. "Kiss me," she said softly. I kneeled on the bed and leaned forward to peck her lips. "I mean, really . . . really kiss me."

I stepped back and slid off my wet jeans. I eased in bed and put her body on top of mine. As I held her face in my hands, I looked deeply into her eyes for a moment and then pulled her face to mine. We smacked lips for a long while, and when I heard LJ, I shook my head.

"He's not going to interrupt me this time. And you're not going anywhere."

"No, I'm not. You know Nanny B got him all taken care of."

"I'm sure she does, but tell me something."

"What?"

"How did you—?"

"Not now, later."

"But what about Coll—"

"Please, not now. I'm here with you, and this is where I want to be."

Just wanting to hold her, I placed her head on
my chest and took deep breaths. I rubbed up and
down her smooth body. I couldn't believe she
was really here. When I was ready to go where
I had dreamed of going for many, many nights, I
moved Nokea to my side and leaned over her. I
pecked her lips a few more times and massaged
her breasts with my hands. When I eased my hand
down and felt how wet and warm her pussy was,
I looked in her eyes, making a prediction.

"We're going to make another baby tonight,
aren't we?"

"You already have LJ, don't you?"

"But I want another one." I kissed her cheeks.
"And another one. And—"

"And if you keep on talking, we'll never get
started."

Now, all she had to do was say the word. I
pulled the soft white quilt over both of our heads.
I didn't plan on coming up until morning. I
opened her legs with mine and laid my goodness
right between the warmth that came from between her legs. After I slid myself inside of her,
she closed her eyes and so did I. I stroked her insides at a slow pace, thinking about how I wanted
to feel like this for the rest of my life. I felt myself
coming, giving her all I had and then some. I'd be
damned if my baby wasn't coming tonight.

Since I never finished up so quickly, I held her
legs together with my hands and kissed down
them. I felt her body wanting . . . needing me,
and when I went back inside of her, I sucked her
breasts that I'd missed so much. She held my

head while rubbing her fingers through my curly hair.

"I love you," she said tearfully. I could hear her heart racing, as mine raced right along with hers. "God knows I never stopped loving you for one minute."

I looked up at her. "Even being married to Collins?"

"Yes, even then. That's why we're not married any—"

"Then marry me."

"No, you marry me." She laughed.

"How about we just marry each other?"

"How about that sounds like a wonderful idea. But you . . . you kind of taking your time with this baby tonight, aren't you? At the rate we're going, we'll never make it."

"I got all night, baby. The Cherry Popper ain't even gotten started."

"What in the hell is a Cherry Popper?"

"I'm 'bout to show you."

"Then hurry it up, because your soon-to-be wife is anxious to get this show on the road."

"Then let's."

Nokea and I made love on and off throughout the night. We both released our emotions because it had taken almost twelve years of our lives to get to this point. That was a long time to be with somebody, and even though we went through the things that we did, there really wasn't any other way around it. The challenges we had, they were put there to make our relationship what it had become. We prevailed, together, and the only

reason we did that is because not for one moment did we ever stop loving each other. That old
saying, when you love somebody, all you have to
do is set them free? Well, even though it hurt me
like hell, I had to do just that. I was only able to
do that because, deep in my heart, I knew my son
and the love of my life would always come back to
me. It's just something you always know.

The following month, which was past the thirty
days required for Nokea's divorce to be finalized,
we had a beautiful and quiet wedding ceremony
on the beach. The only people who were there
were Nanny B, LJ, the Nelsons, and of course, the
priest. As usual, the wind kicked up a soothing
breeze, the sky was a clear blue, and the waves
were sounding off against the rocks. We stood
barefooted in the sand, gazed deeply into each
other's eyes, and held our hands tightly together.
We didn't even care that we wore blue jean
shorts, because it didn't even matter. Our rings
were made from yarn that Nanny B had inter-
twined together, and that didn't matter either. All
that mattered was Nokea was now the official
Mrs. Jaylin Jerome Rogers, and she would forever
be.

Happier than I'd been in my entire lifetime, I
swung Nokea around, kissing her. Once the short
ceremony was over, LJ, Nanny B, Nokea, and I
went for a walk along the beach. I carried Nokea
on my back, and she occasionally leaned down
and kissed my cheek.

"I am so glad the two of you finally got it together," Nanny B said.

"Did you have any doubts?" I asked.

"Yes. With all the ruckus you caused on your birthday, I thought you would die before she got here."

"I was hurt, Nanny B. I was lost without her and LJ."

"Well, you don't have to be lost anymore," Nokea said. "Thanks to Nanny B for calling to tell me how miserable you were. And at the same time, she knew how miserable I was. We owe you one, Nanny, and thanks for not giving up on us."

Nanny B shook her head, and Nokea slid off my back. "I'll race you," she said.

I laughed. "Come on then." I looked at Nanny B. "You too. You could use a little exercise too."

She threw her hand back. "Chile, please. LJ and I gon' go back to the house and exercise our lips on the barbecue I fixed for y'all." She took LJ's hand. "Hurry on back. Don't be out here playing around all day long. The Nelsons planned a dinner party for y'all tonight."

"We won't be long," I said, and then pecked Nanny B on the cheek. I picked up LJ and kissed him as well, then ran to catch up with Nokea, who had already taken off.

As I got close to her, she turned around and laughed. When I reached her, she collapsed to the sand and fell backward. She took deep breaths while on her back, looking up at the sky. I kneeled in front of her and interrupted her thoughts with a kiss.

"What are you thinking about?" I asked.

"I wished that every woman in the world could feel what I feel when I'm with you—that's without all of the drama. Love is such a beautiful thing. If they don't feel what I do, then they're in the wrong place. Many will say that we shouldn't even be together, but no man is perfect, and neither was I. Thank you, Jaylin Jerome Rogers, for making me one of the happiest women in the world. I always knew you could."

I continuously kissed my wife on the lips and cuddled her in my arms for hours on the beach. Afterward, we hurried back to the house and spent the rest of the evening with the Nelsons, a few other neighbors, and of course, Nanny B and LJ. Even Ebay stopped in to give his congrats.

That night, Nokea and I held each other in bed while "Suddenly" by Billy Ocean played on the radio. Holding Nokea in my arms had become my new way of making love to her, and she didn't mind one bit; for we had the rest of our lives together, and that's all that mattered to both of us.


It was almost nine months later, and there I was acting a complete fool at the hospital. I paced back and forth, and Nokea yelled for me to hold her hand. Waiting for what seemed to be a lifetime for this moment, I couldn't even stand the sight. I closed my eyes, as my stomach got weak, and listened to the doctors tell Nokea to push. She screamed, and feeling her pain, I squeezed her hand tightly and leaned down to kiss her.

All of the commotion brought about a baby

girl. She was my first child that I'd seen come into this world, and I'll be damned, I thought, did it take all that? I couldn't stop kissing Nokea, and when the doctors handed my baby girl over to me, I was full of emotions. She was beautiful. She had curly hair like her daddy, and my gray eyes to go with her. She looked more like LJ than anybody, but she did have Nokea's lips. Nokea yelled to take a look at her, but I selfishly turned my back, holding my baby girl in my arms. This was my moment, and it was a moment that nobody could ever take away from me.

Nokea cursed at me, so I knew I'd better hand our daughter over to her. I pulled up a chair close to Nokea.

"So, what are we going to name her?" she asked. "How about after your mother or Nanny B?"

"Naw, that's not gon' work. If you don't have a problem with it, I'd like for her middle name to be Jasmine, like my daughter I haven't seen in years. I could hurt her mother Simone for taking her and leaving without saying good-bye, and you know the private detective I hired never found out what happened to her."

Nokea rubbed the side of my face, comforting me as she knew how to do so well. "It's okay, baby. Keep looking. You'll find her. I think Jasmine is a beautiful name, and whatever you decide is fine with me."

A few days later, we left the hospital with Jaylene Jamiah Rogers. I'd changed my mind because I felt as if Simone and Jasmine were a part of my past. I'd come to grips with the fact that there was a possibility she'd never know me as her father. Either way, I was a proud daddy and couldn't understand how so many men never even had the desire to be a part of their own children's lives. It simply didn't make much sense to me. Throughout my life, having a father very well could have made the difference. Who knows?

When we got back home, there was too much excitement for me. Even Nokea's parents had come to offer their support, which was quite a surprise for her and me. Her father had even given his approval, and told me that he knew all along I was the only man who could make his daughter one hundred percent happy.

Once things settled down that night, I needed some time for myself. Being in my new home allowed me that, so I grabbed a magazine and lay outside on my hammock. I placed my hands behind my head and thought about how far I'd come. A loving nanny, my wealth, two . . . four beautiful kids and a wife who loved me to death. What more could any man ask for? Nothing, I guessed, but only time would tell if a man like me would ever desire to have more.